The Best AMERICAN SHORT STORIES® 2023

Selected from U.S. and Canadian Magazines
by MIN JIN LEE
with HEIDI PITLOR

With an Introduction
by MIN JIN LEE

MARINER BOOKS
New York   Boston

FIRST EDITION

ISSN 0067-6233
ISBN 978-0-06-327590-4
ISBN 978-0-06-327591-1 (LIBRARY EDITION)

23 24 25 26 27 LBC 5 4 3 2 1

Contents

Foreword

THIS YEAR, THE use of second-person point of view made a comeback. I read far more stories than usual from "your" point of view, and although none that appear in the following pages were written in the second person, many are cited in the back of this book. I suspect that this trend has something to do with a desire on the part of writers for immediacy and engagement. What is second person other than a quick way to connect with the reader? After all, we are living in a disconnected time. Heap a waning pandemic that had us all working and attending school at home on a population increasingly isolated by technology, on top of a burgeoning political movement that worships individualism and capitalism and treats social justice and acceptance of diversity as affectations donned by nerds and schoolmarms, and you get a society that is far more fractious than collaborative.

If there's anything I long for lately, it's genuine human connection. If there's anything I read for, it's the same. I look for smartly written characters, humanity of language, emotionally true descriptions of how we do and do not connect as people. These traits are what made me fall in love with fiction decades ago, and they're what I find myself most drawn to still.

The 2023 volume of *The Best American Short Stories* consists of twenty exceptional tales of connection and disconnection. Many of the stories explore the bonds and limits of friendship. In Cherline Bazile's charming, devastating "Tender," two daughters of immigrants become best friends who learn to assimilate in school while enduring traumatic family lives. In "Bebo," Jared Jackson deftly portrays a changing friendship between fourteen-year-olds against the backdrop of gunfire and drug deals in Hartford. Lifelong Soviet friends who live across the globe find their bonds tested upon the invasion of Ukraine in Sana Krasikov's timely "The Muddle." Joanna Pearson's masterful "Grand Mal" presents a woman whose pious college roommate is suddenly murdered. The anxiety-inducing act of sharing one's art with friends is portrayed with acuity and generosity in "This Isn't the Actual Sea" by Corinna Vallianatos, who writes beautiful sentences such as "I was reminded of a sensation from early childhood, of waking from a nap and feeling that the heart, the dense bud of the day, had disappeared and I was left with misplaced time, an hour I didn't recognize, silty and mournful and gray." A cynical copywriter becomes obsessed with a member of a boy band that her friend worships in Esther Yi's wonderfully amusing and profound "Moon."

Family, of course, gives us our earliest training in interdependence. Taryn Bowe's unforgettable and truly gorgeous "Camp Emeline" brings to life a teenage girl who lost a younger sister with spina bifida. Her parents decide to open a summer camp for sick children, and the teenager finds herself simultaneously grieving, growing up, and helping to build the camp from almost nothing. Tom Bissell's searing and whip-smart "His Finest Moment" imagines a well-known writer, "a flirt and a libertine," who must tell his fifteen-year-old daughter that he will soon be publicly outed for a sexual assault allegation. Danica Li explores the impact of distance—both literal and virtual—on a sibling relationship in the topical, savvy "My Brother William." In the poignant "Compromisos," Manuel Muñoz writes of a man considering a return to his family after his lover closes the door to a future for them as a couple. A young supermarket cashier is confronted by her new mother-in-law, who has grander designs for her, in Souvankham Thammavongsa's vibrant, aching story "Trash." A suicidal girl in Nigeria who has long felt unwanted by her parents finds herself face-to-face with gunmen on a bus in Kosiso Ugwueze's transfixing "Supernova."

Magical thinking in the face of grief is another common theme here. Nathan Harris writes in the accomplished "The Mine" of a man tasked with retrieving a body from a South African gold mine despite the objections of the local bush people, who believe that a mythic beast has claimed the body and that it should not be disturbed. Da-Lin's electric "Treasure Island Alley" hopscotches across space and time to deliver a stunning, innovative story of a young girl's grief. A Jewish teenage boy fixates on a mysterious member of his temple after losing his mother in Benjamin Ehrlich's pitch-perfect "The Master Mourner." Sara Freeman's deeply moving "The Company of Others" brings us a woman who explores the limits of motherhood and the echoes of grief: "A parent, I had even heard, is merely a fixed spot on the wall that the child can look to, should she need to regain her balance."

Storytelling itself also figures prominently here. Maya Binyam writes a clear-eyed, haunting story of strangers and the powers of narrative in "Do You Belong to Anybody?" A recent college graduate in Lauren Groff's inspired and delightfully articulate "Annunciation" experiences life-changing grace after driving across the country alone and renting a converted pool house from a mysterious old woman who has quite a lot to tell. Ling Ma's thought-provoking "Peking Duck" explores authorship and language and the differing ways in which immigrants and their children experience words. Finally, the salvation of language and its power to connect disparate lives is plumbed in "It Is What It Is" by Azareen Van der Vliet Oloomi. This brilliant and deeply affecting mourning wail of a story features a downed airplane and a powerful cat who, with the help of Twitter, finds a loving new home.

Min Jin Lee has been an excellent and fastidious guest editor. We share some useful traits for this work: brutal honesty, a passion for good writing, and a desire to see authors supported and protected in our current culture. When she finished reading the 120 stories that I had sent her, she asked if she could include more than twenty. I so wished I could alter the longtime rules, but instead we proceeded to have painful conversations about which stories to let go. This is my seventeenth volume of *The Best American Short Stories*, and I've grown used to these hard decisions. They are made a little less hard by the knowledge that an author whose story came close one year may make it into the book with a future story in another year. I've cited stories by Joanna Pearson, Souvankham Thammavongsa, Corinna Vallianatos, and Azareen Van der Vliet Oloomi numerous times before and was thrilled when Min chose their pieces to appear this year. Congratulations to all of them.

It is possible, of course, to tell affecting, well-crafted stories about individuals battling nature or the supernatural or themselves.

But to be honest, I prefer stories of humans jostling against each other. These encounters come with the dramatic potential of power struggles, love trouble, family intrigue, and a more complicated sense of time and memory. Teenagers frequent these stories, perhaps because adolescence is the time of life when a kind of scrim, a gauzy separation between innocence and knowledge, falls away. Though some of the teenage characters in these pages would be loath to admit it, they do gain invaluable insight from the generosity of friends and family and even strangers. I hope that reading this powerful group of stories makes you too look at the others in your life as well as yourself with a new wisdom and kindness.

The stories chosen for this anthology were originally published between January 2022 and January 2023. The qualifications for selection are (1) original publication in a nationally distributed American or Canadian periodical; (2) publication in English by a writer who has made the United States or Canada their home; (3) original publication as a short story (excerpts or novels are not considered). A list of magazines consulted for this volume appears at the back of the book. Editors who wish their short fiction to be considered for next year's edition should send their publications to Heidi Pitlor, c/o The Best American Short Stories, PO Box 60, Natick, MA 01760, or send links or files as attachments to thebestamericanshortstories@gmail.com.

HEIDI PITLOR

Introduction

Absence of Speech

MY FIRST SEVEN years were spent in Seogyo-dong, a modest
neighborhood in the Mapo district of Seoul. Dad was a marketing
executive at a cosmetics company, and Mom was a piano teacher.
We lived in an unremarkable three-bedroom house, and my two
sisters and I attended the local public schools. The sounds I recall in
my childhood home are the plonking of piano keys by my mother's
students and the crisp Haydn sonatas she played when there was
time to practice on her own. Unlike my older sister, Myung, who
had such a high IQ that the principal of her elementary school
warned our mother never to tell Myung her own score, I was not
considered bright. Our younger sister, Sang, was the lovable baby
and a kind child.

I was so quiet I was silent, a nearsighted girl with wispy hair.
Then again, I do not recall conversations at home. A busy salary-
man, Dad was not around much. Mom gave lessons to neighborhood students, then worked another shift, tending to housework,
cooking, and caring for extended family members who needed
attention. In Korea, a wife and mother who also has a paying job
is just endless motion.

My mother claims that I taught myself how to read Korean before I was four years old and, when we moved to the United States,

somehow I taught myself how to read in English. I don't know exactly how reading happened to me, but I am certain that I had to make sense of letters, words, sentences, and punctuation, because there were so few spoken words in my life, and reading filled that void. I needed to read like a human needs fresh air. We know now that children need to be spoken to, and of course heard, in order to learn and feel loved. My parents were not neglectful; rather, they were occupied with keeping us alive, and there wasn't enough time for a child's interior life. Perhaps our lack of verbal interaction didn't matter really, because stories from books gave me the warmth of feeling, the possibility of growth, and the meaning that I needed from others.

The precious few photographs from my early childhood in Seoul are in black and white, framed by a thin white border. My father must have snapped them on his prized Canon camera. Thus, my memories of Seoul are tinged within a gray scale. Any vivid color and nourishing light in my life then came mostly from storybooks.

Reading in Elmhurst

During the Park Chung-hee administration, my father, a former war refugee from the northern city of Wonsan, wanted to leave Seoul for good. Although my mother had no wish to uproot us, she asked her older brother John, a computer programmer who lived in Queens, to sponsor our immigration, which he did. In 1976, our family of five moved to New York City. For a year my parents ran a newspaper stand, then later operated a stall-like store in Manhattan's Koreatown, where they sold wholesale costume jewelry to street peddlers and small shop owners for six days a week, year-round.

For years we lived in a series of rented apartments in Elmhurst, Queens. Even as a child, I knew that our New York surroundings were not beautiful, not because our home in Seoul was grand or lovely, because it was not. Though Mom rolled up her sleeves and scrubbed away the dirt from the rental apartments, the old linoleum never brightened, and thin layers of grimy paint curled off the walls. The fluorescent tube lights of PS 102 cast an insect green haze over all the schoolchildren, who were not always kind to newcomers. In our apartment building on Van Kleeck Street, water bugs and roaches skittered across the lobby and the walls of the incinerator rooms, and at my parents' rented shop in Manhattan charcoal-colored rats roamed the one basement bathroom— shared by all the building tenants—unafraid of the striped tabby domiciled in the dank underground.

In a blue-collar neighborhood, it is easy to sort out who has less and who has slightly more. I sensed I was luckier than most, because I had healthy parents and kind siblings. We had shelter, nice things to eat, and a predictable schedule. When I was at home with my family, I was safe. However, no different than in Seoul, I remained alienated from other children. My immigrant parents were distracted with the business of settling down and earning enough to get by. My appealing sisters made friends in the new country. They seemed to flourish, yet I could not cross the dark chasm between the outside world and me. I borrowed books from the library and kept reading.

In junior high school, teachers assigned classic short stories. I learned the plots and morals of Langston Hughes's "Thank You, Ma'am," O. Henry's "Gift of the Magi," and Shirley Jackson's "The Lottery." I recall the stories with great particularity because the messages were instructive and understandable to a child, and like vitamin capsules, they enriched me with empathy and irony, as well as exposing me to the savage nature of organized society.

I read and read. I would finish a book then find another. I turned to stories like a seed buried in dirt seeks sunlight. I plowed through fiction because I needed to be somewhere else, anywhere other than my gray childhood—what seemed to me then the dreary life of an unremarkable girl. In the public library, I read through the recommended classics and ended up learning the social codes of Russian aristocrats, the daydreams of listless French provincial housewives, and the heartrending days and nights of the poor in London's cities. I was an immigrant teenager in the 1980s, and through canonical dead American and European writers, I knew far more than I needed to know about the rich inner lives of Black and White adults in far-off places from decades past.

Henry James's downtown Manhattan bore almost no resemblance to my parents' midtown Manhattan, where they were occasionally assaulted, robbed at gunpoint, and burgled. However, I had absorbed the sounds, textures, and scents within James's well-ordered narratives where conflicts were faithfully resolved. I could not forget what I read, and his New York became mine, too.

When I walked past a grand, red-brick mansion along Washington Square, I could envision an heiress pacing across the Persian carpets of her front parlor and hear the heavy rustle of her silk dress. A homely woman could have money, position, and property, yet she could not be certain of being loved only for herself. From James's glowing scenes, I knew that a wealthy father could teach his own child to diminish herself, and it was possible that my immigrant family was the wealthier one, because my father believed I was lovable and capable. Fiction nourished me with worlds far more colorful than my own, and made-up stories gave me a brilliant primer on human motivation.

Apprenticeship and Craft

In high school, my favorite author was Sinclair Lewis, and he had gone to Yale, so I applied there and somehow got in. It didn't occur to me that I could major in English or literature, because the folks who majored in such subjects were the beautiful people on campus. A stolid and plain young woman, I chose to study history, and whenever I could, I took classes outside my major in literature and sociology. Gradually, I could not resist my wish to learn more about creative writing. I had written and published editorials in high school and some personal essays in college, but fiction was something else. Fiction required whole-cloth invention, making up people, places, time, wishes, events, conflicts, and endings. For me, fiction required another level of audacity.

In my junior year, I signed up for a beginner-level fiction class. The professor assigned us excellent short stories to read and, without much guidance, we were told to write our own. I had read many short stories and novels; however, I had not thought much about the differences. For me, they were like various forms of paintings—miniatures, portraits, scrolls, sacred triptychs, ceiling frescoes, or building-sized murals.

Short stories are not novels. Yes, of course, stories are significantly briefer than novels, but no honest novelist would claim that a short story is somehow a lesser art form because one work has fewer words than the other. If anything, having written both forms, I can say that short stories are harder to write well. There is nowhere to hide a mistake in a short story.

Most conventional definitions cite word count as the chief distinction: Short stories range from one thousand to ten thousand words, and well, novels are more than fifty thousand or so. Not terribly helpful, I realize. One can argue that stories will have some intense emotion or a gotcha-like epiphany in contrast to the gradual crisis and resolution buildup allowed in the longer form. I feel like shrugging here because I don't wish to quibble too much about inadequate definitions.

Nevertheless, you and I can agree that short stories and novels are works of narrative fiction. Each requires a beginning, a middle, and an end; each requires the many elements and sub-elements of fiction: theme, characters, setting, point of view, plot, style, voice, conflict, resolution, tone, and narrative time. The old Greeks would demand a protagonist's thwarted wish, her recognition, reversal in point of view, and a satisfactory catharsis for the audience. Fine.

I took my first fiction class, then signed up for another one. I started to read differently. Reading was no longer a retreat or a flight. I began to explore fiction. It felt like playing with found kindling and making tiny fires, and I started to scratch out stories of my own.

In Seoul, there were books in our home; however, in Queens, I read borrowed books from the library down the street and from school. I didn't buy books in stores. There wasn't money for that, and it didn't occur to me to ask my parents for such luxuries. In college, I started to amass books of my own, so I could write in their margins and return to them when I yearned for what I had once discovered there.

In 1950, my father was sixteen years old, and with the onset of the Korean War, he lost his mother, sister, and home. Somehow, Dad put himself through college in Busan, but he never forgot how difficult it was to be a student without money. In 1986, when I was accepted to Yale, Dad gave me an American Express card. I was allowed to buy and keep all of my books and reading packets each term, and he said I could buy as many books as I wanted.

However fanciful my imagination, I had always behaved like a sober child with my limited resources. I saved my pennies, nickels, dimes, and quarters in a wide-mouthed jar, and when the jar was full, I rolled up my treasure in paper coin sleeves to deposit them into my savings account at Chemical Bank. I had a small weekly allowance I saved, and it had never occurred to me to be profligate with my parents' hard-won earnings.

Nevertheless, at Yale, I bought books without reservation. I think I was attempting to catch up with my better-off classmates who had seen every play, knew Latin and Greek, and had visited the Prado and the Louvre. My parents had never taken a holiday in all our years in America, which meant that my sisters and I had not traveled beyond school trips. For the first time in my life, I felt certain that they would want me to learn everything they couldn't teach me, so I bought every kind of book I wanted.

At the beginning of my senior year, I bought a paperback copy of *The Best American Short Stories 1989,* edited by Margaret Atwood, which was not a required text for any class. I read every story, and reread "White Angel" by Michael Cunningham several times. I told anyone who was interested that they had to read Cunningham's story about two brothers from Cleveland, Ohio, and a tragic backyard party hosted by their schoolteacher parents. In 1989, it wasn't possible to know any more about a writer than whatever was listed in the back pages, and his biography didn't matter to me, except that I knew that he was a living author. I had read so many dead writers—all wonderful and significant, but in a way their work felt lapidary—extraordinary classic narratives carved into slabs of marble, the sharp edges of each letter rubbed in with goldleaf—and like any extraordinary work of art, beyond reproach, almost divine.

Unlike the classics of dead writers of my younger reading life, the stories in this anthology felt different and vital because I knew for certain that these writers were working at that moment, and every story had been published only a year prior.

Growing up, I had never met a real writer or attended a reading. Authors didn't visit public schools in Elmhurst, Maspeth, or the Bronx. Through *The Best American Short Stories,* fiction writers became alive and current. Finally, I was reading modern stories.

Not much later, I graduated from college and went to law school. For two years, I practiced law in New York, and in the middle of

1995, after billing three hundred hours in a month, I quit being a lawyer for good. I decided I would try to write fiction, and naturally, I returned to reading with a different level of seriousness. I wrote a terrible novel, which was rejected everywhere. I started to write short fiction again. I sent out my work to literary quarterlies and magazines, and almost always, editors rejected my work. From 1995 to 2006, I collected a thick binder filled with noes. That decade or so was my wilderness, yet, on occasion, I'd catch the possible glimmer of my own aesthetic incandescence—a passage that moved, a character I felt to be true, or a thread of an intrigue that spooled out without effort.

Assessment and Lampposts

When I started writing short stories, I learned just how difficult it was to create the experience of immersive fiction, where life stops outside and the only thing that matters is the conscious dream within the ten to fifteen pages.

I didn't have much good news in my decade-plus years before I published my first novel, so whenever something positive happened, it felt like spotting a blazing streetlamp in the distance on an unfamiliar road. The lamp told me to keep going.

A now-defunct literary magazine called *Bananafish* gave me second prize for a story I wrote called "Bread and Butter" about an aspiring actor and her depressed friend. The cash prize was, I think, $250. A story I had worked on for many years called "Motherland" was published in *The Missouri Review* in 2002 and later became a stand-alone chapter in my second novel. "The Best Girls," a short story based on a news account—I had first written it in college, then later revised it—was published in another now-defunct literary magazine affiliated with the Asian American Writers' Workshop and was included in an NPR "Selected Shorts" reading at Symphony Space in 2004. Fifteen years later, in 2019, I rewrote "The Best Girls" yet again and published the latest iteration in a digital anthology. I wrote and rewrote "The Best Girls" for three decades, from 1989 through 2019. Bananas indeed.

For this year's *Best American Short Stories,* and as she has done for every guest editor before me, Heidi Pitlor, a brilliant writer and gracious literary citizen who serves as the series editor and without whom this anthology would not exist, sent me 120 stories published in 2022. It was my job to read the stories and select twenty for publication. The ones that were not selected to be published are listed in the back pages under "Other Distinguished Stories of 2022."

It is an honor for a writer to edit this annual volume. Nevertheless, I need to express my anguish at assessing fellow writers and leaving off a hundred of them.

In these few introductory pages, I do not see the need to single out any of the stories of the twenty writers chosen, because all of their work is exemplary. You will have the opportunity to savor their wonderful stories in full. Instead, for a moment, I want to throw my lot in with the hundred who didn't make the cut. It is my wish for you, dear reader, to turn to the back of the book and study the hundred stories listed and look out for the work of these writers elsewhere too. Why?

Well, because they are my tribe, and if nothing else, I am loyal to the left-out. If you check page 343 of *The Best American Short Stories 2003*, edited by Walter Mosley, you will find my name and "Motherland" (*The Missouri Review*, vol. 25, no. 6) right above Elmore Leonard's story "How Carlos Webster Changed His Name to Carl and Became a Famous Oklahoma Lawman" from *McSweeney's*. On that same page, you will also spot the names Maile Meloy, Arthur Miller, ZZ Packer, Grace Paley, Edith Pearlman, Annie Proulx, Emily Raboteau, and Roxana Robinson, among others. I was in excellent company. On page 366 of *The Best American Short Stories 2020*, edited by Curtis Sittenfeld, you will find my much-worked-on story "The Best Girls." That year I shared space on the notables list with Anthony Doerr, Louise Erdrich, Garth Greenwell, Yiyun Li, and Carmen Maria Machado. In short, maybe it's also an honor to be an Other Distinguished Story.

It would have been nice to have been one of the twenty writers whose story was chosen, but I remain thrilled to have a story among the 120 selected by the series editor of any year. There were years when I didn't make the 120, and there were far more years when I couldn't get published even for free. None of it matters much in a way, because we write short stories because we want to. We need to, I suppose. The world has tried to discourage us, and yet we have scribbled on.

Gaslighting

I have been a writer for almost three decades. I have been a somewhat successful writer for maybe five years, and even this can be argued depending on who you ask. It has always been difficult to be a writer anywhere in the world. No doubt, there were cave painters who complained about their publishers, agents, or the sizes of their advances. Although we are living in an age when publishing has never been more accessible to any literate person with an internet connection, it is also an extraordinarily tough time to make a living as a writer.

I have some data.

According to the 2020 Authors Guild report "The Profession of Author in the 21st Century," half of full-time authors earn less than the federal poverty level of $12,488. From 2015 to 2020, book-related income dropped by almost half for authors. Authors of Color earned half the median income of White authors. Although the median income of self-published authors increased by 85 percent over the four years since the report's publication, self-published authors still earned 80 percent less than traditionally published authors. Today authors need to write and promote their work while also earning enough income to sustain their writing. Only about 20 percent of full-time authors derive their income from book sales. So what do the remaining 80 percent of authors do to survive?

Writers teach, edit professionally, ghostwrite books, write corporate speeches, copyedit, fact-check, lecture, write for film and television, and/or have full-time or part-time jobs in publishing, marketing, publicity, literary arts organizations, and gosh, anything else. If possible, some become financial dependents or have patrons. One can cobble together an itinerant life of residencies, fellowships, and borrowed sofas of friends, but this is not easy to do. Some high school teachers, accountants, and doctors write fiction on the side. Writers also work as EMTs, security guards, and app-based drivers.

I have at least five jobs: book writer, freelance writer, lecturer, creative writing teacher, and screenwriter. I also serve on two boards, PEN America and Authors Guild, and I try to do what I can for other writers whenever I can, because I know that in my world of books, writers serve readers and other writers.

Every writer I know performs some services for libraries, local bookstores, literary organizations, public schools, prisons, hospitals, community centers, and other nonprofits. When asked, and if feasible, we serve as peer reviewers for fellowships and literary awards. I have judged the Pulitzer Prize, the Kirkus Prize, and the National Book Award. It is always a great honor to serve, yet the honorarium, if any, is never equal to the honor. For those who say the honor should be enough, I wonder how those without means can afford to work for inadequate pay. How can those without financial resources participate in our literary culture? How can our literary culture reflect the real world when we do not include everyone?

Nearly every author is asked to write blurbs and to be involved in the book tours of other authors. Writers recommend reading lists to publications, blogs, podcasts, and mainstream media, and we hold up the good books of friends and strangers on social media, classrooms, and bookstores because we want books to be read and loved. Not every author does everything, but most do some things, and almost always we do it unpaid.

In the book world and in art circles, it is considered impolite to discuss money and time. Yet I mention wages and hours here because I want fiction to matter to all of us.

Again, I ask you to look at the back of this volume. You will see the list of magazines from which these stories first appeared under the title "American and Canadian Magazines Publishing Short Stories." The stories Heidi and I selected this year were published in *The New Yorker* as well as fabled literary quarterlies like *The Sewanee Review* and *Zyzzyva* and visionary online magazines like *Electric Literature,* which is free to the reading public.

Finances have always been challenging for literary magazines; however, the pandemic made their work almost impossible. A 2022 report from the Literary Arts Emergency Fund (LAEF) shows just how difficult it is to write and publish works of literature. Forty percent of the nonprofit literary arts organizations, magazines, and presses that applied for the LAEF had no paid full-time staff. The majority of the applicants with budgets under $100,000 had no full-time employees. They often operate with people who work only part-time, or without pay. Literary magazines rely on volunteer readers to manage the volume of submissions, and when editors work with writers, editors are inadequately compensated, if they are compensated at all. Between fiscal years 2019 and 2021, the quarterlies or publications published almost 50 percent less: from 21,867 works published, their output dropped to 11,591 works.

According to the Poets & Writers database of literary magazines, 773 magazines publish fiction, and only 235 report that they give a cash payment for literary publication.

As for compensation for writers, excluding *The New Yorker*, a Condé Nast publication, the pay for a published short story in the United States ranges from $10 to $300. Many literary magazines give the writer a free copy or two of the publication or an annual subscription as payment.

According to Mary Gannon, the executive director of the Community of Literary Magazine & Presses (CLMP), about 700 of the approximately 800 CLMP members that are literary magazines have budgets below $50,000, and over half of the members have budgets of $15,000 or less.

Well, I think we can reasonably infer that these magazines have no paid full-time staff, and not much money left to pay writers.

But here's the thing: I could not be the guest editor of this extraordinary annual volume unless I published books, and I would not have been able to publish books if I had not published first in literary magazines. I am skipping some steps, but I am telling you how it works for most writers. It's that simple. A literary magazine is usually the first place a writer publishes her story, the first place where she is edited, and that publication is the first thing she can cite on her curriculum vitae or in her cover letter that will get her a fellowship, a literary representative, a teaching gig, or a book deal. Without literary magazines, we could not have this anthology, a treasure that countless gifted and sacrificial individuals have labored over without adequate resources or recognition, all in the hopes that you and I can continue to read modern literature.

Earlier on in my writing life, I would go to an occasional dinner or cocktail party in New York, and if someone asked me what I did, I told them I was a writer. Maybe that's my bad. I set myself up. But, you see, I needed to say that I was a writer before I was published, because I was in fact writing, and I had to convince myself that what I was doing was not just for me. I wasn't writing in a diary or making art which I had no intention of sharing. I wanted to be read. I had something to say, and I wanted to say it in my prose.

Often, too often, the person at the party would reply:

"Oh, how interesting. What do you write?"

"Fiction."

"Can I buy your book in a store?"

"Well, no."

The questioner would look at me with pity.

If I wasn't sitting down and could get away, I would excuse myself and cry in the powder room. With all of my education, I had become someone to be pitied. I was a housewife and mother, and there were years when money was very tough for us. Even when I wanted to teach so we could get health insurance, I couldn't get tenure-track jobs because I didn't have the terminal degrees or the requisite publications. I didn't have the right letters of reference. That said, even if I could have gotten a teaching job then, I wouldn't have made enough to cover childcare.

Lately, even after being published, selling some books, and finding a teaching position, I receive different kinds of pity.

Strangers tell me that they do not read books. They want to talk about television. I love television, but I also love books. I can scan the thought bubble above their heads: Why would anyone want to read when there are streaming services and infinite content? I think to myself: Would these folks replace reading with watching episodes? Reading engages human brains differently than viewing a narrative on-screen. Reading transformed my life for the better, I want to tell them.

Then there are others who read books but enjoy telling me that they do not read fiction. Short stories and novels are not real, they say. They are interested only in the truth. They seem pleased with themselves that they would never read a poem, a play, a short story, or a novel. I adore nonfiction more than most fiction writers. Remember, I trained in history and law. However, I stare hard at this speaker, and I try to control what I say. Decades ago, I would have blamed myself for abandoning a well-paying job to write fiction, just so I wouldn't have had to feel that what I cherish is utterly unimportant to this smug individual. I used to ask myself if they were right and my life was wrong. Not anymore.

I no longer cry in a stranger's bathroom. Rather, I nod, wish the nonreader or nonfiction reader well, and walk away. I do my best not to feel contempt. Contempt is a dehumanizing emotion, and as a novelist, I need to keep my empathy machine in excellent working order. I try to imagine good things for this poor fool. Yes,

I am aware what I just did there. I admit feeling a teensy bit of contempt. Guilty, I am.

In 2022, *Merriam-Webster* selected the term "gaslighting" as the word of the year. As we know, gaslighting is manipulating another person's reality to make her question her sanity. The term originates from a 1938 British play written by Patrick Hamilton, *Gaslight*, which depicts a deceitful husband who makes his wife feel insane in order to steal from her. When someone denies your objective reality for his hidden purposes, you have been gaslighted. It is remarkable that this almost eighty-year-old term has been so steadfastly used in our culture and is only rising in popularity and relevance. I tip my hat to Mr. Hamilton for coining this concept.

The stories in this collection were selected and published in 2022, and I have been thinking of how the word of the year connects with the modern writers of these stories. It occurs to me that perhaps literary magazines, writers, and readers are being gaslighted for caring about fiction, as if we are passionate about fox hunting, reverse glass painting, or the abacus. If we look at the dismal economics of what we love and do, we see that the market has judged us as being out of time or out of touch. If we compare the rise of new forms of entertainment and education with the attention fiction receives, I suppose we are being told that fiction is less relevant. But is that true? Does fiction matter less?

It strikes me that because we can read stories for free in libraries or on the internet, some may view stories as having no value, and I have to disagree with that view. In an increasingly image-oriented world, there is ample data that supports the causal relationship between constructed image in media and poor self-image. Pictures and tweets cannot provide meaning; they are, at best, visual information or news without sufficient context or nuance, and more often they provide only distraction, pithy sarcasm, or forgettable amusement. In a digital world saturated with technicolor brilliance and filtered, unobtainable beauty, modern humans seem unmoored and at sea. We crave stories to tell us who we are. We seek more daylight and purpose.

For those of us who love fiction, we are being gaslighted by a larger world that has lost its meaning and broken its order. We readers and writers know stories save, enlighten, and edify. Without stories, we cannot live well. Each of us would exist dimly, not understanding the value of our brightest moments. Above all, the greatest stories illumine our darkest corners, allowing us to see ourselves because, finally, a candle and a mirror have been brought into an unlit room.

Fiction is a light source in a world that tells us that there is no daylight left. The stories in this annual volume were written by living authors who have struggled and mastered both form and narrative in order to have their say with the original worlds they have created, based on emotions felt and perceived, and they give us our emotional truths, restoring our sanity and providing comfort for the days ahead.

I thank the writers of the 120 stories chosen here as the best of 2022, and writers working everywhere, for the sunlight of your work. I thank literary magazine publishers and editors, slush-pile readers, and patrons of literary arts organizations for your fellowship.

Dear reader, I thank you for your faith, curiosity, and generosity. Thank you for your kinship.

MIN JIN LEE

Tender

FROM *The Sewanee Review*

MY BEST FRIEND doesn't like me much. She said so herself. We were driving to her house so she could braid my hair. I was upset that at the hair store she took her time trying on wigs she wouldn't buy. The braids would take hours. If I wasn't home by ten, my mom would wring my braids around my neck.

In the car, the thick heat, the harsh green numbers on the dashboard that read 5:46 p.m. made me so angry I couldn't move. I didn't bother taking off my jacket. I kept the bag of hair extensions scrunched between my seat belt and my chest, as if it could shield the world from my rage. I didn't respond when she said, I'll finish what I can tonight and do the rest tomorrow after school. Easy.

After fifteen minutes of driving in silence, Best Friend said, It's ninety degrees. Take your jacket off. You have a death wish?

I'm fine, I said.

And that's when she said it. I wish I liked you more.

Then she switched on the radio.

We became friends back in the day, the only two Black girls in all of Lee Elementary. We were losers. Mostly because we had immigrant mothers who wore bulging scarves around their heads and weren't afraid to hit or yell at us in public. They sent us to school with saucy, smelly chicken and rice, which ensured we had no friends, because in our part of Florida no one knew how to deal with difference except to hate it. Soon after Best Friend showed up from Kenya with four large piggy tails and pink barrettes, we sat next to each other every day and pretended we spoke the same language. When the kids made fun of us for being weird, we cursed at them in our respective languages, and the teachers wouldn't say anything because when they tried Best Friend called them racist, the insult her mother told her to use if someone did her wrong. Even after Best Friend realized I understood these kids more than her, that they never asked me questions about living among lions and monkeys, we stuck together, partly out of habit, partly because we liked each other well enough, and partly because we were more like each other than we were like anyone else. We knew how to be mean in a way that was suggestive of love. We knew when to switch to our nice voices, though we didn't do this often. We sang together, shared our lunch, swapped clothes until our mothers found out and warned us that was a fast track for someone to cast a spell on you.

Senior year, Best Friend grew up or whatever and decided who to care about. Which did not include me. And that might have been all right except I care so much that some days I smile so hard my lips get sore. At night I can't sleep.

Best Friend lives with her mom and dad in a three-bedroom house in a gated community. In her living room, I sit near the leather sofa and her legs straddle me. I take the hair out of the packaging, cut off the beige rubber band, and hold out a chunk in my palm. I don't like asking her to do my hair. She thinks I'm embarrassed because I can't pay her. Really, she just braids too tight. She plucks an inch from the pile in my palm, splits it into two strands, crosses them, and presses them into a small section of my hair with her thumb. I feel the pressure on my scalp, even after she releases it. I wonder: when she pulls my baby hairs into the braid, tucks them beneath a hill of hair, repeats, does she know she hates me, and just how much? Is it finger length? Root length? Or maybe the kind that has no length at all because it never stops growing?

She turns on *The Real World*, which is all we ever watch these days because it's good practice for chatting with our new white friends. After Obama got elected, they flocked to her, the white girls who thought she was cool and wanted a cool Black friend so that they could embrace the end of racism in the U.S. We hate them, the girls who used to make fun of our hair and now tell us they love it, who still don't invite us to their birthday parties because their parents like Black people fine now but only at a distance.

That's fine, Best Friend would say, after each non-invite. We'll throw a better party. If someone doesn't give a fuck about you, don't give a fuck about them. Easy.

I don't know why she wants new white friends. The only response she'll give is, They're easier.

I think about that sentence a lot. How it's technically complete, but also cryptic, like it's missing another half. Than you, she means to add. Than you.

Best Friend's braiding away when she says, I hear David likes you?

Dave?

She hums so that it's on me to carry the conversation.

We went on a date. Date-ish, I say. And when she doesn't respond, I add, Maybe a half-date? He didn't tell you?

Dave is Best Friend's only other real friend.

She says, He mentioned he liked you, but I didn't think he was serious.

She digs into my scalp to pull my little hairs into the braid. Before I can say anything, she reroutes. She says, Well I just thought you didn't like white guys.

I don't, but—

And what about Chris? she asks.

I can like two guys, I say. I don't know why I say this. Chris and I have said a total of five words to each other. Before I can take it back, tell her just kidding, she says, So you *do* like David.

Another dig in my scalp, a pulling at the hair. She applies a cool slab of gel to my edges. When I still don't respond, she says, We had sex, you know.

You never told me.

She shrugs.

If I knew, I tell her, I wouldn't have—

I don't like him, she says. I was just attracted.

Okay, well, I don't have to—

Do what you want, Eden. I'm fine with it. David and I are just friends.

Best Friend changes the subject, swift as the next twist, but now my scalp is burning, and I can't stand it anymore. I say, Could you be easier?, and pull away.

Best Friend seems surprised to see me crying, and I say, You know I'm tender-headed.

In the floor-length mirror next to the TV, her eyes go cold. I saw that look yesterday during lunch with her fangirls, who talk all the time but don't say much at all. I told one of them that I liked her earrings. Neon hoops that matched her hair.

I stole them from Walmart, she replied.

I didn't know whether she was kidding. All I could think of was the beating I'd get if my mom found out I'd stolen something. Of course, homegirl didn't stop talking. She said, I don't even feel bad about it. They treat their workers poorly.

Everyone but me and Best Friend vigorously nodded.

Homegirl continued, It was easy to snag them. They were too busy following a Black guy around.

Everyone laughed, but Best Friend and I gave each other a look.

Homegirl added in a whisper to me, Don't worry. It wasn't Chris.

Chris is the only Black guy in our year. For most people that's sufficient cause for a wedding, though no one ever matched Best Friend to Chris.

I excused myself for some milk, and when I returned to the cafeteria table, carton in hand, one of the fangirls had everyone's attention. Best Friend was giggling in response to something surely stupid. I slipped into my seat. Mid-giggle, Best Friend's gaze focused on me. Some kind of haze rested over her eyes, which were hollowed out, replaced by obsidian. The usual warmth in her face was clouded with caution. She was having another conversation entirely. Even as I thought, This is why we shouldn't hang out with white people, I couldn't help but wonder whether she held back when she talked to me, too.

After Best Friend finishes a row of box braids, we take a break from each other: a mutual, silent decision that exiles me to her bathroom. My mom taught me that if you want to know who a person is, check out their bathroom. Best Friend has her own. Coral walls, a dainty window you can stare out of while you pee. Not a single hair clung to the sink. I thought she was a virgin like me, that if I wasn't capable of going there yet, neither was she. Where did she even have sex? At his place? In this very bathroom? Did it hurt? She probably wouldn't have had sex with Dave unless she actually liked him. And she must have liked him for a while, without a word to me. I wash my hands, thinking of her expression as I pulled away. What part of me displeased her? Could I carve it out, little by little?

*

Best Friend's mom gets off work. She sighs when she sees how much of my hair is left. She cooks us plantains and chicken, and then joins Best Friend so they can finish my hair before I have to be home. I'm relieved. Though Best Friend's mom is slender, she has thick thighs, and when I sit between them, staining her stretch marks with grease and gel, I feel cradled. She's much nicer than my mom, and when she speaks to Best Friend, she's warm, which strikes me with envy. Her mom turns on *Passions,* and we watch, engrossed by the faceless Alistair who sends his deranged daughter to kidnap his other pregnant daughter and keep her from marrying the working-class Mexican love of her life.

Hours later, Best Friend's dad comes home. The past few months, he's been gone for weeks at a time. We never talk about it, not my place to ask. We don't notice him until he drops his bag and keys on the coffee table in front of us. He's tall and wears sunglasses, though it's evening and we're indoors. He tries to kiss Best Friend's mother on the cheek. She recoils, her left thigh jabbing my shoulder. He doesn't see me, or maybe he thinks I'm African enough and thus family enough to be invisible. He takes his Black-Berry from his pocket and shoves it into Best Friend's face.

You know why I'm here? he asks. I got a call from your school. Your teacher wants to meet. I asked her what for, and you know what she said?

Best Friend doesn't respond. She fixes her gaze on the TV. Her fingers grow tighter against my hair.

She says you're not doing homework and you failed a math test.

Still, Best Friend doesn't react.

He shuts off the TV. He says, You're too busy watching TV, huh? You have time to do hair, but you don't have time for school.

He insults her in a language I can't understand, waving his hand in a steady beat. Best Friend just pulls and pulls at my hair until I yank it away from her. Her mom pushes her dad away, her legs jolting me, and says, She's acting like this because of you, pig. We're watching TV. Leave us.

She grabs the remote from his hand and turns the TV back on. Best Friend's dad disappears into the kitchen. Best Friend doesn't take her eyes off the screen, even when it goes to the commercials. Her mom whispers something in her ear, and they both turn to me. Best Friend runs her hand through my hair, which is largely unfinished. I get the feeling they're done for the night, which upsets me, though I hold my face. If I went home like this my mom would yell, and I'm not in the mood. Best Friend's mom disappears and comes back with an expensive-looking, earthy scarf that she wraps around my head. Best Friend stands up, and I understand that I should follow her, and she'll take me home. We slip on our shoes by the front door. I pull at the flaps of my Converse and say in a low tone, You sure you can't finish my hair tonight?

She starts to laugh, and then her face becomes serious and she nods without looking at me, not in response to my question but in response to herself.

Just kidding, I say in a high-pitched tone.

She scrunches her lips and opens the door, steps over the threshold, and turns to face me. She looks lovely in the porch light, the bushes behind her neatly shaped.

You're beautiful, I tell her.

She flicks her hand, but she smiles, walks toward her car. I want to stay here a moment, the thick, moist air, the crickets singing of possibility. But she disappears inside the Jeep, and as soon as I slide into the passenger seat she says, I can finish your hair tomorrow after school. We can go to your house.

I'm not allowed to have friends over, you know that.

Best Friend shrugs, My dad's just so—

She's gazing at me. But I am seized by a coolness that makes me avert my eyes, makes my finger press the lock and unlock button again and again.

Terrible, she finishes. Sorry you had to see that.

That was nothing.

Best Friend raises her eyebrows.

Just a heated conversation, I add. A bad day.

Is that so, she says with an even tone.

My mom beats me, I continue. That's why I never take off the jacket.

She says she's sorry. Then she's quiet for a moment and adds, I just wish he was better.

I shrug. At least he provides for you.

Bare minimum. Fathers need to be around, you know?

I don't know. I don't say this though. I lean my head against the passenger window. The pressure on my braids makes me wince. Outside, the traffic light turns red. I watch the crosswalk timer count down three, two, one, the flashing red hand. The light turns green. Two boys in hoodies strut on the crosswalk, taking their time. Best Friend slams the horn, but they don't move any faster.

Words can be a kind of violence, she says.

Not actual violence.

The boys clear the road. She makes a sharp turn.

You've got it good, I add.

Best Friend goes rigid, and I smile in secret.

She drops me off without another word, even when I tell her thank you and good night. My mom is home, still wearing her bright pink nursing clothes. I try to kiss her on the cheek, but she pulls away and says, I'm dirty.

She unravels the rust-orange scarf from my hair, lets it drop to the floor. I look at her feet, which are bare and pointed outward, while she passes her hand through my hair, checking if the braids are tight enough, swirling her hand around the large quarter section where my real hair is twisted into a knot.

Why didn't your friend finish?

I shrug.

She says, You look ugly like that, but the braids are nice. What about school?

I'll wear the scarf.

Hmph, she says. Where'd you get it?

When I tell her, she says, I bet she bought it for one hundred dollars. I could have found it at a yard sale for five.

I like it, I say.

Manman says, Ay. Stop looking at me like that. What are you learning from that friend of yours?

I lower my eyes. I'm in no mood to be hit.

Everything, I say.

I pick up the scarf and head straight to the bathroom, which has stained white tiles and a moldy shower curtain. I pull out scissors from the cabinet behind the mirror, and when I cut the carefully braided hair, it falls into the sink, onto the counter, down my shirt. I unbraid the rest, detach the loose, curly strands from my roots. I wrap the scarf around my head, round up all the synthetic strands, and throw them in the trash. I take off my shirt, stare at my pointy breasts in the mirror, then wipe off the strands of hair that have clung to my chest.

All better.

*

The next day, everyone decides to love me. It's the scarf, which makes me look the right kind of Black—trendy, like Best Friend, but different. I've unhinged myself from our symbiotic relationship. I keep my smile to a minimum, though inside I am thrilled.

I sit in Best Friend's usual seat next to Dave in the back. He's tall with dusty hair, long enough to catch in his eyes. He's not a popular kid exactly, but he's well liked. He knows himself, doesn't try to be anything he isn't. I play brave and ask him on a date. He's already going skating with Best Friend tomorrow, but I could come, too. I remember how she had gone frigid in the car, how she wanted my sympathy without ever having offered hers. I'll be there, I say.

Best Friend gives me a ride home from school.

My mom wants the scarf back, she says.

Reluctantly, I unwrap the scarf and place it in the compartment between us. She eyes my hair warily, and says, You took it out.

I nod, noting that she seems hurt. I lower the visor, finger my hair, which looks like a hill of fluff. We drive in silence for a few minutes. Then she tells me that, by the way, she's orchestrated an ice-skating trip.

I know, I say, Dave invited me.

I know, she says, he told me. I invited Chris and one of my fans, too.

I'll join you all another time, I say.

I already bought the tickets. Group discount.

I can't afford it.

She says, That's okay. It's on me.

Why would you invite both of them? I blurt out.

She tells me she forgot, and she looks so concerned I can't tell if she's lying. I check her eyes and almost see her retreat into a back room in her mind.

She says, Two guys like you. Bigger problems out there.

Oh, now you understand me, I say.

I've never been ice skating before. The arena is colder than I expect and smaller. It's filled with little indoor benches that remind me of picnic tables. Best Friend rents the skates for us both and hands me mine. With the skates on, I'm a couple inches taller, and I like it.

Best Friend glides onto the ice, making a sharp yet graceful spin toward me and her fan, who hovers next to me by the rink's barrier.

Best Friend puts my cheeks in her hands. The smile on her face, I don't recognize the fullness of it. It makes me grin. I say, I didn't know you were good at skating.

There's a lot you don't know about me, Eden, she says with a wink.

Dave makes small circles near us, and when he sees Best Friend skating, he says, Race me? And they're off. But not before she gives him that smile, and I wonder if he always gets that side of her. They loop around, Best Friend in the lead, before I lose them in the crowd.

Look at them go, Fangirl says.

I smile, a reflex that I immediately regret.

She never stops talking about you, Fangirl continues. She says you're sooooo nice.

I can pick out Best Friend in the crowd. She does a tight spin and then skates in the other direction until a line of kids holding hands bury her.

Best Friend emerges with Dave. They're skating slowly, their expressions somber, as if they went off not to race but to have a serious conversation. They fix their faces when they reach us, insisting that we join them.

Fangirl lunges toward them, flailing her arms. She bumps into Dave, who catches her before she falls. Best Friend takes my arm and gestures for me to let go of the wall. I hesitate. But I let go.

I've taught a fair amount of people how to skate, Dave tells us.

How many is that? Two? Best Friend says.

I'm no noob. I can show you ladies how it's done, he says. He launches into a lecture that includes gestures we're supposed to mimic. Before he's said his concluding remarks, a rink guard joins us and says, You can't stand in the middle. Keep it moving.

We giggle, partially because he looks sixteen, partially because he has an unfortunate mustache. Best Friend says to him, We're not in the way. We'll move as soon as we figure out how to skate.

The man-boy broods over us until finally Best Friend tucks one arm in mine and the other around Fangirl and propels us forward in a single stride. We're skating. Ish. Dave skates alongside us, moving slowly so that we can copy his movements. Left foot, right foot, left, two three, right, two three. I'm skating like I have a pole up my butt. As we round the corner, I stumble. Fangirl unhooks her arm before she falls with me.

The cold shoots through my skin, but the fall hurts less than I thought it would. Dave helps me up. I'm sure my heart rate triples as he takes my hand. Best Friend brushes the frost from my pants, laughing.

Chris appears from wherever. He's bumping his head to "Tik Tok" by Ke$ha, singing, Ohoohohoohohoh. When we ask him where he's been, he says he's been here the whole time.

I have a talent for blending into the background, he says. And skating.

Maybe you can teach Eden. She just fell, Best Friend says.

Chris extends his arm, which I take, careful not to look at Dave or Best Friend as we skate by them—Dave, who hasn't taken his eyes off Best Friend since she entered the rink. And can I blame him? Look at her twirl. Her hands know precisely where to go. She's elegant in a way I'll never be, her confidence intensified by the coolness of the rink. And me? Well.

Chris guides me to the wall. He says, Fundamentals.

He begins to teach me with such focus that I yearn for Dave's half-jokes. I pick up the moves quickly, though, and before I know it, I'm skating back and forth along one side of the rink with no trouble.

Last thing, Chris says.

He shows me how to cross my skates as we round the curve. He wraps his arm in mine, and we practice the move together. But when I try and cross my legs, I slip and fall hard on my butt. Chris stumbles but manages to keep his balance. We're laughing, gazing at each other—a look that lasts too long to be neutral. He has warm eyes, I notice for the first time. He takes my hand, and just as he's about to pull me up, I hear laughter. Under his arm I can see Best Friend a few yards away from me. She's fallen, too. She has her hand over her mouth, and she laughs outrageously, a sound she stole from her mother. She must have fallen on purpose. What happens to one happens to the other. As if our bodies were bound together.

You okay? Chris asks.

His expression is so earnest I want to place his head in a pillow-case. I look back at Best Friend, who's looking at me too, only now she's holding Dave's hand. I try to focus on Chris, but Best Friend and Dave are nearby, pulling at my face. I stay my gaze on Chris's hair, which is buzzed too short. We skate for a little longer, hand in hand, quiet. The music changes. I apologize to Chris for knocking him down, but he just smiles.

I'm going to sit down for a moment, I say.

He starts to follow me, but I say, No, you do your thing.

He skates away after a final squeeze of my palm. A woman bumps into me on my way out. Sorry, she says, with a big smile, I got brave.

I rest on a bench, happy to have something sturdy beneath me. I could like Chris. He's a nice guy. At the very least, it feels good to be noticed, especially while Dave and Best Friend skate around like lovers. I don't notice when Best Friend leaves the rink to join me. She puts her hand on my shoulder and squeezes.

I saw you fall. You okay?

I nod.

I'm so happy you came, she says. It means a lot to me.

I fixate on the beauty mark that she drew on her left cheek with her mom's brown lipliner. I'm not sure what to do with her tone. Was she being nice because she won whatever game we were playing?

Me too, I say, my voice flat.

Disco lights flicker across the floor. A siren goes off and an announcer declares that in five minutes, the rink will be closed to kids twelve and under. I glance at my watch. It's almost half past nine. I'll have to leave soon, too. When I look back up, Best Friend seems far away. I can tell that I have done something.

I'm going back in, she says, coolly.

Wait, I say. What's wrong?

I don't like the way you look at me sometimes, Eden.

I don't know what you mean.

She shakes her head and makes for the rink. I'm about to follow her when Dave comes up behind me.

Hey, he says.

Hey, I say.

He sits next to me.

Haven't seen much of you all night, I say, trying to keep my voice from turning bitter.

Yeah, he says, yawning, reaching his hands over his head so that I can see his pale, lean stomach. He reminds me of a fish.

I've mostly been hanging out with the ladies, he adds.

I shake my head and look out to the rink. Best Friend is nearby, watching. I inch closer to Dave. I probably have to go soon, I say.

Bums, he says. I can take you—

And then Best Friend is upon us. She seats herself on the other side of Dave, her arm hanging around his neck, and it's as if I've vanished.

Hey, what's up, Dave says.

Best Friend sighs loudly, You know.

He says, I know.

She says, I felt so good when I got onto the rink. Electric. But then I couldn't stop thinking of all those times my dad took me skating.

A mother plops down near us with her son. The woman who bumped into me before. Her son places his leg on her lap, and she shimmies off his skate. The boy tries to take a sock off, but the mom gestures for him to leave it on.

Best Friend continues, He says he'll stay this time. He won't go back to the lady and their new baby.

Another family. But he's married! The right thing to feel in this moment, I know, is sympathy. Instead, I feel stupid. And embarrassed. Why would Best Friend tell me now, when a boy is stuck between us, blocking the sight of her so that I only have access to her hands—which tremble as she speaks, which float, then sink, then cut through the air, and then lay still in her lap. Why didn't she tell me?

Dave leans back and I can see Best Friend again. Her head's on Dave's shoulder and she's watching me. Only this time she looks younger, vulnerable. She unwraps herself from Dave and says, I have to take Eden home before her curfew.

Dave looks surprised to see me next to them. The rink has mostly cleared now except for our group and the mustached boy-man, who's accelerating toward a group of elderly bachelorettes, who are skating in a line, elbows locked together.

Let's say bye to our friends, Best Friend says as she stands, taking my hand.

Fatima? I say to her.

Hm? she responds, surprised to hear me call her by her name.

But I don't have the words yet.

Outside, my stomach starts speaking, so she ropes me into the Subway across from the rink. I stare at the menu, a bit tired and overwhelmed by the number of choices.

I don't know what I want, I say.

She waits for me to say more.

I point at the menu. I'm talking about the sandwiches. What's good here?

You haven't been to Subway before, she says.

I fake laughter. Of course I have.

We let an older man with a visor go in front of us.

Best Friend says, I bet you'll like the turkey club. And you can tell him what to put on it.

I can choose?

The booth feels private. Maybe it's because it's so close to closing. The lights are slightly dimmed. A few employees wash dishes in the back, chatting. My seat feels comfy.

I'll pay you back, I say to Fatima as she puts her wallet back into her purse.

She shakes her head. My dad gave me a debit card because he feels guilty.

That's nice, I say. I reach for something else to add and settle on, Do you want to talk about it?

She takes a small bite of her sandwich, guarding her mouth with the tips of her fingers. Not really, she says.

That's okay, I say.

I had a good time anyway.

I had a good time, too, I say. Though we both know I'm lying.

An employee in the back cackles. I finish my sandwich, run my tongue against my front teeth to make sure nothing's stuck. Fatima, I say. I haven't been a good friend.

She cocks her head to the side, like she's thinking about it. She takes another bite of her roast beef and chews for a while. I pick at the frayed strings on my jeans. She clears her throat and smiles slightly when she says, No, not really.

If I knew—

You *did* know, she says. You didn't want to know. You want so badly for me to be perfect.

What do you mean? I'm the queen of imperfection.

There, that's it. That's what I mean.

The man who ordered before us emerges from a booth, heads toward the bathroom.

You act, Fatima continues, like me having a bad day is a personal affront to you. I'm allowed to have a hard time. That has nothing to do with you. I don't need you pulling me into some dumb competition. I don't like being pulled.

It's easy to feel like it's not a competition when you're winning.
She scoffs, shaking her head, looks away.

I lean in, whispering, It's hard being friends with someone who
has everything. You fail a test, he's right at your side. You can bring
him back. So what, he yells at you?

Fatima sighs, grabs a napkin, and dabs the tears I didn't notice
were falling down my face.

Eden, she says. Listen to me. Are you listening?

I nod.

If you're always the victim, you lose. Doesn't matter who you're
fighting. Me? she says, crumpling the napkin, I'm not your enemy.
I'm your friend.

When I get home, I lean against the front door, aware of a dull
pain in my backside. Inside, I wrap some ice cubes in paper towels,
seat myself at the dining room table, and place the ice under my
thigh.

The garage door grinds open. I thrust the ice out of sight under the table, though it leaks. I don't want any questions from
my mother. Her socks shuffle against the floor, ungraceful, angry.
She turns down the corner of the hallway, so that I can see her
now, how tired she looks, her wig chomping her forehead by a
quarter. She faces me, leans her purse against the hallway console,
scratches her cheek, and says, Edenia, you know what I would like?

Hi, Manmie, how are you? I interject.

I would like a daughter who cleans the house while I am gone.

She disappears into the kitchen. I can hear her moving the dishes
into one half of the sink. She takes the basin from the cabinet beneath, places it on the empty side, fills it with water and soap.

I did everything for my manman, she says. But you? Your daddy's child. Only care about yourself.

And she keeps talking, though she knows I've shut the door to
my bedroom, though she hears the radio now, my voice singing.
And as I sink into my comforter, I remember the mother at the
skating rink, how sweetly she removed her son's skates. What would
it be like to have a mom who would take me places? We'd go to the
movie theaters, to Subway. And she'd have time to do my hair,
wrap me in her greasy legs, so that when she moved, I did too. She
wouldn't pull with her rough hands, but she'd hold my hair so
firmly. It wouldn't hurt.

MAYA BINYAM

Do You Belong to Anybody?

FROM *The Paris Review*

IN THE MORNING, I received a phone call and was told to board a flight. The arrangements had been made on my behalf. I packed no clothes because my clothes had been packed for me. A car arrived to pick me up. The radio announced traffic due to an accident involving a taxicab driver, a police officer, and a woman whose occupation the dispatcher did not care to identify. But there was no traffic. My ticket was in the breast pocket of my jacket, which was handed to me as I exited the passenger door. Waiting in line, I felt I had no body, but by the time I reached security I was hungry. Inside my carry-on I found two apples and a croissant, which tasted like nothing. The security agent asked me for my name. I gave him my driver's license, walked through the metal detector, and then my body went away.

Before takeoff, a flight attendant announced our destination. Everyone cheered. The passenger to my right asked if I was happy to be going home. He didn't speak our destination's national language, which had become the language of the plane. I told him I was neither happy nor unhappy. He said he understood where I was coming from, because his work had introduced him to people like me. He said that people like me had changed him. It was true that they needed money, but the fact that he gave it to them had nothing to do with who they were to each other.

His real life, outside of our destination, was complicated by ambivalence. Since childhood, his basic needs had been met as if by an invisible force. At first, he believed his mother and father were providing for him, but when they died, he was surprised to feel that he had suffered no loss. He envied the fact that people like me didn't have desires, as we were still struggling to fulfill our basic needs. His own desires felt paralyzing, because none of them were motivated by need. Everything was available to be possessed, which made it impossible to quantify any particular object's allure. He wished he felt more lust for his mistress. I tried to relate to him and understand his concerns.

After takeoff, I unbuckled my seat belt. A flight attendant asked if I preferred coffee or tea. I thought about it but didn't think I had a preference. She tried another language. When she said it like that, I realized I preferred coffee. The guy to my right asked for sugar, and the flight attendant asked if I wanted sugar, too. I said no, and then she switched languages again and gave me sugar anyway. The coffee was delicious. The guy to my right spat it out.

After an hour, the ocean was the size of my window. I looked at the other passengers. Everyone was asleep except the guy to my right, who had begun watching a film on a portable DVD player. On the screen, a strange man with a bald head was standing on a street corner. A woman with a stroller walked by and he asked her to stop. She didn't want to stop. I think she was worried for her baby, who wasn't on the screen but was supposed to be in the stroller. The man said he had a question for her, and her face became open. He said, Do you belong to anybody? She looked flattered. She looked as if she thought the question was specific to her, but after she walked away he did the same thing to the next person, who wasn't even a woman. The next person was a teenager riding a bike. He didn't stop, so the bald man yelled out the question. Everyone was ignoring the strange bald man. He started to look lonely, and then he walked to a movie theater. He sat there and watched a movie about people having sexual relations. When it was done, he decided to walk across the city in a straight line. It didn't matter if there were obstacles. He got to a fence and climbed it, then jumped off on the other side. He got to a building and the security guard told him to show his credentials. The man said, Do you belong to anybody? The security guard didn't answer the question but let him through. The strange bald man climbed up to the roof, walked onto the roof of the next building, and then he fell.

I didn't think the movie was supposed to be over, but the DVD player announced that it was going to sleep. I looked at the guy to my right. I was hoping he would do something to make it wake up. His eyes were open. I said, Excuse me? No answer. To be fair, I had watched his personal movie without permission. He may not have liked that.

I decided to close my eyes. When I woke up, the flight attendant was asking the guy to my right if he preferred chicken or fish. He didn't say anything, which I could relate to, because I also didn't have a preference. If the fish had been fresh, I would have preferred that, but I assumed it had been previously frozen and then cooked in some unidentifiable oil, so comparing it to the chicken, I had no preference. I was thinking about that when the flight attendant began to scream. I assumed she must be having a personal problem. I turned to the guy to my right, wondering if he could understand what was happening with the flight attendant. His eyes were still open, and his head was slanted to an extreme degree.

The flight attendant switched languages and told me the guy to my right was dead. I had watched an entire movie with a dead man without even realizing it. Actually, it was only part of a movie, but still, I was shocked. Another flight attendant asked me if I knew the guy's name. I told her to please excuse me, for although I knew about his problems with his desires, I had not thought to ask for that information.

They made an announcement and asked if there were any doctors on board. Unfortunately, there were none, so a third flight attendant arrived with a first aid kit. Inside were bandages and medicated creams: nothing to help a dead man. I wanted to ask to move to another seat. The flight attendant wrapped the man's body in blankets and put a pillowcase over his head. I didn't think that was any way to treat him, but I recognized that they had no other option, just as I had no other option but to accompany him to our destination. For the rest of the flight, I couldn't do anything but think about my life.

When we landed, I was the final passenger to leave the plane. I wanted to look out the window, but the line to exit had become a procession, and everyone wanted to tell me they were sorry. I'm so sorry, said a man with a backpack. The next guy said sorry in a different language and seemed like he was going to cry. I wondered if I knew him. I didn't like that possibility, so I said thank you and waited for the next. Outside was the country I had left twenty-six years prior, and everyone I knew there. And yet I had to sit and receive condolences for this dead stranger with a pillowcase on his head.

*

In my luggage I found a bus ticket, so I took a taxicab to the bus. The driver knew the general direction of the bus depot but was always forgetting the streets that led there. That was what he told me. Everything was in the process of being built or being demolished, and the constant construction meant that as soon as storefronts, street vendors, and corner buildings became recognizable, they were replaced with other storefronts, street vendors, and corner buildings that were destined to become something other than what they were.

The taxicab driver was a handsome young guy in his twenties. I asked him about his experience of the economy. He told me he had just returned to work from a strike. Fuel was taxed to such an extent that no one could afford to drive. Some people could afford to drive, but they weren't taxicab drivers or the people who hired them, so from his perspective, no one could afford it. The drivers liked to talk to one another at taxicab depots. One day, they agreed to strike the following week. They parked their taxicabs in the middle of the city's busiest intersection, so that even the people who could afford fuel were obstructed from using their vehicles. No one could go anywhere, but people didn't mind, because once they became stuck, the taxicab drivers provided them with everything they needed. Supply trucks bringing vegetables to the city's markets relinquished their stock of corn, which the taxicab drivers roasted over coals and gave out for free.

At first, the government did not respond to the action. The highest officials were transported via helicopter. From above, the traffic jam looked like it might, in time, disperse. But the stoppage did not clear. Taxicab drivers from neighboring regions heard about the strike and left their families to join it. To them, the price of fuel felt even higher, given that they had fewer customers and the same expenses.

The highest officials instructed the middle officials to shut off the internet, which didn't matter, because only a small portion of the population used it (in this taxicab driver's estimation, 3 percent). The lowest officials (the police) surrounded the drivers, their taxicabs, and all the cars that had gotten stuck between them. The police shot one taxicab driver and his child, who had nothing to do with it. The child died, and then the highest officials made a special announcement. They were happy to report that the country

was in a financially strong position, and thus would be able to re-
duce fuel tariffs by one percentage point. They thanked the people
for their continued support, and then they helicoptered away.

The taxicab driver's story made me feel confused. On the one
hand the action was successful, and would improve the lives of all
taxicab drivers. On the other hand, a child, who wasn't a taxicab
driver but was nevertheless related to one, had died. I hadn't expected to hear such a complicated story from a random taxicab
driver, but that's how life was for taxicab drivers, as I had learned
when I started working as a taxicab driver in the country where I
had become a citizen. That was what I told this taxicab driver. He
seemed skeptical about that. From what he had heard, he said, taxicab drivers in the country where I had become a citizen had the
opportunity to grow extremely wealthy, given that the economy was
historically robust, even if it was currently having some problems.
Theoretically, I admitted, taxicab drivers in the country where I had
become a citizen had a regular clientele, and even if they didn't,
they could borrow money from the bank, purchase a medallion,
and eventually make a huge amount of income without having to
drive anywhere, given that the value of taxicab medallions was
guaranteed to increase exponentially as time went on. However, in
my experience, even a guarantee was unreliable, as anything could
happen between the present and the future, including death.

To be honest, I didn't want to discuss my own experience, but
the taxicab driver didn't seem to understand the general points
I was making, so I looked into my memory for a specific example. There was one evening, I said, late on a Saturday, when I was
hailed by two young women, both of them intoxicated beyond belief. I wasn't sure that it would be a good idea to let them into
the taxicab, for I suspected that one of them might vomit on the
leather seats. But the young women were getting into the taxicab
already, and anyway it was my job to drive people wherever they
wished, so I asked them for their desired destination. For some
reason, they started laughing. They told me where they wanted to
go, a place located past the end of the city, some miles down the
highway. Okay, I said, putting the car in drive. I tried to drive fast
on account of the potential vomit situation, but I was obligated to
stay under the speed limit, so my position was difficult.

Eventually, I told the taxicab driver, we got to a supermarket in
the middle of nowhere. I told the young women we were here, not

knowing where here was. I thanked them for riding with me before reading them the fare on the meter. The meter said $20.37, which I rounded down to twenty dollars for the sake of convenience. One of the young women gave me ten dollars, which I was confused by. Politely, I asked for the rest. The other young woman said, Sorry, nigger, and then she got out of the car. I looked around the parking lot, trying to find the person she was talking about. But there was no one there, certainly not anyone she could be referring to by that name. I exited the taxicab and locked the door, with the second young woman still in the back seat. If they could pay only one-half of the fare, I figured, only one-half of them should be dropped off at their destination. The other would have to be deposited back where she came from, which is where I took her, even though she screamed.

That was what I told the taxicab driver. I wasn't sure whether the example I had provided was sufficiently representative of the general experience. While I was evaluating that, he asked me about the value of ten dollars. I told him ten dollars had the value of one expensive sandwich or two inexpensive ones. He seemed satisfied with that.

I asked the taxicab driver about life after the strike. He said that business had been better since then. One day, he would be able to pay off the debt he owed. The debt had been accrued in his teens, when he had worked as a driver for a private touring company. The taxicab driver didn't speak the correct languages and didn't have a driver's license, so he wasn't permitted to drive the tourists, but if there were no tourists in the car, he was permitted to drive the car between destinations the tourists liked to frequent. The distances were long, and often required him to drive all day and night. During one of the taxicab driver's drives, to the battleground where the country, many years ago, had secured its independence, he fell asleep. When he woke up, he was upside down. He lost his job and was charged with damaging company property, the company property being the car. He served two years in prison and was still paying off the associated fine.

On most days, he said, his body felt heavy. In fact, he was very skinny. In the rearview mirror, I noticed that his face carried the imprint of his skull. I looked at him, thinking that he would have looked a little like me if I was a handsome young guy in my twenties. Now, he said, whenever he tried to move his lower body, it split his upper body in half. I told him I was sorry. He said it was all right. It was a bad situation, but he was used to it. I told him I could relate to that. I wanted him to know that I meant it, so I told him about my current predicament, at least what I understood of it. I told him that my brother had had a problem with his heart. It was on the right side of his chest, the wrong side, and had become filled with some kind of liquid. His swollen heart had put pressure on his lungs. On most days, he had trouble breathing, a problem that was exacerbated by the inhospitable environment in which he lived, a town on top of a mountain, where the air was thin and cold. No doctors lived there, and the journey to the nearest hospital required a five-hour drive. My brother wasn't in possession of a car, so if he wished to visit a doctor, he needed to ride a mule, which deposited him at a bus, which deposited him at another bus, which deposited him at the hospital. But my brother never wished to visit a doctor. He believed he could fix his misplaced, swollen heart and all the problems associated with it by buying prescriptions, which he could afford if I would send him a hundred dollars a month.

The taxicab driver said he was sorry. I wasn't sure why he said that. From my description, it was clear that my brother's situation was his own fault. He had encouraged his body to fail him. Even if I elected to fulfill his elaborate requests for cash, my actions would not, ultimately, improve his welfare, given that individuals had no hope of improvement unless they were willing to commit themselves to an alternate way of life, a process that involved changing their habits, desires, and natural inclinations. The swelling of my brother's heart, in addition to causing his breathing problems, had reduced the circulation in his limbs, and so he had no feeling in his fingers and toes. He complained about not being able to dial my phone number. He always pressed the wrong buttons and wound up talking to strangers. They never understood him, and no one wanted to help. He often wasted calling cards that way. He should have needed only one card to make a call, but sometimes it took four or five. That was another reason why my brother wanted money from me.

I intended to ask the taxicab driver about his family, but by then we had reached the bus depot. Instead, I gave him a big tip. He opened my door for me, which wasn't necessary. I walked away and didn't want to turn around. I did turn around. The taxicab driver was gone and had been replaced with other taxicab drivers. I looked at them, wondering if they could tell we shared something.

*

I tried to go inside the bus depot, but there was no inside. The depot was a patch of dirty grass that looked like any other patch of dirty grass, except that it was surrounded by a similarly dirty grouping of buses. The next bus was not due to leave for two hours, and the ticketing agents wouldn't let me into the waiting area, which was just a sectioned-off portion of the dirty grass with some folding chairs. According to the agents, I had two options. Either I could sit on the ground, or I could walk back to the street entrance, outside of which was an internet café. The first option was completely out of the question, so I thanked the ticketing agents and walked in the direction of the street entrance.

At the internet café, I gave the attendant some coins and asked him for a macchiato. He said they had no macchiato, so I asked him for a plain coffee. They had no coffee either. I told him to give me whatever beverage they had, tea or juice or whatever he pleased. He told me that the café sold no beverages. It just sold access to the internet. So I had no choice. I purchased fifteen minutes on the internet.

I checked my email. There was one new message. I opened the message. It was from my wife. She asked if I had arrived okay, and if I had found everything I needed in my luggage. She said she hoped she hadn't forgotten anything. She said she wished she could be with me, but that there was too much to take care of at home. She said she loved me very much. I hit the Reply button and began typing a message. *Thank you for your message,* I typed. *I arrived on schedule. I was wondering,* I typed, *if you happen to know where my blood pressure medication is. If not, please do not worry. I'm happy to give my blood pressure a vacation, just this once.* I read everything over, and then I pressed Send.

I thought to log off the internet, but I still had eight minutes remaining. In my email's search bar, I typed *brother.* About ten emails came up, all of them already read. I opened the oldest and began reading.

Hello brother, it said. *My wish is to extend to you my best regards and greetings. It would be my pleasure to hear more about your day-to-day concerns, relationships, and health.* I thought to exit the message, but I didn't exit the message. *It is a fact that the current debate on the reform of the health-care systems in America affects you, your friends, and all of us family members.*

My personal health has taken a turn since the last presidential election. If you remember, a poor lifestyle is common in my place of residence, and without reliable medical teams, there is no one to help me get better. My wish is to accept from you an invitation in the form of a U.S. entry visa. If you refuse me as a guest, I respect your choice, but I ask that you kindly forward to me some money to see a local doctor. It would please me also to call your attention to the matter of a Swiss bank account. My wish is to have a personal account, for which I would need an initial minimum deposit of $2,000 United States Dollars. My wish is to express to you that a void of attention to personal care and lifestyle could be fatal to a life span. Wishing you a happy day, Your Brother.

I exited the internet and moved to pick up my luggage. Unfortunately, there was no luggage. Not by my feet, not under the computer desk, not at the adjacent computer desk, and not anywhere in the internet café. At that point, I couldn't remember the last time I had had it in my possession. I asked the attendant if he had seen me carrying it when I entered the internet café. The attendant shrugged. He told me that he hadn't been paying attention. I thanked him for his service and left. On the street, I looked at the taxicab drivers, hoping to see someone who looked like me, but they all looked like me, just none in the specific way of the guy who had driven my taxicab. I figured he must have taken my luggage. Perhaps he had meant to or perhaps he hadn't, but in either case, he now possessed it. I went through the bus depot street entrance and reapproached the ticketing agents. I asked them if they had previously seen my luggage, and if so, if they had any idea where it might have gone. They said they were sorry. They saw a lot of people, sometimes dozens within a single minute, and rarely remembered anyone. In this case, they did not remember me. The ticketing agents told me it was still too early to enter the designated waiting area. I did what I was supposed to do, wait, until a ticketing agent announced that the bus was boarding.

On the bus, the woman behind me vomited, and the woman behind her vomited, too. The bus did not seem like it had any desire to stay on the road. After we departed, it tried to roll onto its side. The driver blamed this on the wind. Outside the window, the day was calm. The city had ended abruptly. I turned around and tried to find it, but land got in the way. The roads were struggling to impose themselves. All of the concrete was crumbling or turning to mud.

Soon the bus was hugging the mountains, and when I looked out the window, I saw the carcasses of other buses that had tipped over and rolled onto their backs.

We stopped in a small, impoverished-looking town so that the passengers could use the bathroom. A local food vendor hauled a cart up the steps of the bus and attempted to distribute slices of an elaborate chocolate cake wrapped in plastic. A guy across the aisle got his cake, ate it, and then started heaving into a paper bag. I asked the food vendor to please keep the chocolate cake away from me.

The woman to my left asked for two slices. She didn't look like she should have been able to speak the language, but she did speak it, extremely well. When she was done eating her two slices of cake, I asked her about that. She switched languages and asked me if I understood, which I did. She told me that she had arrived in the region as a volunteer with a foreign aid organization whose aim was to promote mutual understanding. I had no idea what she meant by that, "mutual understanding," but I assumed she would clarify, so I let her go on.

She said she lived among farmers. In the mornings, she surveyed their work and made suggestions for how they might improve the yield of their crops. I asked her what kind of crops they grew. The farmers grew mostly corn, or soy, or wheat, she told me, which were not part of their diet. To make money, they relied on foreign buyers, whom they were connected to through middlemen, a loose grouping of businesspeople in the city who called themselves farmers but who in fact made their money by exploiting real farmers. The meat available to the local population was expensive, and the vegetables provided hardly any nutritional benefit. Babies were born, their bellies swelled from starvation, and then they died.

In an ideal world, she said, the farmers would grow exactly what they needed. (In this woman's estimation, what they needed were things like grains, pulses, and pumpkins.) Ideally, they wouldn't need to deal with the middlemen, the foreign buyers, or even aid workers like her. Ideally, she said, the world would be organized such that her job, her volunteer position, could be eliminated. But in reality, the lives of the farmers were filled with problems, ones even she did not have the training to solve. I asked her what kind of training would be necessary to solve such problems. She told me that a degree in public health would be ideal, but that a degree in political science would suffice. Unfortunately, her degree was in anthropology, which helped her understand the problems but did not give her the tools to fix them.

The bus driver announced that the bathroom break was over. The bus lurched, and the woman settled back into her seat. I asked the woman about the history of the foreign aid organization. She told me that it had been founded by a former president and his wife. The president had retired from politics but was still passionate about exercising his influence, which was why he had decided to establish a nonprofit. His wife would rather have taken his place in politics, but no one liked her, so she couldn't, which was why she had agreed to become the nonprofit's executive director. She ran it like a federal government. The organization's volunteers acted as representatives, and the farmers, patients, and unemployed people whose grievances they arbitrated were their de facto constituents. It didn't matter that the structure involved no voting system, because the nonprofit was run on goodwill.

I asked the woman if she liked the president and his wife. She told me that she didn't like them or dislike them, because she wasn't interested in them as individuals but as representative historical actors. I didn't know what she meant by that, "representative historical actors," so I asked her to clarify. She told me that politicians pretended to have personalities, but their idiosyncrasies were just traits they developed in order to get elected. For most voters, it was less important for a candidate to have a coherent ideology than it was for them to have a dog, a second home, or a sense of humor. It was necessary to cut through all of that, she said, if one wished to have a grasp on one's place in history. She seemed excited by that idea, having a grasp on one's place in history, but then she sighed, so I wasn't sure if she was excited or felt some other emotion. Unfortunately, she said, the American people had no sense of history. They believed that everything that came before them was irrelevant, except insofar as it had given them what they needed. They hoped that their children would have children, and that those children would believe in hardship the way they themselves had once believed in fairy tales.

When the woman had first been sent here by the aid organization, she had felt like she would never be able to communicate with anyone. It had occurred to her that the problems of the farmers were fundamental human problems. Hunger, greed, droughts:

this was the stuff that could be survived only with the accompaniment of faith, the stuff religion was made of. Her problems, on the other hand, were frivolous. She wondered if she would ever be in love. She wondered if her conception of love had been so thoroughly animated by a fantasy of self-improvement that she couldn't help but see it as a story with only two possible endings: one happy, one sad, and in both cases, she died alone. She had trouble saying that, "die alone," because saying it made her cry. I had no idea why it made her cry, because dying alone was just a prediction of hers, which seemed to be founded on nothing. I looked at the napkin on her lap, trying to suggest (without suggesting) that she use it. She picked up the napkin and patted it on her cheeks, which unfortunately left chocolate where her tears had been.

She asked if I had any children. I didn't want to talk about that, so I told her I wasn't sure. She laughed, thinking I was making a joke about being a man, but I wasn't making a joke about being a man, I was just trying to avoid answering her question. I guess that gave her the impression that she should ask again, because she did ask again. I didn't like to lie, but I worried she would never stop asking me her question. I decided to make something up and told her I had a son. Unfortunately, I had messed up, given that that was not a lie. She asked me his name and age. I tried to come up with a random name and age, but I couldn't remember any name or age besides those associated with my real son, so those were what I gave her.

She asked if he had been a good baby. I didn't want to tell her he had been a bad baby, so I told her he had been a good baby, which he had been. I tried to drain my speech of meaning, but she seemed interested in that word, "good," even though she had been the one to introduce it. She asked me to say more. My mind wasn't able to think of any fake things, so I had no choice but to tell her things that were true. On the day he was born, I said, no one died, so we named him Revolution. The woman, looking past my eyes, told me to go on. I didn't want to go on, but I did.

After my son's mother left the hospital, I said, she brought him to the fence. The woman asked me why there was a fence around the hospital. I said the fence wasn't around the hospital, it was around the prison. She looked confused by that idea, prison, but a prison wasn't an idea, it was just a place. She asked, What business does a baby, a good baby, have at a prison? I didn't have the answer to that question, so I told her to disregard the prison, which had significance only insofar as it was the place where I had been sent to die. I hadn't died, so it was insignificant. Anyway, I said, I introduced him to everyone in the insignificant prison, even the ones who had been executed already.

The woman looked as if she had been abducted to a place where she didn't want to go. I think she realized her expression was unpleasant, because she put on a smile and asked about my son's profession. I told her that as far as I knew, he didn't have a profession. Her smile dropped, but then she picked it back up again. She asked if he had children. I told her I wasn't sure about that. I think she thought I didn't understand the question, because she switched languages and asked me again. Again, I told her I wasn't sure.

Her face screwed up, and she looked at me as if she might find something in my expression, something that belonged to me but that she could use for herself. I tried to become completely vacant. I tried to exit my body. She told me my son must love me very much. I couldn't tell if she believed what she was saying, or if she was trying to convince herself that the affection parents felt for their babies reflected back on the parents, turning them into saints. But my son didn't remember being a baby or being loved. My son couldn't remember me outside of what I had done. I left him, and when I tried to find him, he had no desire to be found.

I didn't tell the woman all of that. I just looked out the window at the dry, red plains until the bus driver announced our arrival and the bus came to a halt. Outside, there was nothing to indicate that we were welcome. Again, the station was conjured only by the existence of the bus and, surrounding it, all sorts of passengers, myself included, disembarking.

Smoke was rising from the town. As I approached it, the land became rockier and the road more inclined. At the top of the hill, the road leveled and burst open. There were no traffic patterns. Cars moved wherever they wanted. Drivers shouted, holding one another responsible for a problem they made collectively. Herders walked alongside them, trailing cows with sticks. Goats ran through all of it, seeming to belong to no one.

I wandered onto the sidelines, a strip of concrete where the road met a series of unmarked storefronts. Young men were eating their breakfasts, squatting as if seated on tiny stools. But there were no

tiny stools. Everything was balanced precariously: the tea, threatening to overflow, in one hand; the bread, crumbling, in another;
and the men's weight, concentrated in the balls of the feet, heels
suspended a few inches above the ground. When waitresses came
out with bowls of sugar, each man reached up to receive a spoon
and brought it down to his glass with easy precision. From a distance, everyone seemed to be sitting alone, but when I approached,
I could hear that they were conversing.

Two of the men, one good-looking, the other average, were arguing about history. The good-looking man was adamant that it
was fundamentally cyclical, due to the destructive nature of human
behavior. For instance, he said, flicking bread crumbs into the air,
everyone knew that global corporations were antithetical to human
flourishing, yet they had grown so omnipresent that it was nearly
impossible to envision a better quality of life in their absence.

I looked around for signs of the omnipresence of global corporations, and saw a goat eating some trash. A waitress approached the
two men and asked to clear their plates. But the average-looking
man was busy mounting his rebuttal. History, he said, ignoring her,
tended toward progress. It was defined by the inventive solutions of
ordinary people who learned to recognize themselves as oppressed.
Oppressed people, when they banded together, were forced to come
up with strategies to keep on living. Although these strategies could
never completely relieve an entire society of its oppressive qualities,
and could not be replicated, as each circumstance demanded its
own creative solutions, they did, in time, chip away at the narrative
that ascribed powerlessness to ordinary people in the face of their
leaders' political might.

I wasn't sure which of the two men I agreed with. I could relate
to the first man's point about the immutable qualities of human
beings, who were obsessed with securing their status as individuals
and would justify any number of horrible actions, including war
and genocide, in order to do so. But then I realized I might have
been predisposed to agree with the first man because he was comparatively good-looking. On the other hand, individualism was a
relatively recent trend in history, which passed for universal and
unchanging only because people constantly invoked it as such in
order to excuse their own selfish behavior. So, perhaps I really did
agree with the average-looking man. However, the fact that the two
men were having the exact same debate my friends and I had had

thirty years ago, when we were young, suggested that history was fated to repeat itself after all.

The good-looking man signaled for a waitress, ordered another piece of bread, and then continued speaking. He could understand, he said, the temptation to believe that social change was possible, especially since revolution didn't depend on consensus, but on the will and ingenuity of a dedicated few. But the actual process of revolution was difficult and almost completely contrary to the postrevolutionary life it promised. There was no inherent joy in disavowing the comforts of complicity, in being tortured, or imprisoned, or separated from one's family.

The waitress approached the good-looking man with a piece of bread and held it above his head. The sacrifices people made, he said, reaching his hand up to receive it, achieved significance only if and when they could be viewed retrospectively, from a position of success. The waitress stooped to pick up the good-looking man's old plate off the concrete, and then hovered above him, as if she expected him to say thank you. But he didn't say thank you. He just kept his eyes locked on the average-looking man. With distance, the good-looking man said, taking a bite of his bread, it was easy to see that almost all suffering people had suffered in vain.

I was beginning to get bored and prayed that either the good-looking or the average-looking man would soon bring up the fate of a specific suffering person or group of suffering people. For the time being, I stood near the road and pretended I was waiting for someone. The average-looking man drained his tea. Their argument, he said, was impossible to resolve, because the conclusions they were inclined to draw depended on the assumptions they had made from the very beginning. The good-looking man was able to argue that suffering had no meaning only because he had already established that history did not progress. He, on the other hand, maintained an unwavering belief in the possibility of change, and therefore had no trouble imagining some future point at which the struggles of all persecuted people would be redeemed.

In response, the good-looking man shifted to a new rhetorical tactic: talking about a tragedy that had befallen his own family. His father, he said, had had a brother who resembled the average-looking man, to the extent that both had a false confidence in their own capacities as political agents. The two brothers had been born to a powerful landlord and would have stood to inherit hundreds of acres of fertile land, in addition to cattle, horses, and gold. But the revolution had changed all of that. Their father was stripped of his land and, in the night, members of the military shot down his door and demanded he pay for a second bullet, the one that would go into his head.

While one brother mourned, the other joined a movement that fought for their father's land to be given to the peasants who farmed it. The good-looking man had never met his father's brother, who had been arrested and imprisoned, and had then fled to safety as soon as he was released, abandoning his wife and son. The good-looking man's father had not taken up arms. Instead, he had cared for his wife and child, even after he began to suffer from health problems that would plague him for the rest of his life.

For some years, the good-looking man said, his father had received a monthly allotment of medication, flown in from a country where medications were produced in abundance. But the country that produced the medication stopped providing it for free, and his father's salary was too small to cover the cost. One night, while his father slept, the good-looking man had gone through his father's possessions and found the phone number of his father's brother. The good-looking man knew almost nothing about his uncle except that he was now in another country, being an individual.

So, the good-looking man bought a calling card and went to a telephone booth. A man on the other end said something gruff, and then the good-looking man delivered his speech. When he finished it, the man asked for his name. The good-looking man gave his name, his father's name, his father's father's name, and so on. The man on the other end, who the good-looking man was by now sure was his uncle, said he knew no one by that name, and then he hung up.

By this point, I didn't want the good-looking man to go on talking, but it didn't matter what I wanted, because his story had no ending. The ending was implied by its beginning. The average-looking man told him he was sorry, and handed him a tissue. The good-looking man looked at it, confused, and then appeared to realize that his cheek was damp. He gripped the tissue in his palm, as if having it in his possession was just as good as using it to wipe his face. His uncle, he said, was worthless to him, except insofar as he had provided him with an example of the fundamentally self-serving motivations for all human action. Anyway, he said, it was

in the past. Real problems always arose in the present. He had just
heard this morning that his uncle, who had pretended all those
years ago that like an angel he had no relation to anyone, was
returning to his hometown, just a few miles away, for the funeral.

The average-looking man asked what he planned to do. The
good-looking man placed his glass on the ground and, swallowing
a last piece of bread, stood up to his full height. If I had encoun-
tered him at night, in an alley or some other unsecured place
where we found ourselves alone, I would have been afraid, but as
it was, I must have appeared to him a pleasant stranger, assuming
he had thought to look over at me at all. His uncle, he said, had
probably suffered enough. Suffering was the lot of most men.

The good-looking man and the average-looking man both
stared at a vacant space on the sidewalk, working their brows as
if trying to find a way to fill it. I said good morning. They looked
up at me, then back at each other, and with a simultaneous flick
of their wrists motioned for me to sit. I decided not to. It was hard
to imagine making the long descent toward the invisible stool,
which seemed to me to require balance that my body did not have.
I didn't want to think about what kinds of unfortunate questions
they might ask me, such as how long it had been since I had last
returned home, what were the conditions of my leaving, what had
been my experience of life in prison, and so on. I would have been
happy to talk with these men about my opinions on current events,
such as, for example, my understanding of the world economy in
relation to the economy of the country where I had become a
citizen. But I had no doubt that they would be more interested
in trivial matters like the name of my father, my grandfather, and,
before him, my grandfather's father.

The two men motioned again for me to sit. I walked toward the
traffic and they called out to me, throwing in my direction either a
salutation or an insult. If I had turned around, I could have heard
them clearly, but I stayed facing in the direction I was going. As I approached the blur of cars, cows, and goats, I considered the extent
of my suffering. From what I understood about the nature of pain,
it could not be quantified. Some people liked to measure other
people's suffering, such that they could declare it to be "enough"
or "too much." But even once such a declaration was made, there
was no guarantee that the individual wouldn't go on to feel more
of it.

TOM BISSELL

His Finest Moment

FROM *Zyzzyva*

RIGHT NOW HIS wife was in the bathroom, crying, the door locked. Only moments before, she'd been seated on the edge of their bed while he paced around the room like a public defender saddled with a vividly guilty client. While he talked and explained, she interrupted several times to say "My God" in a voice that ranged from numb to outraged to numbly outraged. He'd been telling her that, for several weeks now, he was in contact with a reporter who worked for a large American newspaper. This reporter, furthermore, was apparently about to publish an article detailing "interactions" he'd had with various women. He knew some of the women's names but not what they were saying he'd done. That's why, he told her, he'd decided to engage with the reporter—to learn the nature of these accusations. The admission earned him his wife's biggest "My God" yet.

There were things he didn't tell his wife. For instance, he didn't tell his wife that the first time the reporter called was April Fool's Day, and how she was thus forced to assure him, more than once, that her questions weren't part of some elaborate practical joke. He didn't tell his wife that the reporter was the first he'd spoken to in years who didn't lead with how much she loved his books. He didn't tell his wife that, after the reporter's first call, he looked her up—young, state-school graduate, usually shared her byline—and became quickly, ruinously certain he could charm or bully her out of pursuing her story. He didn't tell his wife that, when this particular plan failed, he decided to make a note whenever the reporter mentioned a woman's name, so that he could later email the woman in question and begin to contain the damage. He didn't tell his wife that, to his intense frustration, the reporter's questions were oblique-specific micro masterpieces, and, as a result, he was never quite certain which woman was accusing him of what, which made the jocular hey-just-checking-in emails he'd planned to send rather more tactically and rhetorically challenging. He didn't tell his wife he'd spent three hours on the phone with the reporter total, often scoffing and sometimes yelling. And he didn't tell his wife that, during his last call with the reporter, tonight, just over an hour ago, he found himself begging her, please, don't do this.

So while he was, quite admittedly, dissembling, he noticed his wife was sitting like a coiled spring, looking left, to their bedroom door, to escape. He noticed, too, that, despite her obvious anger, she didn't seem particularly surprised. Finally, staring fixedly away, his wife interrupted to say, "Adultery isn't a national news story," after which she tendered her final "My God" and exited the room.

Shortly before all this they'd been discussing what to watch on Netflix tonight, the Indian food they'd order and eat while watching. He felt bad for his wife, certainly. In one moment, she was a good, consuming member of the human race, comfortably bonded to her husband. The next, her marriage was turned so violently inside out that neither she nor he recognized the vascular abomination dripping gore all over their bedroom carpet.

Obviously, part of him knew tonight was coming. Two nights ago, his lawyer—a woman, for what it was worth, whom he'd dragged into this mess far too late to have made a difference— informed him that the piece was "imminent." His publisher and editor, meanwhile, were no longer taking his calls, despite his having denied to them any wrongdoing. Per the lawyer, his publisher and editor were waiting to discover what he was being accused of. Once that was clear, he was told, they planned to take "amendatory" action, whatever that meant. Their gutlessness infuriated him. The dinners, the foreign editions, the awards, the money they'd made off his back—none of it mattered because some excitable child reporter had decided to take aim. Emerson said when you strike at a king, make sure you kill him. Now, one scandalous whisper and the royal guard dropped spears and scattered.

His lawyer referred him to a publicist who specialized in crisis management. Yet he never bothered calling the crisis manager because part of him believed this would all blow over, that his reputation was, as they say, too big to fail. Or maybe it was that calling the crisis manager meant admitting to himself that he was, indeed, in the middle of a crisis. Either way, his hopes were rudely sundered when the reporter called tonight to ask for "any final comment" before her piece went live. It was important to understand that, since April 1, his entire life—every decision, every conversation, every blink and yawn—had been like living with some tolerably horrid condition like tinnitus. In a way, he was relieved the buzzing had finally become a full-blown siren. He would no longer have to pretend that the uncertainty wasn't driving him perfectly crazy, that he still cared one fig about what he and his wife watched or ate.

Now he was standing outside his fifteen-year-old daughter's closed bedroom door. Needless to say, he and his wife had raised her right. *Never send a nude picture of yourself to any boy, ever, under any circumstances. You* are *a feminist. Moderate your social media usage. Black lives matter.* They'd been taking her to marches since she was twelve. A great kid. That's how he always described her to his friends: "She's just a great kid." Which was why he had to get ahead of this. His wife was going to be terribly hurt, obviously, but how would his little girl survive reading what this reporter was, apparently, about to accuse him of? No matter what, his daughter had to hear his side of the story first.

As for his side of the story . . . well, that was complicated, but then so are most worthwhile things. His novels were complicated. Emotionally complicated, anyway. He prided himself on that. He gave his characters, no matter how foul, a fair shake. He loved complicated. You can't write about what you don't understand—he couldn't, anyway—so that meant, for him, becoming a living complication. Formally speaking, though, his novels weren't complicated at all. They all had simple, declarative titles and were rigorously realistic. A hostile female critic had once described his fiction as "secretly conservative," which he often quoted with jollified disdain during writerly dinner parties: "There I go, being secretly conservative again!" Privately, though, he'd been thrilled by the critic's years-ago judgment. A good number of his favorite thinkers and writers, starting with Thomas Jefferson, could be described as "secretly conservative." His favorite thinkers and writers were all men, and sometimes he felt uneasy—implicated, even—

that this was so. He also wasn't sure what to do about it. Back when he used to read to his daughter before bedtime, he always made sure the books were by women. He wanted his daughter to know that the mysterious thing Daddy did in his office all day was something she could aspire to. A few years ago, however, to his lasting disappointment, his daughter seemed to lose her once-fervent interest in books. She'd certainly never expressed any interest in reading his, which bothered him, even though, at the same time, he didn't exactly *want* her reading them, because there were certain scenes and lines of dialogue she'd struggle to reconcile with the good-man masculinity he tried to model and embody. But for him, freedom from life's tiresome meat puppetry was the most magical thing about writing fiction—the way it allowed him to be simultaneously better and worse than he was.

So what *would* he tell his daughter? He'd been unfaithful. So what? So are most people, one way or another. He was a flirt and a libertine. Big deal. So were a lot of successful men. He'd made passes at dozens—possibly hundreds—of women, young and old, over the years, sometimes successfully, mostly not. He'd slipped any of a number of editorial and publicity assistants his hotel room key, and sometimes they showed up and sometimes they didn't. He genuinely loved women and knew they genuinely loved him back. Very occasionally, though, he'd think about the times he'd had a drink thrown in his face, or the emails he'd received over the years subject-titled "Leave me alone" or "Stop contacting me," but that was the cost of doing business. He didn't hurt people. Had he always behaved honorably? No, but he couldn't imagine anything more boring than always behaving honorably. And since when was any of his behavior illegal, much less a matter of national interest? When you got down to it, that's what he really wanted to say to his publisher, editor, and wife, along with all the close friends hours away from writing him off as a monster: *You know who I am. You've read the books. My compulsions, my fascinations—they're all there.* His thirty-year, multi-volume confession had sold hundreds of thousands of copies—and he was the only one who didn't look the other way, the only one who didn't pretend he was something he wasn't.

Early in their conversations, he'd pointed out this hypocrisy to the reporter, who agreed it was "interesting," using a tone of voice that indicated anything other than agreement or being interested. Her condescension enraged him. "I would be very, very careful if I were you," he told her. "Because all you've got is private business between consenting adults." The reporter's response: "I'm afraid that's not quite true."

And then he knew what, mostly likely, she had, and it was nothing he could tell his daughter about or rationalize away. The Incident—that's how he referred to it in his head, almost as if it had been something that happened to him, rather than something he'd done—involved a young woman he met during his last book tour, in Madison, Wisconsin, the day his most recent novel debuted at number three on the bestseller list. That didn't excuse his behavior, certainly, but it helped explain it, at least to himself. It just wasn't a night he wanted to hear *no*, in the end.

The young woman had approached after his reading and revealed that she'd been in touch with him before, through his website, only months earlier, and that he'd given her "great advice" about whether to quit her MFA program. (He couldn't remember what exactly he'd said to her and never asked whether she was still in her MFA program.) When he invited the young woman to get a drink he wasn't expecting her to say yes, necessarily, and was totally prepared to wind up back at his hotel, alone, next to a bottle of room-serviced chardonnay, reading over his most recent novel's ever-growing list of Amazon reviews. But she did say yes. At the bar, he drank too much and she drank too much. "You keep feeding me drinks!" she said at one point, which soured the mood a bit, at least inside his head. He wanted to tell her, "You keep *ordering* drinks." She was having a hard time ambulating by the time they left. His hotel room was huge, so he offered her his couch rather than risk her driving herself home. The first time he kissed her was in the elevator, which she didn't like, so he backed off. The second time he kissed her was when she was on the couch, tucked in, at which point she said she felt sick. What happened next was not, admittedly, his finest moment. He touched her a little bit, after she seemed to have fallen asleep. He kept touching her until she woke up and asked him to stop, but by that point his hand was already in her underwear. If she'd tried harder to push his hand away he likely would have stopped, but she didn't, so he didn't. He already knew she had a boyfriend, because she couldn't stop fucking talking about him at the bar, but he had a wife, so just by

being in a hotel room together they'd already signed their mutu-
ally assured destruction pact. That was how he saw things, anyway.
She climaxed, for the record. He finished himself off in the bathroom, because forcing himself on a drunk girl wasn't exactly his
thing. When he woke up in the morning, with a railroad-spike of
a hangover, she was gone. He never even got her last name—not
until, that is, the reporter said *I'm afraid that's not quite true.* After
hanging up on the reporter, he went and looked through his old
emails and voilà. He then emailed the young woman, casually, al-
luding to their night together in Madison's Edgewater Hotel only
in the vaguest terms. She never responded. That he'd reached out
to this young woman at all was of "particularly grave concern" to
his lawyer. Again, not his finest moment.

When he opened his daughter's bedroom door she was lying
on her bed, wearing pale yellow sweats and a pale yellow sweatshirt
two sizes too big for her, looking like a formless dollop of pancake
batter. Naturally, she was fixated on her phone. His daughter had
been in an uncommunicatively foul mood for the last few months,
which was almost certainly creditable to the awkward phase she
was going through: braces, acne, a recent weight gain. Truth be
told, his daughter's awkward phase was pretty perfectly timed, if
only because there was no beast more hormonally feral than a
fifteen-year-old boy. He wanted to protect his daughter from that.
Thus, when his daughter pranced up to him, a few months ago,
with a pamphlet advertising expensive laser-based acne treatment,
he balked at the price. She reminded him he'd just signed the
movie deal for his still-best-selling novel. When he said that wasn't
the point, she stormed off to her room. He later found the pamphlet inserted under his laptop in his writing office, which was, he
thought, a nice touch. Still, he wasn't about to fork over $3,000 for
an anti-acne laser treatment that wasn't even guaranteed to work.
She had the rest of her life to be attractive.

When he came into his daughter's bedroom, she said, without
looking away from her phone, "You didn't knock." She had him
there, but still: how he resented her pinchy little reminders of
their recent estrangement. So, like a bad actor, he took a big, exaggerated backward step into the jamb, half-closed the door, and
knocked. "Come in," she said, and there it was: the old half-smile
in her voice, affixed at the midpoint between a child's helpless
love and a teenager's practiced disdain.

He sat down on her bed and asked, "What are you looking at?"

When she showed him her phone, he was expecting to see Instagram or TikTok, but no, there it was: the digital front page of the newspaper whose account of him was "imminent." Had the piece finally been published? At once he began to perspire. "Sweetheart—" he said, but there were no more words inside him. Nothing was inside him but some small, impotent creature scratching at the suddenly glass walls of his stomach.

His daughter didn't notice his squirming, hot-bodied discomfort. Which is when he realized: a coincidence. That's all this was. Like the April Fool's Day phone call that started all this. The piece *hadn't* yet been published. His precocious, acne-faced daughter was merely scanning the headlines of the fallen world she'd soon inherit.

"Put your phone away," he said. "Please."

She did.

"I have to talk to you about something."

"Okay."

"It's serious."

She scooted herself upright on the bed. "Okay."

"There's going to be some news coming out."

"What kind of news?"

The mute little creature inside him scratched and scratched. He managed to say, "The book. My book."

"What—are they not doing the movie now? I heard sometimes that happens. They pay for the movie but then they don't make it or whatever."

The movie. He had yet to ponder how this situation might impact the movie. "I'm not sure," he said. "It's possible they won't be making the movie."

"Oh," she said. Then: "That would be too bad."

"Yes," he said. "It would."

"Are you okay?"

"I think so. I just knew that—I knew you'd be disappointed to hear."

"I mean, if it doesn't happen, I'd be sad for you, but . . ."

It occurred to him, then, that he'd be having some version of this conversation for months, even years. He'd have to explain, over and over again, to himself and others, why things didn't work out, hadn't worked out, wouldn't work out. To fight the tears forming in his eyes, he willed himself to think of his daughter, as a child, selling lemonade in their driveway, the sunshine streaming through her pitcher, the pure scalpy smell of her unwashed hair, their life together still an endless meadow of possibility. "But what?" he asked, his voice breaking.

"That's it. I'd-be-sad-for-you-but." She shrugged and then smiled, but tentatively. She knew something was wrong. When she put her hand on his knee, the love he felt from her: It was real. It was real.

She asked, "You're sure you're okay? Are you and Mom okay? I heard you guys arguing before."

He stood. "I'm fine. We're fine."

"You're not like sick or something?"

His laugh was quick and manic, his eyes wild. "I love you, kiddo."

"Love you, too, Dad." But she looked so scared.

"Take care," he said. Then a sad little wave. He'd think about that a lot in the coming months. The last thing he said to his daughter: *Take care.*

He was leaving her bedroom now, passing through the static charge of his own cowardice, wondering if he was imagining the industrious sounds (thuds, zippers) of his wife packing elsewhere in the house. Was she packing for him or the two of them? He didn't have long to wonder about that, because his daughter's phone started pinging with incoming text messages, and then his phone—a hyperactive heart—started vibrating in his pocket, and then the house phone, and his wife's phone, a sensory barrage he barely registered, watching as his daughter lifted her phone to her face and touched the embedded link, which pulled her, without mercy, both away from and into his world.

T A R Y N   B O W E

Camp Emeline

FROM *Indiana Review*

LAKE CHANDELIER WAS midnight blue, vibrating with motor-boats and pontoons, snapping turtles and beavers. Ringed by towering pines and rocky hills, the water shimmered back the sky, stretched out the clouds, sometimes dwarfed the trees. When the settlement money came in, my dad handed me a hundred-dollar bill. I was supposed to use it for something special, he said. The last three years had been chock-full of slick lawyers, collection calls, and outstanding medical bills triggering fresh parental break-downs. By the time we arrived at the camp on the lake, I'd already spent my windfall on twelve bottles of Busch Light. Mr. Morosi sold to underage kids but jacked up the price. My brother, Eli, had spent his settlement money on an acoustic guitar he never played. It was hard to know what to do with death cash. Our younger sister, Emeline, had suffered from spina bifida. She needed a shunt in her head so her brain didn't swell. If her doctors had diagnosed her clogged shunt problem, she would have been eleven, but since they'd missed it, she'd died two months before her eighth birth-day. My parents had spent the last three years waging war against Shriners Hospital for Children in Springfield. A lifetime of court dates later, we were two million dollars richer, the owners of a camp on a lake my parents intended to transform into a summer haven for sick kids.

When we arrived that May, having sold our home in Agawam, seven of the camp's ten cabins were infested with forest mice. A downed tree had ripped a hole through the Mess Hall roof. Nothing about the camp was wheelchair friendly. The girls' bathhouse sat on a raised concrete platform accessed by rickety stairs. The cabin doors were narrow and there were only slim spaces to maneuver between wobbly bunks. The path to the swimming beach was riddled with roots and rocks. Poison ivy was rampant. Even weeks before the hottest, longest days of summer, the mosquitoes were scrappy and out for blood.

That first night, my dad drove the van back into Meredith to buy flashlights and batteries. My mom sat on an army cot in the corner of our cabin, flicking pistachio shells into a bowl. She was someone I no longer knew, either a juggernaut of ferocious energy or a defeated, sunken ship. I missed the in-betweens; giggling, singing Joni Mitchell, licking batter from wooden spoons. I made my mom sadder, I think. I was the daughter who'd survived but look what I was doing with my life. Months before, a friend had snitched to a teacher that I'd jerk off any loser for twenty-five bucks. The principal had called my mom. I'd gotten suspended. My mom couldn't look at me for more than three seconds without turning her face. I left the cabin and walked into the cool, blue night. A giant lawn sloped down to an athletic field flanked by basketball rims, a fenced-in tennis court teeming with weeds. Beyond the court, pines rose, blocking my view of the pebbled beach. The lake was a black slash on the horizon. Without campers, the camp was a ghost town. I could hear loons wailing. "I'm here," they seemed to say. "But where are you?"

The next morning, Eli and I set off to case the property. In the woods, I found a rotted rowboat, a three-legged bench, a torn screen door under a mound of balled-up plastic. Eli found a creepy marionette dangling from a bush, an unstrung tennis racket, a pair of wooden stilts. We dragged our finds down to the swim beach and threw them on top of the heaped-up brush and snapped-off tree limbs we planned to burn later that night. Branches in the water needed to be dredged out. The water was freezing and smelled like bullfrogs. I stripped down to my underwear and T-shirt, waded in, closed my eyes, went under, patting the muck at the bottom for sharp rocks and twigs. I'd read about pets and people who'd drowned in icy water but didn't die, their hearts and brains freezing, needing nothing—no blood, no oxygen—until their bodies thawed.

"You okay?" Eli asked when I came up, shaking.

I nodded, stepping out to dump an armful of rocks beside a dented canoe.

I went back in, finger-raked the bottom for objects and debris that needed to be hauled out. An empty Pringles can, a pair of goggles with a broken strap. Once, I tried to open my eyes, but I couldn't see my hand in front of my face, and for a second, as I crouched low, I couldn't stop shuddering with the certainty that when I resurfaced, nothing and nobody I cared about would be there.

When I emerged, Eli was talking to a guy who looked like he'd stepped off a Nature Channel documentary about leaving civilization to run wild in the woods with bears. His hair was chin length. His beard was speckled with flakes of leaves. I wondered when he'd last glanced in a mirror or washed his clothes. He said he was the camp's sole employee, part of the package my parents had purchased.

"That's my place." He pointed to a small shack leaning over the narrow path that wound back to the Mess Hall.

I grabbed my pants and sweatshirt from a rock and pulled them over my sopping underwear and shirt. "So, you're like a hermit?" I said.

"More like a landscaper," he said.

"Can you buy us beer?"

"No car."

No car wasn't a problem. I said, "Eli can take you in our dad's van."

That evening, the three of us drank at the beach as crickets shrieked and a new moon rose. None of us talked. Eli had doused our foraged branches with gasoline. I'd dropped the match to ignite the blaze. Now we sat balanced atop logs as the fire tore at the air and drove off the insects zigzagging around us.

I stared at the fire's edges, trying to see things that weren't there. Before we'd come to the lake, I'd had this dumb idea that it would be easier to spot signs sent by Emeline in nature. In the wild, there were more messengers. Moths, dragonflies, pockets of cool air, blankets of mist. Off in the distance, I heard a woodpecker drilling into a tree. But I didn't think Emeline would send me a woodpecker. I was waiting for something brilliant.

After a while, I went for my third beer. "Isn't it weird," I said, "for a grown man to come with a camp like an indentured servant?"

Lawn Boy cracked open a new can. "So, who's Emeline?" he asked.

Her name was already painted on the large green sign at the end of the road. Our father's first act of improvement.

"Our dead sister," Eli said.

I said, "Now your turn. Tell us your story, your *real* story."

"Come on, Libs," Eli said. "It's late."

"Where are your people? What did you do to them?" I said.

It was great to be drunk, to say whatever I wanted, to not give a shit about who I hurt.

Lawn Boy sunk into his seat. Eli got up, grabbed an empty, filled it with lake water, and dumped it on the fire. He patted my shoulder. In my mind, the trees began to fall like dominoes. When I tried to stand, my knees gave out. The second time I tried, Lawn Boy grabbed my elbow. The three of us staggered up the path to the cabins. I thought I might vomit, but instead I crashed into Lawn Boy's chest.

"You heard about our money," I said. "Didn't you? You're here to rob us."

"Hey now. Whoa." He held me away. "Don't ruin a nice night."

"What was nice about it? Your beer was shitty. I want my money back."

"I'll take her," Eli said.

Eli slung an arm around my shoulder. He helped me up the hill. At the bathhouse, he steered me into the girls' section, where he cupped his hands beneath a faucet and caught a small pool of water for me to drink.

In the morning, mist rose off the lake. My headache required five aspirin. It was June 1, and we had less than a month to get the grounds ready before the first campers arrived. Saws whirred constantly. Lawn Boy rode a mower over the Great Lawn and across the fields. Eli raked bags of clay over the tennis court, tamping the clay with his feet so it settled flat. I swept the cabins, checked the mattresses for mice and fleas. My mom spent long hours with the insurance broker in Meredith, figuring out how to cover our asses against people like us who liked to sue. My dad planted something of Emeline's in every cabin; the red rabbit stuffy she'd rubbed furless, a nubby yellow blanket, now no more than a tangle of fuzz and string. Eli and I joked that the cabins might be mucked up with pine needles and squirrel shit but at least each one had a freaky shrine to a small dead girl.

"Let's get that in the brochure," I said in my mother's taskmaster voice.

"Front and center," Eli said.

We didn't talk about what we missed. Her wet spluttery giggles, the way she had zero shame. How sometimes, when the three of us were watching TV, she'd start touching herself, making these little soft sighs of pleasure, and when Eli or I said, "Emeline, weirdo, that's private," she'd look at us like we were the dummies. Like she'd discovered the secret to surviving existence. Why on earth weren't we doing this too?

At night, I heard my parents tossing, one of them tiptoeing to the common-area cot that served as a bed or a couch depending on the hour. I walked out of our cabin to the hill that overlooked the lake. The moon was small, but the lake reflected it back bigger and brighter. I looked for the slant of Lawn Boy's roof hidden beneath layers of tree cover. I wanted to ask him if he'd ever made himself into a monster to survive a monstrous thing. What was the worst thing he'd ever seen? The worst thing he'd ever done? Had he ever held another person while they were dying? Come out, I thought. Please come out. I stared at the trees overhanging his shed. It didn't work. All the wanting in the world couldn't make someone materialize.

My parents mobilized a ragtag army of locals to get Camp Emeline into tip-top shape. Angus the Cook, who lived in the double-wide down the road, stocked the cabinets with carbs and condiments. Ursula, head of housekeeping, bleached the shower curtains and unclogged the drains. Mr. Orlov, the stiff, stuffy private school teacher who summered next door, interviewed high school and college students for junior and senior counselor positions. Soon, Reid Tupperman moved into Cabin F. He was a rising junior at the all-boys Catholic prep school in Center Harbor. A diabetic golfer, he was a real-life role model for chronically sick kids. One morning, I found him slashing away at the raised roots that mangled the path to the water. His shirt hung on a nearby branch. His skin was damp. Tiny insects flecked his shoulders.

"I'm Libby," I said.

He reminded me of the B-list boys I'd messed around with in Agawam. Unexceptionally athletic. Marginally cute. Boys desperate enough for physical contact with a girl their age that they were cool with a little shove here, a bite there, a flash of rage and roughness, or no interaction at all, a floppy body on a couch, depending on the night.

I told Reid Tupperman about our nightly shindigs at the beach. "If you give the lawn guy money, he'll buy you beer. No added cost."

A mosquito landed on his neck. When he swatted at the wrong side, I said, "No, there," and brushed the tips of my fingers against his slick and sunbaked skin. I waited for him to say something about Emeline. Every night, our "camp family," as my parents called them, gathered before platters of swollen spaghetti or Shake 'N Bake chicken while my dad said Emeline's name and a brief prayer for strength to install the new boat dock or for guidance to find a crackerjack camp nurse. Sometimes, he wept, as if we weren't among strangers, and I wanted to crawl into my food and die.

"There's another one." I pointed to a mosquito on Reid's temple.

He smushed it against his scalp, leaving behind a bubble of blood.

That night, the four of us—Eli, Lawn Boy, myself, and Reid—drank on the beach beside the fire. Smoke spilled over us, seeping into our hair and clothes. Eli picked a bug bite on his chin. I told him to stop picking it, to let it be. I'd found a letter from Peter Traylor, Agawam's varsity soccer goalie, under his pillow that day. It said: *I'm not a cocksucker like you,*

"Let's burn it," I'd said about the letter. Now, it was already gone. I wished I'd said more, wished I'd said I knew who he was, and it was fine. I'd chew up and spit out the heart of anyone who gave him shit about it.

Lawn Boy drank with his head tipped back, his eyes in the trees. Reid asked if we were always this quiet and boring.

"Pretty much," Eli said.

Reid took another slug of beer and stood, unzipping his pants, pushing them down to his ankles. He wore what looked like swim trunks underneath, shiny fabric with aquamarine dolphins. When

he turned away, toward the trees, fuzzy blond hairs glistened along
one of his calves. The other leg was plastic. Reid's natural leg, the
flesh one, was covered by the most ludicrous tattoo I'd ever seen.
Two huge brown eyes, a snout. That dumb fawn, Bambi.

"What the fuck?" Eli asked.

"Got inked to make a girl smile," Reid said. "Ask me where she
is now?" He pulled his pants back up and buttoned them. "You
guessed it, geniuses. Not with me."

Lawn Boy laughed for the first time since I'd met him. Eli got
up and threw another log on the fire. I stood and made my way
out to the boat dock. The dock was narrow and aluminum. It
gleamed on the lake like a silver T. At the end, I sat and slipped
out of my sandals, dipped my toes into the water. It was too dark to
see if the slippery vibrations beneath the surface were minnows or
sensations I'd dreamt up because I was alone inside my body and
wanted more than anything to brush up against the other side.

After a while, I heard Reid ask Eli about the guitar he always
talked about but never played. Could he run back to his cabin
and get it? Eli dashed off, and Lawn Boy walked out on the dock
and sat about a foot away from me. He smelled of beer and woodsmoke.

"Next time you get wasted and want to take advantage of some
cute boy," he said, "try him." He gestured back to Reid, who was
waiting for Eli.

I kicked at the water. "You're not a cute boy. You're like a
middle-aged man."

"I'm twenty-four," he said.

A firecracker whistled across the lake. He jumped five inches.

I said, "I was a bitch the other night."

"Is that an apology?"

"Maybe."

He said, "When life gives you lemons, you get to be an asshole."

"Is that how it goes?" I asked.

"Who knows how it goes?" he said.

We were quiet, and I heard terrible singing. "Purple Rain."
When I glanced over my shoulder, Reid was arranging Eli's hands
on the guitar, showing him different positions along the finger-
board. I turned back to Lawn Boy. Sometimes, he looked lost. But
other times, in a certain darkness, I sensed he could see through
all my bullshit to the truest part of me.

*

The next night, the mist sank low. Rain pelted the pines above us, and Reid stood and yelled, "Who's swimming?" Eli went after him. They both plunged in. It was good to see my brother letting loose. Within seconds, his hands were on Reid's shoulders, pushing him under.

"Strange night," Lawn Boy said to me, wiping moisture from his cheek.

"You going in?" I asked.

"Nah." He wanted to take out a canoe.

I followed him to the boat rack, where we slid a canoe off the shelf. We carried it down to the water. I sat in the front, and Lawn Boy settled in the back and pushed off. I was such a bad paddler my strokes made it harder for him to steer, so we agreed to take turns. He paddled for a while, and I lay back and closed my eyes. The rain coated my face. The boat rocked beneath me. When the crickets were loud, I knew we were near the shore, and when I could hear the loons wailing, I knew we were moving toward the center where they'd built a nest. When it was my turn, I opened my eyes and sat up. The rain had stopped but the night was still moonless. I dipped my paddle into the water and pulled, guessing we were somewhere near the Christian girls' camp on the north side. I'd known a girl who'd spent six weeks there. Camp Hartland, it was called. By day, campers sang songs about Jesus. By night, they streaked the archery field and used Sharpie markers to label each other's fat.

"What time is it?" I asked.

"Probably time to head back," he said.

But we didn't.

Somewhere in the dark middle, Lawn Boy said, "Everything okay with your parents?"

I said, "Probably not. It's like we're all ghosts, and she's the one who's still here."

"Yeah," he said, as if he'd already drawn the same conclusion.

I heard a fish leap out of the water. I tried to spot it moving, flashes of silver, shimmers of green. I waited for Lawn Boy to tell me something, to explain why he was here on a canoe at a camp on a lake in the middle of nowhere. I didn't think he was a land-scaper. When we'd arrived, nothing about the camp's grounds seemed cared for or maintained. Maybe he'd simply needed a place to stop, to rest, to figure out where to go and how to get there. This didn't sound so strange to me. I asked about his family.

"A half sister," he said.

I told him about Emeline, how something was always wrong with her. If it wasn't her allergies, it was her stomach. If it wasn't her stomach, it was her joints. Sometimes her lungs or vision petered out. She got horrible headaches, saw things that weren't real. I always crawled into her bed when she was frightened. I still didn't know how to sleep without her warmth.

"Are you still there?" I asked him.

"Still here," he said.

His oar dipped into the water, and the boat slid backward.

"Do you know where we are?" I asked.

"Somewhere off Hawk's Nest Beach."

I said, "That's good. We haven't drifted into Canada."

The canoe nudged something wooden. Along the lake's west edge, the trees grew slantwise, their trunks emerging from the gold-brown water like the hulls of sunken ships.

I said, "My parents filed this crazy lawsuit. There was a bump on her head that got infected. She showed it to me, and I felt it and then forgot it. The next day she was in the ICU. Maybe they should have sued me, for like negligence or manslaughter or whatever the fuck?"

"I don't think so," he said. He paddled some more, and the Christian camp's lights receded. "You live long enough, you learn that for every person that's ever died there's a story about how they didn't have to. All the people I've lost," he said, "someone should have been able to save. Couldn't. Pills. Then other stuff. Nothing to do but watch and wait."

I stared at my fingers, coiled around the oar's grip. It felt like we were entering a new body of water, an atmosphere of horrible truths. I wanted to reach back and pat his knee, but I didn't want to tip us. I didn't know how to flip a boat upright if we capsized and needed to turn it over to get back in. "I haven't figured out how to make myself strong again," I said.

He said, "Me neither."

It wasn't long before I heard splashing and my brother's laugh. Up ahead, Eli sprinted down the metal dock and cannonballed into the lake. Lawn Boy had steered us back to shore. How long had we been out there? I didn't know. It was like we'd never left.

If only I'd known no one was missing us, I would have stayed gone longer.

Shortly after our night in the canoe, Lawn Boy came down with a migraine that lasted several days. On the first day, he drove the mower into a tree. My mother ordered him to rest. I checked on him hourly, trying not to be too obvious. A single window offered a glimpse into his shed. Passing, I stalled there, watched the outline of his sleeping body until his chest rose and fell, until his shoulders twitched. On the third day, I lifted the handle and opened his door. His shed smelled like a barn, trapped creature-heat and no fresh air. A belt hung from a nail, and I found a gray towel tossed over a chair and used it to dab his forehead. For a while, I sat on the hard floor beside his pillow, counting his breaths, staring at his things. His watch, with its broken minute hand, a stick of deodorant, a metal spoon. Once, he cried out, and I pressed my fingers to his whiskers, damp with sweat. I wondered if he was here to raid the infirmary for drugs once the sick kids came. Well, good for him, I thought. None of this took away from the fact that he'd made me feel less alone, that he'd seen my ugliness and wasn't repulsed by it. I didn't want to leave him. I wanted to crawl into his bed and cling on tight, but the campers were coming in five days. I had things to do.

That night, Lawn Boy didn't come to the fire. I mentioned a sore throat, said goodnight early, hit the path back up the hill. Soon, I was on the part of the trail that was too far from the beach to catch the boathouse lights, too far from the Mess Hall to catch the glow of the orange lamps. A pale streak flashed through the brush in front of me. I rushed to follow it as it sliced between trees. It stopped at the private beach, where a tree stretched over the lake's edge, shielding the shore from public view. At first, I didn't recognize my mother, naked except for a towel wrapped over her breasts. Her hair ran over her shoulders. She wandered out to the water. She had a beautiful back. Straight and proud, without scars or birthmarks. I'd forgotten this. When she crouched down, the water wet the ends of her hair. I longed to go to her, swim to her, in only the skin I was born in, but there was no going back. This was something no one told you. In a family, you didn't lose one person. You lost one person, and everyone changed. My mother went under. Ripples radiated from the spot where her head had been. I wanted to touch that spot, submerge my fingers. Maybe the water carried her electricity. Maybe, in this small way, we could still connect. I couldn't bear for her to see my spying. I dug my fingernails into a tree. When my mother resurfaced, her hair glistened in the moonlight. I wondered if she was waiting for a sign from Emeline too.

On the night the counselors arrived, Angus the Cook served a banquet of chicken patties. My mother welcomed the staff and read aloud the names of campers arriving the next day. A boy from New Mexico who was allergic to sunlight, a girl from Minneapolis who'd lost eight bones in her face. Two kids with epilepsy, one with leukemia, a crew with asthma. Nurse Shelby, poached from a pediatric clinic in Boston, tapped the point of her pen against her teeth. The counselors hailed from all over the world. Elka was from Norway. Claudette was from France. It felt like an invasion. All through the meal, I looked at Lawn Boy, noticing the way his beard and face changed shape in response to small talk he didn't join in. Halfway through, he got up and disappeared. When he came back, he whispered, "Libs, I got you Kahlua for our last bonfire."

Around nine, it began to pour. Plan B was the boathouse. There, we gathered as rain lashed the trees. We were all sopping wet. I dug through the plastic QuikMart bags until I found the four-pack of premixed Kahlua cocktails Lawn Boy had bought me. Reid unearthed a funnel from a backpack and showed Eli how to raise the cone part high to make the beer gush down his throat. We talked about people we knew who'd gotten their stomachs pumped in high school. Lawn Boy walked to the sliding door. It was open, and you could edge right up to a wall of falling water, break in with your nose, while the rest of you stayed dry. I reached up and touched Lawn Boy's chin. After dinner, he'd shaved his whiskers.

I said, "So soft."

"You're drunk," he said.

"Not quite."

"Your eyes are bloodshot."

I admitted I'd cried a bit on my walk over. I was happy and afraid of happiness ending.

He said he wished it weren't raining. He'd take me out on the lake.

"We could go anyway."

"We could," he said.

But we didn't. I took his hand and looked again at his razed, raw cheeks.

"Do you want to go somewhere else?" I asked. When I glanced back over my shoulder, Reid was kneeling on the floor with the hose of the funnel in his mouth while Eli poured beer into the funnel's opening.

"And leave these monkeys?" Lawn Boy said.

I counted aloud and when I hit three, leapt through the wall of water. In seconds, I was drenched. But he was behind me. A few minutes later, we spilled into his shed. We sat on the floor. He reached under his pillow, pulled out a bottle, and passed it to me.

At some point, I leaned against him, and he looped an arm around my shoulder. I curled into his chest.

"You still awake?" I asked after a while, and he said, "Still awake."

I shifted closer because the floor was hard and I was uncomfortable. The rhythm of the rain on the roof slowed down. He wrapped his arms around me tighter. We were still soaked, and when I started to shiver, he grabbed a blanket off his bed and spread it around us. It smelled like hay.

His chin rested against the top of my head. "Listen," he said. "It stopped."

I did, and it had, the rain. One of the loons wailed. I waited for another to call back. That's why they cried like that, I'd read, to find a mate, or sometimes, if their calls were short and clipped, to locate family, to check if they were out there still, alive. The bed was beside us, and I wondered why we weren't on it, why we'd chosen the hard floor. I put my hand on his chest, where I could feel his heartbeat, and then because I couldn't help it, I moved my hand under his T-shirt, over his sunken belly and the ridges of his ribs. I don't know how long we touched for. At one point, our cheeks pressed together, and my nose grazed his ear, but we didn't kiss, and we kept our clothes on. I said his name, his real name, and he said, "Shh, you don't have to say anything. We can just sit here a while longer."

A few minutes later, a knock rattled the door. From the other side, Eli shouted, "We're taking out the motorboat. Come on."

"Don't crash," I yelled. "Be safe."

Eli shouted back. "You be safe too."

Soon Eli was gone. I waited for Lawn Boy to lift me up to his bed, cover me with his body. I thought of telling him I'd had experiences, lots of them, even though thinking of them now, the shallowness, the numbness, made me feel sick. He patted my head and, when he was done, his hand touched my face, and I thought I might cry but also, I felt stronger than before I'd come here, to this ghost camp, to his little shed.

"God, Libs," he said. "I don't want to hurt you. You're young, and I've already hurt a lot of people. I mean, I have a daughter. I've never even seen her. I'm just barely hanging on."

"Me too."

"No, listen. You're going to make it. Your brother adores you. You're going to find out how to be strong again. I promise. This is what I'm going to do. I'm going to walk you back to your cabin. Then I'm going to say goodnight and walk away."

I watched his back. Even more beautiful than my mother's, I thought. He didn't try to lift his shoulders or straighten his spine, didn't try to pretend for the benefit of other people he was all healed. I stayed on the steps of our cabin until Eli got back from the boat, soaked and shivering. I found him a towel, and he said I'd never believe what they'd seen, a pair of electric eels. "In fresh fucking water," he said. "Neon green." He asked if Lawn Boy had been gentle with me, and I said yes.

Then he went inside, and I went back to dreaming. Maybe someday something would happen between us. Maybe I'd meet his daughter. Maybe we'd fall asleep and wake up brand-new. People could recover from things. Couldn't they? Didn't they?

When the sky began to brighten, I drifted off for a couple more hours, but it wasn't long before cars began to clog the Great Lawn. Minivans with lifts for wheelchairs, big and bulky SUVs. I showered and dressed and went to the top of the hill where Reid sat at a table with a clipboard, checking folks in. Eli hopped from vehicle to vehicle, helping families haul trunks to the cabins where their kids would stay. My dad, dressed in a reflector vest, stood at the top of the hill, directing traffic. I looked everywhere for Lawn Boy, along the periphery, where he often whacked weeds, on the Mess Hall steps, where he lingered, drinking coffee. "Libby!" my mom shouted. "Meet Alexis. She loves friendship bracelets. Her favorite camp food is marshmallows!" Beside my mother, a four-eyed girl squinted in the sun. All these young, expectant faces, echoes of Emeline everywhere.

My mom looked straight at me, but she saw someone else, someone I'd stopped being ages ago.

I ran to his shed even though I already knew. He'd cleaned it out. I lay on his cot and sniffed for his smell. When I found it, my stomach turned. I cried into his mattress and thought of illnesses I could tell the campers I had so they'd stay away. Pink eye, norovirus, strep throat, meningitis. Outside, my mother called my name. "Libby, get out here." There were parents and children she needed me to meet. I wanted to hide inside his shed for the rest of the summer. In sedans, in Subarus, the campers kept coming.

Treasure Island Alley

FROM *New England Review*

THE MOURNING WOMEN are howling. Even with fingers in her ears, Xuan-Xuan hears their loud cries from the big white tent that appeared overnight in the alley. On tiptoe, she peers over the windowsill and looks down three stories to the long line of people holding incense sticks outside the tent. They were here to pay their respects, they said. Her mama had died last night giving birth to a baby, a sister, they said. Her sister would come home but her mama would not, they said, but Xuan-Xuan has her own ideas.

She is in Grandma's bedroom. The smell of old clothes. Spittoon under the bed. She is in her family's apartment building, 58 Hoping Road, Taipei, Taiwan. Mama made her memorize their address on her fifth birthday, a month ago, when Mama and Papa took a rare day off from the family's factory and brought her to the zoo, where Mama got so angry that they came home early after Xuan-Xuan strayed from the peacocks and without telling anyone went searching for the bears.

Cupping fingers around her eyes, Xuan-Xuan pretends to scan Grandma's bedroom with binoculars. The target is the top drawer of the dresser by the bed, where Grandma hides money.

She notices for the first time a hole high up in the ceiling. Next year, a bird will fly through the window into that hole, and even after Papa opens a big chunk of the plaster, he won't find the bird. It will take three days for the bird's song to die, which Xuan-Xuan will remember years later, when she is old and has forgotten almost everything.

The dresser is two, three times her height. She plucks one hair off her pigtails and blows it afloat to invoke her favorite of Monkey King's Seventy-Two Transformations: Size Enhancement. Then she breathes slow and hard, and waits for her legs and arms to grow.

Long minutes pass.

Nothing.

She has to watch again how her fabled hero does it on TV in her favorite cartoon, but there is no time now.

She swings one leg over the ledge of Grandma's bed. Then another. Like a frog, like the fat, stubby frog that managed to climb out of an aluminum bowl in the kitchen, where Grandma has been cooking all morning for the relatives, but—*no!*—Grandma flicked the frog down with her spatula. *Where are you going? The wok's ready.*

Xuan-Xuan climbs on the mahogany headboard and then leans out to pull on the dresser's top drawer. Grudgingly it opens, heavy and squeaky like a pirate's trunk full of treasures. She ignores the gold earrings and jade bracelets, and zooms in on the red envelope. Inside is a stack of Taiwanese dollar bills.

Someone shouts in the stairwell. Papa.

Ma, the feng shui master is here!

Papa thumps up the stairs and Grandma's slippers patah-patah, and then they are talking right outside the bedroom door. Xuan-Xuan grabs the envelope and lands on the comforter, wiggles between the pillows, tries to hide. She waits and waits and grows old . . .

When she is fifteen she will give her virginity to a boy who makes her laugh. At twenty-two she will move to the United States to study biochemistry. She will change her name to Susan and settle in Silicon Valley, and for two decades her startup will be her life. She will marry a white man with a boyish grin and a linebacker's gait, Alex, a venture capitalist. After their divorce, she will become a staunch atheist in search of a religion. At a Silicon Valley meditation boot camp, she will write down everything she knows about her mother on one page with room to spare. On the last day of her life, when she is a hundred and five, she will lie in her deathbed with her second husband by her side, and she will feel lucky despite the sadness that is just beneath the surface of everything.

Time escapes from her fingers and hops, skips, jumps. It's not that difficult really: you wiggle a little and you are there, in a different crevice of time. You close your eyes to the kid in the mirror and open to a face full of wrinkles. You lie down beside your lover, your cheek brushing against the pillow, and there you are again, five years old, hiding, waiting . . .

Finally, Papa thump-thumps down the stairs and Grandma pads back to the kitchen. Xuan-Xuan shoves the red envelope in her Monkey King backpack, and opens the bedroom door a slit. Heat rushes in. Down the hall, Grandma's silhouette shifts in and out of dense smoke. The aromas of three-cup frogs and twice-cooked pork creep downstairs to their factory and drift upstairs to their roof deck, where they keep a German shepherd going insane with old age.

Just yesterday morning, Mama waddled up to the roof deck when Xuan-Xuan was riding her new pink bike and Grandma was hanging bedsheets out to dry. The dog pawed at Mama, almost tearing her favorite blue dress, which clung to her thin frame and swollen belly.

Mama handed Grandma the red envelope. *Ma, for this week.*

Grandma frowned. *How am I supposed to live on this?*

Perhaps . . . you should stop shopping at Japan Imports and Layaways. Mama rubbed the half-moon shadow under her eyes.

You blame me? The factory's broke only after you married my son, because you don't know how to manage money!

Xuan-Xuan tried to get Mama's attention by riding the bike with no hands, but Mama was already stomping down the stairs and yelling, *If you want more money, why don't you go earn it like those girls at Treasure Island Alley?* And Grandma was shouting, *How dare you? I curse you that you fall into that hell!*

The dog pounced and Xuan-Xuan flipped over, taking down the clothesline.

Why is Mama so bad? she said after Grandma pulled her out of the tangle.

Good kid, was all Grandma replied, her face glaring like red-hot coal.

Xuan-Xuan doesn't miss Mama, who never wanted to play, always hunched over a book filled with black lines and red ink, but Mama must have left because Xuan-Xuan sided with Grandma. On TV, Xuan-Xuan has watched Monkey King fight the Lord of Hell to bring people back to life, even erasing his name from the Book of Life Expectancy to become immortal. If Treasure Island Alley is Hell, she will go there to bring Mama back.

*

Outside, Xuan-Xuan tiptoes next to a line of black-robed monks marching toward the big white tent.

Na—Mo—A—Mi—Tuo—Fo—

Their chants sound like *There is no Buddha in the South,* which makes no sense. She slips behind the tent and peeks in through a seam.

Papa, wearing a heavy black suit, is standing next to a big, black stone tub surrounded by towers of beer cans and sarsaparilla bottles and flowers in neon colors. One by one, people bow and give him a white envelope.

Three mourning women wail and throw themselves onto the ground beneath a large photo of Mama wearing that pretty blue dress with little white flowers. The women clutch their hearts and tear at their robes made of rough hemp. Xuan-Xuan can't see their faces, hidden under large headpieces like veils of ghost brides. Their microphones shriek: *Why did you depart so soon? I weep for your children. Come back, come back!*

For a long time, she will believe that the mourning women were hired because she did not cry. Until she leaves home for good, every year on Tomb Sweeping Day, her father will drive her and her sister to the cemetery, and he will buy a stack of ghost money at the entrance. He will teach them how to fold the ghost money, little squares of paper, rough like tree bark, a gold dot in the center. *A deposit for your mother's bank account.* He will weep as he tosses it into the fire, while the girls look on stone-faced. The smoke chokes, and cinders fly like lightning bugs. Only once will she wonder how her sister feels about the date engraved on the tombstone—her sister's birthday, their mother's death day—but she will push the thought out of her mind. It will be decades before she can say to her sister, *I don't hate you. I just don't know how to love you.*

One of the mourning women lifts her head and Xuan-Xuan takes off running, past a Buddhist vegetarian restaurant, a playground where the temple troupe boys are practicing drums, and she skids to a stop in front of Thousand-Big Stationery Store.

Inside, in a glass cabinet, above useless Barbie dolls and fake fire trucks, are Monkey King's impenetrable armor and the cudgel he used to pound the Milky Way flat. The small golden box she needs is on the top shelf. It contains one of Monkey King's precious hairs, to be deployed in the direst of dire circumstances.

She pulls out the red envelope from her backpack and demands, *Give me that box.*

The old lady who owns Thousand-Big narrows her eyes and cranes her wrinkled long neck over the counter like an ostrich guarding her eggs. Xuan-Xuan adds to avoid suspicion, *Oh, and Grandma wants a carton of Longevity.*

Finally, Mrs. Ostrich reaches into the red envelope and pecks out two bills. *Tell your grandma I gave her a discount on the cigarettes.*

Can I have Monkey King's cudgel too, with a discount? she says.

You are your grandma's granddaughter. Mrs. Ostrich tsk-tsks and puts everything including the change into Xuan-Xuan's backpack.

She steps out of the store and a wild herd of elementary school kids just let out of school charges toward her, shoving and cussing each other. She jostles into the dark vestibule of the pedestrian overpass. Dirty words on the wall. Chewing gums and betel nut pulps, sticky under her shoes. She dodges the kids swinging baseball bats and counts each step to distract herself from the sharp vapor of urine from boys and dogs. *One, two, three, four . . .*

By age six, she can count to one thousand. By ten, the fiftieth prime number. She will fall in love with the shape of infinity in high school, filling the margins of her textbooks with that loopy loop that folds in on itself. The idea of something without end fills her with sadness, like lost first love.

In college, she works as a research assistant at the paleontology lab, where she learns to date mummies by carbon-14, which decays by half every 5,730 years. Alone in the lab at night, she blasts punk rock to scare away darkness and dances from tray to tray of bones. The skeletons don't remind her of her mother's, excavated seven years after death per custom and laid out for a day on the marble slab to be picked, cleaned, and sealed in the tomb again. By now her mother seems to have never existed. Xuan-Xuan doesn't know that she keeps death close so it never surprises her again, but on her deathbed years later, she is nonetheless surprised by what flashes across her mind:

7,000,000,000,000,000,000,000,000,000,000,000,000,000,000, 000,000,000,000,000,000,000,000,000,000,000,000,000.

When did these zeros blink down at her for the first time?

She had left Taiwan for graduate studies in the States. A new person on a new continent. She went by Susan because Xuan-

Xuan, pronounced by her English-speaking professors and peers, sounded like wound-up springs.

That night, she had wanted to skip the guest lecture, the annual Big Talk, because she needed to rehearse her closing pitch for the startup competition in the morning, but the judges would be there and so she went. As she scanned the packed auditorium and planned her route to intercept the who's who of Silicon Valley, the lights turned off and the auditorium hushed. All those zeros appeared together on the screen, stretching from wall to wall, blinking, pulsating.

Seven billion, billion, billion, said the guest speaker softly. *The number of atoms in a person's body. In your body.*

The twenty-five-year-old rising star in astrophysics, the youngest addition to Oxford's cosmology faculty, was unassuming in his loose khakis and white T-shirt covered with geometric wrinkles like origami unfolded.

You are seven billion, billion, billion stardust, born in the first second after the Big Bang.

Sitting in the first row, Susan could see the white chalk like new snow on the tip of his straight-edged nose. She felt that he was speaking to her alone.

After the lecture, high on her newly bestowed magnificence as the temporary vessel of billion-year-old stardust, she followed the crowd to the Dutch Goose a mile down the road for sauerkraut and beer. Someone's boom box was playing "Beautiful People" by the Books. *And we genuflect before pure abstraction, 1.05946, twelfth root of two, amen.* She hummed along as the melody looped back where it began. The competition tomorrow and the thesis defense next week receded into white noise.

At the bar, two beers later, she found herself sitting next to the Oxfordian.

Oliver. He shook her hand.

Susan. She flashed her lanyard.

Finalist of the Annual Startup Competition, Oliver said. *You've gone far in the game.*

She shrugged.

When he handed her the third beer, their fingers briefly touched. He said, smiling, *You know two atoms can never touch? The force between them grows exponentially as they get closer? We're actually levitating on the bar stools, you know?* He arched his brows into a lowercase lambda.

But what about quantum entanglement? Lemos et al., 2001. She was showing off.

Oliver blushed, as if they were discussing something other than quantum physics. The nervousness in his voice when he changed the topic would give her courage to track him down years later.

So what's your big idea? he said.

She told him about errors of cell replication, nano-robotic telomerase repair, how death is a disease and a disease can be cured.

How about the beauty of ephemera? Of irreplaceability? he said.

What's the point if we disappear as if we've never existed? she said.

Outside, the night fog had swallowed the stars. A panic set in, as her head started to spin, as if she had been lulled off orbit.

The crowd behind them roared. Two professors climbed on the bar and began downing whiskey shots. Before Susan slipped away to rehearse the pitch, she said hello to one of the venture capitalists sponsoring the prize money, while the giddy crowd counted, *Five! Six! Seven!*

. . . *Twenty-nine, thirty!* Xuan-Xuan counted the last of the stinky staircases and scampered onto the pedestrian overpass. Far away, the old temple warps under the noonday sun like a mirage in the Taklamakan Desert, where Monkey King fought the demons. Somewhere behind the temple, behind the market, behind Snake Alley that is behind the market, is Treasure Island Alley. Hell.

A whiff of pee, wet fur, zoo. A homeless man is splayed out on the ground, neck-to-toe under a disgusting comforter. Not moving. If he is dead then she'll have to save him in Hell too. She checks his face, twisted and sunburnt. Suddenly the man mumbles. Xuan-Xuan barely escapes his fingers, which jab the air as if he is interrogating someone in his dream.

She runs downstairs to the other side of the road, weaves through the market, resists food carts selling fried tofu and popcorn chicken, and dodges people slurping noodles while walking, until a giant snake freezes her in her track.

The snake that dangles off the arched entrance of Snake Alley is thicker than her thigh and longer than the longest pipe. Sharp fangs, green scales, and very dead.

Papa has taken her here before, for a Chinese New Year banquet with his factory workers, but which way is Treasure Island Alley? She wants to ask the boss man of One Snake restaurant, but a group of men blocks the entrance. They look like the bank men who come to Papa's office every week. Leather briefcases and sweaty armpits. *Dozo,* they say, bowing to let each other enter first, and she realizes that they are Japanese tourists.

Twelve bowls of double penis soup! their tour guide yells in Mandarin as he directs the men in and switches to Taiwanese to whisper to the waiter, *These horny dogs need extra potency for later.*

Finally, only one man remains outside. Big-bearded like a wild boar.

Little friend-rr! the Japanese man says, his foreigner's Mandarin gurgle-gurgling like there's a baby bird in his throat. *You like-rr Doraemon?*

Of course, she thinks. The robot cat is the hero of her second favorite cartoon.

Want to see Doraemon's magic pocket? he says and unzips his bag.

Xuan-Xuan reaches for the bag, because Doraemon's Anywhere Door can open straight to Treasure Island Alley so she won't have to waste time while Mama's body grows stale.

Suddenly someone snatches her hand. *Don't you dare touch this one,* the woman hisses at the man and drags Xuan-Xuan down a narrow alley. The woman doesn't let go until they stop at an opening where several alleyways converge. Xuan-Xuan has never seen this woman before. Fake eyelashes, sequin miniskirt, and heels as high as footstools.

Where you live? What you do here? The woman fires the questions so rapidly that Xuan-Xuan feels a familiar heat shoot up her chest, like when Mama got angry.

One by one, strange women step out from shadowy doorways and circle her.

Lucky Mei-Li picked up a stray! Their red mouths are full of teeth, their eyes wild with crayon colors.

What you thinking? The Japanese could kidnap you to be a comfort woman like they did to her, Mei-Li says and points at a very old woman in mud-caked pajamas squatting by a house corner. The old woman dips her head and hugs her broom.

Comfort woman? Such ancient history. Better the Japanese than penniless Kuomintang veterans! says a girl who has been painting toenails on a stoop. *Kidnap me, please!*

You wish! You're stuck in Treasure Island Alley!

Xuan-Xuan knows she can't ask these women about Mama because they are the minions of the Lord of Hell she has been expecting. She's seen them so many times on TV, in disguise to seduce Monkey King from his missions. Her heart thumps. She grips her backpack and eyes the alleyways.

While the women shriek and bend with laughter, falling over each other, Xuan-Xuan escapes down an alley. She runs past one barred window after another, searching for Mama and peering into dark rooms, where strange creatures with men's heads and women's feet moan and writhe under comforters.

It happens fast, between blinks and tricks of light. First, she hears a scream. Then she is straining to see into a room where someone is shouting, *Stop it! I can't breathe!* In the room, in a pool of sunlight on the ground, is Mama's favorite blue dress, torn. *Let me go!* Mama screams. Xuan-Xuan shakes the window bars but they do not budge. She crawls into the room through a hole for dogs at the bottom of the concrete wall, scraping her hands and knees.

On a bed in the tiny room, a man is sitting on Mama's face and growling, *I paid you, bitch.* Xuan-Xuan bites down on the man's buttock, her strength all animal.

Rat, rat! the man yells and jumps off the bed.

Rat, rat! Mama also yells, and Xuan-Xuan sees that the woman is not Mama but a naked girl with purple glitters on her bruised eyes, a bad soul that has been punished.

Then Xuan-Xuan is lifted up by her backpack, kicking air.

Let her go, you beast! The girl beats the man with bare hands, and Xuan-Xuan falls on the bed.

In the darkness that is all perfume and sweat, she rummages in her backpack and finds Monkey King's cudgel, but the man swipes it away. As she dives for it, he yanks her legs.

Save me, Monkey King!

Suddenly the man yelps in pain and doubles over. A broom is beating his back. The old comfort woman has appeared from nowhere, looking twice as big and half as old, her dirty pajamas whipping, and she beats the man with her broom, again and again.

You crazy whores! the man shouts and flees the room. The old woman gives chase.

Xuan-Xuan runs after the old woman, convinced that she is

Monkey King. Rounding a corner, she is suddenly out on the street, out of the maze of Treasure Island Alley. In front of the old temple, a throng of worshipers is coming and going. She searches the faces crushing toward her, but Monkey King is gone.

Later, years later, she will doubt if any of this really happened. The blue dress. The pool of light by the dog hole. Cinematic spotlight of reconstructed memory. Perhaps she can't bear the failure? Perhaps she wishes she really had gone to Hell to search for her mother? She will decide that she never looked for her mother, never wanted to, for many years.

And in those years, she rarely leaves the office. That is where she and Alex have their last argument over the phone. By then the divorce is merely a formality. Time has softened him and hardened her armor. *You never let me in, never let anyone in,* is the last thing he says to her. She sends her father's call to the voicemail. *Xuan-Xuan*—the name feels like a stranger's—*your grandma is dying and your sister is not doing well.* She doesn't go back to Taiwan because there is the next fight for the next round of funding to pursue another dead end in her quest to eradicate death.

On the eve of her forty-second birthday, after the last investor walks away, she turns off the office light for the last time. She is ten years older than her mother ever would be. One day she will be another pile of bones under a marble slab. What's the point? Returning to her house, long emptied of her ex's things, she binge-watches two decades of missed TV shows.

Afternoons slide into evenings. Evenings creep into mornings. Then all day it is evening.

One night, the moonlight wakes her. She steps outside for the first time in weeks wearing unwashed yoga-wear. The moon walks her north, past the midcentury houses of her neighborhood, then gated mansions, then clusters of high-rises, then car washes, car dealers, car repairs, along forty miles of El Camino Real.

Twelve hours of walk later, she is in San Francisco's Chinatown. In front of a breakfast shop, people huddle against the chill wind from the bay and sip steamy rice milk in Styrofoam cups. On a rooftop, a crackly old radio is playing.

She finds herself in front of Eternal Light Kung Fu Academy, its storefront windows covered with flyers for tai chi, qigong, and something she has never heard of, laughing yoga. Inside, ten, twelve

Chinese grandmas and grandpas are lying on tatami mats with their legs up in the air, happy baby pose. *Hah hah! Hah hah!* They pump their bellies like mechanics warming rusty engines. An old man with a shock of white hair and a tiger-stripe scarf walks up and down the aisle prodding the old folks with his cane. *Louder, louder!* he says.

Somehow, all at once, they burst out laughing—roaring—laughing like it's all funny, like to live is funny to die is funny to love is funny to hate is funny, their lungs choking with funny.

She opens the glass door, yearning to lose herself in this lunatic bin.

Welcome, the old man shouts in Mandarin above the chorus of laughter. He points his cane toward a free spot.

Susan lies down and opens her mouth. Nothing comes out. She tries again, but what comes out sounds like the cough of a mouse.

The old man hobbles over and kneels between her legs. He presses his palm into her navel and she chuckles. Then, somewhere between *ahh* and *aargh,* she starts to cry.

There. There. If you can't cry, you can't laugh, the old man says. *But there's more.*

He wedges his fingers between her ribs and digs. Just below her heart, he finds an ancient obstruction, a wad of grief, which Xuan-Xuan pelletized and wedged in when she was five. A dam breaks loose. Tears gush out. She tumbles down the waves, thrashing, kicking, trying not to drown. In the roaring laughter that envelops her, she cries till time disappears.

When she wakes up on the tatami mat, the old man is gone, and the grandmas and grandpas are asleep, their snores one soft rumble. She struggles up. Her legs wobble, and her body feels foreign as if what held her up all these years has gone out with the tears.

She staggers home.

In her living room, under a stack of magazines by the fireplace, she finds the piece of paper from the meditation boot camp, where she scribbled down the few things she knew about her mother: accounting major, loves animal channels, type O negative . . .

She sits by the fire and writes silly questions she would ask her mother if she could: Ocean or mountain? Your worst lie? What would you name your bar?

Her pencil hovers like the needle of a record player abruptly stopped. She studies her hands. They have green veins like her father's, but her father says that her heels are rough like her mother's.

She may have her father's eyes, but he says she has her mother's mouth. She makes up answers, knowing that half of them come from her mother.

Then she folds the paper corners to center, the way her father taught her to do with the ghost money, and tosses it into the fire. It unfurls and blossoms. A white rose aflame. In a minute, it is ash.

Mother. She tests the word.

Mother. It tastes like a horn melon, musky with a hint of sour.

Mother.

Perhaps the truth is this: that past and future are concepts the mind makes up to take refuge from the present. Perhaps all of time is one. Send a word back to when you were that kid, not yet strong enough to fall. Say *you'll be okay.* Send a word forward to that moment you dread, your last moment, say *I'm here. I'm with you.* If you are lucky, you will feel all of you cushioning your fall. And if you are very lucky, you will realize before it's too late that what is the point is really the wrong question.

From the temple, Xuan-Xuan retraces her steps home. She climbs the pedestrian overpass distractedly. Where is Mama? Maybe she needs to go west, like Monkey King's journey, maybe recruit an entourage, maybe their German shepherd, old but still with good teeth. But how long does she have before Mama's body becomes too stale for the soul?

Suddenly something grabs her. She looks down to see the homeless man by her feet, his dirty hand on her ankle.

Where's you going? the man rasps and grins. Wide mouth no teeth! She screams—

She will have a century of recurring dreams about this homeless man, and she dreams of him now, in the last moment of her life, as the nectar of opioid drips into her vein, as all her moments collapse into one, and Oliver, her frail Oxfordian—wasn't it yesterday when she found him again?—sits vigil by her side.

Let go of me, in her feverish dream she begs the homeless man. *I have no more time for your game.*

The man laughs. *Stupid girl. All these years and you don't recognize me?*

He flings open his dirty comforter and unfurls a tail in stripes of brown and black. She blinks and the man changes. First, he is the old comfort woman, then the old man at the Kung Fu Academy, and then he is a thousand images of a thousand people.

Monkey King stands before her, not much taller than she is. His windblown fur sticks out from underneath his yellow kung fu suit. A face full not of lines but of furrows.

You have seen death, but you've never seen it in the right light, he says, twirling his thousand-pound cudgel with his thumb. *I'll teach you the way of immortality, the greatest trick of all mankind.*

Then his images begin to chant in unison, *Na—Mo—A—Mi—Tuo—Fo—*

She bursts out laughing. *You're kidding.*

This is no joke. Monkey King taps her head with his cudgel. *Repeat after me.*

She gives in, too tired to argue, certain that this, all this, will end soon enough.

Na—Mo—A—Mi—Tuo—Fo . . . Bow to the Buddha of Infinite Light. And now—

Wait, wait, she says, suddenly panicky, but only a gurgle escapes her throat. The dying note of a bird's last song. She feels Oliver's hands. *Two atoms can never touch.* Then the girl that she was, twenty and alone in the lab, twenty and feeling old, is saying to her, *Don't be scared, you're only going where your mother has gone . . .*

Monkey King guides her hand to pluck a hair off her head. The gesture of his Seventy-Two Transformations. With her last breath, she whispers her last bit of magic:

Now . . . Watch me disappear . . .

Her seven-billion-billion-billion particles break away—a liberal amount of oxygen and carbon, some hydrogen, nitrogen, calcium, a pinch of sulfur, phosphorus, potassium—and they race toward another cosmic lottery to become a hummingbird, a copper tin, a speck of dirt in Treasure Island Alley, a little girl, who flees the homeless man and runs into the swell of chants and cries from the white tent holding her mother's body, and she screams to a stop in front of her family's building—

Grandma appears at the top of the stairs, a spatula still in hand, a baby swaddled to her chest.

Where have you been?

For a few moments that feel like forever, Xuan-Xuan does not know.

BENJAMIN EHRLICH

The Master Mourner

FROM *The Gettysburg Review*

MY HEBREW SCHOOL teacher used to tell us that God is everywhere. In fact, I remember her saying exactly that—"He is *every*where"—elongating the *every* for what seemed like eternity while waving her ancient hands over our tiny classroom in the basement of the shul, which was meant to represent the totality of universal space. Then she smiled, wide and yellow. Morah Lev's black hair was always pulled back tightly atop her head, forcing the skin of her wrinkled forehead taut. Behind her skull, the thin strands of her hair converged into a long, firm braid that hung down to the bottom of her back. She used to tell us that she had three hearts: the organic one inside her chest, the one that was her last name (*lev,* the Hebrew word for "heart"), and an additional, symbolic one, for bravery, located somewhere in her gut. Boys and girls both asked if she had ever killed anyone back in Israel. She simply said yes, as though we had asked her if her name was indeed her name. She once told us that she was a spy for the Irgun during the War of Independence and that for one cold night in the desert she was ordered to entertain British soldiers on the piano until her comrades could plant strategic bundles of dynamite. "In my dreams," she said, her bony pointer finger poised like a gun to her twitching temple, "I still see the blood and flesh on the white keys." Then she began to tickle the air, mock playing the remembered instrument. She laughed the laugh of youthful amusement. We did not laugh; we were frightened. None of us was even a bar or bat mitzvah. The boys did not wear deodorant yet, and the girls did not wear makeup. Morah Lev wore three different colors of lipstick at once: blue, in a line around the outside, orange, in a stripe across her upper lip, and deep red, the color of blood, closest to and often on the enamel canvas of her twisted teeth. Without ever having met Morah Lev, from only my scattered transmissions in the car on the way home from Hebrew school, my father mentioned that she sounded "colorful." By then, his voice had become like that of an AM disc jockey after midnight who would rather be in bed than be heard. This was after my mother passed, during the time when I realized that God is not everywhere; Bernie Bernstein is everywhere.

Once, in the grocery store, I nearly drove my shopping cart right into him as he was examining arthritis schmears in the fluorescent glow of aisle eleven. My mother was still sick, and they only carried her medicine at the pharmacy of the big chain located in the next town, where our black hats and black coats stood out. I was reckless then; I pushed fast and turned tight. I tried to gather some speed on the checkered tile so that I could jump on the rail between the two rear wheels and make the cart buck and whinny like a steel-wire bronco. All of a sudden, with the climate-controlled breeze flowing through my wispy payos and puffing up my oversized white dress shirt, I saw that I was heading right toward a man in a pinstripe suit with a kippah attached to his head. I was frightened, but the man was as calm as a tree. He simply raised his hand, and I swerved into a head-high pyramid of medicated foot powder. Each bottle teetered, but just one fell, hitting the floor with a sharp smack and a brief cough of white dust.

"You're Henry's son, aren't you," he said with softened vowels that echoed a German accent. This could have been a question but was not a question. "Drive the cart, do not let the cart drive you," he added. His beard was white around his chin and jaw, but the hair became darker as it crept unclipped toward his dark eyes. As though preparing to pray the amidah, the silent devotion, he bowed from the waist and picked up the fallen plastic container and handed it to me.

Outside, my father's car was parked in the fire zone with the flashers on. For a moment, I thought something could be wrong, but the thought passed away like most of my absurd notions. My father, of course, was asleep in the driver's seat. He possessed the miraculous ability to slip into a nap in any setting. In shul, while the congregation was made to suffer through sermon after sermon, my father would slip into some other, somnolent realm. I always wished I could go with him. Even when an errand lasted as few as five minutes, my father was always asleep when I returned, always upright with his chin bouncing off of his chest, sports talk radio blaring. My father had been a runner, and people in the community knew him as one, or rather, as having been one in the past. He had run half-marathons twice a year the decade before I was born.

That day outside the store, the pavement was wet, but the sun was out, and it was baseball season, and listeners were calling in to rant about a shortstop who had lost his magic powers since turning thirty-eight. "He can't cover no ground like he used to," said Louie from the Bronx. My father looked peaceful. I said to myself, "God Almighty, will I end up like him?" And God Almighty said, "Of course." I got into the car and closed the door, which woke my father. "Dad," I asked, "is there a man who wears a pinstripe suit who goes to our shul? I think I just ran into him."

"You mean Bernie Bernstein," my father said, which could have been a question but was not a question. "Yes, he is a very important member of our community." Then he yawned and shifted into reverse.

As my mother got closer to her end, I began to accompany my father to Shabbat services in the main sanctuary of the shul. I did not count as a man toward the ten men necessary for a full minyan; I was a spectator. The sanctuary was a cozy room with stained wood and glass, where the pews squeaked, "Please!" and "No!" with the standing up and sitting down and standing up and sitting down of indecisive-seeming obedience. Each man in the congregation had a wild beard and shuckled back and forth almost violently while his lips danced through memorized prayers. The women were in another room. Bored, I spent most of the time playing with the fringes that dangled from my father's tallis. I tugged them, pretending they were levers that opened the ark or did some other unexpected trick. I eagerly awaited the singsong tune that meant the last prayer in the service and my relief. Slumped in my seat so that my suit and tie bunched uncomfortably, I saw all of the men gather around Bernie Bernstein, shaking his hand as though congratulating him on another week. He beamed, and his teeth were so white that I wondered to whom they really belonged. Bernie Bernstein took each hand in both of his own as if to cup and contain some fragile, flying thing. A cage in search of a bird.

After my mother passed away, during the seven days of shiva, it either rained or had just stopped raining or was about to rain for all of the days but one. The one non-rainy day was the day Bernie Bernstein paid his call. Perhaps it was the third or fourth or fifth day, but it was definitely not the first. I know because I had already learned to open the door with my face prepared with a mourner's mixture of pale sorrow, stiff resilience, and a hint of eye-smiling gratitude for the offering of yet another of the inevitable and innumerable fruit baskets. And I remember that I was surprised to see the eyes and smile of Bernie Bernstein. He wore the same pinstripe suit, black with subtle gray lines. His tie and handkerchief were the bluish color of veins beneath skin.

"My condolences," he said, his eyes moist and serious, taking my one hand in his two. He did not wait for me to welcome him into the house, beelining directly to the whitefish salad that the women of the sisterhood had provided for us. The quasi-sexual way in which he sucked the flesh from between his perfect teeth disgusted me.

My father sat on the floor, hugging his knees in a customary torn shirt and listening to his running partner, or former running partner, Harold Morton. Harold was talking about this phenomenon called barefoot running, which supposedly prevents injuries and increases endurance, at least for the Kenyans. My father was not napping, but I could tell he was not awake. He was in a different realm. I came to understand that this new realm was where he lived, and our real realm was the one he visited. I tried to shout, Dad! Come back! But it was as if he was in a place where sound could not travel. My sound, at least, was inaudible to him. My father stopped running after my mother died. He said he had a bad heart.

My mother had always been dying. My strongest, earliest childhood memory is of her doctor, Doctor Kaplan. He exists to me as a small, thin man who wore short-sleeved dress shirts, oval glasses with gold wire rims, and a kind of hat that I have never seen another man wear in real life. It was round and fat and, I imagined, hard and hollow. I liked him because he gave me a lollipop whenever he came to the house. After my mother passed away, Doctor

Kaplan left our community to move to Florida to be near his son, a doctor as well. They were very close. Years later, I saw his hat in an old movie about horse racing my father made me watch. In the movie, it sat on the bedside table of a degenerate jockey who was murdered for winning a race he was not supposed to win. I had almost no memory of my mother, but I remembered this hat, which I had desperately wanted to rap with my fist. I was forced to admit to myself then that the whole ordeal had seemed to me, as a child, to be no more than the loss of lollipops. It was as if my mother was stowed on the other side of the curtain in the sanctuary, separated from me, beyond my vision. But this jockey in the movie was twisted and bloodied, and I thought about the suddenness of some deaths. You never find out who kills the jockey. My father must have been bored because his eyes were closed.

My father, whose name was Henry Singer, descended from longer-surnamed shtetl dwellers from the morasses of Eastern Europe. I guess I am descended from them too, although I never liked to think so. My father made a modest living in the schmatta business, fabrics and such, which has ceased to exist. He worked hard, but then all of a sudden he looked up and nothing was like it used to be. In the town where we moved after it was time to sell his business, a small town with a smaller Jewish community, he was unhappy. He was unhappy before my mother started dying. He was unhappy if I bought jumbo-sized eggs to use for breakfast. He would click his tongue twice before cracking the shells and watching them fry. At first, I bought this variety by accident, but after a while, I started to do it on purpose, maybe to help him adjust but really just to shift him out of reverse.

I soon learned that Bernie Bernstein had been in the schmatta business too, and I figured that was what they talked about every Saturday after services. Bernie Bernstein and my father had a lot in common, it turned out. Before I knew it, Bernie Bernstein became my father's only friend. When I watched them speak, my father became more energetic than I ever saw him, widening his eyes and shaking his swollen face back and forth, while Bernie Bernstein merely stood there, pinstriped and expressionless. Sometimes he nodded intermittent affirmations with his eyes closed. They began to meet for lunch on Wednesdays to talk about the old days and the Old World.

I started to see Bernie Bernstein everywhere. Kissing the hand of a newly bat mitzvahed girl and the cheek of her mother in the kosher bakery, tickling the chins of babies in strollers on the sidewalk, recalling to grade-schoolers that he used to know them when they were only *this* tall. It seemed I was seeing him impossibly frequently. Once, from the window of the kosher deli, I saw him helping an older woman into her car, easing her into the driver's seat as though it were a scalding bath. Then I turned toward the counter and immediately saw him shaking shoulders with the owner. Could Bernie Bernstein possibly be in more than one place at one time? I wondered. I asked my father about this, and he laughed, his chin kicking back so that the great and terrible sound was released to the heavens. "Bernie Bernstein is an unusual man. Perhaps he has found a loophole in this dimension." My father could be quite funny when he felt the world was funny.

I decided that Bernie Bernstein was a fraud and that I would expose him. At the end of Shabbat evening services, it was the tradition of our congregation to invite the young boys to lead the final prayer—Adon Olam, the singsong one. Even though I was in high school, I marched up to the front with the kids. From my position behind the bimah, I spotted Morah Lev, who always wore a black beret and black trench coat and sat in the back row. She winked at me, and I shuddered. The kids started into the song with gusto, and I imagined my own voice, lower than the rest. I began to hum but did not utter a word. As we finished, my eyes were on Bernie Bernstein, who was already receiving his weekly congratulations. I made my way down from the bimah and toward him. My heart was hot. The other congregants peeled away, and suddenly there I was in front of him. Looking at his well-tanned face, I realized that I had no idea how old he was. He could have been anywhere between thirty and three thousand. I tried to shake his hand harder than he shook mine.

"Mr. Bernstein," I said in an unprecedentedly friendly tone. "Do you have an identical twin? I feel like I see you everywhere."

His breath became slow and noisy, like a struggling car. He closed his eyes, and I saw that his eyelids were pink. "I had a brother," he said. "He was murdered at Bergen-Belsen."

My face flushed with shame, each individual blood vessel burning. I understood that hell itself was that heat right there. Every Friday night and Saturday morning when Bernie Bernstein silently rose for the mourner's Kaddish, joining my father and me and the rest who recite for the dead, I had seethed. I realized then that everything I thought I was I was not and everything I assumed I would be I would never be and everything I assumed I would never be I would most certainly be. My father had recently become the only member of the congregation to drive to shul instead of walking, which was a violation of the rules of Shabbat. He said it was because he was too heavy for his own legs. After I confronted Bernie Bernstein, I told my father that I wanted to walk home, alone, which I did slowly, training my eyes on the ground, trying somehow to see below it.

It was late when I returned home, but I did not see my father's car. It was not in front of the house in its usual place. I checked the garage, and there it was, resting in the dark. Inside, my father had already gone upstairs. I sat in the living room. The only light in the house came from the television, which I turned on but kept silent.

There was a knock at the door, hard and hollow. I was not immediately sure that I heard it, in the way that one is never sure about a thing he does not expect. But then I heard it again, just the same. I got up from the couch and crept across the wooden floor, old and warped, which cried, "No! Stay!" I always tried to be quiet because my father did not like to be disturbed upstairs. Although it was late and I was not totally alert, I became so as soon as I opened the door. It was Bernie Bernstein, in his pinstripe suit, a kippah attached to his head. He was panting, and his shirt was torn. He had been looking for me. The air in the starry world was fragrant with invisible rain. The crickets chirped.

"I am sorry, Jacob," I heard Bernie Bernstein say as he handed me my father's keys. I turned around and sprinted up the stairs.

SARA FREEMAN

The Company of Others

FROM *The Sewanee Review*

I SPENT THAT first afternoon alone, without my family, on the terrace of the Café Ti-Loup, in a pleasant state of half-reading, half-listening to a couple arguing, to a father and his adolescent son sharing a moment of taut silence, glad for once not to be contributing to the ambient family discord but bearing peaceable witness to it instead. I was getting ready to leave my table when I saw her, walking on the other side of the street, and into the *caisse populaire*. The similarity was so uncanny that it wouldn't be right to merely call it a resemblance. No, in that instant, there was no doubt in my mind that it was her, my mother, as she had been the year of her death, nearly twelve years before—tall, fair, the same proud, inquisitive nose, the dark, expressive parentheses for eyebrows. I drank three large gulps of water, standing there above the flimsy outdoor table, trying to steady my hands, which were now cold and shaking, the nails drained of their pink. My mind immediately set to breaking the spell: the hair was different and I didn't remember my mother being quite so tall. And yet I could not convince myself that it was not her. The waitress asked me if I needed anything, she was hoping to give the table to someone else, and I managed to say absentmindedly: *Non, tout va bien, mademoiselle, allez-y,* and step out onto the sidewalk, where I stood, agitated, like a dog tied to a lamppost, waiting for its owner to return from an errand.

Moments later, my mother emerged from the bank again, her head down, as she placed a large wallet, with its old-fashioned ball clasp, the very kind I suddenly remembered she'd always carried, back into her handbag. As she lifted her head my error was revealed: the nose was all wrong—flatter, broader—the eyebrows thicker and far darker than I'd first thought. The entire effect was unpleasant, and I was reminded of the time when in a restaurant some years earlier on Saint-Denis, out for dinner with my husband, Bertrand, I had ordered a cheese soufflé and found, past the miraculous and airy dome, the slimy amniotic soup of raw egg beneath.

That queasy feeling, a tightness at my jaw, remained all day. By the evening, even the apartment had begun to bear the signs of my nausea, of this close call with another realm. I opened the door to my daughter's room and turned the lights on and off and back on again. What did I hope to find there? My mother, smiling, her teeth in their gentle disarray, her heavy breasts, her unyielding blue eyes? In reality, I found nothing but the indelible traces of my daughter—opposite to my mother's old-world austerity—the bright colors of the feather boa that she had worn at Halloween slung over the headboard. Dafna was a girl of accessories, talismans, shells collected and arranged, collages she'd made tacked to the corkboard, memories of herself.

I had collected nothing as a child, not a rock or a doll.

We had spent the days before Dafna's departure for summer camp shopping and packing, finding the perfect sleeping bag and flip-flops, the myriad toiletries that pleased her. Under regular circumstances, I would have let Bertrand take care of this part of the preparations, but I must have felt a certain amount of guilt about the plan from which I had excluded myself entirely. He would drive her to the camp just north of Quebec City; he would pick her up. And in the interim, he would take the opportunity to visit with his mother, who had been recently widowed and was desperate for the company of her favorite child. There had been some talk, when the plan had first been devised, of my going with them, staying with Bertrand in his mother's house, but the accommodation was uncomfortable, a lone cot that we would have to share like much younger versions of ourselves. In those first years together, I had welcomed the discomfort of this sleeping arrangement and its forced physical closeness verging on siblinghood, which, having grown up as an only child, I found nearly erotic. Or perhaps, to put it simply, I had been hungry, in those early years, for any excuse to be physically close to Bertrand. His nearness, from the beginning, had seemed like a kind of concession granted to me by some stroke of luck or circumstance.

His mother, it was no great secret, had never especially liked me. She had couched the feeling as linguistic in nature, cultural in kind. My French, at age twenty, had been so halting and internal, I could not blame her for finding me an odd and abrupt successor to Bertrand's most recent girlfriend, a francophone classmate in his PhD program, whom he had been with for the better part of a decade. But it was my refusal, a few years later, to christen our daughter, which I justified would have ostracized me permanently from my own Jewish family, that had been my first unpardonable sin. My open insistence on speaking English to Dafna, even when we visited Quebec City, had surely not helped my cause either. But even after it had been clear that my efforts had failed—Dafna had not spoken a word to me in English since she had started public school in French two years earlier, and there were increasingly vociferous stirrings about wanting to be confirmed—Bertrand's mother's disapproval had broadened, like a kind of generosity, to include the farthest reaches of my decision-making: my choice to work only part-time as a homework assistant in an English boys' school, my preference not to dye my hair, even after it turned, shortly after Dafna's birth, prematurely salt and pepper.

I would not have said, at the time, that summer of 1992, that my family was falling apart, only that we were at something like an impasse, that it was true that my eight-year-old daughter's sizable will had recently flourished and seemed aimed at annihilating me. My husband, despite his efforts at fairness, firmly sided with our daughter, and so a fault line had emerged, and I had found it easy to simply give myself over to it, to fall into this trench in my own family life. And yet the problem was that I could not remember a time before this one, the arrangement before this one. I could not recall ever having been pleasantly and easily at the center of my own life, at the center of Bertrand's attentions. Like all small familial tragedies, it seemed, that year, as though it had been there all along, this truth, waiting to live out its inevitability. For months now, I had wanted this time alone, advocated for it. In our ten years together, I had asked for almost nothing from Bertrand. This is not to say that I had been a particularly good wife, only that my badness, if you could call it that, had little to do with making actual demands.

*

On the phone that evening, as I described the encounter with my dead mother, Bertrand was patient, as he always tried to be when I recounted something that he found irrational. After a lull in the conversation, he asked:

"Do you miss her?"

"Dafna?" I responded, irritated by the question.

"I meant your mother," he clarified.

"I don't think it's that," I said, and brought up an inconsequential improvement in the apartment, a shelf I hoped to install in the bathroom while he was away. "That's a good idea," he said, knowing, just as I did, that I was not likely to complete such a task without him. Bertrand, before hanging up, said *je t'aime*, as he always did, and I put down the receiver very softly as I heard the words taking on their worn-in shape, preserving the possibility, for his sake, that I simply had not heard him.

But even after we'd hung up, I could not dislodge Bertrand's question. A jagged crumb at the back of my throat: Did I miss my mother? To miss someone suggests a past shared, a present remembered. I could think only of a half-dozen times Bertrand and I had talked about my mother in the decade of knowing one another. I had met him in my second year at university, just one year after her death. I had categorized it then, her passing, as a kind of perceptual trap, a sleight of hand, the world playing a cruel trick on me. Nothing that talking or revisiting might resolve or clarify. We had had a fight the last time I'd seen her, a small thing made infinitely bigger, so small in fact that later I could not, when it came time to remember it, locate it—the exact slip of the tongue, the single look or gesture, the mismanaged instant that had made me leave the apartment and return to my residence hall across the city without saying goodbye—this moment that had led me to wish, in the private way that only eighteen-year-olds can, that my mother should go ahead and die, that I could only start living when she did, and that she should actually, ten days later, do it, and so very swiftly at that: the lung had clotted, the heart had stopped. For the days and weeks and months that followed, I believed that it was me who'd done it, that the wish had been enough; mothers murder their daughters and I had murdered my mother. And so it had stayed that way, my mother's death: a room in the house I refused to step into, a devastated place that existed nearby but that I would not, for any reason whatsoever, ever wish to visit.

*

The next morning, I drank my coffee quickly and ate a few dry crackers with jam before heading outside, eager for the loose company of others. I had slept badly, stuck on the image of the stranger's face, the exact moment of distortion, my mother's vanishing point. I walked south on Saint-Laurent, and east down Rachel, all the way to Parc Lafontaine, where I had not been in many years. Later, I would ask myself why I'd chosen this park in particular, this walk, when so many others were available to me. It was one of the side effects of parenthood, this small radius of the city I now inhabited: apartment, school, pediatrician, dance studio, and soccer field. Perhaps that day, I would later justify it to myself, I had simply wanted to expand that circle, to walk beyond its reaches to see what I might find.

I wore a light blouse and skirt, and from time to time I caught sight of a pale leg and was surprised to find that it was my own. I stopped by the pond, where the ducks were placidly gliding, then dunking their heads, flapping their wings maniacally, their animal repetitiousness on delirious display. I settled on a bench just outside the perimeter of the playground and watched as a few children played on the swings and monkey bars. Their noises were comforting—gleeful yelps that carried the distant pleasure of children not your own. A little girl, five or maybe six, a little younger than Dafna, sat with her legs spread wide in front of her. A teenager was with her, no more than sixteen or seventeen, crouching nearby. She had dark kohl around her eyes that had smudged, lending the impression that she had not slept the night before, or had wanted it to appear that way. She looked somehow unformed—the body, the face, still in search of their shape. How strange it seemed then, suddenly, that we should ask adolescents, the most unreliable of creatures, to care for our children. The babysitter held her cigarette away from her body and that of the child and rose from time to time to take a long, sensuous drag, which she blew out in messy, unprocessed puffs. She coughed, looking around as though she had lost something of some importance to her.

The two moved wordlessly, in a functional sort of apathy. The babysitter pressed her ringed hand into the little girl's, urging her to write something with the thick chalk. The little girl made a single circle on the ground and promptly dropped the piece of chalk, looked up at the babysitter, who rolled her eyes. The babysitter gave the child another colored piece of chalk. The girl hesitated before bending over and making another circle—larger this time, but only timidly so—to surround the first one. This went on, until the little girl declared that she had no more colors. Exasperated, the babysitter sighed and said, "Use your imagination." The little girl picked up the same color and began to reverse the chromatic order of the circles. It was impossible not to find in the scene a real suspense, not to be compelled by the childish hand—steady, rhythmic, making its imperfectly concentric circles.

She was a pretty child, with dark, almost black hair, cropped right beneath the ear and parted on the side with a short fringe that revealed dark, astute eyes. She appeared odd to me that day, but I wouldn't have been able to explain why. I have always had an uncanny ability to remember faces, to see them once in public and locate them again, often even able to remember exactly where I have seen them first—on the metro, at the supermarket, behind the counter at a coffee shop. But this was something else: a feeling I had of immediate interest, of unfounded complicity, the kind I had only ever felt those few times in my adult life when I'd met a woman I wished to befriend.

My daughter, it was true, was the kind of child who required constant attention, who, presented with the suggestion of an activity, would immediately reject it for another—her own, usually—which she deemed more interesting. It was one of Dafna's gifts to me that despite preferring her father's company, she did not let me out of her sight. When I was in another room, she always yelled out: "What are you doing? Come back." Often, when I joined in whatever activity she'd decreed, she commented impatiently: "Why are you doing it like that? Daddy doesn't do it that way," and so on. I had read enough child psychology to know that this was normal enough, that a parent, at this phase, is in essence sacrificial, that she must, in order to inspire the child's long-term confidence, survive her own destruction. A parent, I had even heard, is merely a fixed spot on the wall that the child can look to, should she need to regain her balance. I knew this all in the abstract, of course, but in practice, I was not a dot on the wall, an immutable shape on the horizon, and I found that the destruction merely had the desired effect of destroying me.

This little girl, on the other hand, was perfectly content to work slowly and consistently with only one object in mind. Having

located another color from her collection, the child looked up
and met my gaze, smiled, then returned to her necessary, purpose-
ful task. The babysitter, on her second cigarette now, was oblivious
to the interaction. She got up and pulled at her jeans, which, belt-
less, revealed a lower back etched with deep purple stretch marks.
Having seen the split skin, hidden and then revealed, the body's
cruel logic on display, I felt new empathy for the babysitter, who
said something inaudible to the little girl before walking away in
the direction of the public restroom, a good distance away from
the playground.

Under the canopy of the ugly stucco building stood a boy the
babysitter's age, maybe even younger than she was, his hands dug
into his pockets, the wiry body curved inward, waiting for her.
When she arrived, he shuffled from one foot to the other. They
did not kiss or touch, but from time to time, they laughed, never
both at the same time, in a courteous sort of call and response.
When they said goodbye, it was with rushed urgency and a stern,
flattening embrace.

The babysitter returned, making a loud, unrelenting phlegmy
sound before spitting into a bush. She began picking up the chalk
and pushing it into the box in a messy tumble. She was in a bad
mood, as though having gotten what she'd wanted, it was impossible to return to what she did not. The little girl had just finished
her final circle when the babysitter took her hand firmly in her
own. "*Allez ouste*," she said in her disgruntled tone.

Before leaving, the little girl turned toward me and made a
barely detectable shrug. She was sharing, I read in her expression,
the knowledge of her own circumstance: childhood, its injustices
and absurdities, its imposed companions. I smiled back, warmed
by the welcome sense of complicity. I had been a child once, the
kind who knew what childhood was, the orchestra of rule and
routine, discipline and disappointment.

I slept in my daughter's bed, in her sheets and their waning scent
of her, every night that week, but I did not exactly miss her. One
night as I was courting sleep, however, an image of her returned
to me, complete, with the precision of a photograph. The summer
before, at the cottage of our family friends, my daughter in her red
and pink polka dot bathing suit, arms akimbo, surveying the placid
lake. She holds her head high; there is a slight tilt at her hip. She

is seven, but already poised and somehow easy, both aware and dismissive of her audience, an actor or an executive in the making. My husband calls out: "*Vas-y ma belle.*" I wait for her to turn back, to look at us, to ask us for permission or encouragement, but she does not; she doesn't need anyone's blessing to do exactly what she wants. When she has finally made up her mind, she runs and dives in, swimming in that feverish but efficient way of hers, yelping from time to time. She is not a technically good swimmer but can thrash around for hours, noisily, exuberantly. I never learned to swim myself, but I always watch and clap, congratulate her on her progress, shaking out the sand from the towel and handing it to her, drying her off until she insists I leave her alone.

I remembered this moment as I lay in bed, because it was in that very instant, a year before, that I first came across the phrase in its entirety, one that had been seven years in the making, a slow accumulation of proof, and for days afterward, I couldn't help but repeat it, those three words so nearly perfect in their strangeness and their accuracy of feeling: *not my daughter.*

Not my daughter. Of course, it was ridiculous. You could doubt paternity, sure, but maternity was an entirely different story. I had seen her come out of me, held her sticky mass to my bare chest, marveled even then at her separateness, her otherness. How to explain that her growing up had been, from the beginning, a kind of growing away. There was her complexion, of course, her almost white hair, her startled blue eyes, her limbs, which were long and lithe, and her skin, which tanned easily, everything opposite to me. And everything else too—every gesture, expression, habit, every belief was her father's or her very own; it often seemed that I had lent her nothing of myself. *If she's my daughter, she'll turn and look at me,* I had thought, standing by the water that day, testing the gods of love. But she hadn't. The thought had been freeing, the phrase a door I had stepped through and into a brighter, more hopeful future. If she were not mine, then I could move on and away from her too.

The little girl from the park appeared to me that night: on the ground, marking the small territory of her mind. Her face immediately familiar, known as in a dream. Where did I know her from? I found that I could almost touch the place where I had first seen her, and there it was, the place: sleep. I had figured something out, or everything out, but awake now, moving into the kitchen—

the early morning sounds of the apartment heightened, distended by fear—I found only an unnatural shadow, the source of which I could not identify, the curtains swaying in the breeze. In the reflection of the hallway mirror: a clavicle trying to break through the pale envelope of skin, hair matted to one side, deep lines around the eyes and at the forehead. I had never been beautiful, as Dafna was already becoming. In my twenties this had seemed like a disappointment, that even being young, I was not especially lovely, but now I was glad of it, relieved not to be weighed down by the extra promise implied in beauty, the need to cultivate and preserve it, to maintain its particular illusion.

I witnessed the accident on a Friday. By then, my midmorning trip to the playground had become something of a habit. I sat nearby as the girl played, mostly alone, with her chalk, her beads, her plasticine. The babysitter often disappeared for long stretches to meet her boyfriend under the nearby arches of the park's pavilion. And so, in the absence of proper care, I reasoned, I could be useful, serve as the child's temporary guardian. That day, I was already seated on the bench when the little girl arrived, walking and then skipping in order to keep up with the babysitter's quick clip. She was wearing a pretty short-sleeve shirt, with a delicate red and purple floral print and a rounded collar, with some shorts that fell below the knees, which made her seem, for an instant, like a boy out of a medieval portrait: crabapple cheeks, the neck unnaturally choked and elongated by the tight collar. The whole outfit suggested a mother, one who had imposed a whimsical but inappropriate aesthetic onto her child. Dafna had insisted very early on choosing her own clothes, clashing with a kind of maniacal enthusiasm, refusing even to wear socks that matched. The babysitter was also dressed differently that day, not in her regular, loose-fitting jeans but in a pale silk dress with spaghetti straps that dug into her rounded, pocked shoulders. She would be going straight out afterward—a date with her boyfriend, or a walk on Sainte-Catherine with her girlfriends.

First they played on the swings, then the little girl tried to drag herself across the monkey bars. The babysitter signaled her departure, and the little girl moved from the cement slab toward the large pyramidal rope structure. There were two other children climbing with ease—an athletic brother and sister—whose mother seemed only distantly interested in their activity. I stood up from my seat and, arms crossed, observed the little girl, nervous about her new endeavor. She began her ascent slowly, looking up at her hands and down at her feet with great care before any small step up or to the side. She had decided to do something that scared her. My heart beat faster for her, a tightening of my throat in antic- ipation of her next deliberate move. I was proud of her. When she had climbed halfway up, I contemplated clapping, but I decided against it; I was not her mother, after all. Her hands were trem- bling now, her shoulders in her ears, her body suddenly seized up in fear. Her breath quickened. With her chest heaving, she turned around and seemed, in that moment, to be looking for someone— for me. I smiled and waved and, nodding at her, mouthed "*Vas-y.*"

Go on.

With a surge of bravery, she began climbing, this time more confidently. Her eyes must have been closed, or her focus so pre- cisely on the feeling of her hands clutching the rough rope that she didn't notice that she was moving into the path of another child. The boy's foot mistook the little girl's small hand for the soft ledge. Then her yelp, tumble, and her body splayed on the ground.

I was next to her then, lifting her into my arms. She looked up at me, eyes full of tears, but still lucid. A look of recognition, which, despite the strangeness of the situation, made this feel like a reunion, a moment we'd both been waiting for. The little girl's breath was heavy; she was too stunned to cry. There was a gash above her eyebrow, and I used the white cotton shirt from around my waist to stop up the wound. "*Ça doit faire mal,*" I told her. *It must hurt.* She nodded *yes,* and then began to cry quietly. A small crowd had gathered, and we were all crouched around her on the bench now.

"*Ça va, ma belle?*" the babysitter asked now, back from her tryst, hovering behind me, her voice breaking, so much softer and more girlish than I'd expected it to sound. I pulled my shirt away from the child's forehead to inspect the wound, but returned it imme- diately, finding that the bleeding had not yet stopped, the gash deeper than I'd first assumed.

"What did you do to yourself?" the babysitter asked, inadvertently blaming the child. *Blame me,* I thought. Hadn't I been the one to encourage her to climb higher? The babysitter gave the child a forceful, determined hug and rubbed her head like a dog's. "Let's go home now," she said and tried to gather the little girl in her arms.

"You'd better go call an ambulance. She may need stitches," I heard myself telling the babysitter. She looked up and considered me for the first time. She seemed about to say something, to resist my orders, but then the child let out a heavy, chesty sigh and began crying again. "Go on," I said, pointing to a phone booth just outside the park and the babysitter ran toward it. In these moments of crisis, with my family, it was my husband who moved without hesitation, who told me what I must do. I welcomed this new role, this rediscovered muscle not fully atrophied yet.

"What's your name?" I asked the little girl, no tremor in my voice.

"Elle," she said, wiping her tears with the backs of her hands.

"You're going to be fine," I said, and took her small, clammy hand in mine.

Soon the babysitter returned and declared: "I called. They are on their way."

"Good. Well done," I told her, with newfound authority.

The front of the babysitter's silk dress was now stained by an expressionistic smear of blood. While we waited for the ambulance to arrive, she nervously dabbed at the front of the pale, delicate dress. Up close, the choice of outfit seemed all the more indecent, as though the girl had, in some hungover haste, simply forgotten to get fully dressed that morning.

"She's going to kill me. It's *her* dress," she muttered to me, as if I would know what she meant. "The mother's," she added in a whisper that made the word itself seem obscene.

"If you wash it right when you get home, there's a good chance it'll come out."

"I've never done it before," she said, swallowing her tears, "borrowed her clothes."

As the ambulance left, carrying the wounded child and her babysitter, it was the babysitter whom I was most worried about. She appeared, in our final moments together, pale and fretful, her eyes searching wildly for some comfort. The real drama of the situation revealed itself: some private shame this girl had about borrowing another woman's clothes, about wanting something *for* herself when she was being paid to give *of* herself. Before she climbed into the back, I moved toward her and said in a low voice: "You can always throw it out."

My daughter did write. On Monday, after my lunch at the bakery, there it was, amidst a pile of bills, an envelope with my own hand-writing on it. Her message was short. Three lines, in English, which came as a nice surprise: "I forgot my T-shirt the one with the pink stripes. Can you send me some candy too? Thanks."

That afternoon, I walked east in search of a gift to send along with the T-shirt and some candy I had bought at the pharmacy. My daughter and her friends adored the souk-like stores along Mont-Royal, and I often accompanied them there, impressed by the decisive, knowing leanings of their tastes. I settled on a scarf, one that had a few gold threads woven into it so that it shimmered in certain lights. She would like this effect. For Christmas, my hus-band had bought her a book of optical illusions entitled *Masters of Delusion* and she had sat there for hours, pulling the heavy book away from her nose and then back toward her, yelling from time to time, "I got it, I got it," with infectious jubilation. It was rare for her to give herself entirely to a reality other than her own, and this world of graphic distortions and discoveries, for a few weeks at least, had seemed a refuge from the tyranny of her wants.

In the street, I reflexively walked east, finding myself pulled back to the playground. Blocks from the park, I caught sight of them from behind: Elle wearing the same shorts as the day of the accident, but instead of the babysitter by her side, a woman, tall, elegant in a long linen dress, a few gray streaks in her dark hair that rippled with light. I hurried toward them. When I said, "*Pardon*," Elle turned around first, and there was an instant of joy in seeing her ruddy cheeks, those clever, doleful eyes that I had come to know. Then the jolt of dark, unsightly threads protruding, spider-like, from a few stitches above her eyebrow. The woman turned to greet me. There are faces that are so familiar, so intimately known, even if you believe that they have faded, you encounter them, and your knowledge is there, uncreased, every shadow and plane left intact and as devastating as before. She pushed her hand out. "Maude," she said, but of course I knew that already. Her smile was unchanged: at once shy and self-assured. I had looked, over the years, at dozens of photos of that face, tucked in the pages of Bertrand's red and white Editions Gallimard, photos whose angles and intricacies I had studied for the proof of something, every-thing that I could not be—his past, his first love, his match and companion in everything. My hand somehow made it over to hers. I spoke politely. I amazed myself with my poise. I explained that I had been there the day of the accident, had waited for the ambu-lance to come pick Elle up. I had a child of my own, a little older than Elle, I offered up, as if to justify my concern, my presence at the park. Maude did not appear to recognize me, as I had recognized her.

We had met, in person, only twice before. First on McGill's campus, where Bertrand had introduced me, before anything had happened between us, as one of the students in a course in which he was a TA. She had looked me over once and instantaneously deemed me unthreatening: too young, too Anglo, too plain. The second time, when Dafna was not yet one, we'd bumped into her at the Jean-Talon market. She had been alone, inspecting some punnets of blueberries—it was August then. She was visiting from Montpellier for a family wedding, she had explained to Bertrand, smiling, so obviously glad to see him, taking his hand in hers, as if once you've held a hand enough times, it is always yours to hold. She had made, it seemed to me then, an effort so subtle and efficient not to look at me or Dafna—whom I was carrying face pressed to my chest, curls out—that afterward, I did wonder if I'd actually been there to witness the encounter.

When she asked me my name now, on the crowded sidewalk, I emphasized the English pronunciation, one I hadn't used for at least a decade, *Leah*, not since before I'd met my husband, when I'd first made the change to the French *Léa*. It was a pathetic at-tempt at dissimulation, even then, as though a single vowel could make a difference between being oneself and not. I noticed, as she spoke, a new tautening of her syllables, which gave the overall impression that each word was being articulated to itself. I guessed that this must be from all the years she'd spent in France. Elle tugged at her mother's arm and then whispered into her ear. *Invite her*, she said, and then I was with them, not standing on the street anymore but walking as if with old friends, up the block and to the left, climbing up the steep steps to the third-floor apartment with Maude, Bertrand's Maude. I pictured it: thrusting my hand out and declaring it: Léa Parent, Bertrand's wife, the woman who came after you, or maybe it was in fact between you. Wasn't it both somehow? Instead, I sat on the couch and drank her water, its energetic fizz clinging to the slice of lemon with diseased enthusiasm. The apartment was bright with gleaming white walls and windows so tall that looking at Maude's face, just a few feet ahead of me, it was the sun itself that I saw. Their relationship had been frayed already, I had comforted myself, a tooth so loose it needed just the lightest of tugs. Elle settled in the corner of the room at a little table set up just for her. Maude stood and moved toward her, kissed her on the head. I had done the tugging, sure. Had held the bloodied tooth in my palm.

I had never wanted anything before that moment, not a single thing.

"Twenty minutes in your *cahier* and then you can play," Maude said to her daughter, feigning authoritarianism. Elle opened her exercise book and started working, pencil dutifully moving across the page. Everything about them told me that they got along not by decree but by effortless complementarity; they had, despite the impositions of biology, chosen one another.

Maude was near me on the couch now. It was impossible not to notice the separate, competing elements of her face. I was drawn in by her mouth, her teeth, that gap. I had so idolized that gap, which had held, in my eyes, some sliver of truth, endlessly enticing. I had pictured Bertrand looking at it, loving it, wanting never to be separated from it. She brought her voice down to a whisper: "I had to fire her. She didn't even call me after the accident. And then the strangest thing happened: I found my dress crumpled in a ball in the kitchen garbage. Had she told me the truth, that she'd borrowed the dress, then I don't think I would have been angry, but the deception . . ."

I was nodding now, trying to show my empathy, wondering if my face looked as mask-like as it felt.

"I didn't get angry. I don't have the time for anger these days . . . I just got divorced."

"I'm so sorry to hear that," I said, trying to sound surprised. Although of course I knew about the divorce. Bertrand had told me, weeks before: Maude was back and she had taken possession of the old apartment, her grandmother's, near Parc Lafontaine, the same one he and she had shared for five years. He had told me that Maude was living alone with her daughter now, that she and the French father had split up. Maude had called Bertrand like an old friend might: *It's me. I'm back.* Just like that. He had told me. He had made no secret of it. I had heard it and then just as quickly unheard it, a window opening and immediately closing shut.

"What about you?" she asked. "Married? Happy?" she asked, with a dry little laugh.

I nodded yes, "Happy enough." *I'm very unhappy,* I might have told her then, if I had been an altogether different person.

She asked me where I worked, and I told her the name of the school.

"I'm a pedagogue too," she volunteered. "I'll be teaching at the high school in the fall."

"That's wonderful," I said, although of course it wasn't. The Maude I knew was not a high school teacher. She was a poet and a translator. She had been, I had known it nearly immediately, more brilliant than Bertrand. And yet she had been the one to drop out before completing her dissertation, to stay on in France after what was meant to be merely a summer away, the same summer Bertrand and I had become a couple.

"Well, how lucky that you happened to be there when Elle fell," she said, regarding me with uncomplicated gratitude.

"Very lucky," I said, feeling my face redden.

I had dozens of questions, but none of them came to mind; instead I half-listened, not knowing what to do with the time: it would be over too soon. I did not want to go without saying something, something of importance, and then it was time for a snack, Maude told Elle, and when a single thought did come to me, *you can have him back,* I was already outside, remembering now that I had forgotten the bag containing the scarf, which I had laid next to me on the couch, and then it was gone, the thought, the purpose, the scarf, in the muddle of our encounter, and now the front door was shut, a blue, endlessly dark blue door, much darker than my daughter's room where I pulled the curtains shut, even though it was only four in the afternoon, and even then, it was still not dark enough in the room, so I lay under the weight of her floral duvet, the one we had chosen together, and I wept, oh what a fight there had been about this duvet, a battle at every turn. She wanted this one, but in a different color. *Your eyes will be closed, you won't have to look at it anyway,* and she had cried and told me I knew nothing about duvet colors, nothing about her.

As I was falling asleep, I remembered, for some reason, the coat

I had worn the year I'd met Bertrand, a hand-me-down from my cousin Cindy, the exact feeling of it against my neck, its heady smell of mothballs and smoke. It was double-breasted and too large at the shoulders and waist, but I had liked it that way then. I had worn it until Bertrand had told me, "I've always disliked that coat. We should get you a new one." Ten years on and I was stylish now, wore clothes that were streamlined and in neutral, innocuous colors. I had found in the photographs of Maude, I could admit it now, with some remove, a certain necessary inspiration, a blueprint of what I might, in the absence of my own idea of myself, become. At nineteen, I had had no particular style of my own. But I had given the coat away with so little resistance, and now it seemed a mistake, the error of an unknowing person—not myself. The regret around the ugly coat took on that night a kind of urgency, so that I woke the next morning with a sense of having misplaced something crucial. It was like the dream I'd had for a whole year when Dafna was a baby, where I forgot her everywhere: on a park bench, in the car with its windows rolled up, or even once, on one of the arms of the giant crucifix atop Mount Royal.

I spent my final days without Bertrand and Dafna stocking the pantry with Dafna's favorite treats, tidying up my side of the bed of its piles of half-read books and magazines. I imagined a future in which they returned and I was someone else: easy and lithe, impervious to Dafna's moods, effortlessly familial. Like Maude and Elle, mother and daughter, unquestioning, happy together in their bright living room. I stayed away from the park, from their apartment, although the bag containing Dafna's scarf did trouble me, a loose thread that threatened to snag. It would be easy enough for Maude to find me. I had told her the name of the school where I worked. I pictured her calling and finding out my last name, Bertrand's last name, *Parent*. Surely then she would make the connection. Surely then she would feel suspicious, angry even. I felt oddly buoyed by it, childishly perhaps, this possibility of being found out. By Maude, by Bertrand. I pictured the scene: confession, apology, catharsis. Perhaps even a reunion between Maude and Bertrand. An object brought back to its rightful owner. A library book checked out and then returned, slipped back into the stacks. And then what?

On my final afternoon alone, I gave in and walked past Saint-

Denis and east toward the park. It was cool now, September announcing itself in the breeze. It always hit me, in this season, a
necessary reminder after summer's amnesia: the city's arctic un-
dertow, its melancholy pull. It was in this season that my mother
had died, in this season that I had met Bertrand. I had spent that
year, between her death and what felt then like the beginning of
my life, stuck in a kind of static disbelief, my mother an echo in
every step, a shadow in every room. I found her everywhere: in the
pert sound of a cashier laughing at Steinberg's supermarket; in a
pair of hands, veined and bare, folded in a lap on the metro; in my
own reflection, caught in the darkened window of the university
library, the same furrowed concentration she used when she was
sewing, a figure folding inward on itself. I could not picture, then,
a future in which someone might say *you* and mean me.

I sat on the bench by the playground and watched, but no child
was Elle: her sweet self-sufficiency, her knowing tentativeness, the
wound above the eye that would become a scar. If I saw her, then I
would know what to do. Instead, a tangle of children—not Elle—
yelling, elbowing, stepping on each other's toes, skinning knees,
parents rising to intervene and returning to their seats, their practiced reactivity. Afternoon shifted into evening. Nothing left to find
here in this playground, emptied of children. A few couples and
groups of friends sat around on blankets eating their late-summer
picnics: baguettes and pâtés, olives and sardines. On the way back,
I walked past Maude's apartment and looked up to find that the
windows were dark, save for a lamp left on farther indoors. They
were out with friends, no doubt, with other children, in a large
house nearby, I imagined, all the doors swung open, each room
bright and airy and humming with life. I did not want to go back
to our darkened apartment.

It was easy enough to imagine: packing up the small collection
of books that belonged to me, my clothes, making my way to my
father's apartment, living there until I found a place of my own.
Bertrand would be upset, of course, but mostly inconvenienced
by the disruption that my absence would cause. Others would be
surprised as well, that it was *I* who was leaving *him*. For years, when
anyone asked about how we'd met, I had said, with such unflinch-
ing, fated certainty, that I had seen him and simply known. Known
what? All those years, telling of this moment of prophecy, I had
omitted, consciously, unconsciously—what did it matter now—the

most significant part. He was not the only one I had seen that day. Maude had been there too. They were sitting together at the café on Saint-Urbain, his head a mass of fair curls, her profile just a sliver, both of their attentions rapt, their perfect reciprocity, their undeniable ease. It was from this image—one that fundamentally excluded me—that I had fashioned my own hope. I must have thought then that a life was something you could slip into for a while, like a piece of clothing or a story.

Back at home, I placed my shoes next to Dafna's white sneakers with pink laces and a single Velcro strap at the top, her favorites. She had outgrown them in the spring; in fact, we were still looking for a suitable replacement, had been to multiple stores in various shopping malls, yet she had not fallen in love with any of them. When we had first bought them, she had spent a good hour sitting cross-legged in the entrance, pulling open the strap, and closing it shut, once and then again and again. She'd placed a chair near her and instructed me to sit on it; then she had taken a bow, as though she were about to perform an exquisite solo. The scratching sound, repeated, sped up and then slowed, had made an excruciating sort of music. I had asked her, after what felt like longer than was humane, to stop, too abruptly no doubt, and she had thrown the shoe in my direction and yelled, "You don't even respect me," parroting some adult speech, from television, or from Bertrand and me. I had responded, quickly, thoughtlessly, "You are so obstinate." I had said it and remembered the word immediately, stashed away and then recovered, untarnished; the same sharp tool my mother had so often used on me. Hadn't it been the undertone of every one of our fights: my selfishness, hers? My obstinacy, hers. I couldn't help now, shoe in hand, opening and closing the Velcro strap, laughing about it, how right Dafna was, how satisfying the sound was when you were the one making it. Dafna's infuriating resolve. Something of mine, perhaps. I could feel my own resolve falling away, as I moved into the kitchen and opened a bottle of beer, drank a few bitter sips. She would grow out of it, or I would grow into it. The light from the answering machine flashed. I moved toward it, pressed Play. *We miss you,* their voices called out in English, in unison. My husband, my daughter. They must have been in Quebec City by then, at Bertrand's mother's house. They said it three times in a row, as though they knew that I needed it, this emphatic reminder. We miss you. We miss you. We miss you.

graduation, my two brothers, who were still in high school, could not be trusted to resist having a party in a house vacant of parents.

This was why, after walking across the stage and tossing the mortarboard and hugging my friends, I came back alone to my dorm room, dodging my roommates' families, who were loading all their stuff into cars. I closed the door and looked for a long while at my own neatly packed boxes, the stripped mattress. I took my toiletries, *Moby-Dick* from the box of books, a sleeping bag, a pillow, a hiking backpack full of clothes, and slipped out, leaving everything else behind. I didn't say goodbye. I told no one where I was going. I didn't know until I was outside in the softly setting New England sun that I was turning toward the West.

I had been given my grandfather's enormous Buick when he died, and there was still a packet of his pipe tobacco, a tube of his mustache cream, and a little bowie knife in the glove box. These three things summoned the ghost of him into the car as I drove, and it seemed to me that he was protecting me when I stopped to rest for a few neon-lit hours in a truckers' lot outside a highway strip joint, or when I cruised some small-town grocery store for the cheapest and most abundant calories. I had only a pocketful of change and a half tank of gas when I rolled around the curve and saw San Francisco in its dark glitter before me. I'd visited libraries along the way to check an internet bulletin board, where I had advertised the Buick for sale, and it happened that I arrived an hour or so before I had agreed to meet the car's buyer in a hospital parking lot. I pocketed the bowie knife, and felt a pang that I was trading my grandfather's ghost for a paltry thousand dollars in cash, but told myself that surely the dead desire the living to eat.

For a month, I had the upper bunk in a Chinatown youth hostel, a life swept clean of family and friends, an emptiness that I could fill in whatever way I wished. I wished to go hungry until dinner to save money, to walk the hills of San Francisco, asking at every bookshop and bar for a job. Nothing was available, at least not for me. When I squint back through time, I can see her again, this restless, ill-clothed, stringy-haired, half-starved girl who could not, for shyness, look a bookshop manager in the eye.

At night I lay in my top bunk, listening to the two shiny Brazilians assigned to the bottom bunks as they pulled their mattresses to the center of the floor and had gentle, wet, endless sex. Once I had to go to the bathroom, and when I tried to climb down soundlessly a hand grasped me around the ankle, and a voice from below invited me to join them. In the bathroom, I stared at my face in the mirror, trying to see if the new person I was becoming was someone who would have a threesome on the floor with Brazilians so beautiful it was hard to see their faces for their glow. I decided that I would instead be a person shivering in her pajamas on the disgusting puce couch in the common room. I regret this decision, as I regret all the times in my life that I turned away from living.

My money was dwindling, and I submitted my résumé to a temp agency. I went in on a Friday to take a typing test, and before I left I was offered a job all the way down in Redwood City, starting on Monday.

For hours in the library afterward, I scrolled the internet bulletin boards for a place to stay, and when I had almost given up I saw Griselda's ad for a converted pool house in Mountain View. The rent was cheap, because the renter was required to do assorted daily chores, some, Griselda admitted in the ad, unpleasant. Men were preferred. I ignored this last bit and took a bus south, and walked a mile, and saw the cottage for the first time in a kind of spectral dusk. The place sang to me in a register straight out of the fairy tales I'd loved as a child. It seemed a place built for Titania and Puck and little volatile men who grant three wishes.

There was an enormous dog guarding the gate of the big house, an English mastiff of more than two hundred pounds that opened its mouth as if to bark but gave only a series of dry coughs. Griselda had had his vocal cords removed, she would tell me later. She looked astonished when I said that seemed cruel, that it was like taking away a human's ability to speak, and she responded that this was nonsense, that of course dogs couldn't speak. Also, surely, she said, it was less cruel than kicking him when he barked too much. I rang the bell outside the gate and waited, then rang it every five minutes until finally the door opened and a shadowy figure emerged who pulled at the dog's chain until he backed up, then looped it around something so his orbit was small, and at last she stood before me, peering out the gate.

I had never met a person like Griselda in my life. She was as tall as I am, rather tall for a woman, but I saw her as a strangely wizened child. Her blunt inky bob was held back on one side by a plastic barrette, and though her face was round, its skin had wrinkled into a topographical map. Her eyes were sunken, their positions vaguely semaphored by eyeliner that fell in crumbs down her cheeks. Her neck was extremely long and her body, in descending, swelled ever outward from her fragile shoulders until it ended in two purple ankleless columns overflowing a pair of cracked patent-leather slippers.

Who are you? she said. What do you want? I heard even in these few words her German accent, which also seemed like evidence that she belonged to the world of the Black Forest, wolves, dark magic.

I told her that I was there to rent the cottage, that I was quiet and responsible and punctual. I handed her my résumé through the gate. She did not take it but looked at me for a long time and told me that I wasn't a man. I said that I knew I wasn't a man, but I could do whatever a man could do, that I was as strong as a man, which certainly wasn't true anymore, after my month of starvation. Griselda sighed.

Ah. So she is a feminist, she said. I was a feminist once. But then the robbers came at night. And there was no man here. And they tied me up and took everything I had that was good.

This gave me pause; in the pause, I saw the little house suddenly begin to slip away from me, and so I said, What, they even stole your feminism? Then she blinked and her face widened; it was a miraculous sort of unpleating, and she laughed a large, loud laugh and clicked her tongue, and said, Well, yes, fine, fine, fine, you take it. I don't know why but I like you.

Tonight, I said, quickly, and held out the roll of cash that was my entire worldly fortune, save twenty-three dollars and sixty-four cents, which had to keep me until my first paycheck.

She sighed and took the cash and removed the key from her key chain and put it in my palm. Tonight, fine, she said. Tomorrow you begin with the chores. Gladly, I said, and without even looking inside the cottage I ran back to the bus stop, rode it northward, sprinted uphill to the hostel, packed my things, spent a second in the kitchen considering, then threw into my backpack the dustiest of the pasta and rice and ramen and cans of beans and bulk boxes of Chinese green tea and the crusty oil and salt and pepper, all things that other hostel dwellers had left because they wanted them to be used, I reasoned, knowing, even as I stole this food, that I was beyond the pale.

The cottage was cloaked in darkness when I returned. I opened the door, and the place seemed to embrace me. I didn't turn on the light. I saw sharply outlined by the moonlight a woodstove, a kitchenette, a shower and toilet behind a glass wall. Best of all, stretching across the entire ceiling there was a vast skylight, showing the huge oak's muscular branches and the stars sharp between them.

I went out the back. I found that Griselda's pool had been filled with white gravel that glowed in the moonlight, and that the roots of the tree made a smooth and beautiful stool and table. There was a sound inside the tree like a soft, low, constant hum, which I took to be the movement of the tree's sap in its immensely slow circulation, or its long and meditative respiration, or even the way the tree sang to itself in its gladness at being so strong and so alive on a chill bright night like that one.

Inside the cottage, of course, there was no mattress, only my sleeping bag. I slept on the carpet and woke in the morning to a shower of light falling through the oak branches, falling warm and good upon my face.

Griselda's tasks for her renter were, as advertised, unpleasant. She showed me how to unlock the gate, how to fill the food and water bowls for the mastiff, how to scoop up the huge quantity of poop he left on a strip of Astroturf at the end of the range of his chain, and how to spray down the acrid expanse until the smell and the flies were somewhat mitigated. The dog watched me from a bamboo thicket that was pressing itself against Griselda's sprawling nineteen-sixties ranch house. It was a ramshackle place in this neighborhood of neat and lavish mansions. I was also to scrub the dog down once a month or so. Griselda said airily, waving her hand, He stinks! And though it was true that the dog needed many consecutive washes to stop stinking, he and I looked at each other and tacitly agreed that I would not be the one to bathe him. He weighed far more than I did and his teeth were long and yellow.

Why, I ventured to ask, when I was safely away from him, watering geraniums in the giant pots in the courtyard, was the dog always on a chain?

But, instead of answering, Griselda sat down in one of the wrought-iron chairs she had scattered there and asked me if I knew that she was the daughter of an industrialist in Germany. Very, very wealthy.

Pins! Some kind of pin nobody else in the world could make. When she was a child, every Christmas Eve, after the department store in her town closed for the night, it would open just for her, little princess Griselda, and she was allowed to run up and down the aisles and choose any toys she wanted. How magical it was in that empty store, with its sweet evergreen boughs and oranges and the smell of Feuerzangenbowle in the air!

I listened, thinking it was odd that, when Griselda spoke, she seemed not to be telling a story but rather to be reciting something that she had memorized verbatim.

Perhaps, I told myself, she loved to tell stories to create a past she never had. And who was I, who had just erased my own past, to blame her for this.

It took me two hours to finish my chores that first day, and would take me an hour every day from then on. When I was done, Griselda hefted herself upright with a grunt, saying, Wait, I have something for you, and disappeared into the house. She came out with a huge jar, the size of a human head, half full of honey.

A sin what my wealthy neighbors throw out, she said.

Wait, I said. You found that in the trash?

Well, yes, she said, but don't worry, it is not poisoned. I had some in my tea this morning. And look at me, I am still alive!

That Monday, there were twenty temporary workers like me assembled in the conference room of a squat, despondent yellow brick building that was the Department of Human Services in Redwood City. We had been hired by a consultancy firm to help digitize and streamline the social workers' files on each child in the system. I hovered near the bagel table during the orientation PowerPoints so that I could slip as many bagels as possible into my backpack, each a whole meal I wouldn't have to buy. In the shadows on the other side of the table, there was another woman poaching the bagels, and I disliked her immediately, partly because she kept snagging the ones I was about to take and partly because she offended my aesthetic sense. She had long pale unkempt hair to her waist with a fuzz of dandruff in the center part, a strange orange tint to her lips and fingernails, and was wearing an avocado-and-tan striped high-necked shirt-and-skirt combination that would not have been fashionable in the seventies, when it was first imposed upon the world. Her glasses were enormous, with yellow lenses that darkened when she stepped outside into the sun, and which gave her a cagey look in any light. There was a thick funk to her that reached out to me even across the table. Anais, she had written on the nametag sticker on her chest, though she looked more like something biblical, a Judith or Esther or Hagar or Zipporah. A prophetess, a martyr, a believer who loved the ache in the knees after a long session of prayer.

When in the afternoon we were paired off with sample folders, each containing a fictional child's case notes, so that we could practice either keying in answers to an online questionnaire or creating a five-hundred-word narrative of the child's life, I watched with growing unease as all the people I wouldn't have minded being paired with went off together, until in the end I was left with Anais.

She sighed, looked me over with narrowed eyes, and said, Ugh, all right.

All right, I snapped back, though being her partner was not in the least all right.

We sat side by side at our paired computers. She blazed along with the data entry, but because I was vain about my writing I was so slow with the narrative that I was only a few sentences in when time was called. Anais leaned in to read what I had written, and I held my breath and tipped myself away from her smell, and finally she said, No, no, this won't do. You're being too fancy. You got to be simple, clean, in and out, get it?

I must have looked as stung as I felt, because her voice softened. She said, You got to understand. We're about to see some pretty heavy stuff with these kids. Neglect and hunger and rape and broken bones and a bunch of other bad stuff, and if you're writing all that fancy prose you're going to feel all that badness in you. But if you're sharp and cold it won't get to you so deep. You see what I'm getting at? You need to protect yourself, sweetie.

I have always had difficulty with tenderness that comes to me unexpectedly. Perhaps it was also true that by then my beautiful solitude had slid a little into loneliness. My eyes filled with tears. Anais leaned even closer, and put her hand, stinking of something strange, on my face and said, Oh, sweetie, you'll be okay.

When we were given our first real folder to process, I saw that Anais was right: the child in it had a life that was relatively good compared with many we would see, but still, a great horror radiated out from between the lines. There were many different social workers' notes documenting the discipline problems of this small boy, the diagnoses and medications, the cycling into and out of foster homes, all the way back to the initial trauma and the separation from his mother, who had been deemed unfit because she had left her baby with a paramour who had somehow broken the little boy's leg. I wrote my narrative as quickly and cleanly as I could, then, while Anais was finishing the online form, went to the bathroom to cry. But once I stood there in the stall, resting my head against the cool metal, I couldn't. Something was stuck inside me, huge and uncomfortable.

When I returned to my desk, I understood where some of Anais's odor came from. She had taken a small container of orange powder from her battered pocketbook and measured out a careful spoonful. I watched, astonished, as she swallowed the powder down, staining her tongue and teeth orange. Turmeric. It's my medicine, she explained, daring me to say something.

Witnessing this only added density to the enormous immovable object inside me. When I got home to the cottage, I had the idea to put on my running shoes and go out into the delicious coolness and try to run the bad feelings off.

I went through the expensive streets of Mountain View in the dusk, and though I could not yet run far, and I still couldn't cry, the lump inside me dissolved enough that I felt relief.

I returned to the cottage to find a gift from Griselda outside my door: a beautiful armchair. On the note, in a spiky and elegant hand, she wrote that she had noticed I had no furniture yet in the cottage, and that someone like me always needed a separate place to sit and think.

The following months became a plait of four strands: the dark horror of my job, with all those damaged children who burned beyond their folders into the world at large; the increasingly long and ecstatic runs I began to take every night after work; Anais, my coworker; and Griselda, with her stories and her gifts of rescued castoffs.

One morning, as I scooped up dog shit, Griselda told me that she had once been a model in New York in the nineteen-sixties. She showed me a torn-out magazine photo of a dark-haired woman who, except for the extremely long and elegant neck, looked nothing at all like her. She said that back then she went to parties all the time, really scandalous parties, and she knew everyone—Lou Reed, David Bowie, Andy Warhol. In fact, she had been in a sex film of Andy's. But under an assumed name, of course.

Oh, of course, I said politely, scooping, scooping.

But, as much as Griselda spun her stories around me, Anais, who had begun to interest me, was resolutely silent. She had pinned above our shared desk a photo of a tiny child of three or so, with long red braids on either side of her face. She was so striking that I had to mask my surprise when Anais told me that the girl was her daughter, and that her name was Luce.

Afterward, I glanced at Anais's face surreptitiously throughout the day, seeing this woman whom I had believed to be a spinster, or uninterested in sex, suddenly as a mother. I was so young, with the distorted vision of youth, and had assumed from the way she dressed that she was much older than me. I saw now the dry skin of the emaciated where before I had seen wrinkles. I saw a young woman wearing the thrift-store costume of a much older woman. I began to sense that she was hiding something.

We were, finally, given our first paycheck. At last, I had enough for rent and food; the extra left over felt luxurious. I began to buy fruit from a food cart to supplement my peanut-butter-and-jelly sandwiches at lunch, a little clamshell of beautiful fresh strawberries and watermelon with some mint sprinkled in. There was a kind older social worker I sat with in the sun while I ate this fruit, a comfortable woman named Shelley, who talked about her grandchildren and the weather and books. During those months, Shelley became a good acquaintance, if not a friend. I had no friends. I wanted none.

But one day I felt the joy of my extra money and bought a second clamshell of fruit to take back to Anais, who, as far as I could tell, only ever had soup she sipped from a beige plastic thermos.

I handed it to her, and she looked at me, wary of my gift, then a softness settled into her shoulders and she said a quiet thank-you, and ate the fruit slowly with little grunts of appreciation, saving half of it to take home to her girl.

After that, things were more balanced between us. I had grown used to her turmeric-swallowing. She grew comfortable enough with me not to hide that as she worked she was listening to the voice of an evangelical minister in her earphones. I had heard of this man—my roommate in college, a former evangelical, spoke scathingly about him, calling the minister a charlatan and a hypocrite and a serial seducer of young boys. I had committed to my dispassionate life, though, and didn't mention the rumors to Anais. Who was I to ruin her pleasure in this form of God? I liked it even when, once in a while as she listened, she nodded with a radiant smile on her face.

Soon she began to use the landline in front of me, which we weren't allowed to use—it was for the actual social workers, who resented us—to talk to the mechanic who was always fixing something or other, carburetor, hose, tire, on her Vanagon.

Vanagon? I asked. She smiled, then seemed to make a decision and took her wallet out of her pocketbook, and from it pulled a photo of a boxy olive-green Volkswagen van. My home, she said proudly. I bought it cash, and so I don't have to pay rent. It's got everything, a bed my girl and me share and a table and a little kitchenette and a toilet, but the shower's broke and I'm saving up to fix it. We can up and go whenever we want. Say there's another earthquake, which there will be, mark my words, all we do is get in the Vanagon and drive to somewhere safe.

Then she seemed to regret having said this much, and to all my questions afterward she frowned and shook her head.

I am sure I would never have discovered what Anais was running from if I hadn't come back from the bathroom one day to hear her on the landline, pledging a thousand dollars to the evangelical charlatan's overseas ministry. I must have let out an incredulous sound, because she looked at me and made a furious face. She said that she would send a check, and slammed the receiver down. Then she stood up, quivering with rage, and said loudly that it was her money, she could do whatever she wanted with it.

All the other temps stopped working to look at us. I said, You're right.

For the rest of the morning, Anais typed on her keyboard so hard that I was afraid she might break it.

This was our six-month anniversary of the digitizing project, and we were, surprisingly, over our quota. Our supervisor, a sweaty new college graduate, who looked like all the frat boys I had gone to school with, celebrated our achievement by buying us a stack of pizzas and a sheet cake. He also forgot where we were and the gravity of what we were doing, and brought a couple of twenty-four packs of cold beer.

I watched from across the room as Anais stood silently in a little knot of people, sipping a beer so fast that it was clear to me she had never in her life drunk one before. I don't think she would have had one now if I hadn't upset her so deeply that morning. I watched with dismay as she opened a second beer. This she drank even faster, and I watched her give a little burp into her fist, and the people in the ring around her all at once leaned back a little, perhaps because of a sudden waft of spice.

There was a speech I didn't listen to; I was watching Anais wobble, her eyes grow a little loose behind her thick lenses. I made my way around the room until I was standing right behind her. The speech ended, everyone applauded and began shuffling out of the conference room, and I caught Anais's arm as she made to move but tripped on nothing and began to fall.

She looked at me. Uh-oh, she said. I steered her into the bathroom so quickly that I was able to pull her hair back into a bun at her nape before she vomited into the toilet.

She retched and retched, neatly, like a cat, except for in the first torrent, when some puke had splashed back up onto her chin, her glasses, and the high seventies bow of her shirt. She sat, bleary and sweating, on the side of the sink while I wet a paper towel and wiped her face, then ran her glasses under the water and tried to clean the bow by dabbing it with a fresh towel. I saw that it attached to the collar of her shirt with a series of tiny buttons all the way around, and began to unbutton them one by one.

She watched me. Without the glasses obscuring her face, she looked young, my age. She was not unpretty, I saw with surprise.

I undid the last button, and took the end of the bow to pull it open, but she put her small hand over mine, squeezed, and looked me in the face. Then she pulled the end and the bow fell away. Her neck was scrawny and pale. Across it there was a raised purple scar that stretched from beneath one ear all the way to the other.

Almost killed me, she said. Luce's dad.

I saw then why she was so wily, so secretive, why she lived with her child in a van, why the ability to escape trumped every other need.

So now you know why nobody gets to tell me what to do ever again, she said.

I thought about what to say while I washed out the bow with hand soap and hot water, then held it under the hot-air dryer. The fabric was shiny, synthetic, thin from wear, and didn't take long to dry. I had found nothing to say by the time I began buttoning it back around her collar.

Gently, I tied the bow in a great loose loop that swallowed up Anais's angry scar.

Then Anais leaned forward and kissed me gently on the lips. She tasted like turmeric and beer and vomit, and I moved my head away.

But, as I did, her face changed, a horror entered it, and she snatched up her glasses and ran out the door. I spent some time cleaning up the bathroom. When I came out, she had left a note on my keyboard: Sick. Forgive me. Won't happen again.

I didn't get to tell her that it was all right, that though I didn't want it to happen again, either, I didn't mind that it had taken place once. By the next day Anais had built such a strong wall around herself that I was never going to be able to reach her again. Not once during the next few months did she speak to me about anything other than work-related matters. I tried to get her to talk about Luce, but she wouldn't. She was gone, closed. I had done some violence that I wasn't at that time capable of understanding.

As the silence between us grew, I began to be unable to sleep at night, thinking about Anais's girl. Every day, her little flower of a face looked down at me from the photo above the computer; when Anais was in the bathroom or slowly measuring out her turmeric, I would look at her and think about how she sent her money to that disgusting evangelical charlatan. And then I would think about the Vanagon that she could never keep running properly, and what would happen if Luce's father found them when the vehicle was going through one of its many sulks. If they would be able to get away from him. If Anais would be too holy to fight him off if he were to try to murder her again.

After a while, I had thought about Anais and her daughter so constantly that I grew angry. It began to seem wildly irresponsible for any mother to waste her money on religion and vehicle maintenance, to fritter away the means by which she could get an actual apartment, not a box on wheels, to choose not to build up a safety net to protect her child. There was only a flimsy aluminum door between the tiny girl and all the danger in the world.

As if sensing my anxiety, one weekend Griselda told me a story about her life. Once, she said, in the nineteen-eighties, a very wealthy lover got so mad at her while they were on his yacht in the Caribbean that he slipped her a mickey, and when she woke up she was floating on a raft out at sea, sunburned and wearing only a bikini. She floated like this for a week or so, lost in the blazing sun during the day and the stars at night, surprised by two sudden rainstorms that put enough water in the bottom of the boat to keep her alive, circled by sharks, until she thought that she would simply jump into the waves and let the sea take her down into its hungry depths. But then she was rescued by a family with a sailboat whose father had wanted to write a book about their year on the seas. They thought they'd caught a mermaid! They carried her to a hospital in the British Virgin Islands, where a doctor fell in love with her, but she had to break his heart and go back home to her daughters, who were teenagers and hadn't even realized she was gone.

That sounds like a difficult experience, I said, as neutrally as I could.

Oh, indeed, that was a very bad experience, Griselda said contemplatively. But, once I was out of the hospital, the hush money from my lover who had made me a castaway was excellent.

And she smiled her wide, gorgeous smile that was like an explosion in her face.

One Friday, after Anais gave a curt little nod and said, Happy weekend, and slung her pocketbook over her shoulder, I followed her, though without at first meaning to. We were going in the same direction, and I simply continued on past my bus stop, drawn almost against my will. She walked with her martial step through the scorching streets of Redwood City, probably not wanting to spend money on bus fare. I stopped, watching from behind a tree, as she entered a cinder-block day care, and came out holding the hand of her daughter. She was smiling down at Luce, and the girl was talking excitedly up to her. They walked slowly for a few blocks to a library, and I lingered at the window of a convenience store across the street, pretending to agonize over a rack of gum, until they came out again, the little girl with a book tucked under her arm.

I followed them as the road twisted into a copse of bay laurels and cypresses, where I saw the Vanagon hidden by the thick shade.

There was the flicker of a kerosene light in the window. I saw that the night had begun to deepen. There was the smell of cooking— garlic and some kind of starch, like pasta. But seeing the dark forms of Anais and Luce moving in the light made me ashamed of myself, and I quickly left the copse. In self-punishment, I walked the three hours back home.

This should have been the end of it. I should have let the distance sit between us. But I had not yet learned wisdom, and silence had not yet sunk into me as deeply as it later would. That week, I was sitting out in the noontime sun with the social worker, Shelley, eating cut fruit with mint, and talking about Anais, about Luce, about the Vanagon.

Just between you and me, I confided, I think she's an excellent mother, but I'm worried about her daughter. I think it's not impossible that she doesn't take the girl to get her shots. The preacher she listens to doesn't believe in vaccines.

And Shelley nodded slowly, smiling, which at the time I took to be agreement with my assertions of confidentiality, but which I came to understand did not commit her to anything like silence, or discretion, or inaction.

I ask myself now if some part of me wanted Anais to be jolted; if I wanted, obscurely, to force her to find a solid place for her child. If I knew that she and her daughter might be separated. I would never have put it like this to myself at the time. There are moments in our lives when our sense of our own goodness is so shaky that we build elaborate defenses against the possibility that we may be far worse than we fear. I have come to think that I had a secret intention, held at the very center of my actions, so small and dark that I pretended not to see it then; I could not see it even a decade later. It is only now, when I know myself to be good and bad in equal measure, that I can glimpse it, if barely.

As I took care of the mastiff that weekend, Griselda sat in the courtyard in a plastic chair, soaking her feet in a tub. She was telling me another of her tall tales, this time about the period when she taught philosophy at Princeton, back in the seventies and eighties, and had an affair with Derrida—or was it Nagel? It's astonishing how things get confused as one ages, she said. I filled the water bowl, half-smiling at the idea of Griselda as a philosopher when her thinking was so muddled she couldn't get her lovers straight.

Then she said, with her eyes closed and her face turned up to the sun, In those years, I felt the world stirring within me. I was so *alive* then.

I turned off the water, and said, quickly, Yes, that's exactly how it is, exactly. I told Griselda that I had felt that way ever since I moved into the cottage eight months ago. Every day, I sit with my tea out under the oak tree, I told her, and I press my ear to it and hear the way the world and the tree seem to have found a resonance within me. It is like a triangulation—the world, the tree, and me.

Then I saw a bee land on the chair close to Griselda's bared shin, and I said, Careful, bee.

She bent and looked at it, then looked across the yard, at the geraniums, where more bees were crawling in and out of the vivid red flowers.

I watched as slowly her eyes lifted above the wall of bamboo, to the top of the great oak tree, and she held her hand in a visor and squinted, looking there for a long time, frowning.

When she dropped her hand, in her face there was something like pity. Ah, she said. I'm so sorry. It's not the resonance of the world, or whatever you think it is. It's bees.

I couldn't believe that I had missed them in their thick orbiting of the top of the tree, where there must have been a hollow. Griselda forbade me to go into my backyard, saying that she was sorry, there were legal issues. One of her former tenants had been stung and had an anaphylactic reaction and had to go to the hospital, and now she was bee-shy as a landlord—she couldn't afford such hospital bills again!

She brought me a gift of six beautiful amber-colored drinking glasses in apology, so that I wouldn't have to drink out of old pasta-sauce jars anymore, and that night I sat on the cold woodstove to drink my tea from an amber glass, and felt a longing to be next to the tree as usual.

I woke on Sunday morning to a feeling that something was wrong, and stood blearily in the shower, trying to understand what it could be. At last, I lifted my eyes to look through the skylight, where, at the top of the tree, a man had belayed himself and was spraying the hive, a can of chemicals in each hand. At the moment I looked up, he was looking down at me, but was oddly faceless, which I couldn't understand until I had screamed and cowered on the floor, and crawled naked out of the shower, and thrown on my clothes and run out into the driveway barefoot, my hair dripping.

Griselda was standing colossal there, supervising the spraying from below. Oh, don't worry, she said. His name is Gabriel, he does handiwork for me sometimes.

Yes, unfortunately he did have to spray at this time in the morning, she said. It is when the bees are sleepy and won't sting so much.

Yes, he has a face, she said, I just made him wear three pairs of my panty hose over his head to protect himself.

And at last she said, impatiently, Ah, Liebchen, he doesn't care for your nakedness. He is up in a tree being stung by *bees*.

On Monday morning, the tree did not hum its happiness.

At work, there was no Anais. She did not come in, did not even call to say she wasn't coming in, my supervisor complained. My cubicle felt lonely and the face of the little girl looked down at me, an accusation there.

When after work I walked all the way to the little grove of laurels and cypresses, the Vanagon was, of course, gone. There was an indentation in the soil in the shape of Anais and her child's life.

The next day, though I stood outside the day care and waited to see her, Anais did not come to pick up her daughter, and the women finally locked the door. It was clear that the child had not come in that day. I grew so concerned, I could hardly sleep.

After a few days of standing on the street, watching, I summoned the courage to go into the day care, which smelled like paste and piss and crackers, and asked the lady in charge about Luce and Anais; a window slammed shut in her soft face, and in Spanish she called the other two child-minders over and the three of them stood in a ring around me defensively, saying that Anais was gone, that she did not want to be found, that I had better forget her.

The state had come around asking questions, the lady in charge said. I wasn't someone sent from the state, was I?

Oh, God, no! I said. I am not a threat, I wanted to say. Then I understood that to any woman on the run the fact that I was there, trying to find her, meant that I was indeed a threat.

And so I began to come home from work directly, to change into my running clothes as quickly as I could, and I would go out into the late afternoon and twilight and night, trying to spot

Anais's van in the towns all around Redwood City, my heart lifting every time I saw an olive-colored van, and crashing down again when I understood that it wasn't Anais's, that she had gone somewhere too far for me to run to.

I began to run farther and farther at night, in expiation, but also still looking for her.

I am so sorry, I wanted to tell her. I am not someone you need to run from. I would never harm you. I would never ask the authorities to take your child from you. You do not need to fear me. But she had gone somewhere out of reach of my contrition.

A month passed, and then another. My body had become whittled with all the running. The bees came back, and I didn't tell Griselda; I just sat in the chilly bright mornings drinking my tea and listening to the low song inside the trunk. I took care of the mastiff before work every morning. Some days Griselda joined me and told impossible stories from her life, and other days she would leave a gift on my doorstep: a bottle of hot sauce, an expensive face cream, barely used. The only thing marring my happiness was the black spot, the sin, of having sent a traumatized woman bolting out of her life. For this, I still cannot forgive myself.

On one of the nights I spent running through the cool dark streets looking for Anais's Vanagon, Griselda shuffled to my door while I was gone to deliver a water-buckled copy of *Life and Fate* that she had discovered tossed by a Mountain View neighbor. She had seen my stash of books and knew how much I loved to read, she wrote in the lumpy copy, signing her full name. When she was returning through the gate, the mastiff, a strange puppyishness perhaps overwhelming him, rose up on his hind legs, all two hundred pounds of him, and put his two great paws on Griselda's shoulders, knocking the old woman down. In falling, she hit her head on one of the enormous geranium planters and something shifted and bubbled up inside her skull. The fall had also cut her scalp deeply, and a black pool of blood slowly grew on the stones behind her head. The dog would have barked his alarm, but could not. He skulked into the bamboo thickets, knowing he had done something terribly wrong. That night, I ran so far that I couldn't run anymore, and I walked home, cold and nearly blind with exhaustion. I picked up the book off my mat, entered the cottage, took a long hot shower, and slept until midmorning. When I came out to feed and water the mastiff, I saw through the bars of the gate the purple soles of Griselda's feet facing me. I rushed to her. Griselda was still alive, her eyes glassy. She was speaking. Oh, she murmured. It's you, the sun is bright. *Wer rastet, der rostet.* No, I am not fond of organ meat.

I ran inside, picked my way through the fetid piles of junk among which she must have burrowed for so many years, unable to feel, yet, the shock of the mess, and found her phone and called an ambulance. Then, back outside, I tried to press a towel on the wound of her scalp, but the blood had already clotted. She had rips on the shoulders of her nightgown, where the mastiff's claws had fallen, and a few bloody scratches on the skin beneath. The dog watched from the shadows, his chin on his paws.

While we waited, Griselda spoke, and amid her wild talk, her nonsense words, the long phrases in German, the directives to call her daughters, whose numbers were in the book by the phone, and to please please please, Liebchen, tidy up before the ambulance comes, she said two things that I later wrote down.

She said we have art so as not to die of the truth.

She said that in every human there is both an animal and a god wrestling unto death.

The first was Nietzsche. The second I have found nowhere. I think it was Griselda's own philosophy.

Griselda's daughters arrived while she was in the hospital. The doctors had induced a medical coma to help her brain heal, but the prognosis wasn't good. I had sent the mastiff to the pound; he had to be dragged out to the truck by two men, coughing his sad, soundless barks. He strained toward me as he passed, putting his cold nose on my leg, but I was too young to find in my heart any forgiveness for a murderer. I met the daughters when they at last came to their mother's home, after forty-eight hours at the hospital, when they were too exhausted to sit vigil at Griselda's side any longer. They saw me waiting as they pulled into the drive, and got out of the car spiky with rage. Why weren't you here to check on her, they yelled, these skinny women dressed in expensive black. Why was that awful dog not under control? Why didn't anyone tell us she was so far gone? I kept my eyes down and said nothing. They went into Griselda's house. I couldn't move my body. They came out again, their faces crumbling at how their mother had been living. Sorry, they said. We're so sorry. It's not your fault. We're just so sad.

They stayed in a hotel for a month. One of the daughters would sit by Griselda, who was swollen and absent in her hospital bed, while the other put on work gloves and took armfuls of trash out to the hired skip. I stopped going to my job so that I could help with the clean-out, gathering up the newspapers and all sorts of things her neighbors had put out for trash and she had saved. We slowly uncovered the excellent furniture that had lain for so long beneath it all, which the daughters would be selling. We found treasures: Picasso prints, original Stickley chairs. One day, I unearthed a painting that had fallen behind a headboard in the guest room. Is this a Mondrian? I asked. The daughter gave a little crow. Oh! she said, it's here. We thought the robbers stole it. She hugged it to herself and took it back to her hotel room, and though I wanted to see it again, and would not, my hands still felt warm after having touched something so beautiful.

Only later did I realize that the daughter had mentioned the robbers, which meant that Griselda's story about them was likely true. I hadn't believed it. In truth, I hadn't believed any of her stories; they were all so composed, as if she had made them up long before. The daughters warmed to me, and began buying me sandwiches when it was time for lunch, and so one day I asked if the other stories that Griselda had told me were also true.

The daughter I was with that day, the one who wore expensive European glasses with tiny blue frames, looked at me with surprise. What stories? she said. I told her about Griselda's being the daughter of the industrialist in Germany, and how the toy store was opened just for her on Christmas Eve. Of her modelling career and of Andy Warhol. How she had been lost at sea for two weeks. How she'd been a philosopher at Princeton.

Then I saw, briefly, in the daughter's face a look of such yearning that I stopped talking. Yes, she said at last. All of this is true. Griselda doesn't lie, has never lied in her life.

Huh, I said.

No, you don't get it, the daughter said, blinking quickly. It's just she never talked about any of it—*any* of it—with us. Even when we begged her to tell us. And yet she gave those stories to you, a total stranger.

Griselda never woke up. A truck came and took away the skip filled with junk. An auction house came and took away all the furniture. It turned out that, underneath the furniture, the roots of the bamboo thickets had been pushing up through the terra-cotta floors. Griselda was cremated without a service. The daughters gave me one of the lesser Picasso prints and said I could stay in the cottage rent-free until the place was sold. I found a job as an administrative assistant at Stanford, basically a receptionist, with excellent health care.

Two months after Griselda died, a year into my quiet life alone in the cottage, I felt a disturbance in the air in front of my desk at work, and looked up, and standing there was a woman, and that woman was my mother. She wore a floral dress I had never seen before, and was cupping her hands to her mouth.

My mother said, I found you.

She had tracked me down through my Social Security number, which I'd given when applying for my job at Stanford. I left the office early. My mother looked deeply uncomfortable as we toured the cottage, and then she suggested that she rent a hotel room in the city. At first, there was a tension between us, a hesitancy, but she had always dreamed of San Francisco and had never been able to visit, and here she was, her face full of wonder, and the warmth between us returned, sweetened. We spent the weekend sightseeing. I have pictures of my mother on a trolley, eating a bread bowl full of chowder, in front of the Golden Gate Bridge in a sweatshirt she had to buy because she hadn't counted on its being so very cold in California. We split a bottle of wine the night before she flew back home, and she confessed that she thought I had been sucked into a prostitution ring or was on heroin or something, and she was going to have to rescue me, drag me home to that cold house with the wind coming through the drafty windows and too many children to a room.

No, I said. I'm finding my own way to survive.

For a long time she had nothing to say to that, then at last she gave a little shiver and said, It is so cold here. Aren't you so cold? I knew, obscurely, that she wasn't talking about the weather.

At the airport, she hugged me and cried, and just as she was about to go through security I watched as the new mother I had seen all weekend—bright, laughing, eager—changed physically, bending down to take off her shoes and coming up slightly slumped, shoulders rounded, as if already facing her chaotic home, her baffled husband and noisy children, and all the heaviness that awaited her there. I held my breath, but she didn't look back before she disappeared through the gate.

*

I had to leave the cottage not long after this. I moved away from the Bay Area a few years later. Life came for me, swallowed me up. I created my own family, and it has become my true north, which turns me in its direction no matter where I find myself, no matter all the changes that draw with astonishing swiftness over the face of the earth. Surely Anais's little girl is an adult now. I tell myself that, with a mother as loving as Anais, surely she is fine. Still, the cottage, and Griselda's slowly sinking house, and even the vast and perfect oak tree, all of which took up an entire city block of the most expensive real estate in the country, must have been crushed and replaced by buildings meant for wealthier and more prosaic souls. I once lived in golden light in California, that light lived within me, and though it returns for spells here and there, that same golden light has never been with me as steadily as it was that year. In fact, there are often times when my life seems so small that the darkness in me has no outlet, and it keeps circling, faster and faster, tighter and tighter, until it seems that there is nothing but darkness, endlessly spinning. My emergence from these times is painful and very slow. I have to go far away to recover myself. My family has weathered these flights of mine before; they have learned to accept them, because in the past I have always returned, and, when I do, I am a mother who sees her children fully.

In this pale apartment on another continent where I have come to be alone now, I have been waking, to my surprise, into brightness and peace, marvelling that beauty could come so suddenly, after such deep and, I believed, permanent shadow. Grace is a gift undeserved, yet given anyway. In these hills I finally feel again that deep yearning, not for anything in particular but for the wild whole-being gladness that I knew for the first time in the cottage covered in moss and ferns and the shadow of the oak tree, where my freedom overwhelmed me. Sometimes when I am doing nothing but listening to the birds that nest in the crags of the nearby castle, I think about how there are, constellated through the countryside all around this place, churches full of Madonnas, paintings and frescoes and sculptures. There are a thousand Madonnas here, with a thousand different faces. Each Madonna wears the face of a particular mortal woman whom the artist loved. Each woman is one in whom the animal was briefly overcome by the god that lived within her.

The Mine

FROM *Electric Literature*

A BOY HAS died in the crypt. (I'm told this is what they call the
bottom of the mine, now: the crypt.) Benji, my surveyor, has come
to tell me the news. As he stands before me, I notice that grime
has crept into the folds of his face; that his overalls are stained
with streaks of mud. The air-conditioning in the trailer seems to
unnerve him, bringing him to flinch as it cranks to life once more,
a steady breeze causing his shirt to flap upon his chest.

"This is a problem," I tell him.

Benji nods, knowingly.

"When can he be retrieved?"

"The others refuse to go. They are afraid."

"Afraid?"

He shakes his head, as though disappointed in himself. "They
believe there is something evil in the deposits. That the dead boy
has been claimed by a monster. That it would be wrong to bring
him back up."

The air conditioner stops and the trailer falls silent.

"I see," I say, for many of the boys who work in the gold mines
are from the bush, and I know their beliefs to be primitive. Even
my own father—who grew up under a hut in a village he came to
disdain—took to such nonsense on occasion.

What must be understood is that the executives are to arrive
later today. They come to tour the grounds periodically, and there
cannot be a corpse rotting away, no matter if it is unreachable, no
matter if they will never glimpse the horror themselves, for there

are many horrors here, and all of them must be hidden on the day these men come.

"Take me to them," I say. And Benji, his shoulders falling in acquiescence, opens the door to guide me out.

Few are familiar with the brightness of the sun after a morning spent underground: emerging from the deposits, the sudden prick of heat upon the skin building to a burn, as if in time it might torch you to cinder. I worked the mines when I was younger, under the supervision of my father, and so I know the sensation. Nowadays, I mostly see its power on the faces of the miners when I approach them. They work tirelessly, noiselessly, and yet their fatigue can be gleaned from the way their knees buckle when their wheelbarrows falter on a ridge of stone; in the slouch of their shoulders when the pickaxe grows too heavy on their back as they carry it to storage.

The mine shaft is before us, workers steadily flowing out of the elevator in their yellow hats and suspenders like bees exiting a hive. Benji has us turn towards the smelter—its innards, bright as lava, sending swirls of heat into the air as it is fed endless quantities of ore. The boys in question are lined up under the break canopy, awaiting my arrival. Sweat masks their faces, and I know the feeling of wanting to undress under the weight of the heat: to find the nearest source of water and jump. (There is a perversity here, for when their shifts end, they will find only the chill of the night; and by the time they take to their showers in the barracks, the shiver of the cold will be as unwanted as the sweat that came before it.)

There are individuals versed in retrieving bodies from the mine. It happens, perhaps twice a year, and it must be handled with great care and discretion. It is reported to the attorney for the company that backs us, a man I have never met and know only as a voice. It is of the utmost importance that the matter remains confidential—including the payment to the dead man's next of kin. So in such an instance, when the boys who are trusted with the task are reticent to do it, the occasion has become delicate enough to require my full attention.

"Boys," I say. Benji stands at my side, his arms tucked into the pouch of his overalls. I pace before them like their superior officer, telling the same story I have told so many other employees, perhaps these same ones. "Did you know that I worked these very mines when I was your age? That what you fear, I once feared? That my own brother died under rockfall? I had only waved goodbye to him the very morning of the accident. If I had not been holed up with my father, learning how to manage the books, I would've died alongside him. In a sense, we, too, are brothers." I point at them now. "Tethered by this place. But as I did my duty back then, you must now do yours."

I stop, then. I face a boy who is staring at me with great resolve. The sun has broken his face into a leathered mask like that of a man twice his age. He is so dark that his skin matches the blacks of his eyes, and it is the yellow of his pupils, the ravages of some burgeoning disease, that shines brighter than the rest of him.

"The body is in the crypt," he says. "Where the scientists go, we do not."

I look to Benji, who nods in confirmation. "They say he went on a dare," Benji tells me. "He fell from the path as he descended."

So this is what they mean by the crypt. Scientists overtake a segment of the mine each winter, examining microbes in an astonishingly deep vein of earth. The dig goes so far underground that it often makes the news. The boys fear what might be found there. It is wholly irrational, for it is merely another cavity of dirt, but I now understand the problem.

"I need this taken care of quickly," I say. "I will double your wage for the day."

The boy who spoke stands tall now, defiantly taking the shirt laid upon his shoulder and wrapping it upon his head as he steps into the sunlight from beneath the canopy.

"The Grootslang lives in the crypt. We do not go there."

"*The Grootslang*," I say, under my breath. An elephantine being with a serpent's tail. Bush folklore. More nonsense in a day far too full of it.

"It will make you see great horrors," the boy says. "Torment you in ways you cannot imagine."

I breathe in, and smell the tobacco on the boy's breath—then there is the stench of the heat, of the day's work, like hot piss emanating from his being. I turn to the mine elevator. On certain days, exhausting days when I stay long after the rest have gone home, I have eyed my brother there—waving, beckoning, as though I should come to him. The darkness coalesces then, absorbs the specter whole, and it is gone in an instant. Is this their fabled monster? A child's fear of the dark?

"What is your name?" I ask the boy.

"Felix."

"Felix," I say. "We will speak again soon. And Benji."

Benji turns.

"Make sure the men carry on working as if nothing has happened. As it must be. Appearances and what have you."

My employer has called to inform me he is on his way, so I know to wait for him in my trailer. I sit there, twirling my pen, thinking. I had asked Benji if there were any others who would retrieve the body, but all those who might take on the job have formed a pact behind Felix; he is, Benji told me, a reformed criminal, a man who knows death and does not flinch from it. I will need his help. I have to reach him, somehow. Make him do what must be done.

There is then a knock at the door, and they do not wait for me to answer before coming in. There are six men in all, led by Ross Fletcher himself, the face of Tibor Holdings, the largest mining outfit in all of South Africa. He is wearing a polo and khakis. They are all wearing polos and khakis. After this meeting, Mr. Fletcher will take them to a golf course two hours away, an idyllic place of combed sand and green fields, and the other men, prospective investors, will tell their colleagues that their money will not be scrutinized once entrusted to such a conscious enterprise as Tibor Holdings.

"Nicholas!" Mr. Fletcher says, his hand springing towards my own.

"Sir," I say.

His teeth are immense, his pectorals full, and when the air conditioner turns on once more his nipples appear with a sudden wakefulness.

"These men are from London, Nicholas. They're eager to see the facility."

The men, wary, hands behind their backs, nod to me. I nod back. Once this is done, Mr. Fletcher's presentation begins, an exchange we have had so many times it's taken on the air of theater.

"This photo, behind Nicholas, that is his father. He was a surveyor here, a wonderful worker . . ." The men are nodding again, eager to consume this narrative. I look back at the photo myself. These visits are the only time I do so. My father in his church suit, his bony jowls and thick lips, eyes beaded, like he cannot make out the photographer before him. The pride in the straightness of his back. *Look at me,* he used to say. *A twig of a man. An African from the backcountry. Yet look at what I have done. Think of what you will do . . .*

The men are staring in my direction. It is my turn to speak. "Yes," I say. "I thought nothing would stop my father from working until that tragedy took place. The loss of my brother was too much to bear. He never stepped foot near the mines again." I do not say that my father was a near-mute after the accident; that the few words he shared after it were put towards the task of getting me to quit my job right alongside him. That my refusal to do so was the greatest shame of his life behind the guilt of letting his firstborn die.

Mr. Fletcher steps forward, now. He is adjacent to my desk, and I allow him the spotlight.

"The least we could do was give Nicholas the chance of an education. In short order he returned and took us up on our offer to become the first African captain of a mine. He runs the entire production. His story is remarkable. I would say it's one of Tibor Holdings' proudest achievements."

He does not say that though this is the only mine of its kind, it is a mere token of significance. I am an obedient and nothing more, a man paid to own the deaths of others.

His hand—a fleshy mound, soft and child-like—is on my desk. The thought of this slab of wood, this wood he owns and allows me to borrow, brings to mind my dinner table at home. My father had it made of African teak, large enough to sit twelve, running the length of the dining room. He would sit at its head, relishing his authority, deciding who would give their thanks before the meal, declaring his need for another helping and expecting the dish to be placed before him. My brother and I would sit on opposite sides of him. Often, as my father told stories, or gave commands, I would rub the swirling knot of wood upon the table's underside, as though it might give me strength, some means to escape my father's scrutiny, the next command I did not wish to answer to, the next piece of wisdom he would quiz me on in the days that followed. I feel for it, now, under my desk, that knot, knowing it is not there; knowing there is no reprieve from the moment that is upon me.

"We'd love to take a tour inside the mine," Mr. Fletcher says. "Where are the hard hats, Nicholas?"

The room has grown so hot I feel the need to disrobe, to lie upon the floor and discover the coolness of each vinyl tile I might find there. "We are, unfortunately, conducting a safety review of the mines," I say. "It is a full-scale, top-to-bottom effort. We can't have any visitors inside."

Mr. Fletcher's gaze finds me, and I feel my insides flinch. His coolness, his ability to show no feeling, frightens me.

"Did you not know we were coming, Nicholas?"

"It is a terrible oversight, one for which I apologize. It will not happen again."

He is still hiding his teeth, and soon begins to crack his knuckles despondently, some vague assertion of power.

"You will be spending the night at the Prince Grant Estate, no?" I say. "Why do you not take the tour tomorrow, when you come back this way? We will be ready, then."

"The mine is quite a detour . . ." Mr. Fletcher eyes his guests, but they are silently shrugging, for this is vacation for them, and it would appear they don't wish to take on any further responsibility than that of a guest. ". . . So be it. Tomorrow afternoon, then. We will work off our breakfast with a walk in the mines! What could be better?"

The men laugh at this so loudly the trailer shakes. There is absolutely no reason for them to laugh this loud. Mr. Fletcher squeezes my shoulder—as though pinching a child's cheek—and leads them out. He does not look back at me—only waves with the back of his hand.

I arrive home at night, the moon bright in the cloudless sky. The veranda sits empty, the wooden shutters on the windows open just enough that I can glimpse movement inside. Although it is beautiful, I have always found this place strange—a whitewashed, colonial home my father had built some distance from town, beside a marsh that holds no life. I have no idea why he enjoyed such desolation, but I am of the impression he treated this place as a sanctuary of sorts; a place he could rule when he had so little power to his name.

I exit the car, and at the sound of my daughter's voice I can feel my shoulders fall limp, a pressure escaping me.

"Who is this intruder at my home?" I ask. "I'm calling the police!"

She runs wildly, wobbling to and fro so recklessly that I nearly break down in tears. It is remarkable that this can happen every day. That I might never grow tired of seeing her sprint towards me with no care except for the wish to feel my arms wrapped around her.

"It's me, Lila," she says, her face falling into the crook of my neck.

"Lila?" I act stupefied. "But my daughter could not grow so much in a single day."

"I have!" she says.

A silhouette is before the door. The child's nanny. Lila's mother and I, although not divorced, live apart. She is a nurse in town with a condominium near the hospital. She works in marathon shifts that last days; she then takes Lila for extended periods, however long she wishes. When she brings her back I often mention that she looks fatigued, that she should come in and rest, and she tells me that I should feel the same sympathy for the mine workers who frequent her clinic with such exhaustion that they cannot keep their eyes open long enough to speak in full sentences. I then once more appreciate the distance that separates us.

Imani, the nanny, informs me that Lila finished her homework earlier in the evening. I see my daughter's books spread out upon the dining room table and nod. The lights are on in the kitchen, in the living room, as I prefer it. There is no reason a house of such bounty, of such beauty, should be shrouded in darkness. I wish to see it all: the family portraits on the wall; the cabinet with my diploma; my father's medal of service; the bowl of appreciation that Benji delivered to me after his promotion (inscribed as so: *To a fine man, my boss*); the long couch with fluffed pillows that I often fall into with a tumbler of whisky.

"Would you like some dinner?" Imani asks.

The smell of the spices wafts through the air. She is often making some recipe from her home village, some obscure stew with game meat, the sort of offering you envision being stirred in a cauldron.

"What is it?" I ask. "I imagine you have made something . . . unique for us."

"Not really, no," she says. "Just tacos. Lila's favorites. Would you like some?"

"That would be nice." Lila is pulling on my pant leg. She asks to draw with me in the dining room while I eat. I tell her to go there. That I will join her soon. When she is off, I inform Imani that she may retire for the night when she has prepared my plate. I then excuse myself to go shower, to cleanse myself from the remnants of the day.

As I eat, I watch Lila draw beside me at the dinner table. I wipe the long curls of her hair from her line of sight, smile down upon her as she pokes her tongue from her mouth in concentration.

"Scrunchy, papa."

I retrieve a scrunchy from the living room, attend to her hair, putting it up before returning to my meal. I love the child's hands. I think of my father's hands, as rough as the paws of a feral dog, callused over as though boils festered at the root of his every finger. My own calluses have disappeared over time, and there appears to be some evolution, some law of good, that will afford my daughter's hands to be forever soft: saved perhaps, for gesticulating orders to a boardroom full of executives; or for leading a classroom. She will not be dull like her father. She will not have his scars. The opportunities are endless, and it is the income from my work that has allowed this. There is a life of wrongs made right by this fact, and the nature of this truth is something her mother never understood.

I sit back in my chair, the very chair my father once claimed, and take in the sight he assigned himself when building our home—the marshland that faces out from the back of the property, a small bed of murky water that strings itself to the greater body of the Limraso River. It was a walk my father and I would take on occasion, prattling along the riverbed when it was dry, each footstep locked in a vice of mud, our hands playing against the surrounding reeds. If he was in a particularly good mood, our strolls would become a game of tag. I recall him running ahead of me, out of my line of sight, yet I could make out his head atop the grass, floating off in the distance, bobbing as he sprinted away. When he had reached a clearing, he would turn and point to me with a mocking laugh, and I would enter a sprint knowing he would turn and escape me once more.

The water is high, now, and the marsh appears as a pond might, the surface twinkling, spotted with the reflection of the stars, and it is no coincidence that my father has come to mind in this moment, for there is a figure—right there, if one looks closely—floating above the marsh, a sculpted void that cuts through the darkness, a shadow that presents itself in the shape of a human, lithe and decrepit, wavering, as though it might disintegrate in the wind.

The figure, as though sourcing life from the light of the moon, molds flesh, grows real, and before I can look away, lanky limbs have protruded from this shadow form—a single hand has risen up from its arm. It points to me before vanishing.

"Papa," I hear my daughter say. "The picture is done."

I do not look at my daughter, nor at the marsh, but rather I close my eyes, feel under the table, once more seeking the knot of wood from my youth; and when I cannot locate it, as though time has grooved the table's contours smooth, I abruptly stand, so quickly my daughter drops her marker.

"It's time for bed!" I say.

"Papa?"

"Come now," I say.

"You didn't look at the picture."

"I will look as I tuck you in."

Lila waits as I put my dishes in the sink, standing with her head cocked, the picture limp in her hand. I return, leading her up-stairs, each step creaking as we ascend. I'm eager to remain calm, to think of anything beyond what I have witnessed. It is a saving grace that there is life in every corner of this home, pleading to be freed; the walls bleed memories, and they consume you at every turn. To take a step, to touch the handrail, to open a door, offers access to endless recollections: my father's hand upon my backside as I run from punishment; a glimpse of my mother slipping into her bedroom to nap away the afternoon. Even as I enter Lila's room, meeting the sweet smell of her candy-scented hairspray, the brightness of the walls, a child's yellow, I cannot help but strip away the paint, the years, and envision the bedroom that was once mine and my brother's.

I have her under the covers. Safe, her eyes finding my own as I look over the picture she's set on her nightstand. There is nothing to it. Lila and her mother and I, holding hands, in the manner all children draw families, one row of stick figures. One row of smiles.

"Your hand," Lila says.

It is trembling.

"Something has come over me," I say. And once more, as my mind scrambles for relief, I am lost to the past, thinking only of the silence of my home, the strange quality I felt lying where Lila now lies when I was a teenage boy, of how peaceful it was with my brother dead and gone. Not smelling his odor from across the room. My contempt when he would rise for a glass of water, rousing me when I had only just fallen asleep. Such guilt knows no bounds. Even now, I have the urge to sell this place and start anew elsewhere, only for it to be undone by the shame once more, as I envision the home razed to rubble by its future buyer. This image transforms in my mind to that of my brother somewhere in the shaft of the mine, the walls closing in on him. Rock crushing him flat.

I put the picture down and rise up from the bed.

"Shall I leave the night-light on?" I ask Lila.

"But you always tell me I must be brave, papa. That I should keep it off."

I am peering out the window. There is nothing but darkness.

"We can make an exception," I tell her.

"I'm brave," she says.

"Of course you are," I say, leaning down to kiss her forehead.

I turn off the night-light and say goodnight without even waiting for her to do the same. I walk briskly to my room as though there is something to run from. And yet before I enter, a noise (could it be laughter?) filters out from Imani's bedroom, opposite mine. I listen to muffled sounds, and before I can stop myself, I find that I am knocking on the door.

The noise quits. There is a shuffling, the sound of objects being moved. I have never done this before, knocked at such an hour, but something has unsettled me. The floor trembles with some unseen fragility, and the walls of the hallway narrow. Sweat has leaked down the span of my back and into the cleft of my behind. I am not well.

"Imani," I say.

Her voice is nothing more than a peep. "Yes?"

"May I open the door?"

The room is spotless, the bed made, the walls unadorned. Imani is on the floor, sitting before the trunk pressed against the front of the bed. The phone, its cord snaking from the wall, sits on her lap. I'm not surprised by the arrangement. I often used to eavesdrop on her conversations. That was until I heard her, once, speak of my marriage. Saying how I was to blame for the dissolution. The certainty in her voice as she gossiped still rings in my ears whenever we speak. Our distance from each other has been sealed ever since, and if it wasn't for her closeness to Lila, she would no longer be here. But the question at hand feels urgent. It must be asked.

"I have interrupted something," I say.

"It's my mother," she says, pointing to the phone with an index finger. "Is that okay? You told me it would be okay to call once I have finished—"

"It's fine. Perfectly fine."

Her eyes are doe-like. Her skin shines pure. She is a different person here, left alone in this space. A young woman that laughs and cries, I am sure; a young woman of great vibrancy, of complicated personality. A young woman I am now intruding on. And just as quickly as I have spotted this hidden person, I notice her eyes contract, her smile fade, and I realize I have worried her. Not by my presence, perhaps, but by what I might need. By the news I might bring.

"I only have a question," I say. "I wish . . . to have your opinion. I have heard of a beast. A mythic beast. I believe they refer to it as The Grootslang. Do you believe in this thing?"

The phone erupts in noise, and Imani listens for a moment before lowering the volume, apologizing to me for the interruption. "It is nothing." Her smile is false. "My mother has outbursts."

I mutter something indescribable even to myself, some show of acknowledgement, realizing in a single instance how little I know of this girl. That she has an aged mother who screams on the phone; the strange quality in the spartan nakedness of her walls; her ability to hide in my own home and remain so quiet.

"You tend to your mother," I tell her. "It is late. I should get some rest." I go to leave, but she says, "Sir," and I turn back.

"I do believe in it," she says, with a confidence I find haunting. "But I believe in many similar things. It is only part of our tradition, to believe in the evil that is born from our wrongdoing. It is the mark of our people, no? My mother tells the story of when—"

"That's all and well, Imani," I say. "I believe I am too tired to hear such things right now. Perhaps save it for Lila, if it is not too frightening. I shouldn't have asked."

The start of her answer was more ridiculous than my question. She looks down, then. Her legs, lanky and child-like, are sprawled in a knot beneath her. Her pajamas so large the tops curl over her hands, the bottoms fall over her feet. It is unbecoming, to be speaking to such a young woman in so serious a way. And the moment, if there was one, is gone.

"Goodnight, Imani."

"Sir."

I leave the light on in the hallway as I head to my bedroom. She will turn it off when she sees it's been left on; by then, I hope, I'll be long asleep.

A phone call wakes me. It is Benji. There is trouble, he says. I should arrive as early as I can. I dress in the same clothes I wore the day before to save time. I decline the oatmeal Imani offers me and leave home before Lila wakes.

It is Benji who sleeps in the barracks, overseeing the boys. I can count on one hand the times he has contacted me so early, and almost all of them involved the birth of one of his children or a matter of equal urgency. I can only imagine how much conflict he must deal with on his own, with two hundred young men in such close quarters, and yet not once has he asked me to be involved in a single quarrel.

The sun is only now rising, and one can glimpse it between the twisted forks of the leadwood trees, bright gasps of orange that follow me as I pass other cars. Soon I am on site. I wind down the path into the bowl of the mine, the descent silent enough to feel like I am floating in my car. As I park beside my trailer, Benji is already approaching me. I wait for him, his legs swishing slowly in his overalls, and as he draws near it is difficult to ignore what lies behind him: an endless stretch of yellow uniforms and yellow hard hats—my workers, standing listlessly as one, staring at me.

I step out to greet him. There are whiskers of a mustache, and this is perhaps more foreboding than the sight of the workers. The man is always clean shaven.

"Perhaps we should speak in my trailer," I say.

Benji nods solemnly. "To keep up appearances, sir."

"Yes, Benji. To keep up appearances."

I offer him a bottle of water from the mini-fridge. He declines, and is already speaking as I take a seat behind my desk.

"The worker who has died is beloved. Very well thought of. He has a wife, an infant, a little girl. The others are aghast that his family has not been notified. That he has been left in the crypt—"

"*Do not* call it a crypt," I say. "It is a site of *science*. For heaven's sake, they are returning in a few months to resume their work. I will not surrender to such language. You shouldn't, either."

Even I realize how strange my outburst is. Benji blinks once, a cautionary measure, before continuing on. "The others cannot believe he has been left to rot in the site of science. The more religious believe a cleansing should take place in the mine. All of them believe the body must be retrieved immediately. They will not work unless it is done. It is a protest, sir. An organized protest."

The words are supposed to strike fear in me, but I do not share his concern. In fact, I clap my hands together joyously at the development. "Benji!" I say. "This is good news! Let them do their ritual. Let them get the body. Bring the candles, chant the chants. Whatever must be done." Already I am thinking of the coroner arriving in an hour's time; that this will be taken care of by mid-morning, before Mr. Fletcher has even finished his brunch at the Prince George Estates. The mere thought has brought me to near-ecstasy. "How quickly can they manage the job?"

Yet Benji merely slouches against the wall, his hands clenched in a ball against his chest. The pouches beneath his eyes are so evident, so full, that I wonder if there might exist a procedure to drain them. He appears defeated.

"They won't do it themselves." His voice is so low I can hardly hear him speak. "They believe you have made a bargain with The Grootslang. Brought it into existence."

"Not this again." I realize that it is pity that drives Benji's words. That he is worried about my end, not his own. The task before me is clear. My charge as a leader. The call I must answer.

"I will go," I tell him. "I will retrieve the body myself."

There is a sense of resignation knowing what lays ahead of me, and I find that my voice is calm as I ask the other workers where I might find Felix. I smile at them politely. I even offer one man a handshake. And yet when my eyes fall upon Felix himself, under the break canopy, casually eating chips, I am quickly overcome by anger. His eyes, still black as night, are strangely tranquil, looking upon me with an empathy so perverse I have the urge to strike him.

"You are leading a protest," I say. "I should have you fired. I should put your name on a list. Did you know there's a list? A list of men who will not get hired at any mine. You have made quite the error."

His eyes are fixed upon me, and his mouth seems to move independently from the rest of his face. He speaks in one tone, a single string of words, as though all of them, each connected to the one before, have been in a line in his mouth, awaiting my arrival to be unspooled.

"It is you that brought The Grootslang upon us. Your conscience lies with Peter, and so the beast calls your name."

"Who on earth is Peter?" I ask.

He shakes his head, and I realize my mistake too late. "*The boy,*" he says. "The boy who died."

"What do you want," I ask. "If you were to go down with me—to get the body and have the men return to work—what would you ask for in return?"

He speaks so quickly it's apparent the thought has been on his mind for some time, if not since the beginning of the whole ordeal. "I wish to be a surveyor. To be paid like a surveyor. To have Benji's power."

"I could use another. Consider it done." My willingness to compromise takes him off guard. And for the first time his eyes wander from me, and I know they have landed upon the elevator at my back. His cheekbones, sharp enough to draw blood, suddenly twitch, and I wonder if it is from the fear that courses through him: the same fear now coursing through me.

"The sooner the better," I say.

He takes the cap lamp at his side and places it upon his helmet. He mumbles what appears to be a prayer and then smiles wickedly.

"Whenever you are ready," he says.

I turn my face towards the elevator. There is nothing inside that might save me from what is to come.

In the mine, it is always night. Illumination is key, and yet permanent installations of any lighting system are too burdensome a cost. A few lamps are made use of throughout the primary shaft, the active workings. The rest of the journey must be done by the cap-lamp alone, a light which shines forth seemingly from one's own skull. A third eye, the miners call it. We do not need our lamps yet, but I know we will soon.

Felix is beside me, the folded stretcher tied to his back. The length of the mine runs before us. To stand still, to witness the thing in silence, creates such overwhelming awe that it exacts the dimensions of a living being. To feel the rock wall is to feel it throb, no different from a pounding heartbeat.

"This is it," Felix says.

The elevator is thirty minutes to our rear. We have walked some ways. And now we see a small brow of the wall, a crevice expanded to the size of a small human, where the scientists made their own way.

We dip through the hole and find ourselves facing what feels to be an impenetrable shroud of darkness. There is no up or down. Before us is infinity, and there is a pull to it, like the tug of a rope around one's chest. I quickly reach for my cap-lamp, which casts a bright beam down the length of nothingness before me.

I have surveyed the maps left by the scientists, and so I know to follow the path before us, turning once we reach the far wall. The descent is slow, a sloping trail like any other, and yet there is no end to it. Neither of us look to the side, where Peter has surely fallen, for it is clear the light will meet nothing but further darkness, more dust skittering in the air from the wall of the cave like insects in flight.

"Two miles," I say.

Felix says nothing.

"There is nothing to fear," I say. "It is a jaunt in the mine like any other. Like all that have come before this one."

"But you are scared. More than I am."

"Don't be ridiculous," I say. "I do not fear creatures that lurk at the bottom of a mine."

"It is not just in the mine." His voice is low and certain. "Is that what you have taken from the legend?"

"I do not *know* the legend. I do not *wish* to know the legend."

"The beast is born from our wrongs. It is in you. Just as it is in me—"

"You *must* quit. I refuse to believe that you go on like this in your private life. That you speak to those close to you in the manner of an ominous sage, dispensing wisdom. I have no time for it."

A moment, and then the boy speaks once more in a mutter. "You only ask me to stop because you believe my words are true."

"Is that so?" I ask, holding a hand upon the wall, moisture dripping under my sleeve.

"It is as I said. It is in you, just as it is in me. And perhaps you fear that more than the rest. That we are no different from one another."

My legs wobble with fatigue. The temperature rises like a warning. And quite suddenly there is water beneath our feet, puddles and ankle-deep mud, announcing the end of the descent. The bottom of the mine.

We stop at once. Total darkness does not speak to what lays beyond this point, what extends before us. It is an absence. A void. The senses, beyond the mud gripping my feet, have nothing to register. I am afloat, wholly and totally, and I only become bound by the touch of Felix, prodding the small of my back.

"We must backtrack to where he would've fallen," he says.

"Just a moment to rest," I say.

But he is already moving. I cannot keep on with conversation. It is as though I am progressing through the cycles of sleep, inching towards a dream, a flurry of babble erupting from some crease of my brain that I cannot access on my own volition. I wish for it to stop but it will not. It is then that the sounds meet me: uproarious laughter, recognizable at once as the men from my trailer, Ross Fletcher's investors, voices jarring enough to make me turn to seek out the source, and yet in the time it takes me to wheel around the noise has minimized itself to a piercing howl, and then nothing at all, and soon Felix is asking me if I am all right, and by then it is only my heartbeat I can hear, so loud that I wish to scream so I might mask the noise of my own terror.

"Are you okay?" Felix asks again.

"Perhaps we should turn back," I say. There is a desire to sit down. To scrunch up into a ball and allow the mud to envelop me. To be done with this business. Yet as the thought passes, I hear Felix gasp, and I look up, quickly, to find the outline of an object standing before us.

"The scientist's equipment," Felix says.

It is a light of some sort, crane-like, perched against the tunnel face.

"Why would they leave it?" Felix asks.

"They are returning," I tell him, but the sight has emboldened him, and he is running forward now.

"Felix, wait," I say.

I do not move. I adjust my line of sight to keep him alight, and he is now upon an enormous box, sturdy as the shell of a turtle, unwieldy upon the ground.

"A generator," he says. "They have left their generator."

With my cap-lamp, I can make him out before me. Alone in the abyss. So far from me, yet in the great chasm of darkness that binds us, we are closer than any other humans might possibly manage in so vast a space. He has a cord in hand. I can feel dust coating my throat; my body seize. The sound of a motor, of a howling animal, blows over me like hot air. And in the time it takes to blink, the time it takes to gasp for a single breath, a crushing light illuminates the mine with the force of a detonation. There is Felix, his back to me. Behind him, a table of fathomless dimensions; a table of African teak that runs on endlessly into a darkness that supersedes the light. The table is crowded with men. It is only immediately behind Felix, at its head, that I spot my father facing me, his eyes wide with terror, his lips sewed shut, maggots squirming through the stitching, his finger pointing at my chest. Beside him is my brother, his cheeks broken into his skull, blood spilling from his forehead, beckoning me with fingers limp as noodles, flicking towards me pathetically. There are hundreds of miners behind them, standing stoically in their yellow vests. They are all staring, all silent, rotted and grotesque, and it is as though I am looking in a mirror reflecting itself, for I can see it go on so far that the illusion plays upon itself, and at the far end, a dot lost in a canvas of horrors, I spy a figure that could only be myself, for when I raise my hand up to cover my mouth, it is the only parcel of space that moves, and it is then that the light dies, and darkness consumes the crypt once more.

"The body," he says. "It is right ahead of us." I hear then, the sounds of him cranking the generator once more. Yet this is of no use. The crypt remains black.

"Did you not see it? Follow me, Nicholas. This way."

I turn, then. And the voice I hear, demanding I return, calling me back, is only an echo by the time I have stopped running.

*

I am home before lunch. Felix has retrieved the body. The coroner, I know, is on his way. Full working production of the mine on offer before Ross Fletcher has arrived; just as I hoped.

And now there is a strange comfort to the sound of gravel crunching beneath my car, the sound that signals my return home, to this small plot of safety. Imani greets me at the front door. Her arms are crossed. A stalled and baking heat lingers in the air and I wipe my brow as I approach her.

"What is wrong?" she asks.

I say no words, but rather turn from her, sit on the steps of the veranda, looking off upon the road from which I have just arrived from.

"Tell me," she says. "Something is the matter."

"Please sit," I say, tapping the tiles of the stairs. I cannot help but smell the scent of flowers that leaves her, so welcome after a day at the mines, and I wish to thank her, and yet of course I do not, knowing she could not even begin to understand how welcome her presence is after all that has come to pass.

"You have me worried."

"What if nothing is wrong?" I ask. "What if things are finally right?"

"But you are here. You should be at work—"

"I have put Benji in charge. He is a fine man. And he has a new surveyor to lead. A very capable fellow. A brave man who has made right by me. They will work well together."

The trees in the distance are countless, lifeless, so scorched by the sun as to be left without a single leaf. The expanse of dirt is the color of iron. It is endless. And yet from here there is a remarkable nature to the sight; the landscape in the distance converging with the bank of the sky, like two segments of a painting in contrast. A brilliant design. One that will repeat itself endlessly. And the reassurance I draw from this is so great that I feel my shoulders fall, my neck go slack, for the first time since exiting the mine.

"It is strange," I say. "I don't know when Lila comes home. How do I not know?"

"The bus pulls up in an hour," Imani tells. She points, then. Down the road. "She will run from there. Just as she runs to you when you pull in."

To think I have not once seen the sight of my daughter running from the road up ahead. I imagine it to be even greater than when she greets me after a long day at work, my little dust devil in motion, her lunch box bouncing against her side, her hair one bobbing mess. I know that I will wait right where I'm sitting until I witness it. There is nothing else I wish to lay my eyes upon. Nothing else that might save me from the terrors I have witnessed.

"I should continue cleaning," Imani says.

At this, the phone inside begins to ring. I know instantly it is Ross Fletcher, ready for his tour. Wondering, no doubt, where I have wandered off to. I tell Imani to let it ring, repeating myself once more as it goes on, and on, until finally it is quiet once again.

"Stay here," I then tell her. "Please. Sit. Just . . . just until the bus comes."

She shifts beside me, the bracelet on her wrist clanging like a chime.

"Tell me," I say. And the words feel random, yet ordained, and altogether urgent. "Tell me your story. Of this village you hail from. Of your family. To have someone under my roof I know so little of. It seems wrong, no?"

A wind pulls over us. Imani looks at me with uncertainty.

"My grandmother hails from a small village south of here. She's told me many stories, yet most of them are tall tales, as you might put it, although I often wondered if they were true . . ." She does not know what she is allowed to say, and yet silence will not do. Not now. Not with what I have seen still playing in my head. "You really wish to know, sir?"

My heart is pounding. Yet somehow, so far from the mine, so far from my past, I am at peace.

"Imani, it would be an honor to hear them told," I say. "Carry on. End only when you find it right to. You have my ear."

Her voice overtakes the air; the wind. Finally, I am able to close my eyes and keep them so. And all that is left to do is listen.

Bebo

FROM *The Kenyon Review*

BEBO AND I used to kick it. Then we didn't. But the fact that we once did gave Enis the idea. Practice had ended, and we were parked with our gear on the curb outside the Quickie Mart where Enis's dad worked. Fall came quickly that year, gave summer the boot without notice. By the time we made the fifteen-minute walk from the park, crossing the last practice field—the one with grass so thin, so patchy, it reminded us of our coach's balding head—and down to the corner where the store sat, two buildings over from the Boys & Girls Club, across the street from the other convenience store, the one that gave Enis's dad headaches because that one had a gas station and his didn't, which cut into the business, the sun had almost clocked out for the day.

"Ain't that Ralphie?" Enis said, pointing with the metal baseball bat he stole from our coach's bag two weeks earlier. After swiping it, Enis slipped a fiver from his dad's store register, rode his bike to the Walmart on Flatbush Avenue, bought a pack of red bat grip, swapped out the black grip that was peeling from the one he stole, and came to practice the next day like it wasn't a thing. When Coach pressed him, referencing the missing bat and asking Enis how he got his, daring him to lie, Enis lifted it to Coach's eyes. "Does this look like the same bat to you?" he said, holding it by the barrel, moving it left to right, taunting Coach and flaunting the brand-new tape job.

"Yeah. That's him," I said, pushing down his bat with my hand. Ralphie and his boys were across the street, holding court in the parking lot of the competing convenience store. It's where they served the zombies who skulked around corners and down alleyways. Where they had fast exchanges with cars that pulled up slow. Where they leaned into the windows of those cars, touched fists, and made baggies disappear from one hand and reappear in another, like magic.

It was one of their usual spots, aside from the lot behind the pizza place where they set up shop on weekends, which was five minutes north, off of Henry Street, directly across from one of the dorms owned by the private college that existed in its own little bubble. That was where the white kids from the college, who made up more than half of Ralphie's customers, sleepwalked to for late-night pizza. It was owned by this Greek guy who gave Ralphie and them scraps of whatever he had left over: frostbitten mozzarella sticks, days-old wings, the occasional salad tossed together with lettuce he was half a second away from trashing. Anything to make Ralphie and his boys handle their business away from the front entrance.

"You think he'd let me run with him?" Enis asked.

"Run with him?"

"Join his crew," Enis said, standing up and tossing the bat to me.

I caught it, squeezed it. It was my first time holding the bat since Enis lifted it. It was padded, felt stronger. Made you feel like you had more control, something we all itched for.

"Why you wanna do that?"

"Why you asking questions instead of giving answers?"

I rolled the bat over in my hands, dragged the barrel across the cracked concrete.

"We need the money," Enis finally said.

I glanced at Ralphie and his boys, looked back at Enis.

"Probably not."

"Why not?"

"Wouldn't trust you," I said, and Enis knew what I meant. He was one of the few white boys in the neighborhood. Looked like he'd been pulled straight from a Disney movie.

"You're dirty for that."

"You asked."

Enis ripped the bat from my hands and got into a stance: front shoulder tucked, back elbow high, the bat at a forty-five-degree angle like a jacked-up antenna. We were both fourteen and had played on the same baseball team since he moved to the city two years earlier—since he seeped into my life like a gas leak.

Enis lived two doors down, with his mom, who never left their apartment, and his pops, who hardly spent time in it. Moved here from Wisconsin by way of Bosnia. He told me the stories. Which family members were killed during the war. How his mom and pops carried him through forests, trudged through rivers. The bodies he remembered, the detached limbs iced over like frozen meat.

"Hartford ain't shit," he once told me. We were throwing rocks over the fence in his backyard, which was nothing more than a patch of grass the size of a chalk outline for a game of four square. "We had nothing. Less than nothing. And more to be afraid of. This place don't scare me," he said, and for whatever reason, I believed him.

"What about Bebo?" Enis asked now.

"What *about* Bebo?"

"Keep up." Enis extended the bat with both hands, measured the distance between the end of the barrel and my head. "Ralphie's his brother. Bebo can put in a good word. Shit, we'll *make* him put in a good word."

"We?"

"Yeah. We, Collin," Enis said, swinging the bat so close I could lick it. "Ain't Bebo *your* boy, Collin? *We* will grab him after practice."

I never claimed Bebo as my boy. But we used to orbit each other. Our moms were friends. They worked in the same plaza on Jordan Lane. Bebo's mom bagged groceries at Stop & Shop while my mom peddled cheap sneakers at the Payless three stores down.

They ate lunch together, rode the bus to and from work together. When they hung out outside of work, Bebo and I did too, both of them dragging us along to their ladies' nights.

I'm an only child, what my mom calls her best accident from her worst mistake. And though it ain't work out with my dad—who I haven't seen in years, but last I heard stayed with his sister who lived no more than fifteen minutes from Mom and me—to this day, Mom will bring up how she regrets not giving me a sibling. How she's afraid of leaving me alone in the world. Point being, Mom liked that Bebo was my age. We were forced together.

This was how it was until Enis appeared, which was around the same time Bebo's mom disappeared, sent away to The Retreat on Retreat Avenue. No one calls it that anymore. But when I heard Bebo's mom had been committed, I looked it up. Learned it was one of the first hospitals of its kind. Learned the grounds were designed by the same guy who did Central Park. Learned that it went through a number of names before landing on The Institute of Living, a decent name, sure, but The Retreat sounds better. Gives the illusion that you're only on vacation.

With Bebo's mom gone, I only saw him around the way, at school or practice or wandering alone, moving from corner to corner, street to street. He didn't seem to mind being alone. Once his mom left, he left in his own way too. He was never a talkative kid. But those days, he hardly spoke when spoken to. Instead, he looked at you like how a dog looks at itself in a mirror: empty, without recognition, which spooked most kids. Brought to mind the rumors about his mom, the whispers our teammates believed were true.

I never saw the signs, and I never asked Mom about it. But there was always chatter about the voices Bebo's mom was said to have heard in her head. How she was spotted walking down Jordan Lane, onto the Berlin Turnpike, and in the direction of oncoming traffic, until a state trooper pulled her over. That she was the reason Bebo walked with a limp. That she injured him during one of her episodes.

None of it was true, and though I never added on, didn't talk shit about Bebo or his mom, I never stopped our teammates either.

On the day Enis decided we'd go to Bebo's apartment so he could have a word with Ralphie, we came up from behind Bebo after practice. Enis had his stolen bat in his right hand and joked about Bebo's belly button that poked out from a white T-shirt two sizes too small.

With his back to us, Bebo packed up his glove in a Nike string bag. He took off his cleats, slipped his hands inside, and clapped the dirt-caked spikes together like they were flippers. He threw on a pair of worn black slides, hooked the bag over his shoulders, then turned and saw us.

"What you got planned tonight?" Enis asked before Bebo had a chance to breathe. "Can we come through?"

*

Bebo lived over in Dutch Point, down by Colt Park. Back in the day, it was a place to get your fix, or catch shouting matches, or go to sleep knowing it wasn't firecrackers you heard outside your window. On the way down, Enis buzzed music from his phone. A few weeks earlier, he started dating this girl who kept headphones dangling from her ears like jewelry. Whatever he played was because of her, and when I asked what he was listening to now, he just looked at me, bobbed his head off beat, said, "You know, it's that good shit."

Halfway to Bebo's place, Enis paused his music and made me stop with him at the stand of an old woman who sold homemade empanadas from a grocery cart. She mouthed the price while holding up bony fingers wrapped in skin that looked like it was melting. I scraped up loose change from my backpack to snag two each for two bucks, and when I turned to ask Bebo if he wanted anything, he was half a block ahead.

Enis and I took our food and trailed his footsteps for a handful of blocks, past Washington and down Jefferson, across Main Street and Wethersfield Avenue. On my last bite, I spotted the Suit Man muttering to himself in his usual uniform, a run-down gray suit he wore without a shirt. His chest hair was long, coiled like a Slinky. And he clutched a briefcase to his chest, as if it held important papers. We all knew it didn't.

Since we were kids we had heard he once was a big-shot lawyer. That one day he lost everything, including his mind. Now he haunted the city. Drifting without a purpose. Lurking when you didn't know he was there.

Bebo strolled past him but Enis stopped, so I stopped too. He pulled a green olive from what was left of his empanada and pitched it at the Suit Man.

"You hungry?" Enis shouted.

The olive hit the Suit Man on the side of his head. He paused for a second, looked around, then went back to muttering.

"You hear me?" Enis yelled. "I said, 'You hungry?'" He threw the rest of his empanada at the Suit Man, hitting his briefcase, ground beef and crust exploding into the air.

Enis turned to me. "You try to help the crazies and look what you get." I hesitated but gave him the laugh he waited for. "You know something about crazy people, don't you?" Enis yelled to

Bebo, who was now at least ten yards ahead of us. We jogged up behind him.

"You can't wait?" Enis said. "It's a good thing you got that bum foot."

Enis smirked at me, mimicked Bebo's walk.

"Why you walk like that anyway? I mean—is it true?" he asked, which made my chest tug.

"Enis," I half-whispered.

"What, Collin? I can't ask him a question? He don't gotta answer. I just wanna know if what they say is true."

"What they say?" Bebo said over his shoulder, surprising us both.

"Like you don't know. You hear what they say. You're crippled, not deaf."

Bebo kept limping ahead.

"Jesus, man. Can't nobody talk today? That your mom messed you up when you were a baby. You were crawling in the kitchen or something, and your mom thought you were a rodent. Grabbed the closest thing she could find, a hammer on the kitchen sink, I heard, and started hacking away, trying to kill it, kill you. She caught your foot a few times before Ralphie heard you screaming."

Bebo turned around. Bum leg or not, he was a big kid. Tubby, sure, but a growth spurt from the previous summer gave him a cool three inches on us. He pigeoned his head from front to back.

"What's that? Is that a yes?" Enis said.

Bebo took a sharp inhale through his nose, then hawked green phlegm that landed between Enis's feet. From the corner of my eye, I saw Enis's fingers tighten around his bat. But after a few long seconds, he did nothing, and Bebo hobbled forward.

When we hit the last block before reaching Bebo's place, we saw Ralphie from a distance. He was shorter than Bebo but had a lean body with muscles that fit together like puzzle pieces and a beauty mark on his left cheek that made him look nicer than he actually was.

He had changed from the kid I knew when his mom was around. The kid who played MASH with neighborhood girls to prove he was destined to marry them. Who threw water balloons at friends he'd see walking by the front window of his apartment. Who walked his brother home because their mom worked late and their pops didn't care.

A year earlier, on my way home from practice, I saw this kid walk past Ralphie and his boys in a pair of fresh-out-the-box Air Max 97s. *Mistake number one.* Ralphie shouted, "I like those kicks." The boy stopped and said thanks, all smiles and stupid pride. "I just got them." *Mistake number two.* "Word," Ralphie said, rubbing his hands together as he walked toward the boy. "Yeah, those are clean. Those are clean." And the boy stood there, cheery. *Mistake number three.* Even I knew once Ralphie said, *I like those kicks,* there were two options: fight or run. In a matter of seconds, Ralphie robbed the kid's sneakers. After, his boys stomped the kid just for fun.

"You think Ralphie's gonna come home while we're there?" I asked Bebo.

"That's his brother, ain't it?" Enis said, jumping in. "He'll come to his own place."

"I'm just asking."

"Well, you asking stupid questions."

"It's not a stupid—"

"Yeah," Bebo said, cutting us both off. "He'll show up. He always shows up."

From the street, Bebo's place wasn't as welcoming as ours. The city hadn't finished cleaning up the units they knocked down. Trash and broken concrete lined the sidewalks, junkies squirreled around in abandoned buildings, and dirt floated onto my pants from the muck that kicked up from Bebo's dragging foot.

Inside, it was worse. The living room was full of dishes caked with grease, half-emptied beer bottles with gnats hovering above the lip, old magazines of naked women with cigarette burns where their nipples should be. We made our way through the maze and walked past a closed door where someone snored inside.

"My dad," Bebo said, reading our looks. "You ain't gotta worry about him."

We entered the bedroom I knew Bebo shared with Ralphie. Enis and I sat next to each other on the wood floor while Bebo stepped back out. Hanging on the wall was a two-year-old calendar with the day's date circled. Next to it was a series of fist-sized holes. There was one bed, one window, and a small end table with a desk lamp tucked in the far-right corner. A chill leaked through the window, and in the dim light, Enis's breath hung in the air like fog.

"Can you relax?" Enis said, standing up, then sitting on Ralphie and Bebo's bed.

"I am relaxed."

"You don't look it."

"Well, I am."

"Then stop looking around."

"It's getting late and you know my mom's gonna—"

"Chill out for once," Enis snapped. "Can you do that? Look, if you want, when we leave I'll walk with you to your place and make up some shit about how I needed your help with something, and how we played video games or did homework or whatever the fuck you want. I'll tell your mom it's my fault that you didn't call to check in. That I'm the reason you're late."

I brushed Enis off, pinched a dirty, soggy sock next to my leg and lobbed it farther to the side, over by the door, just as Bebo walked in with a bottle in his hand.

He twisted off the top, took a swig, and extended his arm to Enis.

"You drank before, right?"

"Who do I look like? I don't know about Collin, but me?"

Enis took a sip, coughed it back up, and I couldn't help but laugh.

"You think that's funny? Here," he said, shoving the bottle to my chest.

I read the label, smelled the burn before it could slide down my throat. It was almost at my lips when a cockroach scurried out of the sock I had pitched to the side. The cockroach crawled over my leg, and I jumped to my feet, spilling half the bottle down my shirt.

"Now *that's* funny," Enis said, laughing fist to mouth. "Ain't that funny, Bebo?"

Bebo ignored him, watched the cockroach. It stopped and moved, stopped and moved, as if playing a game. Bebo knelt down and put his hand on the floor, palm up, ready to receive it like the Eucharist.

"There you are," he said, as the cockroach crawled onto his hand.

Enis leaned over, picked up the bottle from the ground, and forced down another mouthful.

"You raising cockroaches?" he asked between coughs.

Bebo laughed.

"Nothing like that. They come and go as they please."

Bebo seesawed the hand with the cockroach while it crept between his fingers.

"Come and go as they please?" Enis said. "You ain't making no sense. Collin, tell this kid he ain't making no sense."

I took a seat next to Enis on the bed, my eyes scanning for whatever else might scamper across the floor.

"You know, my mom was taken today. A couple years ago today," Bebo said evenly, still standing.

"What?" Enis said.

Bebo motioned with his head to the calendar on the wall.

"My mom. She was—"

"Yeah, I heard you. That's why you let us come over? So you wouldn't be alone with cockroaches on the day your mom was put away?"

I jabbed Enis in the ribs.

"*What*, Collin? You think that's normal? It ain't. Just like his mom ain't."

"It's not true, you know," Bebo said.

"What now? What's not true?"

"What they say about my mom—at least about my foot."

"Oh, it ain't?" Enis mocked.

"I was born like this," Bebo said, placing his left hand next to his right, letting the cockroach bridge across. "One leg is shorter than the other."

"And?" Enis said, taking another drink from the bottle, then putting it on the floor. "The one thing about her that ain't true. You know, I really—"

But before Enis could finish, Bebo started listing facts about cockroaches. That there were more than four thousand different species, and the one on his right hand, an American cockroach, could grow up to two inches long, and ate just about anything.

"They're opportunistic eaters," he said. "And can squeeze into tight spaces, and like dark, moist areas, which is why I keep that sock wet. It's also why I missed the game last week."

"*Now* what you talking about?" Enis groaned.

Bebo took his second pull from the bottle. I still hadn't taken my first.

"I couldn't sleep last week. Every time I put my head down and felt myself dozing off, I kept hearing this noise. I checked my room. Nothing. Then I went into the living room to see if Ralphie was home. All I found was my dad knocked out in the recliner with his arms dangling all still-like, like he was dead, his middle finger dipped inside the mouth of a bottle."

Enis snatched the bottle in the room from Bebo, took another drink.

"I went back to my room and got into bed," Bebo continued. "But again, once things were quiet and I was lying down, I heard this noise. This clicking. Then I noticed that the sound was coming from one side of my head, from *inside* my head. My right ear, to be exact."

"Stop," Enis said. "Just stop."

Bebo laughed as the cockroach crawled up his arm.

"I had one of these guys inside my ear. The doctor took it out in pieces. First its legs, then parts of its shell."

"What was the clicking like?" I asked before thinking. "That noise."

"That's what you're worried about?" Enis slurred.

"Hold on," Bebo said.

He guided the cockroach onto the end table, then left the room.

"A freak," Enis said. "That's what he is. And I'm gonna let him know too. Let him know, then we're leaving."

When Bebo returned, his hand was in his waistband.

"Is he touching himself?" Enis asked, leaning on me. "I swear to god, if he's touching himself."

I pushed Enis off me just as Bebo sat down to his left.

"Now relax," Bebo said, then pulled out a gun.

"*Easy*," Enis said.

"Collin wanted to know what the cockroach sounded like."

"So you grabbed a gun?"

"Ralphie's gun."

Bebo lifted it and pressed the muzzle against the side of Enis's head.

"It sounded like this," Bebo said. "When you cock and uncock it, that clicking sound."

Click. Off. Click. On.

I held my breath.

"Now imagine this sound inside your head."

Click. Off. Click. On.

"You hear it, right? You hearing it?"

After the fourth or fifth time, Enis found his voice, told Bebo that he got it, and that this shit wasn't funny. Bebo took his sweet time, but eventually moved the gun, and I finally exhaled, saw the wet under Enis's armpits.

Then Bebo stood back up, picked up the bottle, took another sip, and placed the gun to the side of his own head.

"You want to know another fact about cockroaches?"

Click. Off. Click. On.

"They ain't like us. Don't die easy like us. If this went off, I'd bleed out in minutes."

Click. Off. Click. On.

"But see, if you take off their head, cut it off or put a hole in it or something, they'd survive for at least a week or so. They got different systems. Their body would clot itself. Ain't that something? They'd survive, but we'd die something quick."

Click. Off.

Bang.

Enis dropped to the floor, pulled me down with him.

"That's just the front door," Bebo said, laughing wild and wide.

Enis and I hustled to our feet. Bebo tucked the gun into the front of his boxers and rolled the bottle under his bed. We slinked out into the living room, peeked around the corner. No one was there, and Bebo's dad's door was still closed.

Then Bebo went to the window, and we followed. It was dark out now, but in the streetlights' glow, we saw Ralphie and his boys in an argument with a group of guys none of us knew.

"Where you going?" Enis shouted.

Bebo stopped, already halfway to the front door.

"He's probably looking for this," he said, patting his waist.

"And?"

"And what?"

"Just wait."

"You two can wait."

And that's what we did, almost hiding, while Bebo trotted out to Ralphie like a proud pony, gimpy foot and all. Ralphie spotted him, and watching through the glass pane that separated Enis and me from them, we saw Bebo fight through the group of boys who were shouting like they were about to go to war.

"We're out," Enis said.

I glanced at him and saw that his knuckles were pale, strained from squeezing the window frame.

"We're out?"

"That's what I said."

On the street, Bebo reached into his waistband as Ralphie's hand patted his chest, pushing him away.

"Bebo ain't my friend," Enis said. "And he ain't yours either."

We all know that person. The one with enough charm to convince you to love them more than yourself. Who can convince you to do what you know is wrong.

Enis was mine. Enis was wrong. Either way, we left.

We slipped out the front door, through the screened-in porch, and down four uneven steps. Bebo clocked us as we slithered past. I ignored him. Told myself that I was minding my business. Kept my head bowed, hanging like a wilted plant.

"There he goes again," Enis said, sounding annoyed, a few yards from Bebo's apartment. "I bet he's hungry now."

I lifted my head and saw the Suit Man standing across the street. With one hand he picked at his 'fro, a grayed-out heap of strands that looked like they were stretching. With the other, he held his briefcase against his side, as if he was ready to go to work.

He glanced at us, then at Bebo and the group, then back at us—his eyes appearing to linger on me, like he was judging me. Like he knew I was ditching my friend.

Once, when Bebo and I were ten, before his mom was out of the picture, we spent an afternoon riding our bikes near the community center in the park. Our tires flattened dead grass and sprayed through sprinklers. We popped wheelies and coasted with no hands. With no one around, we sped down the gravel hill that led from the jungle gym to the baseball field without a fence. I lost my balance and fell off my bike. Glided down the rocky slope like it was a Slip 'N Slide. I felt nothing until I looked down and saw the blood leaking through my ripped tank top. Then I looked up and saw the Suit Man. He stood in the distance, watching as Bebo patted my chest, then patted his own, like Ralphie would do to him years later, except Bebo wasn't pushing me away.

"Look," Bebo said at the time, smiling, the red staining his shirt. "My handprints look like turkeys."

Now, leaving Bebo's place, I didn't turn back when Enis and I rounded the corner and flinched from what sounded like a car backfiring. Not even when Enis burned out in a sprint, ditching me to face my mom alone. I shuffled the entire way back home with the weight of the Suit Man's eyes following me like a shadow, knowing I should've stayed with Bebo like he had stayed with me.

"You're good. You hear me? You're good," he said that day in the park, placing both hands on me, steadying my shaking shoulders. He tapped me on the chest with the back of his hand. Brushed off the dirt clinging to the blood dripping from my chin. Tilted my face up so he could look me in the eye.

"I got you, Collin. You're good," Bebo said again, and even then, I knew it wasn't true.

SANA KRASIKOV

The Muddle

FROM *The New Yorker*

SHURA WAS TRYING to reach Alyona and Oleg, first over Skype and WhatsApp, then Facebook, on which Alyona kept an account she barely used. It should not have been so hard to get hold of them. Alyona had not posted recently, but she'd checked her messages, Shura could see that. Maybe she thought Shura was being dramatic—hadn't she always thought so? With her digital silence, Alyona was making a big show of her own calm, doubling down on her refusal to treat anything as a catastrophe. Well, goody for her, Shura thought, and shut her laptop. If Alyona wasn't panicked, why should she be? It was day three and there were still no Russian boots in central Kyiv. There was the battle at the Hostomel airport, and a rocket had crashed into a building in Obolon, but that was not near where Alyona and Oleg lived, in the Shevchenkivskyi district. From the security of her own house in Croton-on-Hudson, Shura tried not to think about the last conversation she'd had with Alyona. It had been a rather unpleasant chat, but now there was a war on and it seemed unnecessary to be holding a grudge, one of the very few they'd had in their sixty-odd-year friendship.

On day five, a reply came over Skype. "We're alive." Two words in a pale-blue bubble. It should have taken the tension out of her lungs, but it only agitated Shura more. She'd expected a bit more emotiveness—did they have groceries? Were they spending nights in their building's basement, or in the metro? *We're alive.* The bare minimum.

She would write back, Shura decided, but not yet. She dialled

Pavel's number in Toronto instead. "All right, Pavel," she said briskly. "What's going on with your parents?"

"They're waiting it out in the apartment."

She gathered from his voice that he'd understood her meaning. Not *Are they okay?* but *What's wrong with those two?*

"Why aren't they on their way to Toronto?"

Shura could hear Pavel exhale. He'd likely been asked this a dozen times by now. "Have they become patriots all of a sudden?" she said, unable to resist.

But he wasn't hurt, having some of his own bitterness to shed. "Last time she was here, Mama said she didn't find Toronto 'cozy.'"

"Meaning what—it's too Canadian?"

"Too Ukrainian."

"Oh, for heaven's sake." Oleg, to be sure, was Russian, the son of a colonel. But Alyona was Ukrainian, on both sides, as she'd proudly told Shura when they were girls. Her father's family was from the Vinnytsia area; her mother's, from Donbas.

Pavel said, "Mama I understand better than I do him. She's always been under his thumb. But I think he'd rather spend his old age living on canned *tushonka* than accept help from me."

Pavel had been more of a joker when he'd arrived in Toronto, twenty years ago. The long shift into a Canadian had turned him, Shura thought, more earnest, and a touch more righteous.

"Oh, Pavel." She sensed that he would tell her more if she egged him on a little. But she hesitated, not wanting to give the impression that she was disparaging his mother. "So what's their situation with groceries?"

"No worries about that. Last time we spoke, she was making veal *the French way*."

At School No. 6, French had been Alyona's favorite subject, and, by extension, Shura's. Chattering in broken French was how they got to pretend that they were more than provincial Soviet schoolgirls in a quasi-industrial railroad city. In their sixth-grade production of *Cinderella*, Alyona, with her shining blond head and biscuit skin, was cast as Fée Marraine, the fairy godmother. Shura, slight, pale, with dark braids and eyes that could narrow suspiciously, had played an evil stepsister. Alyona was one of only five Ukrainian kids in their class of twenty-nine. *Zhidovskaya shkola*—the Jew school— was how the Ukrainians and the Jews both referred to School No. 6, a neighborhood Russian school known to be one of the best in the city. Not a snide designation, just fact. There was a Ukrainian school in the same neighborhood, so parents had a choice. Alyona's parents, engineers at the mechanical plant, had chosen the Jew school.

All Shura remembered now of her French was that song they'd sung at the top of their voices, walking home. "*Les Russes veulent-ils la guerre?*" Do the Russians want war? A refrain that, fifty years later, could land you in prison. Alyona had kept up her French, reading classics in the original. When Shura had spoken to her by Skype last year, while Alyona and Oleg were living in Toronto (no, not living, only visiting, as it turned out), Alyona had been working through a copy of Colette's *Le Blé en herbe.* Into the corporate-issued Mac that Shura had inherited in her retirement, she'd nearly shouted, "What are you doing with *that?* You're wasting your time. It's Toronto, not Quebec! Start practicing your English."

Foolishly, she'd imagined herself and Alyona forming a study group the way they'd done as girls, a tight unit to beat out the boys in their class. She advised Alyona on the best language software and told her that she would dig up her old ESL coursework from night classes. She'd held on to it, sentimentally, even after her daughters had left home and she'd decluttered the place. "I'll mail you everything," she promised overeagerly, too pleased to have her friend on the same continent to hear her demurrals. "I have my grandson here if I need to practice conversation," Alyona had said. "And, anyhow, I prefer to work on my French."

Shura had never asked what it had taken Pavel to get his parents Canadian residency cards. Years of paperwork, she imagined. Regular checks mailed to lawyers. And yet, after only three months in Toronto, they'd packed up and flown home. "Not for us" was all Alyona had told her.

Shura could understand Alyona protecting her pride—she certainly had enough of it. But practicing her French? It made no sense. She would have thought her friend more pragmatic than that.

They'd sat at neighboring desks since the first grade, Korolenko and Kravetz, their friendship alphabetically predestined, but it wasn't until the second grade that they'd become close. Their teacher that year was young and rigid, without the heavyset authority of their first-grade teacher, who'd hand-selected children for her class, ensuring that the brightest (in her clairvoyant estimation) would remain with one another until their college entrance exams. By contrast, the young teacher exercised her rule through public embarrassment.

It was March, and they were starting their painting unit. (Shura's father had bought her a new watercolor set, the waffles of pigment arrayed in a tin like tiny gems.) The assignment was to paint the spring outside. The teacher brought in an easel with her own painting, a primitively pastoral scene with a leafy tree supporting a yellow-breasted bird, and a blue pond accommodating one duck. Two clouds, major and minor, floated toward a conical sun wedged in a corner. Shura had not understood that she was supposed to copy directly from the teacher's example. She'd made the mistake of looking out the window, where spring had arrived in a wash of mud-streaked sidewalks and oily puddles. In truth, she'd hewed closely to her teacher's design, altering only the palette, graying the blues, daubing brown along the picture's grassy bottom edge. She'd covered the sun with a gray cloud.

Moving down the rows of desks, their teacher had stopped and, with pincered fingers, lifted Shura's wet paper as an example of what the others should not do: muddy their colors, soak their parchment with water, fail to pay attention to the assignment. Shura had sat wordlessly, her cheeks growing hot. It was true she'd used too much water, but the charge of not paying attention to the assignment seemed utterly unfair. "But I did paint the spring," she protested, turning to the window as proof. The young teacher, still looking at her picture, had declared, "This is not spring. This is a muddle."

That afternoon, Alyona and Shura walked home together, and Shura's outrage unleashed itself in her gait. She didn't avoid the mud on the sidewalks, despite owning only one pair of school shoes, which her mother would have to scrub that night. She made herself leap in puddles, as if the damage to her wool stockings and coat would stand as proof of the treachery that the spring was capable of. Each time Shura was about to jump, Alyona would take a step back, protecting her own neat ensemble. Yet she did not tell Shura to stop. "You saw! You saw!" Shura kept insisting, because it seemed to her that only Alyona did not think her crazy, even if Alyona herself had decided to ignore the world outside the window. Finally, seeing that Shura's tantrum would not end without some concession on her part, Alyona said, "She wanted us to paint spring as it *should* be." Her voice was filled with quiet, tidy exhaustion at having to deliver an explanation too obvious to be spoken aloud.

Only it hadn't been obvious to Shura. For the next eight years of her schooling, she'd learn to adopt a kind of vigilance toward herself, to ferret out what a teacher really wanted from her, to stop herself before her hunger to excel tipped over into intellectual extravagance. She found it helpful to follow Alyona's lead in this regard. Later, when Shura began to study computer science in Leningrad, the word "requirements" would come to mind whenever she thought of her friend (studying the same subject in Kyiv). She thought of Alyona's ability to ascertain the implicit expectations of a task while ignoring anything unnecessary.

The conversation that had left a bad taste in Shura's mouth, a week before the invasion began, had been about bread. Shura was watching the massing of troops on the border with a growing dread and had called Alyona.

"You aren't worried?"

"About?"

"War."

"Is that what you all are placing your bets on?"

"You all?" Shura said. "It's me you're talking to."

"Your media, then, putting chips on different squares on the calendar."

These didn't sound like Alyona's words—perhaps they were Oleg's. "So you're not placing a bet, then?"

That was when Alyona said it: "Why? In Kharkiv, their hands are already tired from baking *karavai*."

Shura wasn't sure she'd heard correctly. Did Alyona understand what she'd just said? *Karavai?* Did she mean the bread and salt with which some Ukrainians had greeted the Germans back in '41? "You mean celebrating the takeover? What about you—are you baking *karavai*, too?"

If Alyona was taken aback by the sharpness of Shura's voice, she didn't show it. "You know I never bake," she said. But they'd both felt a shift then, as if each had suddenly discovered something distasteful about the other and wanted to get past it as quickly as possible.

*

After that conversation, Shura had slept badly. Plenty of her friends in North America had relatives or old classmates still in Ukraine. But none of them, as far as she knew, had mentioned anyone speaking the way Alyona had. Shura *was*, in fact, placing bets on a war, and the morning that it finally happened she felt so weakened that her vision blurred from an abrupt drop in blood pressure. She had experienced these sudden drops occasionally since the conclusion of her chemo, three years before, an uncommon but not life-threatening side effect. For the first time in two years, Shura wondered if things would be easier now if she hadn't retired, if her mind had blocks of code to occupy itself with, instead of the movements of troops and tanks across three separate fronts. After her treatment, she hadn't gone back to work, and she'd been surprised at how quickly many of her friendships thinned out without common deadlines and office gossip. Still, life was too short to code yourself into the grave. Throughout the years, she and Alyona had been in touch sporadically, but during her recovery they'd started talking again almost every week. Until now.

On days six and seven, Shura tried Skyping Alyona but couldn't reach her. On day eight, she called Pavel again. He said that his parents had packed up and headed to their dacha. He couldn't vouch for the reliability of their internet when they arrived.

Shura did not want to second-guess herself. Most likely Alyona was busy escaping the city. Perhaps her devices had died. And still Shura felt that Alyona's failure to give her updates was payback for their argument about *karavai*, when Alyona had accused her of not having a clue about what was really happening in "the East."

"They act like they're the cops, roaming the streets after dark and stopping anyone they want, asking for papers," Alyona had said of the Ukrainian militias. "They say they're hunting separatists. You get a mass riot in America every time one of your police tries half the stuff these fascists pull."

"Really?" Shura said. "Are they shooting people?"

"Well, they're not exactly walking around *unarmed*. And they're anti-Semites."

She suspected that Alyona had thrown in the anti-Semite charge to press her buttons. "Are they pogroming?" she inquired.

"Are you out of your mind?"

"So it's just words."

"You think that isn't enough? The police let the nationalists run rampant. They're afraid to stop them."

"In Kyiv?"

"Not here, but . . . even here they come out on Independence Square in their sunglasses and stupid bandannas, and their wrong-side-up swastikas painted on their cars."

"Democracy is messy," Shura said, though she wasn't sure why she was defending Ukraine to a Ukrainian.

"Democracy, are you kidding? They've colonized the state. Our Nouvelle Droite."

Alyona sometimes used French when she wanted to make a point, but "colonized the state" hardly sounded like her.

"How could the fascists have colonized the state," Shura said, "when your President is a Jew? And the defense minister, too."

"You think *that* proves anything? Your Trump was practically a Jew himself with his Kushners running the shop. Did that stop him saluting *your* neo-Nazis when he got up on a balcony?"

Shura had complicated opinions on this matter but kept them to herself.

"Zelensky's afraid they'll topple the government if he doesn't kiss their asses. You should hear them talk. An army of lions being led by sheep. Big deal, Jewish President—we change Presidents every five years."

"Better than every twenty-five," Shura said.

On the evening before day eleven, NATO was still rejecting a no-fly zone and the nuclear plant in Zaporizhzhia had been seized, but that morning Shura felt as though her body had somehow acclimated to the new state of alarm. She was squinting at the expiration date on a vitamin D bottle when Skype's cartoonish jingle rang on her laptop. "Alyona, where are you?" she shouted as the screen revealed, behind Alyona's halo of pulled-back blond hair, a narrow kitchen with old metal dishes stacked on hanging shelves. "Are you at the dacha?"

"We arrived two nights ago. Pavel said you called him?" Alyona hadn't wanted to Skype from Kyiv, she said. "Too noisy. Hard to talk over the sirens."

"Right."

"A mess." She made a few limp hand motions like waving a lazy goodbye. "Oleg and I are tired of this whole muddle."

Her face looked puffy, dark satchels of exhaustion under her eyes. It was always unsettling for Shura to see a woman like Alyona not looking her best. At school, the boys had all been in love with her, but Shura hadn't really understood the measure of Alyona's beauty until she'd come to America and watched *Tootsie* at a party thrown by one of the seasoned immigrants, who'd screened it for the new arrivals as a kind of cultural tutorial. Watching Dustin Hoffman's love interest, played by Jessica Lange, had suddenly made her feel both nostalgic and comforted in this new land. It was as though Alyona had appeared onscreen, with the same soft brown eyes and feathery waves, the same slow smile. Now Lange was skinny and Botoxed, her fine features sharpened into aggressive angles, while Alyona's, each time Shura saw her, seemed to be blurring and becoming more lost in the fleshiness of her face, her softening jawline.

Oleg's meaty head entered the frame as he crouched down to say, "Greetings, Shurochka!"

"How are you two?"

The couple glanced at each other, an inscrutable message passing between them. "No worse for wear," Oleg answered. Which meant what, exactly?

"Where are you, again?"

He gave the name of the town, in the Zhitomir area.

"It's really quieter around Zhitomir?" Shura said, powerless to keep the distress out of her voice, as she quickly typed in the city on Google Maps, employing the Ukrainian "Zhytomyr," the more guttural sound of which she still felt too pretentious to say. Hadn't they been shelling Zhitomir all night?

"Tell her to take a breath," Oleg said. "We're nowhere near the city."

Alyona confirmed. "Not even close."

Shura liked Oleg well enough, but he had a way of making you feel slightly foolish for asking reasonable questions—either giving you an excessively long and detailed answer, and getting impatient if you wanted to hurry it along, or else making some joke of your inquiry so that you felt it was superfluous. Their dacha was closer to Kyiv than to the Belarus border, he now explained, giving the full coordinates. Still, it seemed odd to Shura that they should have travelled in that direction, with troops still filtering down from the north. "How long do you plan to stay?" she asked.

"Oh, the usual—probably through September."

Shura tried not to let the surprise show on her face. Pavel had been right about them making no plans to leave.

"Do you have food with you?"

Oleg was silently laughing at her again. "We brought plenty from Kyiv, even red wine. Packed the whole car."

"I suppose you'll grow the rest, then?"

"Well, sure," Alyona said. "We'll need to get the ground ready for planting soon."

"In March?"

"Why not?" Oleg cut in. "The carrots and dill we can plant already. We can start the seeds for the cabbage and squash in the greenhouses."

Alyona gave him a look. "You know I like to use those for the strawberries." For a few moments, the screen seemed to freeze.

When the connection returned to normal, Alyona was talking about moving the tomato pots indoors.

Shura said, "I guess you've got it all sorted out." She wasn't sure what game they were playing, chatting as if it were another spring at the dacha, as if Alyona and Oleg had retired to the countryside for a vacation instead of fleeing a city under attack. Then again, what *should* Alyona be doing? All day long, Shura watched the news on YouTube, zooming in on crowds flooding into train stations, people shouting, "Please, please," and conductors shouting back, "No space." Occasionally, someone begged for a mother with a child to be let on, as in the war tales she'd heard growing up. Except this time everything was in bright color. She could hardly blame her friend for not wanting to be stuck among all those jostling bodies. And yet she could not help thinking that these people had nowhere to go, while Alyona did—to her son. It baffled her. "All that planting sounds like a lot of work," she said.

Alyona gave her Jessica Lange smile. "It *always* is."

The next day, she called Pavel again. "There are flights from Warsaw to Toronto. If they can just get themselves to Lviv first—all the trains are running, I've checked the schedules."

"Aunt Shura, they *know*."

"They're almost seventy years old, and that estate is at least an acre! If the Russians move another few inches south, your parents are going to be feeding three types of squash to those bandits."

"My father is impenetrable. If it was just her, I could convince her to come back, get some proper care. But as long as she's around him . . ."

A feeling like embarrassment fluttered through her at his words. She thought of Alyona, with her sense of decorum, hearing them talk like this. "What happened, Pavel? Why did they leave Toronto so soon?"

She hadn't dared to ask this question before, and he was quiet for so long that she had to say his name again.

"I don't know where to start," he said. "He's contemptuous of the way I live. He said that I do nothing but work, I barely see my child. It's true, I had a tight delivery schedule when they were here—the company had just gone public. I was managing a new team. I didn't argue with him. He started going on about how when he and Mama were working at the Informatics Institute, they never kept anyone past six—how after work there was a *life*, culture, a theatre circle, a chess club—people *did* things together. I said, Papa, I'm sorry my e-commerce firm doesn't have a chess club, I'm sorry it doesn't have an a cappella group."

"What did he say?"

"He thought I was mocking him. He said, 'Your problem is you believe that the whole world wants to live like you.' I was foolish enough to think I could prove him wrong. We had a party, a few friends from work, but mostly my wife's from the Ukrainian church, people who helped us out when we first came. We started talking about Crimea, Donbas. He got up from the table and left the room. I thought, Good riddance. But then he came back. He sat down, lifted his glass, and started singing one of those old Russian-veteran songs—'We Need Only Victory!'"

"Was he drunk?"

"Not at all. He was trying to get Mama to sing along with him. He was waving his hand up and down like a choirmaster—to get her to harmonize."

"And did she?"

"Oh, yes. She may have been a little embarrassed at first, but then she did it. She got into it, or pretended to. I can't tell with her anymore. She did her best to carry his tune, like she always does."

"What do you mean *always*?"

"He talks to me about how *I* live." There was a river of grievance waiting to come out now. "His mother waited on his father, and on him, hand and foot, and when *she* died he expected the same treatment from Mama. Couldn't care less if she had her own job or life."

"He's a man of the old generation," Shura said, disingenuously. She thought of her husband, Misha, donning volleyball kneepads to clean the kitchen tile. Oleg might laugh at that. But then he wasn't exactly a gentleman of leisure. He did most of the work at the dacha, Alyona had told her: planting, fixing pipes, rigging the internet, building a sauna.

"That isn't why," Pavel objected. "It's because they ran the show, those Russian military guys. They still expect everyone to roll over for them. He feels hurt that my son speaks only English and Ukrainian."

She understood now that Pavel had forsaken his Russianness completely. "But your father *knows* Ukrainian, almost as well as your mother."

"I explained that they teach the language at Sunday school, but Papa shook his head. He thinks our church is a bunch of *banderovtsy* stuck in a time capsule, and that groups like them fund everything that's wrong at home. But I think what really kills him is that the community here has done more for me than he ever did."

Or *could* do, Shura thought. What good would Oleg's family connections have done for Pavel after the great collapse? The economy had still been reeling when Pavel had left on a summer work visa to pick fruit on a farm in England, when he'd befriended some local guys at an internet café in Cambridge and offered to write code for them, when he'd been hired by the startup they worked for, then by the corporation that had bought the startup and transplanted him and his young wife to Toronto. That his father dared to judge him for having clawed his way to the life he had must have felt exceedingly unfair. But how fair was it to judge his parents, Shura thought, who'd had so little to offer him?

"My wife and I had a big fight that night. The next day I told him that if he ever did that in my house again he was free to leave. When I woke up the morning after, they were packing their suitcases."

"But you said your mother needed medical attention?"

Her diabetes had worsened, Pavel admitted. Alyona had had appointments coming up.

Preoccupied with her own health, Shura had not pressed Alyona on her diabetes, which Alyona always played down, perhaps not wanting to compete over their ailments. Shura regretted this now. "They wouldn't even wait until the next doctor's visit," Pavel said, his voice strained with helpless petulance. "Mama said she could get it all in Kyiv."

"But she's not in Kyiv now."

"They loathe the city almost as much as they do Toronto."

"But why?"

"The Ubers, the new street names, the ads in Ukrainian and English. Last time I was there, everything annoyed them." It had never looked so modern, Pavel added. Like Prague or London. They'd changed the parking rules, put up those stone planters so cars couldn't nose up on the sidewalks anymore. But his mother had kept stubbing her toe on the planters, almost as if she didn't see them, or didn't want to. "What frightens them is that there's no trace of anything Soviet anymore. I can't get through to her, Aunt Shura. Maybe you can."

Shura felt panic touch her chest. "What are you asking, Pavel?" she said, suddenly switching to English.

"She needs care. She listens to you, Aunt Shura."

"You mean she should come alone?"

"It's the only way."

When she hung up the phone, Shura reminded herself that she'd agreed to nothing. She wasn't completely sure what Pavel had asked her to do—persuade Alyona to go to Toronto for medical care, or to stay for good? Because it also sounded to her like what her friend's son was asking her to do was break up his parents' marriage.

Shura had never given much thought to Alyona and Oleg as a pair, though initially she had found Alyona's choice perplexing. In the letters they exchanged throughout college, Alyona had not once mentioned Oleg. Then, in her second-to-last year, she'd written to Shura to announce that she was getting married. Oleg was a year ahead. They'd known each other as acquaintances but never dated. One day, late in his final semester, he'd asked to walk her to her dormitory. He'd been hoping for a while to speak to her, he said. It was not hard for Shura to imagine a boy taking months to work up the courage to approach Alyona. But Oleg was not timid. On their walk, he laid it out simply. He wanted to marry her. His father was a colonel in the Soviet Army, and his parents had a three-bedroom apartment on the Right Bank in Kyiv, and would help them get their own place soon. He'd given Alyona one day to decide.

"Only a day?" Shura had been a little stunned to confirm this when she'd come home from Leningrad that July, to attend the wedding.

But Alyona saw this as a sign of character. "He said twenty-four hours should be enough time."

"What did you like about him?" Shura ventured to ask. She'd meant besides his Kyiv residency papers.

"He's tall. And he has confidence."

Of course, a colonel's son had the confidence of his position, but Alyona had meant more than that. She meant certainty about what he wanted from life, and what he was entitled to. In this case, her.

Shura had always thought of Alyona's ability to intuit what was required of her as a kind of mental elegance, something of a piece with the physical elegance. But a different memory had come to her then: in high school, they'd made a pact to travel to Leningrad and sit for their university exams together. After they'd already bought the train tickets, Alyona announced that she wasn't going. Her father wanted her to go to a college closer to home. Shura had known even then that Alyona would not argue with this.

Nonetheless, Shura did not think that Pavel's version of his mother as the long-suffering wife was accurate. Whenever Shura had returned to Ukraine for visits, it was always Alyona who'd picked her up at the airport, in any kind of weather, first on the bus and later in her own car. At the train station in Kyiv, while Shura waited for her connection back to the town where they'd grown up, the young women would drink tea and talk. Alyona had seemed happy, or at least content. "I have a lot of freedom," she'd admit, almost guiltily. Shura assumed she was referring to her roomy apartment, close to Oleg's parents, and to the fact that Oleg's mother took Pavel to day care every morning and picked him up, and also did the grocery shopping and errands. (Shura's own life, except for these brief trips home, had been a series of increasingly narrow constrictions. She'd married Misha, her college sweetheart, and moved to his native Azerbaijan. Not even to Baku, but to an industrial town that made the one she'd grown up in seem like a botanical garden.) Later, however, she had wondered if Alyona's allusion to her freedom had meant something more.

Sometimes Alyona made references to a colleague, a man with whom she ate lunches that stretched into matinées at a nearby movie house. Just a friend from work, she said.

The last time Alyona and Shura had met in Kyiv, Shura had confessed that she and Misha had received permission to emigrate, and Alyona, in turn, had confessed that her friend's wife had died abruptly, a few months earlier, and that he had asked her to leave Oleg to be with him. They had not acted on their affection and she was asking Shura what to do.

Maybe it was the giddiness of knowing that everything in her own life was about to change that made Shura say, "Do it! Pavel is in high school. If you don't now, when?"

"Yes, you're right." Alyona had breathed slowly, bracing herself, it seemed, for escape. She'd taken the wide collar of her blouse and raised it to her face, knuckles at her nose as if protecting herself from a freezing gale, though it was June.

When they got back in touch, two years later, Shura learned that Alyona had stayed with Oleg.

"I thought you loved him—your friend."

"I do."

"But?"

"He doesn't have the same, I don't know . . . force of will."

Shura hid her disappointment. She liked the idea of giving up everything for a great love. (She believed, in a private way, that she'd done just that for Misha.) But Alyona wasn't interested in talking about a decision once it was made, and Shura let it drop.

"So, what have you planted so far?" Shura asked when they spoke next, on day sixteen. Alyona said that she'd sown the beets and carrot seeds and spring onions. She wanted to plant spinach, but there was a shortage of fertilizer, so she'd settled for peas.

"All that in two weeks?"

Alyona smiled, glad at Shura's exaggerated awe. "Well, then, what have you and Pavel been talking about?"

Shura hesitated. "We were talking about your health. He said you need an update to your blood-sugar monitor."

"You don't know the whole story."

"You're right, I know nothing," Shura admitted. "But it sounds like he wants to take care of you."

Alyona said that they could take care of themselves well enough. Indeed, they could, Shura concurred.

Privately, it made Shura manic. Those goddam vegetable gardens! She'd grown up on a little homestead herself—right in the middle of their town—helping her parents tend a sizable piece of property that had been in the family since before the Bolsheviks, complete with apple trees and chickens. Shura's parents had wanted her to "inherit" this patch of soil they'd somehow managed to hold on to under the system. (Did they really think she, an only child, a professional, would have time to tend any of it?) Not until her midforties did she acquire a taste for gardening again, after she and Misha had saved up and moved to their house in Croton. They'd bought across the street from a woman named Trish, who worked as a real estate agent and was obsessed with helping her neighbors keep their yards nice in order to maintain the neighborhood's property values. Trish had been generous with her time, showing Shura which boxwoods were better for light and for shade, how to keep her grass from yellowing.

When the war started, Trish had come over with a basket of begonia bulbs and said, "Are you *all right?* Tell me what I can *do.*" Her eyes as plaintive as if she'd just learned that Shura had cancer again. It was how all her American friends spoke to her now, calling and asking what they could *do,* flexing their empathy muscles. Shura appreciated it, even if it felt infantilizing. What she liked about this country was the unfailing optimism of its people, the faith they had that something could always be *done,* that things could be improved. They were certain that, with enough aid, enough sanctions, enough deprivation, "the regular Russian people" would take it upon themselves to overthrow the Turd. It didn't occur to them that these same "regular people" might take a vengeful pleasure, even a national pride, in their own deprivation and humiliation. That this pride could propel them, at a moment's notice, to head to their little dachas and plant their little gardens, to pickle and can their vegetables until Armageddon.

Harder to explain was the sentiment of some of her Jewish immigrant friends, who in spite of shaking their heads compassionately, in spite of sending money to Ukraine's Army fund, said among themselves, *But, still, are we supposed to forget?* They meant Bandera and Shukhevych and the Odesa and Proskurov pogroms and all the rest of it. Oh, how Shura detested that "but, still." In the chemo room, she'd watched Zelensky's victory—a kind of sunlight trickling into her veins along with the drugs. The surprise was not just that they'd elected a Jew but that this seemed of so much less consequence to the Ukrainians themselves than it was to the press. It had made her feel that the world really could change, that its surprises were worth sticking around for.

Shura had started calling on Tuesdays at 7 p.m. Alyona's time, noon hers. This was the hour, Alyona had told her, when Oleg was usually out visiting a neighbor for a drink.

"How's settlement life going?"

Alyona said she'd been up since dawn pruning fruit trees. It seemed to Shura that her enthusiasm had somewhat waned. She said two of the greenhouses had torn siding and finding replacement plastic was turning out to be a nightmare.

"Well, at least you did a lot of the ground planting."

"That's true." Alyona sighed. "Then again, fish, meat, and butter don't grow in neat little rows, do they?"

It was a sign, Shura thought, that Alyona was letting her guard down. The self-sufficiency she'd opted for wasn't without its burdens. Still, it was not the same as being captive. Something Shura could not explain to Pavel: that when you reached a certain age, when you'd peered down that canyon, your mate, if they happened to still be alive and healthy, was the luck you held on to by your fingernails.

The next time Shura called, Alyona picked up right away, instead of returning the missed call. "Did you see about O——?" Shura said, naming the town they'd grown up in.

A look of naked worry crossed Alyona's face. "I heard something. What happened?"

"They bombed the railway station."

Even if Shura hadn't been compulsively following the war, she would have heard about the bombing on Facebook, where her old classmates posted news like this within minutes of its announcement. Still, it was strange that she knew more about each round of shelling from her kitchen in Croton than Alyona, forty miles away from it. "Schools No. 5 and 2 also got hit," she said.

"Anyone inside?"

"I don't think so."

"What about No. 6?"

"No, ours is still standing."

On the screen, Alyona sat, her shoulders fallen. She was looking away from the camera, toward what must have been the window, the last of the day's pink sun touching the wooden posts of her chair.

They were making progress, Shura thought. Sometimes, after Oleg turned in for the night, Alyona called her. They avoided talk of the war, instead recalling moments of their youth. "Remember Felix Smolyar, in the green brigades with us?" Shura said.

"Not too bright with numbers?"

"He wrote me from California, asked if I was still in contact with you."

"He did?"

"We all thought he was a dummy, but turns out he had dyslexia."

Shura asked if she remembered their second-grade teacher, the one she'd argued with about painting spring. Alyona shook her head. "You don't remember telling me I should paint spring as it *should* be?" She didn't know why it should sadden her that Alyona had forgotten. "You always did insist on your way of things," Alyona finally said.

It was April now, and through her bay window Shura could see her tulips peeking up, her daffodils already blooming. She thought of the news analysis she'd heard that morning, that all Ukraine needed to turn the war around was tree cover. The country had a long tradition of guerrilla warfare. Once everything was in bloom and the forests dense, the Russians were in for a bitter slog. She repeated none of this to Alyona.

Shura couldn't remember when she'd stopped counting the days. Maybe after the Russians had been pushed out of Kyiv and thousands of Ukrainians had returned. Each week, Alyona seemed closer to changing her mind. One evening, watching Shura scoop ice cream into a bowl, Alyona said, "What I wouldn't do for some of that."

Shura stopped moving the spoon toward her mouth, feeling the illusion of their proximity suddenly disappear. "I'd love to give you mine."

"We couldn't take any in the car. It would melt, that's all."

"I bet you could make some."

But Alyona said that she was almost out of cooking butter. What cream she could get her hands on, she'd make into that first.

"You could go back to Kyiv for a bit," Shura suggested.

For a long moment, Alyona didn't speak, looking somewhere past the camera. "There's not enough fuel in the cans for leisure trips," she said. Meaning, Oleg wouldn't do it.

"Anyone you could get a ride with?" Shura knew she was treading on delicate ground now. "To get some supplies," she added.

Alyona was gazing out the window again. It would be good for her, Shura thought, to be in a city that had just won its freedom, however precarious. "You have a cousin in Kyiv, don't you?"

Alyona seemed to consider this. But there were parallel creases between her eyes when she looked in the camera again. "You don't know what it's like to be treated as an enemy because you want peace," she said.

Was it the cousin she was talking about, or Pavel? Shura couldn't say. But that night, calling Pavel, she said, "If she felt she could have a place to herself, in Toronto . . . it might be easier to persuade her to come back."

He said that he had already put his parents on a list for subsidized apartments in the greater Toronto area. There was a housing help center he could appeal to. He could guarantee their rent. The problem, he explained, was that filling out more paperwork wouldn't do the job. They had to show up, physically, at various offices. Or at least Alyona did.

But Shura found herself unable to talk about this with Alyona, their common ground now being, quite literally, the ground. Shura shared her own difficulties with her dry, rock-filled soil, the challenges of untangling perennial tubers. "Planting is not so bad," Alyona said. "There's hope in it, at least. It's the weeding I can't bear. It's endless." She presented her pale arms to the camera so Shura could see the map of red scratches from thickets she'd tried to rip out. Her knees were rubbed raw, she said.

Shura suggested a hot bath to soak them, and knew her mistake immediately.

"What in? I can't fill it with more than five centimetres of warm water, or he says we're wasting heating oil." But suddenly Alyona looked embarrassed by her complaint. "I've lived through worse."

"Well, of course you have. But you don't have to anymore, right? You have options this time."

"Options?"

"Stocked shelves. Good health care. It's nothing to laugh at, at our age. You need to be taking walks, not digging a spade in the ground eight hours a day."

"Sounds like you and Pavel have been talking about more than just my health."

But Shura was tired of being coy. "Look, he's found you an apartment. In your kind of situation, you'll go right to the top of the line." She didn't know how true this was but hoped it was true enough.

Alyona swung her head in an I-don't-know gesture. It wasn't enough for her to have the facts. She had to be seduced. "Change is hard only at first, but then it's just . . . life," Shura said. "Look at me. I've done it three times already."

"You think I haven't lived through enough changes?" Alyona's face was amused and cool, and Shura saw her own error. Of course she'd witnessed bigger upheavals just staying put.

"Look, even if Oleg wanted to leave Toronto that doesn't mean you have to . . ."

"Oleg?"

"Pavel said they were quarrelling . . ."

"Yes, and they would have gone on quarrelling for eternity if I hadn't said we were going home."

Shura felt something like a tremor in her breastbone. "*You* wanted to go back?"

"I just wanted peace, Shura. Pavel invites friends over who he knows will make Oleg upset. What can we do? We're there at his goodwill, so he reminds us."

The irony of this struck Shura like a blow to the temple. Her blood pressure was doing funny things again. How silly of her to think that Alyona was being kept in Ukraine against her will, that she'd lived too long on the milk of others' admiration to know what she really desired. That, like her country, all she needed was an opportunity to decide her own fate. "Leave or stay," Shura said. "You'll have to adapt either way—it's never going back to how it was, you know. The country won't let itself be occupied."

Alyona almost, but not quite, laughed. "It already is," she said. Did Shura think it was free? That it wasn't already occupied by an army of government consultants? "By ones like Hunter Biden sitting on every board?"

It wasn't that Shura was shocked by this parroting of worn propaganda. Shura had no wish anymore to argue about the particulars. What she had failed to see was that in Alyona's view the choice was always between two compromises. The idea of an unadulterated liberty was another sham Shura had fallen for. Had Alyona always felt this way, or had it come from a lifetime of making her bargains and sticking with them? Before they hung up, she said, "You'll forgive me if I don't want to end my days in a waiting room, holding out for Canada's promises."

Shura's aversion to that term—waiting room—still rises in her throat five days later, while she sits in her oncologist's waiting room, expecting to be called in for her marker test. The words make her think of the Turd's latest speech, accusing defectors who have left Russia of selling out their mothers for a chance to sit in the waiting rooms of the West. When the tests come back normal, she takes a long, sustaining breath, then tries to Skype Alyona. No answer. She tries the following day. Maybe they have lost their jiggered internet. Maybe they have gone back to Kyiv. She is too embarrassed to call Pavel, not that she'd ever tell him that it was his mother's decision to leave Toronto, or admit what her last words to Alyona had been. "And yet who could have imagined you, Alyona Korolenko," she'd said, "living out your days as a farmer's wife?" In her parting shot, she'd gone after the one thing she'd known would make Alyona turn away: her vanity.

For weeks, she continues to hope that her friend might be the one to call her, for once. That Alyona should feel so out of place outside her country, or in it, strikes Shura as a failure of imagination much worse than her own failures of discretion. In her garden, on her knees, Shura breaks up the soil, mixing in the compost, removing the winter mulch. Afterward, she washes her hands in the kitchen, where the birds can be heard tweeting from a dogwood in bloom over her deck. The season, as it should be, has arrived at last.

My Brother William

FROM *The Iowa Review*

THE FIRST TIME I threw out my back was in New York City, shortly after college. I was moving apartments and went down trying to lift a mini-fridge from standing position. Idiot idea. There was a wrenching feeling and I suddenly found myself on the floor, fore-arm braced, as the muscles of my lower back went into a spasm. The pain was immense. Swallowing, in its totality. Later, when I was immobilized in bed, Will conferenced in and listened to me yowl. The grainy pixilated loom of his face on the screen of my laptop. Long after my friends left, he stayed on. He was doing work, I knew, or if not working, gaming, or if not gaming, scroll-ing through social media, corresponding simultaneously on three platforms with his legions of online friends. He didn't say much. Just kept me company. Occasionally he looked over at me and I would see him tapping on the screen. Hey, he said, hey. Don't die. I'm supposed to go before you. Order of succession. Sib dibs were called and sib dibs were inviolate, he reminded me. Never mind that no one had ever died of a back injury.

I was an ambitious young kid. That's why I lifted miniature refrig-erators from standing position, because I couldn't be bothered to squat down and get my legs under me; I couldn't stomach the wasted seconds. It infuriated me to be in the condition I was in for the two days I was bed-bound. Really it made me mad as hell. How could my body be so weak? I was twenty-one. I had an in-terview with a newsweekly upcoming, my first full-time gig out of college, and spent the daylight hours punching my pillow to keep from crying and mimicking the facial expressions of the actresses in daytime soaps as I recited answers to imagined questions. On the third day I felt much better, could spoon soup directly from a can into my mouth and call that dinner, could piss into the toilet from a more or less orthodox position. On the fourth I left the building and went to the interview. Afterward, I sat for an hour in the ground floor lobby, pretending to read, but really waiting out my back, waiting for the pain to ease.

In those first few years I didn't travel so much, so I only got to see Will once a year or so outside of the Christmas holiday, when we both went home to visit our folks. Will had been out of college for a few years and was making bank. He was working for the tech companies in San Francisco as a software engineer, but to what ends I wasn't sure, it could've been anything, games, social media, the dark web organ trade for all I knew. He was always closemouthed about the specifics. Because of an NDA, possibly, but maybe also out of genuine loyalty—that would've been like him.

After the weekly, I went to a website that put me to use covering city and state politics. I spent a few years chasing around after smarmy politicians and glad-handing with lobbyists and legislative aides. They were all the same, liberals, conservatives, no matter their agendas. In the course of tracking down a story, I met my girlfriend, Kylie, a reporter for a rival newsgroup. In a daring maneuver she tried to poach one of my most trusted sources, forcing me to out the source to intervene. In my admiration I asked her out for a drink. In the following years, my back didn't bother me so much. I chalked it up to being in love.

Even though we didn't see each other in person that often, I was close to my older brother. Had been since we were young. Closer to him than to our parents. There was a special bond there. We cried when we were separated at school and the other kids made fun of us for it. Now we kept up over the phone, texted constantly. If I had to describe him to someone who didn't know him, I'd say he was a quiet, sweet guy. Kind of shy—not like me, the loudmouth. Sensitive. Reclusive. But brilliant. That was in both of us, I guess—the high-octane brains good at thinking. But there was also in both of us the neuroticism that comes with being good at thinking. The tendency towards living too much in our own heads. As if the universe were a thing housed entirely within our skulls.

Towards the end of my stint with the website I flew to go visit him. He showed up an hour late to the airport in a taxi. I hadn't seen him in a year. His curly black hair, his solemn dark eyes, were the same. He was in rumpled khakis, an untucked shirt. I didn't care. I hugged him, glad as hell to see him. In the taxi back I kept asking questions about how he was, how life was, gripping the back of his headrest and flicking his earlobes like I was his kid sister, but his answers were distracted, monosyllabic. He was on his phone, answering his work emails, he said. I sat back, feeling annoyed now. When my girlfriend was on her phone while with me I had a habit of grabbing it from her and stuffing it in my bra.

He walked us up to his apartment, on the fourth floor of an apartment complex in the industrial outskirts of the city. The elevator was broken. I didn't understand why, if he was making so much money, he was living here. But I didn't ask. We pushed into his apartment. Even though it was a blazing day outside, inside it was dark. The blackout curtains were drawn. In the kitchen the yellow fluorescent lights shone on a countertop heaped with cereal boxes, crumpled burrito wrappers, stacks of unopened mail. There were storage boxes shoved against the wall, corners sealed with tape, untouched from his move from a year ago. There was no dining table, no shoe rack, no food in the fridge except a giant unlidded tub of margarine, but there was a videogame console and a projector set up in the living room on which the games could be played. I was shocked. I hadn't visited my brother's living arrangements since he'd been in a raucous all-boys dormitory in college. I knew my brother was a bachelor and a technologist (formerly derided as a nerd, now elevated into the ruling class), but I hadn't expected this.

At night I set up my sleeping quarters in the living room. Billowed a sheet over the sagging futon. Will retreated into his room. Said he needed to take care of something. The door was open though and when I went by on the way to the bathroom I saw through that he was at his screen. He was talking in a singsong way to a girl, a girl whose round pretty face glowed, lunar, on her webcam, dominating his screen. When I asked him later he said it was his girlfriend. I asked him if she was from around here. He didn't know, he said, he'd never met her.

*

It was at around this time that my work took off. I broke a big story about a city politician's suspect campaign contributions. It led to a shouting match at a council meeting, a press frenzy, the state attorney general threatening indictment. It elevated my name to be connected with the story, which, though sordid, brought about important changes in the regulatory scheme governing campaign finance. I was proud. Got my picture taken and everything.

In the course of my work I thought about technology too, of course, since I was in the media, and was, like my brother, constantly online, scrolling through my social media feeds, talking to lots of people at once, connecting and transacting and commenting and liking and prospecting. Like him, I was in the business of producing online content, but unlike him, I found the whole thing troubling, in addition to inspirational. What was troubling was the extent to which we were becoming dependent on our screens, the refractory effect on our attention spans—consciousness becoming like the trillion bits in a kaleidoscope which every ten seconds was given a vigorous shake—the compulsive repetitive refreshing of our feeds, the extent to which life itself seemed increasingly concentrated in the lit glowing squares in our hands.

It was necessary to play the game, which I did and did well, but I played it so that I could achieve an end. My brother played it for love and love alone.

The end I achieved was that I was hired on by a prestigious national magazine to write features. Being hired on by this magazine was the terminus point of many a career. Yearly its staff racked in journalism awards and fellowship grants, book contracts, top prizes in the field, plum speaking engagements. When I got the call I nearly had an aneurysm. What I felt was beyond joy. At thirty-one, I felt, I had peaked.

I remember I had a long philosophical conversation with Will about all this stuff. He loved to have these conversations. It thrilled him, invigorated some fundamental view he had of life. It started when he said that it was not all bad, that there were people who derived only benefit from living the best parts of their lives online. This was not nor should it be a controversial statement, he said. Take, he said, a mother of twins with severe disabilities, who wakes at five every morning to prepare for her kids' days, and who every night before bed escapes the hardship of her existence through engagement with an online community populated by diverse individuals from all around the planet. For an hour each night she has access to virtual worlds that she could not otherwise have as a being with corporeal and financial limitations. For an hour each night she can live elsewhere. When she emerges, she emerges refreshed, ready to love and care for her kids, not exercise bitterness and acrimony upon them. Would we deny her these avenues of living, he said, simply because they were looked down upon by society for being quote unquote not real?

So you're saying people with disabilities benefit in particular, I said.

Yes, he said.

But aren't her needs a reflection of the failures of the real world? I said. A real world whose social structures are inadequate to take care of her kids? What I meant was that even if virtual life was beneficial for individuals, the benefits reflected an external failure of society in providing for those individuals. She wasn't getting her needs met in real life, necessitating dependence on a virtual one. We shouldn't applaud the virtual life—we needed to fix the real one, which was broken.

Will nodded thoughtfully at this. That's true, he said. But in the meantime what are you gonna do? Deny the lady her brief slots of carefree existence?

The vast majority of users aren't disabled, or mothers of disabled children, I said. I felt a pain at saying this, of insecurity, thinking of my own weak back.

Everyone has something to escape, Will said.

For the longest time I didn't, and then, in a short span of time, I did. The start of my time at the magazine was not the triumph I imagined it to be. As a junior staff member, I was assigned to report on the environment. Later I would have the seniority to create my own assignments, carve out my own specialty, but for now, there I was, taking notes at the foot of hazardous dump sites with a wet rag wrapped around my face, interviewing climate change scientists weary of repeating the same conclusions to gridlocked parliaments and ineffectual bodies of Congress, reading boxes upon boxes of documents on the effects of deforestation and mountaintop strip-mining. At around the same time, after six years together, I broke

up with my girlfriend. It was the first of many breakups that occurred between us, but I didn't know it at the time. I thought I had
lost her forever.

It was the first dark age of my life. I sank into what I now know
was a black depression, but what at the time only registered as a
bewilderment of mismatched socks, lost keys, a numbing inability to get out of bed. I felt blurry, dissociated. I had difficulty following the trains of simple conversations. With my plummeting
mood my back weakened. There were days when I had to leave the
office at noon because it hurt so much to sit in the office chair.
I asked for accommodations to work at home, for special equipment to work while lying down, but when insurance denied my
chiropractic claims as medically unnecessary I lost track of the
other requests in the ensuing scramble to pay the bills. During
the nights the pain kept me up, interrupting my nightmares, the
visions of bombed-out redwood groves and raging wildfires. The
lack of sleep worsened everything: my mood, my back. My back in
turn made it hard to sleep, which worsened my mood. And on and
on in a vicious cycle.

At the same time, Will and I began talking less. He was absorbed
into his work on the West Coast, and it was really the whole coast
now, since his work was flying him up and down to speak at confer-
ences, to give workshops. Our calls and texts dwindled to once or
twice a week, then once or twice every few weeks, then once every
month or three. He was aware that I was going through a hard time,
but I didn't tell him how bad it was. It wasn't my way to appear weak.

Will wrote an article. With my help, my contacts in the field, he
published it. What was real and what was not real? he said. Emotional pain was registered in the brain as if it were physical pain.
Anyone who had a broken heart knew how much worse it hurt
than a sprained ankle, and for longer. The centers of the brain that
mediated experience registered each experience as a constellation
of electrical signals. So what did it matter what source acted upon
the brain to elicit an experience? If reality was your brain lighting up in particular configurations, then shouldn't anything that
elicited the lighting, be considered real? The arbitrary categories
into which we divided our experiences, he said, were limiting us.
We should liberalize our understanding of reality. Recognize that
the physical world was only one among an uncountable number

available to us. Life, after all, he said, was lived only in the mind; and the mind was limitless.

My back got better. After a medical leave of absence, I changed to another division. We got a new editor-in-chief, then an infusion of funding from a well-known progressive foundation. As the token lesbian on staff, and with my new editor's encouragement, I started writing features about women. Hard-charging female artists; queer firebrands; Midwestern homemakers suddenly deciding to run for office in the middle of changing their kids' nappies. It was still hard. So much of reporting the news is about trouble, about suffering. Ambulance chasing, as it were. There's no news like bad news. But there was a new hopefulness in me. I think it had to do with interviewing these women. They suffered too, like everyone, in singular and unprecedented ways, but that didn't stop them.

At the same time that Will was going deeper into his life's work, I was going deeper into mine. After the depression lifted, something happened. I felt as if I were living life for the very first time. The vividity of the world astonished me. I was newly ushered into it, like a child. I walked down from my apartment to Tompkins Square Park and sat under the trees, which were going gold-green, orange, bright red, and I sat there dumbfounded, underneath this canopy with the birds flitting in it like grace notes and the leaves drifting down to heap in colorful dry-rustling piles at my feet. I smelled woodsmoke on my walks by the river. The nights went cool, and the stars showed. I walked around as if naked, all my defenses stripped from me by pain, and finally the pain eased. I remember my first real breath—the first moment of relief after a long period of suffering. On an ordinary Tuesday evening, by the jazz club, the silvery notes wavering. It pierced me right through.

After that autumn I rebounded. I went into the world and I talked to people from all over the country, Texan mechanics, high-society ladies in Charlottesville, refugees fleeing the latest military coup in Myanmar or Syria or Ecuador, young kids in a pediatric oncology clinic who held their parents' hands as they sobbed, scientists and lawyers working doggedly for climate reform. I wrote furiously. I was convinced of something. I was convinced that the world was not beyond saving. That it had ugliness in it, but also a savage and innocent beauty that redeemed it. My despair had shown me the depths to which I could sink, but it had also shown me the extent to which I believed in my work as an entrance into what was true. The truth was that I believed that the real world was not to be jettisoned, turned away from, escaped. As hard as that world was, it was precious, because it was all we had.

In the middle of this I got back together with my girlfriend. Within a year we were engaged. In the spirit of my rejuvenation I swore to love her forever, believing that our differences could be resolved with counseling and mutual effort. The wedding was held at a lakeside chalet, strung with fairy lights, on a warm summer's night. It was like something out of a dream. I, who never cried, cried and cried. My parents came, my friends and old classmates from all over the country, a few of my ex-lovers, now friends, and even some of the people who I had profiled over the years, whose careers I had elevated, whose faces and companies I had helped make famous. The only one who didn't make it was Will.

Will was elusive for that long stretch of years. I knew the surface reason was that his work was demanding, but secretly I thought that it was because our life paths were diverging, mine taking me deeper into the real world, him taking him deeper into worlds of his own creation.

The reason he had not been able to attend my wedding was because he was chairing an important conference in Amsterdam. At that point we had not been close for several years. The division that had appeared between us, when I was reporting on environmental disasters and he was immersed in creating brightly colored digital environments while real ones flooded and burned, had widened. Some years I forgot his birthday. When we emailed each other we signed our names formally, and addressed each other using complete sentences, rather than the exclamations and rows of smiling faces we had employed before. One day I saw in a headline that he had secured $10 billion in funding for a project looking to develop virtual reality environments as a means of treatment for military veterans with PTSD. Prominent technologist clinches major Department of Defense contract, the headline read. I immediately forwarded the link to my parents. They were happy for him. In truth, I was too.

The one area of my life that did not yield to my determined optimism was the relationship I had with my wife. In the half decade after our wedding, our old patterns of dysfunction surfaced again. Old hurts, old fights. I remembered that night I had first seen her, resplendent in a dress, her hair cut in a pageboy, her smoky cat's-eye eyeliner. She was still as beautiful and as lively to me as when I'd met her more than fifteen years ago now, but the patterns of behavior in which we were locked seemed impossible to break.

Worse, as my health fluctuated, so did my limitations. There were times, increasing in frequency over the years, when she did all the lifting and moving and the climbing and stooping around the house, ferrying in the groceries, handling the laundry, while I lay with my back against a heating pad, playing her inspirational music from my laptop and trying not to feel guilty; when we couldn't go on the hikes or extended walks we used to love and had to stay inside, alone together in front of our respective screens; or when she became angry at me because I insisted on exceeding my restrictions in pursuit of a story. Those were the worst, those fights about what I couldn't do, what she wouldn't allow me to do, what I nevertheless insisted on doing.

Finally we agreed to a trial period of separation, after which we would regroup and determine what to do next. I moved out of our place into an apartment out in Queens, a two-bedroom above a health food storefront that sold ginseng in stapled baggies and insect shells pounded into a powder. I was distraught, so I escaped into my work, taking on new assignments on the regional effects of climate change, ones that didn't require quite so much travel. How ironic, I thought, that in our separation I was listening to my wife after all.

The separation stretched out. Two years, then three. I continued to limit my travel and reported only one story on international relations, a climate change summit where the signatories tore up their hundred-page agreement at the eleventh hour. It began to feel like my back was preventing me from keeping up my expertise on our deteriorating world, which infuriated me at the same time it drove me to panic. At the same time I wanted to show my wife I could operate within the bounds of safety, of acceptability. In an attempt to distract myself I began drafting a manuscript for a book—a memoir. I had a physical therapist for my back, regular ergonomic evaluations. I exercised it faithfully and regularly.

None of it did any good. My wife and I tried on several occasions, and failed on several occasions, to reconcile. I resigned myself to waiting to be served with divorce papers. I was forty-five years old.

Funny, I thought, in one of my black moods. There were all these statistics on how often men left their female partners when they got sick, and how often women left their male partners who got sick too. But no numbers on women who left women.

There was one time in that period of years where I got to see Will, I mean really got to see him. It was during the holidays. For once, I wasn't traveling for an assignment; for once, his work was in a lull. We went back home, to our folks.

Our folks lived out in Nevada. My mom was an accountant; my dad a school administrator. Both were retired by now and in their late seventies. They were good people, homespun, folksy yet unsentimental, content to live out the remainders of their lives in the small town where they had raised us. Their only bewilderment was how their progeny had gotten out and become so radicalized, what with the reportage in far-flung places and the trafficking in alternate realities. When Will talked about his work my mom and dad nodded in tandem, smiling encouragingly, not understanding a single word. Most of that time we spent talking about health problems, like my dad's wobbly knees, which had recently necessitated a walker, or my back.

I arrived home driving a rental car because I didn't want my parents to come out and get me. The morning was typical Nevada; hot, blowing hotter. Little swirls of dust leapt and cleared on the sidewalk. I got out of the car and swung my luggage from the trunk. Wheeled it up the entranceway, listening to the wheels rumble, feeling very young and very old at the same time.

Will opened the door. He looked questioningly at me for a moment, as if I was not the sister he expected, but then his face cleared, and he smiled in recognition. He looked good. He was heavier, his gut carried in front of him like a bowling ball, and his hair was going, but he was wearing a fitted suit jacket, which I had never known Will to wear. It made him look almost like the capable executive he was, and his voice when he spoke was humorous and spirited. He gave me a big bear hug. Showed me the Fitbit strapped to his forearm with a pink wristband. The meatspace body a priority after all.

After our parents went to bed that night we stayed up talking and catching up. He asked how I was. He asked after my estranged wife. About my work. When I talked he was entirely there with me, listening. It was a part of being a leader, I suppose. Making people feel heard. How ironic that in all his work on alternate reality he had gotten very good at concentrating himself in this reality. There is a special person who can effect that kind of presence. It is a luminous thing. When my brother had achieved this ability, I was ashamed to say that I didn't know.

I asked about him in turn because that was my job, asking people about their lives, but also because I suddenly really wanted to know. Not know in the superficial way that people expect to know when they ask, how are you? and are given one of maybe two possible responses, both entirely facile and likely untrue, but know in the deep way that something is known, like the face of someone you love, even as it changes beyond recognition over the long years.

He got very serious then, going quiet. His gaze went beyond me for a moment, and he nodded to himself, as if coming to a decision. He said then that his company was in trouble.

What kind of trouble he didn't say, and continued to decline to say, as we spoke of it over the course of the night. I was worldly enough to know that Will wouldn't bring up a trifle. This was something serious—a government investigation or irreversible financial insolvency. We stayed up until two—far too late for both of us. He seemed uneasy, but resigned. I was more afraid than he was. Here was his life's work, its viability hung in the balance. We talked about how he felt, the fees for the law firm he'd placed on retainer. He said don't tell Mom and Dad, I don't want them to worry. We parted a few days later, a few days before New Year's Eve, and promised to keep in touch.

Then a long period when I didn't hear anything from my brother. I asked my parents and they said he was responding sporadically, that they'd last talked to him while he was on an airplane to Hong Kong, the Wi-Fi sputtering in and out until it disconnected.

My back was acting up, as it did with greater and greater frequency as the years wore on. I attempted to contact my wife but it seemed that she too was out of reach, traveling in another country perhaps, or busy with new and exciting endeavors that didn't involve the contemplation of our failed relationship. I began to sink again, at first imperceptibly. My interest in my work faltered. When any number of manual exercises failed to strengthen my back, I fired my longtime physical therapist, irate. I spent long weeks in bed, working from home, shakily levering myself in and out of the bathtub, or onto or off of the toilet, and ordering takeout of days' worth of meals at a time. I tried to cling to the old exhortations which had buoyed me but it was hard to believe them as I once had.

In the middle of the night, the thought would come to me: Maybe, I thought, my brother was right. Maybe it was better to be elsewhere. Anywhere but here, in this difficult, riven world.

On a whim I accepted an assignment that took me out to Guatemala. The immensity of all that greenness right outside, monolithic; the hotel room's windows fogged with humidity. The hotel concierge eyeing me, a woman traveling alone. I was too unwell to do this story but I went. There was something important to cover, some story that I needed to tell the world. If I didn't tell it things would get worse. The old raring daring in me, never extinguished, flipping the finger to the limitations which barred me.

But jet-lagged, lifting my luggage from an inconvenient position in my room, I felt the muscles of my back distort in that now-familiar way. I went down onto the ground, ungracefully collapsed, and lay there counting out my life in increments of ten. Deep breaths. When I could move again, I crawled to the bed. Heaved myself up into it somehow.

The bed was lumpy. Unideal, my physical therapist would say, even dangerous, for my current condition. No matter. Nothing to be done. I fumbled the phone off its cradle and called staff up and they came with cold compresses, speaking rapidly to each other over my becalmed form, shaking out pain medication into my open palms which I swallowed down dry, choking. They got my knees up under a mound of pillows. One of them brought me my cell phone, my laptop. These I had him place on the bed next to me. There was an air of confusion, of multiple people speaking over each other at once. At last a course of action was decided on. It was too late in the evening now, they said. They would call the doctor first thing in the morning.

They left. The room was suddenly quiet. Outside the air itself seemed green-tinted. Like being in an algae-darkened aquarium. The spasms came on in waves, rhythmic. A punishing music I didn't want to hear. I twisted and sweated into the bedsheets and cursed my bad timing. Here I was, in a foreign country, lacking health care access, with rudimentary language proficiency, no friends or family within a thousand-mile radius. It occurred to me that I might be in real danger.

I stayed up all through the night, compulsively checking the battery of my equipment. My phone still had juice. I didn't want to call my parents, didn't want to worry them. It was, I knew, five a.m. in New York. I called my friends in New York and left messages. I called my wife; no answer.

If it was five a.m. in New York, it was two a.m. in California. I thumbed through my contacts and paused on my brother Will. Our last conversation, the history said, was six months ago, over text. I hit Dial.

A spasm gripped me and I almost dropped the phone. When it passed the phone was still ringing. After three more rings it went to voicemail and Will's voice filled the room.

I left a terse message, then hung up and laid in bed. I looked up at the ceiling. My mind was all twisted up with ugly, fearful thoughts. I was totally alone. I tried to quiet my breathing but couldn't. I was afraid.

An hour passed. Then the screen lit and without thinking I grabbed it. I could have cried. It didn't matter who it was as long as it was someone. I held it right in front of my eyes to make sure I wasn't hallucinating from pain and exhaustion. The screen showed my brother's name. I put him on.

His voice filled the room again—the real one. I put the phone against my sternum so I could listen more easily and so I could feel its warmth against me.

Hey, Will, I said, almost lightly. It was easier to conceal my fear now that I was talking to someone.

Why are you awake? he asked.

I'm in . . . a bit of a pickle, I said.

He laughed. Yeah, he said. In a tone of voice that said: I figured.

Can you just stay on the phone with me? We don't have to talk or anything. I'm in Guatemala right now, I said.

Okay, he said, sure.

I felt calmer. I heard him tapping on his keyboard. The tapping made me feel better, like I was twenty again, crying and bemoaning my condition with Will on the line listening. After a while he

Peking Duck

FROM *The New Yorker*

I.

IN MY FIRST years in the U.S., my parents take me to the library to encourage my learning of English. With my mother's guidance, I check out ten, fifteen books every weekend. Though I gravitate toward picture books, my mother pushes me to start reading more advanced chapter books. "Just the words themselves should be enough," she says. "If you can't think up the image on your own, then that's a failure of imagination."

This is how I come across *Iron & Silk,* recommended by a librarian as an adult book that's easy to read. It's a memoir by Mark Salzman, a wushu enthusiast who was among the first wave of Americans accepted into China in the early nineteen-eighties. He travelled to Changsha and taught English at the Hunan Medical College.

Salzman recounts how, during one lesson, he asked the students to read aloud their essays on the topic of "My Happiest Moment." The class consisted of middle-aged teachers brushing up on English. The last to read was Teacher Zhu, who wrote about attending a banquet dinner in Beijing years before. "First we ate cold dishes," he read, "such as marinated pig stomach and sea slugs. Then we had steamed fish, then at last the duck arrived! The skin was brown and crisp and shiny, in my mouth it was like clouds disappearing." He recounted other courses of the Peking-duck dinner: the duck skin in pancakes with sauce and scallions, the meat with vegetables, the duck-bone soup and fruits.

At the end of his reading, Teacher Zhu set down his essay and confessed to Salzman that he had never experienced this. It's someone else's memory, he said. "My wife went to Beijing and had this duck. But she often tells me about it again and again, and I think, even though I was not there, it is my happiest moment."

I've never had Peking duck, but it was once a near-iconographic image. In a past life in Fuzhou, it represented some reality other than the one of daily congee and pickled turnips, cabbage and boiled-rib soup. On TV in the evenings, I saw it in soap operas set among the wealthy, in commercials filmed in Hong Kong. After I moved to the U.S., however, I forgot about it. Flipping through picture books, sometimes I conflate Peking duck with similar-looking things: a turkey in a story about the origins of Thanksgiving, the roast chicken that's part of a hallucinatory dinner that appears to the little match girl, foods she's fantasized about but never tasted.

2.

It's winter when I move to the U.S., where my parents have been living for the past few years. In the airport after we deplane, a woman lunges at me with so much excitement that I draw back toward my grandfather, my escort on the trip. The sliding doors close between us just as I recognize her, faintly, as my mother. I'm seven, and have not had a mother for two years. But I have had a grandma, whose hands, ruddy fingers inlaid with gold and jade rings, patted me reassuringly before I fell asleep at night. Next to her warm, snoring body, I drowsed on a bed overlaid with bamboo mats that kept us cool in the subtropical heat. When it got even hotter, my grandma hung bedsheets all across the concrete balcony to block out the sun.

It's December, possibly, off the top of my memory, when I arrive. There are sensations that exist for me only in English, many associated with winter, that I experience for the first time when I move to Utah. There is the sensation of walking underneath pine trees, of wearing a too big puffy coat, of destroying the clean surface of snow after first snowfall, of buying discounted items in a white-tiled Osco Drug redolent of harsh detergents, the scent of which I will always associate with being poor; overcompensatory cleanliness. The sensation of my mother dragging a wet towel across my face to wipe off dried congee, and the sensation of wet skin drying in the stiff, cold air outside. We live in a one-bedroom apartment that is very tidy, but sometimes ants come in through the bathroom. I sleep in the living room, where, at night, I still hear my grandma's phantom snores.

In someone else's home, a two-story mansion nestled in the mountains outside Salt Lake, a VHS cassette of *Bambi* plays on the TV while actual deer come through the backyard, pulling at the garden foliage with their teeth, and we are separated from them only by a sliding glass door.

My mother points outside. *Deer. Tree. Teeth. Eats.*

I repeat the words, then put them in sentence order: *Deer eats tree with teeth.*

The English lessons take place inside the mansion, where my mother is employed as a nanny to a toddler named Brandon. The home, which has a lobby-like foyer and an elevator, is imposing enough that not even Mormon missionaries bother us. Either that, or it's too isolated from anywhere else to be worth the trek. When I first arrive in the U.S., my mother takes me with her to work every day, my father driving us half an hour outside the city before swinging back to campus to resume his grad studies. At the mansion, our days are geared around my learning English. We watch *Sesame Street*, though it's too babyish for me even then, so I can learn the alphabet. I keep a daily journal and write three to five sentences in English every day.

When her charge is napping, my mother goes through ESL workbooks with me at the kitchen table, books she's found at school-supply stores. One question set asks you to come up with the first letters of similar-sounding words. *Mouse, house, blouse. Pill* and *hill. Bell* and *knell. Pail* and . . . She gives me hints. "The letter you feel in your nose," she says, and I understand that she is talking about "n." *Nail. Pail* and *nail.*

When a salesman comes to the door, he has a hard time understanding my mother. She tells him to come back later, when the owners are home, and he takes this as an invitation to come inside, to demonstrate his cleaning sprays. Peering over the railing, I think maybe he's willfully misunderstanding her, hoping it will result in a sale. My mother, noticing that I am spying, tells me to go into the other room.

I'm not sure how my mother teaches me English, when her

facility with the language is hesitant and halting. Unlike my father, she didn't learn English in China, and even after living in the States for years she is not fluent or even proficient. Cashiers at grocery stores stare at her blankly, the Mormon missionaries who show up at our apartment give up trying to convert us, and the sellers at yard sales shake their heads and over-enunciate, saying loudly, "I can't understand you." Despite this, her imperfect, broken English serves as a scaffolding for my own.

The winter that I touch snow for the first time, I also taste ice cream. In the kitchen, we review the fridge and pantry foods in English. My mother names every item, foods I've never heard of: Minute Maid orange-juice concentrate, Yoplait strawberry-banana yogurt, Farley's Dinosaurs Fruit Snacks, Lay's potato chips, Surfer Cooler Capri Sun, Lunchables. I repeat each word after her. They hover in a vacuum, with no Chinese correlation. And we're not allowed to eat anything, so I can't associate word with taste.

There is, however, *bing ji ling,* which up until this point I have seen only on TV. My mother sneaks me some from a rectangular paper carton. Breyers French Vanilla. It's denser and sweeter than I expected, eggy in flavor, fuzzy with freezer burn. To my surprise, I don't like it at all and feel nauseated by its smell. But I have to like it, because I saw ice cream on TV back home, where all my friends and I fantasized about how wonderful it must taste.

Ice cream is my favorite food. I write these words in the journal my mother gives me to record my first days in the U.S. English is just a play language to me, the words tethered to their meanings by the loosest, most tenuous connections. So it's easy to lie. I tell the truth in Chinese, I make up stories in English. I don't take it that seriously. When I'm finally enrolled in first grade, I tell classmates that I live in a house with an elevator, with deer in the backyard. It is the language in which I have nothing to lose, even if they don't believe a thing I say.

3.

During one semester of my MFA program, we begin every work-shop with a discussion of a piece from *The Collected Stories of Lydia Davis.* That week's piece is called "Happiest Moment." The work-shop, which takes place every Thursday evening, is held in a building typically reserved for the hotel-management program. The instructor reads aloud the entirety of the story:

> If you ask her what is a favorite story she has written, she will hesitate for a long time and then say it may be this story that she read in a book once: an English-language teacher in China asked his Chinese student to say what was the happiest moment in his life. The student hesitated for a long time. At last he smiled with embarrassment and said that his wife had once gone to Beijing and eaten duck there, and she often told him about it, and he would have to say the happiest moment of his life was her trip, and the eating of the duck.

The instructor looks at the class, eight students scattered around a conference table in a fluorescently lit seminar room. "So, what do we think?"

We talk about the way the story frames and reframes an anecdote. Thom, whom everyone calls "the plot Nazi," likens this device to a game of telephone, where the story is transmitted from person to person. "The wife tells her husband the story about eating Peking duck, the husband shares the story with the teacher, laying claim to it as his own happiness, the teacher writes a book incorporating this story. And then, in this piece, the writer describes what she read in a book, which is recounted by the narrator. It's being reframed once again."

We talk about the reframing and what we think the writer is trying to achieve. I tell them about *Iron & Silk*, which contains the same anecdote. "The Lydia Davis story doesn't give credit to the Salzman memoir, but I can't imagine that it *isn't* a reference to that book."

Matthew, the only other Asian student in our program, has read the book, too. He says, "This idea of framing and reframing the same anecdote raises a question: Can the writer, who's retelling another's story, really assume authorship? And, going along those lines, can Mark Salzman assume authorship for his student's story?"

We kick this ball around for a bit—discussing the difference between appropriating someone's story and making it new through retelling—without drawing much of a conclusion. At some point, Allie, the star student, declares, "By writing the story, the writer naturally lays claim to it." To which Matthew responds, "But we know that's just an excuse. Authorial license never justifies appropriation."

In the ensuing silence, the instructor smiles. "Well, these are all great points," she says smoothly. "Since we're running out of time, we need to get started with workshop." She turns to me. "Let's begin with your story."

4.

My workshop story follows a Chinese immigrant nanny through the span of a Friday, when she brings her young daughter to the mansion where she is employed. The piece is written from the nanny's perspective, as she moves through a seemingly ordinary workday, which is interrupted by the arrival of a door-to-door salesman, who persistently tries to sell her cleaning products. The day culminates in her losing her job. Her daughter observes the proceedings.

"Well," the instructor says brightly. "This is a very interesting story. Let's open up discussion. Any thoughts?"

Thom always speaks first. "The way English is rendered in this piece, it's kind of artificial. I mean, the first-person narration reads too smoothly and is too well articulated for a protagonist who's not fluent in English."

Others in workshop echo some of Thom's sentiments about the inherent awkwardness of rendering the experiences of such a character in English, but there's no consensus on how to solve this issue. Someone suggests that it could be written in Chinglish instead, but another student counters that this would play into stereotypes. "Using Chinglish would exaggerate the character's inarticulateness, and flatten her into an immigrant trope."

From the far end of the conference table, Matthew clears his throat. Somehow, I've been waiting for his response. "Whether the story is written in English or Chinglish," he says deliberately, "it's just a tired Asian American subject, these stories about immigrant hardships and, like, intergenerational woes."

I can't look at Matthew. His thesis is a Western novel that, in his words, interrogates white masculinity. The few times we've spoken outside class, he's talked mostly about his summers in Taiwan, which he spends playing basketball with his cousins. He continues,

"It also doesn't help that this is a stereotypical representation of a female Chinese immigrant."

There is an uncomfortable silence. The instructor clears her throat. She says, "For those of us who may not be familiar, can you expand on this stereotype, Matthew?"

I look at him.

"Yeah," he says. "Like, when the salesman invites himself inside, she just goes along with it. She's very passive. It fits into representations of these meek, submissive women we see all the time. It's unrealistic." He doubles down. "It's a kind of Asian *minstrelsy*."

When no one wants to speak, Thom does. "Is this story auto-biographical?"

"The writer isn't allowed to answer during workshop," Allie points out.

There is another lull in the room.

"Well, I found the story *so* interesting," the instructor interjects, forced cheer in her voice. "It shows how differences in cultural assimilation, in English fluency, can alienate this immigrant mother and daughter from each other." Her voice rises. "And then there are these *startling* moments of tenderness . . ."

5.

My mother drinks only water in restaurants; any other drink order is an unnecessary expenditure. Because she is my mother, I do the same and order water, even though she's long ago given up on lecturing me about frugality. A few weeks before my book release, I take her out to a fancy Chinese restaurant, a half-empty banquet hall with roast ducks hanging in the front window. The restaurant is famed for its Peking duck, which is ranked the second best in the world, according to a travel magazine.

When the waiter comes, I order for us in English, the usual dishes. "So, we'll get B16, C7, and F22. To start, we'd like A5 and A11."

My mother sets her menu down, looks at me. "Is that how you order? Like a computer."

"Okay, sounds good." The waiter, a Chinese teenager in Air Force 1s, also answers in English. "I'll get those appetizers out first."

Before the dishes arrive, I give her an advance copy of my book, a story collection with a vaguely Chinese cover image of persimmons in a Ming-dynasty bowl. "It comes out next month."

"So this is the final copy? I'll show your father when I get home." She studies it skeptically, as if it were a lottery ticket that will never yield, frowning at the marketing copy on the jacket flap. "Haven't these stories been published already?"

"Some have. They're just all collected in one book."

"People can just read them for free somewhere else?"

"Have you read any of them already?"

"I looked at the story about the nanny you sent me." She slides the book into her purse. "So, where do you get your ideas?" She asks this in a lightly mocking tone, pretending to be an interviewer.

"For the nanny story? Well, it's obviously based on your job in Salt Lake."

Though we start off speaking English, all conversations with my mother eventually move toward Mandarin, the language in which she is the most agile, firing off insults and embedding her observations with acid subtext. Though I am no longer fluent in Mandarin, I try to accommodate. Her English is awkward and mangled, and it's not easy to move through the world shielded from the unkindness of others by only their thin veneer of liberal respectability.

The teenage waiter returns with the appetizers and the main dishes together, setting down mock-chicken bean curd, lotus root, garlic pea shoots, mapo tofu, and salt-and-pepper smelt sprinkled with tiny diced jalapeños. It all comes out so quickly that I wonder about the quality. Topping off our water, he asks, "Is there anything else I can get you?"

Not bothering to switch back to English, my mother asks for a little side dish of chili bamboo.

"I'm sorry, what?" he says.

"A2," I tell him, and he rushes away. My mother helps herself delicately to a bite of pea shoots, then the smelt. "Do you think the food is good here?" I ask her.

"I like simple food," she says, neither confirming nor denying. Maybe it was ridiculous to come to a restaurant famed for its Peking duck and just order regular dishes. Neither of us likes duck though, with its fatty skin. She pretends to correct herself. "No, no, that's wrong. What I *should* say is: I love it, honey! This is the best."

"But you would never say that."

She smiles her Cheshire-cat grin. "But I don't want to be like the usual Chinese mother, someone who is never satisfied, yells at her children, and keeps saying *ai-yah* all the time."

Now I understand. "Do you think it's you in these stories?"

"There are so many mothers in your stories, what am I supposed to think?" My mother is suddenly indignant. "But they're all so miserable. Does there have to be so much suffering?"

I look down at my plate, a mound of rice covered with gushy mapo. "Well, they're not all about you. I wasn't trying to capture your experience."

"You weren't trying to capture my experience," she repeats, as if to herself. "Then why did you write them?"

I'm surprised by this question. "Well, the nanny story was more based on you, compared with the others. It was about what happened to us when you worked as a nanny. I wanted to show how terrible—"

"But how would you even know what happened? It happened to *me*, not to us. You were too young to understand. And you weren't in the room. I made sure of that."

"I was in the hall, listening. And you told me when I was older. The details were very disturbing."

My mother is smiling incongruously. "But, see, you're not tough. You need to be tough. He was just a silly man. You made him seem almost dangerous."

"He was dangerous, very unpredictable. He was nice one moment, then scary the next. The things he said to you, they were very hurtful."

She sighs a little. "Look, we're not like Americans. We don't need to talk about everything that gives us a negative feeling. I wouldn't move forward if I just kept thinking about it. But I do move forward. I set a good example for you. And you had a great childhood."

I take a sip of water. We've been over this before. There's no point in setting the record straight for the millionth time about my childhood, the school bullying. The worst part was how my mother used to encourage me to lie to her, to pretend how great things were. She would phrase her questions like "You're popular at school, right?" or "You have a lot of friends, right?," priming me to answer the way she wanted. She couldn't not have known that I was lying, but she wanted to bathe in the lies. She needed to believe that I was thriving in the U.S., that my happiness came at the cost of hers, rather than acknowledge the fact that we were both miserable in this country together.

Instead of arguing this time, I simply say, "My therapist says that it is always better to acknowledge reality."

She flinches at my mention of therapy, which, predictably, closes the conversation. As we pick at our food in silence, the TV in the background plays a compilation reel of food-show segments featuring the restaurant. In one clip, the host tells the audience that Peking duck goes as far back as the fourteenth century. He looks at the viewer, breaking the fourth wall. "So remember, when you take a bite of that mouthwatering barbecue, you're eating a piece of history."

The waiter comes back. "How is everything?"

"Great. I think we're actually going to get the rest of this boxed up," I tell him.

My mother turns to him. In Mandarin, she gives elaborate instructions on how she wants the leftovers wrapped so that I can take them home.

He waits for her to finish, then smiles in embarrassment. "I'm sorry, I don't speak Chinese."

6.

I am making lunch for the children when the doorbell rings. Because the house is in a remote area outside Salt Lake, it's unusual that we receive guests. Sometimes I ignore the doorbell, the same way I ignore phone calls to the house. Let people go to the answering machine or leave a note. They're not here to talk to me.

But today I feel restless. I take the elevator down to the large foyer, where I open the door.

"Good afternoon!" It's a man carrying a clipboard and a caddy of cleaning products. "I just have one question. How clean would you say your home is?" He holds up the cleaning spray, and informs me that I can take it today for a one-week trial, and if I like it there's an installment plan for the entire set . . . His enthusiasm makes him speak very quickly and I can't catch everything. "Just try it for a week! And then I can come back in seven days to see what you think."

In his jeans and plaid shirt, he doesn't look like a salesman. His long, dirty-blond hair and goatee aren't well groomed, either. He's looking at me, then past me, at the gleaming, tiled foyer, which amplifies our voices, the elevator leading up to the second floor, the upstairs railing. He's taking everything in.

"No, thank you. I'm not the owner." I smile politely. He hesitates. "So are you the cleaning lady?"

"I work here. I don't clean." I don't feel the need to specify that I'm the nanny, looking after two children, my daughter and a boy named Brandon. "You come back later. The owners come home. Maybe they buy."

"Oh, okay." After a pause, he resumes. "This product works for everyone, though. It can go on all surfaces. Let me show you." He walks past me, into the foyer, and begins cleaning the wooden bench next to the elevator.

I worked for a cleaning company when I first came to the States. During the training, the manager told us trainees to crouch down when we were wiping floors with a rag. And then he looked at us, all these women cleaning on their hands and knees. Why would we not use mops and brooms? I'm not a dog, so I quit.

The man in front of me kneels to polish the legs of the bench, and soon he is on all fours. It's strange that he doesn't at least feel shame in this position, a position he voluntarily assumes. Maybe he wants me to feel sorry for him. "Very nice. It's very good," I tell him. "Maybe we buy later."

He looks up. "They don't sell this in stores, ma'am!" When the elevator comes—did he press the button?—and opens its doors, he walks inside, spraying down the metal handrail, the two-button panel. Unsure of what to do, I step inside with him. There is dirt under his nails, and his clothes carry the smell of gasoline, making me think of farming equipment. The elevator feels very small with two people. He asks, "What are you up to today?"

"It's very busy day. I make lunch now."

"Well, I could use some lunch, too." He smiles at me. When the doors open, he steps out, marvelling at the rest of the home, its view of the valley and the mountains below. It's good that my daughter is not within sight, is in another room. And Brandon, whom the man does not notice, is still sleeping on the sofa.

I follow him, a bit helplessly.

"I haven't eaten all day." He seats himself at the kitchen table, sliding my coupons off so they fall to the floor. It's when he looks at me, a kind of leer on his face, that I finally realize the situation has become unusual. "So, what kind of Chinese food can you cook me?"

"I don't cook Chinese food," I say, somewhat formally.

"Come on, play along." It is his first sign of impatience. "What about moo shu?"

"Mushrooms?" I know what he means.

"No, moo shu. It's a dish. It's listed on all those menus."

"Oh. I don't know." I shake my head.

He is annoyed. "Come on, now. I'm not asking for the real thing. I'm asking for you to play along."

"I don't eat moo shu where I am from in China," I say calmly, and that seems to placate him. Of the two of us, only I can be the expert on this. Before he gets too angry, however, I tell him, "I can make egg and tomato."

He hesitates. "Is that like egg foo young?"

"No, egg and tomatoes. I stir-fry with rice wine and sugar." It is my favorite quick dinner.

"That doesn't sound too good." After a pause, he says, "What about Peking duck?"

"I don't have duck. But how about kung-fu chicken?" I am just making up names.

He hesitates. "Okay," he finally says.

"This is *real* Chinese cooking," I warn him. As for what kung-fu chicken is, I don't know. I wanted to say wushu chicken.

In the fridge, there is a leftover roast chicken. I shred the white meat with my hands, afraid of using a knife and revealing where all the sharp objects might be. I make a soy-oil-sugar marinade, then stir-fry the chicken with some green onions, which I also tear apart into jagged pieces. The result is maybe a terrible stir-fry version of three-cup chicken. What matters is that it passes as Chinese to his taste.

There is a wall phone in the kitchen. I calculate the risk of calling 911, but decide against it. It's too obvious. He'll see me. According to the clock, it is two-forty-five in the afternoon. The parents, who own a Mormon jewelry company, usually get home early on Fridays, around three. All I need to do is distract him for the fifteen or twenty minutes until they return.

"This is good," he says, after taking the first few bites, and I feel sorry for him, that he can't tell that what I've cooked is actually a mess, sprinkled heavily with five-spice from a dusty bottle, using old soy-sauce packets I found in a drawer of takeout menus. I wouldn't serve it to anyone I cared about. And he thinks it's good. I almost wish I had made it better.

Then he puts his arm around my waist, and I stiffen. "This is all I want, you know?"

"You want some tea?" I move beyond his reach.

"I want beer. You got any beer?" Feeling bolder, he gets up and begins to root through the fridge himself. My daughter peeks into the doorway of the kitchen, a little confused. Irritably, I gesture for her to hide herself, and she does.

"I get it for you!" I half scold him, which he seems to like. "Finish the food."

He sits back down. "Yes, ma'am." We are playing house, I realize, the same way my daughter plays it with the Taiwanese boy next door. She brushes the doorway with an imaginary broom and scolds him for tracking dirt into the house. He pretends to watch TV and acts grouchy.

When I place a cold can before the man, he tells me to pour it into a tall glass. As I do this, he tells me earnestly, "I can take you away from here." He points out the window, to an indeterminate spot in the distance. "I live in a cabin, out there in the woods."

Where he's pointing, all I see is a row of snowcapped mountains. I often sit here alone, while the kids are watching TV, and look out the triangular window, built to align with the roof. It is my favorite part of the house, with a view of the sunset in the late afternoons. I can estimate the time of day by the way the light looks. Sometimes I think the landscape of Utah is the most beautiful I have ever seen. This view may be the only thing that anchors me to this job, to this new life my husband insists on pursuing.

The man says, in a voice low and wistful, "Do you want to come with me?"

"I will think about it," I say, as if deciding whether to buy his cleaning sprays. I feel more afraid than I sound. "I'm very busy. People rely on me." It's all so logical. I stop short of filling in the details. That my husband is a PhD student in math, in his second year. That he is paid a small stipend. Until he graduates, I work to help support the family. I went through a string of jobs before landing at this one, the most leisurely one, the one that feels like passing time more than all the others. I am almost thirty-five years old.

"Oh. That's a pity." He looks down at his beer. His voice changes. "But I'm going to be honest. When people see you, they can tell you don't belong here." He rushes into his next sentence. "Now, I'm not trying to offend you, and you know how you're different, the way you look and talk. You're obviously not from here."

"Hmm." I pretend to consider this.

He taps on the window, indicating his home in the distance. "But where I live, it's far away from anyone. And I'm completely self-sufficient, you'll see. I have a water pump, I have my own electricity. There's no one around to judge me." He turns to me. "So, do you think you'll reconsider?"

"I don't think so."

"Well, why the hell not?" His agitation is a little splash of hot oil.

"Do you know what I used to do in China?" I say, looking out the window. Not at anything in particular, the trees and the mountains and the road winding through them, carrying, in the distance, the mother's car, painted a shiny beige shade that I think of as champagne. She will be home soon.

Maybe it's because of the sight of that car, knowing that someone is coming, that I tell this man more than I would normally, more than I've ever told my employers. How, in another life, I worked at an accounting firm, where I managed the accounts of the mayor and other prominent local officials. There weren't as many high-rise buildings in the city then, but our office was in one of them, and we worked on an upper level. I made more money than my husband, whom I was only dating at the time. For two years, he wrote me long letters, revealing a passion I barely glimpsed from him in person. During reeducation, he, along with both my sisters, was sent out into the countryside to work. Hard labor, manual labor. I saw their hands when they returned. But not me. I stayed in the city because of my job, which was deemed crucial to the Party. I stayed in the city and looked after my parents. Sometimes it felt as if I were the only young adult who lived there. I liked that time very much, when everything else—marriage, children—was something that had been planned but nothing I had to think about in the day-to-day. I liked knowing that my life was following a track without having to accept responsibility for it.

When I'm done, I turn away from the window. Who knows how

much he even understood of what I've said? I can't communicate the complicated things in this language.

"So, are you a Communist?" he asks, looking at me curiously.

I know there's no answer except no. "No."

"Good, because we don't like Communists in this country. You know what we do with them?" I can't tell if he's joking. I've always thought those old American movies about the Cold War were just movies. He stands up, his face a scowl. "Do you know what we do with Communists?"

I don't say anything. It is the first time I feel afraid. I look past him, and I see my daughter standing in the doorway again. I am filled, suddenly, irrevocably, with anger. "Get out of here," I tell her in Chinese. "Go, go into the other room." When she doesn't move, I raise my voice to a scream. "Get out!" I yell, and she rushes away.

The sound of the garage door opening fills the room.

When my daughter first came to the States, she would insist that I tell her a bedtime story every night before sleep. This was a tradition her grandma established when she lived in China without me. So I tried to make up stories, simple fables with a moral lesson. Except when I got to the end, my mind would go blank. What's the lesson here supposed to be? I would always lose track, thinking she'd be asleep long before the story finished. But she would wait for the conclusion, and if it didn't satisfy her she would ask a lot of questions. She wanted the story to make sense, at a time when my own life didn't make any sense. Shortly after, I began taking her to the library. I would read her picture books instead, and that solved my problem with thinking up endings.

The ending of what happened that day is that, as soon as the salesman hears the garage door opening, he panics. Cursing me, he stands up quickly, the fork and knife dashing off the table. Watching him rush out the door and then downstairs, I think, This is so easy. This problem of this stupid stranger is so easily solved despite all the fear I felt.

Then the wife comes through the garage door. She looks at the messy kitchen, the cutlery that scattered across the floor as he bolted up to leave. I explain everything, relieved. Then she asks me a lot of questions. Questions like: Did you invite him inside? Did he misunderstand, maybe, your English? Why didn't you ask him to leave? Did you offer him food? When he forced you to cook food for him, why didn't you just say no? Why is there beer open in the kitchen? Did he also force you to give him a beer? What made you afraid of him? Did he have a weapon on him? How did the food get all over the place?

I'm answering her as well as I can, but in the middle of my answers she interrupts with another question. And so my English falters, becomes distracted and nervous. When she can't fully understand my responses, she looks over at my daughter, who is only too eager to translate.

My husband, who has arrived to pick us up, watches intently from the kitchen doorway.

The mother says, more to herself, "I have to figure out what to do."

"What about calling the police?" my husband suggests.

"Well, it's tricky, given the arrangement we have worked out . . ." She trails off.

"We're legal U.S. residents," he says, thinking that he's clarifying.

But I know what she's referring to. Even though we have our green cards, I'm not their legal employee, and they pay me under the table. "Let me talk it over with Dave when he gets home," she finally says. "He should be getting back any minute." She glances at the clock, then at me. Indicating the mess in the kitchen, she asks, "Well, can you clean this up now? Then you can go."

"No." It's a reflex, how quickly I say this.

"What do you mean?" She's looking at me. Does she really think I'm going to drop everything to clean her kitchen? While my husband and daughter look on?

"She wants you to clean up, Mom," my daughter says in Chinese. She thinks I can't understand.

I look at my husband. I want him to intervene, to defend me. He opens his mouth, then closes it, unsure. He is an agreeable person, but his problem is that he wants to please everyone. That's how you survive here, he told me. But just because he wants to live in this country doesn't mean I have to eat shit.

She purses her lips. "But that's your job."

"No. I take care of Brandon." All the times that I've wiped down the countertops, the stove, the inside of the microwave at their request—I have tried to be a good employee, going above and beyond, but cleaning is not actually part of my job. They pay me less than what a trained nanny would cost, what a maid would cost.

She doesn't say anything for a moment. "Someone has to clean up. And I didn't make this mess," she says.

I don't say anything.

"I'll do it," my daughter announces, grabbing the paper towels. I yank her arm back, and she yells in pain.

"Maybe you can talk about it on Monday," my husband proposes.

"Bye, Brandon," I tell the boy as he squeezes his warm body against mine. I give him a little hug. I am not coming back on Monday, I decide. Maybe that will turn out to be a lie, but it's a lie I need in this moment. Without looking at anyone, I go out the front door and sit in the passenger seat of the car, waiting.

It is several minutes before my husband and my daughter come to the driveway. "You shouldn't have done that," he says, grimacing as he gets into the driver's seat and starts the engine. We drive downhill. My daughter chimes in from the back seat, "Brandon's mom is very nice, Mom. She just wants to know what happened."

In the rearview mirror, I study my daughter. When I first learned that I was having a daughter, everyone in the family was so disappointed. In China, a boy is always better, if you're going to have one child. But me, I was secretly happy. A boy, at best, can adore his mother, but a girl can understand her. When the doctor told me it was a girl, I thought, Now I will be understood. That was my happiest moment. The idea of a daughter.

"Don't talk to me about things you don't understand," I tell her now.

She blinks, doesn't say anything. She makes herself very quiet, as she should, and gazes out the window. Good, I think. Don't look at me.

As if by instinct, she looks up. Our eyes meet in the mirror. Then she looks away.

MANUEL MUÑOZ

Compromisos

FROM *Electric Literature*

MAURICIO WOULD STOP and buy the oranges on his way back into town. He would need them as a treat for his young daughter, Rocío. She had the unfortunate gift of sensing unease in a silent room and he had to appease her. Last August, right at the start of third grade, he was sent to pick her up from school and Rocío noticed the stricken look on his face as he drove. She had seen it, but not understood it. At home, his daughter could hear how angry and hurt her mother was, but she understood only that it meant Mauricio would not stay at the house any longer, that her father would come only every few days. Even now, deep into January, Mauricio didn't know exactly what Alba had told the kids. Their older son, Alonso, was in high school with his own troubles, and if he missed having Mauricio around, he never let on. Rocío was different. Since December, Mauricio had had restless nights, sitting up in the thin bed of the one-room he was renting in Kingsburg, one town over. The hours got later and later, closer and closer to dawn, and he couldn't shake the sense that he had made a terrible mistake. The restlessness had decided for him. He would have to come back. He would have to ask forgiveness.

On the morning he decided to ask Alba to let him back, the January fog had not lifted, and he had to wait, along with everyone, for the density to break. The Saturday traffic was slow and heavy and impatient, people late for their second-job shifts, their errands. On days like this, he knew, no one would have time to stop for the old Mexican woman who sold the smallest of the winter oranges from under a white tent at one of the rural intersections outside of town. She would stand near the edge of the road some-times, waving for customers to come, which they did out of pity or loyalty. "Mírala," Alba used to say, before they had kids, on their way to spend the day walking the Fulton Mall in Fresno. "That's going to be me one day," she said, "when it's all over."

"She's somebody's mother," Mauricio would say, which was the kind of thing they said to each other as a private reminder to be kind to those around them. This is why Alba had married him, he knew, why they had started dating in the first place. Alba had sensed in him that same dutiful nature that made her the respon-sible one of three girls in her family, just as pretty as her chola sisters, who lived for cruising Mooney Boulevard in Visalia, their mother always yelling at them. He knew what it meant, even way back then when they were in high school and had only coins in their pockets, to pull over at the white tent and buy the old woman's last bag of summer fruit.

This morning, though, the old woman wasn't there. When Mau-ricio pulled to the side of the road, the figure rising from behind the stand was a young man in a black jacket, reaching for a paper bag in anticipation. "¿Cuántas?" the young man asked, even before Mauricio reached the stand—not unkindly, but it was clear he already wanted to be done with the slow morning. The oranges were small and hail-scarred and the two crates were near full. "Media docena," Mauricio answered and he watched the young man count out six oranges for him, pushing past the ones that didn't look bright or plump enough. He saw, at the foot of the young man's chair, a plastic bucket with pink carnations.

"¿Se venden?" he asked, pointing at the flowers. It was too early in the year for flowers, but the nurseries must have started sending them out for the high school fundraisers. He could pic-ture the cheerleaders at the basketball games with handfuls of them, the boys saving their money because this was how to show love. The more you gave, the more it mattered.

The young man raised the bucket to the table and shuffled the stems, the pink carnations already a little limp. "¿Para su señora?" he asked. He had a handsome face, now that Mauricio could study it closely, distracted as the young man was in handling the flowers, clean-shaven, his cheeks a little rough and ashy from the chill of being outside. He counted a half dozen as if he had already de-cided for Mauricio, his hand on another stem, hopeful.

"Sí," Mauricio said, but he was responding to the young man's face, the young man's insistence, a decision made for him without him even agreeing, as decisions had always been. Hadn't it been that way in dating Alba in high school, a pairing that sometimes felt like it had been willed by everyone else around them? Hadn't it been that way with Pico, the man from the beginning of summer, who did nothing but ask Mauricio questions undercut with gentle urging. "¿Un trago?" Pico had asked him. "Anda . . . un trago," he decided for him, just one drink, from behind the counter at the Woolworth's on Fulton Mall, handing Mauricio his purchase without ever having asked, like this young man had, if it was for his señora. Pico hadn't cared. Pico had probably seen his wedding band, but hadn't bothered to look at it again, his eyes locked on Mauricio the moment he had entered the store.

"¿Algo más?" The young man slid the bag of oranges across the table, along with the flowers, and this time he did sound unkind, aware of how Mauricio had been studying him and how much he didn't appreciate it. Mauricio shook his head and the young man quoted him the price—Mauricio knew it was too much, but he couldn't refuse now, not with the way the young man stared at him. He fumbled the money across the table, realizing only when he started toward the car that he had forgotten his change. He felt himself rush to the car, turning hurriedly toward town but seeing the young man out of the corner of his eye, one last time, hands back in his pockets.

"¿Algo más?" Pico had asked the same thing at the Woolworth's, but Mauricio had heard it differently then. It wasn't meant to rush him along, but to draw him forward. Maybe this lotion, Pico suggested, never once saying it was for any señora. The Woolworth's cosmetics counter was hardly more than a single case with nothing expensive in it, but Pico had come from behind it just the same to show some things to the man who had wandered in from the open walkways of the Fulton Mall. Men walked past the windows all day and Pico must have known how to spot the ones like Mauricio, and he knew how to speak to them in Spanish, the better to suggest something that was already understood. "Anda," Pico had urged, and Mauricio only resisted the invitation by staying in front of the counter, a dumb smile on his face. He had waited for Pico to clock out at five and they walked on the shaded side of the Fulton Mall. Even for late May, it was already scorching. People lingered on the benches and the edges of the central fountain, cooling off. Their eyes followed Pico. Out in the sunlight, Mauricio could see that Pico's hair was brassy from a dye job. He could complete the picture that the eyes all around them were forming—one boyfriend picking up the other after work, Woolworth's badge dangling from the fingers of the younger one, a small gift tucked under the arm of the other. A drink didn't seem right anymore.

"Come," Mauricio ordered, turning west when they hit the edge of the mall and they walked by the Canada shoe store and the Mexican record shop to the Crest cinema on the corner. "The movie's already started," the young woman in the booth said, looking at both of them for a moment before sliding the tickets through the mousehole. The lobby was empty by then, the carpet muffling everything except the bubbling juice fountain and the hum of the air-conditioning. Mauricio felt more at ease and they made their way past the closed double doors in the theater, where, eyes adjusting to the sudden darkness, he felt Pico's small hand reach out for his in the dark as they sought out seats in the back. He couldn't tell how many people were in the theater—not many though, and so he let Pico's hand remain in his, too soft to the touch and damp from the walk outside. It was a loud comedy, a Mexican pratfaller whose name he couldn't remember, and in the clatter of overturned restaurant tables and policemen slipping into muddy street puddles and a loudmouth kid who made the dark theater choke with laughter, Mauricio felt Pico's hand reach over to his belt buckle, his fingers unzipping his pants and slipping inside. Did it matter if the dark theater could hear the squeak of the vinyl seats, the Woolworth's bag crinkling? At first, Mauricio thought it did—it did matter—two men who walked into a theater in the middle of the day, one of them with brassy, dyed hair, the other one older and who should know better. But then it didn't matter, and the hinges of his chair creaked as he spread his legs and let Pico do what he wanted. When Pico felt him start to come, he gripped Mauricio harder and let out a little laugh of triumph, a giggle almost. Mauricio moved to get Pico's hand out of his pants, afraid someone would finally turn around to see them, but Pico held firm, drawing his fingers around the stickiness and grinning at him. Nothing was funny on the screen, but it didn't matter. That's how life was, Mauricio thought, the things that brought some people to laughter.

Pico sent him home after that, a mess in his pants even after he went into the theater bathroom and wiped himself clean. He knew he'd see Pico again. Or try to. The summer went on like that, the drives to Fresno longer and longer, and Alba, he knew, reluctant to ask him questions, her back turned to him at night with a deep sigh. What did it matter? he kept asking himself. He had one answer in his children. "I'm somebody's father," he said aloud to himself, in the darkness of his one-room in Kingsburg, trying to remind himself of parental pride, the joy in children that everyone claimed, but he couldn't feel it deep down. He would never say so. Some things shouldn't be asked. He could sense a better question in Pico, a truer answer at a back table at La Fiesta, where the bartender warmly poured them drinks and left them alone in the dark shadow of the nearly empty bar. "No, no, no," Pico had said, when Mauricio dared to let slip what he had been thinking about. Mauricio had it all wrong. "You already made your bed," Pico told him. "I'm not asking you to leave anybody."

Pico didn't mention it again, but he had been firm enough, and it reminded Mauricio that he had, in fact, made a decision a long time ago. It had been a bad one, he knew now. To think that marriage could settle him into the calm he knew he needed, that it would help him rise over his own dishonesty. He didn't have the courage to ask Pico if it was his marriage or the children that he saw as an uncrossable line. He knew Pico would never offer more than drinks at a back table at La Fiesta. He could listen to Pico talk about the night classes he was scheduled to take at the community college during the summer session or the trip that he was saving for to visit his mother in Los Mochis, right on the coast in Sinaloa. But they were Pico's plans, only his. He didn't talk about them in a way that invited Mauricio to even imagine about sharing in them.

So he knew, then, that he didn't have anywhere else to go. As he approached the house, he saw Alba spot the car from the living room window, perplexed to see him driving up on a Saturday morning. He watched her silhouette move into the kitchen to greet him from the side door of the house—she didn't like him using the front door anymore, where the kids would know immediately that he had arrived. At the side door, she could speak low to him if things turned harsh, or block him out entirely if an argument threatened to erupt. She could study his manner, the look on his face, and figure out if she was up for anything that took too much effort. She'd grown wary now, when, back in high school, she had been the timid one, clerking at the furniture store on Tulare Street. Mauricio had gotten to know her after he'd been hired part-time for deliveries, going up to the front counter with signed charge slips that she needed to stamp and file away. In those brief encounters, Alba would smile timidly at him, and it was something that he knew what to do with—an interest that he wouldn't have to act on. She was years from knowing the truth about him, years from being able to see through him.

So when he parked the car and saw Alba already standing at the threshold of the side door to the house, he didn't reach for the carnations. He left them sitting on the passenger seat. He took only the bag of oranges, tucking them under his arm as if they were just a newspaper, but he could see Alba's eyes trained on it, judging whether or not he could come into the house. The closer he got, the sharper her look became, her eyes so trained on the bag that he sensed that it was his heart in judgment. She was in no mood to make any guesses, he could tell, so he held the bag out to her, his arms outstretched.

"What's this?" Alba asked, not moving from the threshold, the door behind her as if he were a vacuum salesman.

To answer her simply, with just the one word—Mauricio knew what it sounded like, the thinness of his intentions. So he stood like that, reaching out for the long moment it took Alba to accept the bag, open it, and look inside. She was judging him and maybe she had the right to do so, but as she peered into the bag, he couldn't help but notice that the resentment on her face had no trace of the fact that she, too, had once left the marriage for a small stretch. It had been a surprise, very early on, before the kids. She had taken up with Nepo, who worked for city garbage collection. Nepo had been several years ahead of them in high school, but Mauricio hardly remembered him. That was how big the town was—people measured themselves by the years they did or didn't go to high school and the circles they ran in. Only Nepo's name was memorable to him. Not what Nepo looked like or if he was in a marriage or if he had kids or why Alba had gotten together with him at all. She was gone only two months and she quit Nepo before she could fall in too deep. "Out of respect," Alba had said, "for my vows." She had humbled herself in apology when she said that, hands crossed at the kitchen table, head bowed. And maybe this was why she scowled at Mauricio now for returning on a Saturday morning, blocking the door and his view into the house in case their daughter wandered into the kitchen. Maybe this was why she saw the oranges and knew what he was trying to do.

"Lookit . . ." she said, sounding just like her chola sisters, the ones who had told her from the beginning that he wasn't the man she thought he was. Giggles, one of them went by, and La Troubles, the one who could do nothing but complain. "Lookit," Alba said, "I mean it when I say I just want you to be happy."

She didn't even give him a chance to speak. Maybe it was better that he didn't say aloud what he felt he should say, but knew wasn't true. *If you want me to come back,* he had decided to say, sitting on the edge of his bed at dawn. *For the kids.* Self-sacrifice was deeper than love, he had thought, and maybe Alba would recognize that. Mauricio had felt so sure, but facing Alba now, the door still half-closed behind her, he couldn't explain himself anymore and didn't know what to do.

"You don't need to ruin your life," Pico had told him. "You just need to live it."

From the kitchen, he could hear the footsteps of their young daughter coming into the kitchen, stopping to contemplate who was at the door. Alba closed the door a little tighter behind her.

"Listen," she said, lowering her voice. "Why don't you go pick up Alonso for me? He's rehearsing for a quinceañera right now at the Veterans' Hall."

He nodded at her, knowing not to say anything to alert their daughter to the sound of his voice. Alba slipped behind the door and shut it quickly behind her. He didn't know if she wanted him to simply drop Alonso off, if she wanted to talk things over or not. Maybe it wasn't something to settle in one conversation. The gesture was everything, he decided, a first step at least. He drove over to the Veterans' Hall, where, noticing that no other parents were waiting in their cars, he guessed he had arrived too early. He made his way to the long lobby entrance, where a woman holding a bucket and a damp rag pointed at one of the benches. "It's dry," she said. "It's clean," she said, "if you want to sit down." Mauricio nodded at her and sat down to wait. He could hear the faint footsteps of a group practicing their dance steps in the main room, and the woman continued her patient work of wiping down the scratched, lacquered wood of the benches, of the display cases

with medals and American flags. She moved slowly through the
length of the long lobby, the brick walls faded and chipped, her
hand moving the damp rag in a reverent circle over the bronze
plaques and the framed pictures of all the hometown boys who
had come and gone. She was a widow—she had to be, Mauricio
decided, of someone in one of the black-and-white pictures on the
wall—for her to dutifully clean what no one ever really noticed.
A trace of Pine-Sol lingered in the air and it reminded him of the
faint smell of the back of La Fiesta, the bar dark and secret, but
here the lobby was filled with winter light. Something was amiss,
Mauricio thought, and it took a moment for him to realize it was
the sound of the dance steps, the faint offbeat of someone out of
sync.

He rose from the bench and peered through the skinny window
in the door leading to the main room. There was Alonso, in a pink
vest and bow tie, the girls in wide, full ball gowns. Like the rest of
the boys, he was having trouble maneuvering the dance steps with
all of that fabric.

"The main girl's not even there." The cleaning woman had
joined him at the door, peering through the glass. "Which one is
yours?"

"The tall skinny boy," he said. He could see what girls liked
about Alonso, his height wobbling him, his head a little too big
and his shoulders too narrow, but steady somehow, sure of himself.

"Ah," said the cleaning woman. "He looks like you." They
watched the group move through the routine, Alonso the only boy
to get the dance steps correct that time. "He's good," she said.
"He's got a right and left."

"You know what time their rehearsal is over?"

"Soon," she said. "They've been at it for a while. And you know
teenagers can't do anything for very long if they get bored." She
turned back to her cleaning and, not long after, disappeared
from the lobby altogether. Mauricio watched the group rehearse,
Alonso focused enough to not notice that he was being watched
by his father. Mauricio returned to the bench to wait. He could
hear the footsteps echo in the lobby, now that he had nothing else
to focus on, and he could hear the lack of unison. He thought
he could almost hear the sighs of frustration as they had to work
through it one more time.

At the entrance, two girls walked into the lobby. One girl wore a long denim skirt—a church girl—and she held open the door long enough for her friend to maneuver a stroller inside. They walked past Mauricio, close enough for him to see the baby inside the stroller, kept warm by a lime-green blanket. The girls beelined to the skinny window. The girl in the long skirt held her gaze the longest, the other already bored. "He looks so cute in pink," Mauricio heard the girl in the long skirt mutter. He wondered for a moment if she could be talking about Alonso, but something told him that he wouldn't go for a girl in a long skirt. Alonso wouldn't go for someone dutiful. He was smart enough to know why his parents had split up.

The girl with the baby took a quick look through the window. "What a dumb color," she said, and returned to fuss with the baby, who made little noises of contentment from her attention. It brought an involuntary smile to Mauricio's face—he could feel it form as he watched the girl tuck the lime-green blanket tighter around her baby. "Qué vida," he remembered Pico saying, after Pico had asked him if he liked having kids, "not that I'd ever want them myself." The girl happened to glance up at Mauricio and met his eyes with a flash that reminded him of how the young man with the oranges had looked at him. She turned her back to him. "Let's go," she said to her friend.

"They're almost finished," her friend said, her hand clutching at her long skirt. "I just want him to talk to me again."

"He's done with you," the stroller girl said. "Don't you get it?" She said it with such authority, such knowingness, and she pushed the stroller toward the lobby entrance so that her friend could see that she was serious. The girl in the long skirt turned to watch her go, clearly torn by the dancers not yet finishing and her friend already at the exit. She finally pulled herself away and followed her friend. Mauricio caught her eye briefly and was surprised to see her eyes welling up in tears. She seemed ashamed of herself and he wanted to tell her that there was nothing to regret for feeling however she was feeling. But it wasn't his place to do so. He wasn't her father.

When the dancing stopped, the teenagers started to file out. The girls all held the bells of their gowns as they made their way through the lobby, the boys wandering outside one by one, no one to answer to. Mauricio couldn't decide which of them had been the object of that girl's affection, which one could have been worth so much pining. All of the boys wore the same pink vest and bow tie, but the formality couldn't hide that this one was chubby, that one dull and bored looking. Alonso was last to step out. Scanning the lobby, he seemed surprised to see Mauricio there. Alonso fixed his eyes on him, trying to hide that he had been waiting for someone.

"Hey, Dad," he said. "What are you doing here?"

"Your mom sent me to pick you up."

"Oh, uh . . ." Now Alonso looked again at the bustle of the lobby, at the girls milling in and out of the bathroom, tied up in the drama of not getting their gowns dirty. "I was going to hang out with some friends, actually."

Mauricio lowered his voice a bit. "I know, but . . . right now, what your mom says, goes."

If Alonso had thought about protesting this, his face didn't show it. He started toward the lobby doors, not in any hurry, or with the impatient distance that he sometimes had when the entire family was together in public places. He kept pace with Mauricio, nodding his chin at a couple of friends who didn't stop to chat with him when they saw he was with his father now, and they made their way out to the parking lot.

Not too far away from the entrance, the two girls stood waiting, and when the girl in the long skirt spotted Alonso, Mauricio knew then that his son was the one she had been waiting for. Alonso didn't acknowledge her, but he quickened his pace to the car. Mauricio could tell that this was something he didn't want to share. It amazed him how transparent teenagers could be in their feelings. Everything was written in Alonso's suddenly hunched shoulders, as if he was trying to lower his height, make himself small and unnoticeable. It was so easy to detect. But wasn't it always so easy to spot someone pulled helplessly along by who they really were? He could still see the faces of Alba's chola sisters all those years ago, Giggles and La Troubles, sitting in the back of a Buick Skylark. The two older guys sitting up front. Mauricio had been unloading heavy boxes in front of the furniture store when the Skylark slowed down, as if the guys had wanted to give the girls a look at him, make him aware of just how big his arms had gotten from all the lifting. The chola sisters looked him over, their eyes telling him that all that muscle was wasted on a boy like him. The guys in the front seat of the Skylark laughed as they sped away. They left Mauricio standing with the weight of everything suddenly so overwhelming and sharp that he had to set his box down and wipe his brow. They saw through his look of deep concentration, of focusing on the job at hand, his single-mindedness. They detected his avoidance, his studied endurance nothing more than the look of someone with too much to bear.

In the car, Alonso moved the carnations from the passenger seat so he could sit, but once they were in his hand, he regarded them closely. "Who are these for?" he asked, hesitating, as if maybe he wondered for a moment if the flowers could be for someone besides his mother.

"Those . . ." Mauricio sighed. "Well, your mother doesn't really like carnations."

"Does this mean you're coming home?" Alonso blurted out.

Mauricio started the car, but other parents had arrived in the parking lot now, so they would have to wait their turn to get out. "One step at a time," Mauricio said. "Maybe," he said. "I don't know."

He turned to see if the girls were still hanging about and they were, slowly making their way to the opposite end of the parking lot, the girl in the long skirt looking directly at their car. It wasn't any of his business, but he was Alonso's father. "Is that your girlfriend?" he asked. "Why don't you give her those flowers?"

Alonso laughed. "Stupid shit," he said, and he sounded like what Mauricio imagined those two guys driving the Skylark would have sounded like, crude and ready to make fun of everything. But as Mauricio started to turn out of the lot, Alonso said, "Okay, yeah . . . let me," pointing at the girls, and Mauricio pulled over a bit to let the other cars pass. Alonso bounded out with the carnations in his hand and when he got to the girls, sure enough he offered them to the one in the long skirt. Whatever was between them, Mauricio could see it from across the distance of the parking lot, something innocent that he envied. If innocent was the word. What was the word for it? He rested both hands on the steering wheel, patient as he watched Alonso hand over the carnations, the girl in the long skirt reaching up to receive them, her face crumbling into joy. Compromiso, he thought. He remembered. What Pico said when he told him he was in love. "Impossible," Pico had said. "You can't fall in love with someone with too many obligations.

A few, yes, because we all have some. But if you have too many, love is impossible."

Someone behind him honked impatiently but Mauricio waved them to go around. He was watching Alonso speak to the girl in the long skirt, nothing to hide anymore. It was so easy and clear to see, the way the two guys driving the Skylark had seen him, the way Giggles and La Troubles had laughed. The way Pico had spotted him at the counter of the Woolworth's from the moment he had walked in. The young woman in the Crest movie booth, handing over the tickets. The bartender at La Fiesta who always gave them a free round, no questions asked. The young man with the oranges, suddenly aware that he was being looked at. Alba at the door just a while ago, staring him plain in the face. Or Alba, really, from the very beginning, looking up from the delivery receipts and ignoring everything her chola sisters warned her about. How life could have been so different if he had been a little braver about what he was feeling. He felt for the girl pushing the stroller, bending down to her compromiso, then rising up again to see if the conversation had finished. Not yet. And so she nudged the stroller just a bit, back and forth, back and forth, waiting and waiting, though Mauricio understood it was already too late.

JOANNA PEARSON

Grand Mal

FROM *The Kenyon Review*

MY FRESHMAN ROOMMATE, Karlie, claimed that if you were being attacked, you had to throw a fit: fall to the ground, froth at the mouth, growl, fling your arms, spout gibberish. She demonstrated vividly, and with an ease that suggested she'd previously employed such a tactic successfully. She looked like a Holy Roller, someone in the grip of ecstatic revelation—nothing like an actual epileptic. I knew because my father suffered from epilepsy. But an attacker would hardly know the difference, Karlie promised. The exact details wouldn't matter. So go bananas with it. Vomit, if you're able. Let your eyes roll back in your head. The attacker would be so startled, so wary of whatever dread affliction or malevolent spirit had seized you, that he'd scamper off, harmless, into the shadows.

In another of the most vivid memories I have of Karlie, she's presiding over a group of our dormmates, passing out piping-hot break-and-bake cookies straight from the toaster oven along with hand-annotated chapter summaries printed from a book called *I Kissed Dating Goodbye*. The girls, glossy-haired and chirruping like a cluster of morning songbirds, sit cross-legged atop her loft bed, sprawled across her lavender comforter. They perch on my desk, straddle my desk chair. Cooing abundantly, they fill the room with soft exhalations and murmurs of assent. Their sweet breath combines with the scent of fresh-baked cookies, mango body lotion, and tropical fruit hair conditioner to turn the air madly, clashingly fragrant, like that in a fine ladies' boutique. Karlie, her very name like a filigreed pink greeting card, is leading a small group derived from a large, all-campus evangelical organization. She has a way of noticing the friendless and ushering them toward her, cultivating some secret specialness they each possess until it blooms. Already, at age eighteen, she holds herself with an unflappable maternal authority. Even then, as it's happening, this is a scene on which I can gaze but never truly enter, stuck outside, Little Match Girl–style, my fingers icy against the metaphorical glass of a specific sort of faith, or lack thereof, that blocks true access. I have a chemistry exam looming. I am the sort of girl who takes looming chemistry exams seriously. There is no space for me—my seriousness, my worldly anxieties—here, in my own blessèd dorm room. I must trudge back to the library, but not before my roommate pauses and smiles. Karlie knows my type and pities me, handing me a cookie for my troubles. Even in this dismissal, she glows with a sanctified warmth. Everyone is a bit more radiant in Karlie's presence, and I am not immune.

This moment occurred, of course, before Karlie went through a phase of rebellion—a personal rumspringa during which she discovered drinking and the fact that *blow job* did not mean blowing gently against the nether regions of a person you love. Those were the innocent early days, when she still used terms like *front bottom* instead of *vagina* and collected lip balms flavored like pineapple soda and endorsed books that argued godly young women should refrain from kissing anyone until their wedding day. Submission to the right sort of authority, Karlie told me, was glorious. Liberating, even. It was a doublespeak so calm, so self-assured, that I envied her certitude.

Despite all this, Karlie possessed a brutal practicality. While her providential faith armed her with untroubled optimism in many respects—God would guide her through that Spanish quiz she hadn't studied for!—she had an array of strategies when it came to certain exigencies. She was a collector of tips gleaned from Oprah, ways to jab a pickpocket in the throat or how to escape from a trunk in the event of a carjacking. She could change a flat in the time it took AAA to show up; she could remove a stain from white linen with her own spit. God would nod approvingly. She was prepared: pink Mace, a dainty purse-sized first aid kit, double-sided tape to secure a bra strap, emergency tampons, granola bars, a Swiss Army knife.

Not three years after we met, Karlie was dead.

It happened during the latter days of Karlie's apostasy, when she'd reportedly started to consider a return to the fold as prodigal daughter. Her story would have made for an excellent faith journey, real road-to-Damascus stuff for the fresh converts. But that night, she'd gone out drinking. It was the end of winter break, early January, most students yet to return to town. According to those who'd accompanied her, Karlie had stayed out until the wee hours. When no one heard from her over the next two days, a friend finally went to check her off-campus apartment. She found Karlie's body right there on the living room floor. Violated. Murdered. The apartment showed no signs of forced entry. It appeared she'd invited the killer, whoever he was, into her home—welcomed him, even. The story of her murder was covered salaciously by reporters for months.

We were no longer close at that point, but my friends knew that Karlie had been my freshman roommate—that she'd left me little prayer notes and Easter baskets and had generally treated me with all the love and attention a kindergarten teacher might bestow upon a reluctant student. During her time in the wilderness, I'd met up with Karlie once or twice for a drink, leaving at the point when she began to get flirty with whichever frat boy happened to be standing nearby. Her business, I figured. Whichever version of her I got, who was I—lonely and awkward, still overcoming the stutter that had plagued me throughout my childhood—to judge?

"She was magnetic," I told my friend Sari. We were studying together in the stacks not long after Karlie's death. "She wasn't supposed to end up like this. She didn't deserve it." Even though I hadn't bought into everything Karlie believed, I still thought of her as fundamentally *good*—a genuinely devout person, someone merely trying on wildness for size.

Sari made a little sucking sound through her teeth and looked hard at me. We knew better, of course. *I* knew better, or should have. Nobody deserved to end up murdered. It wasn't right to turn Karlie into an old-fashioned morality tale, an innocent led astray. But it was also hard not to fall back on old habits, not to provide myself reassurance, to seek out the fatal flaw and correct for it myself with numerous precautions. Never be a woman out alone, in the dark, after drinks. Never invite the enemy in. Punishments abounded.

I thought of Karlie's trick. I wondered if she'd even had the chance to try it: a practiced series of convulsions while she uncapped her Mace. I told Sari about this, but she just shook her head. We volunteered for an intimate partner violence support line; we were minoring in women's studies. We were already practicing our world-weariness. We thought we knew things.

"Come on, Joy," Sari said. "You know it doesn't work that way. I mean, I could argue that the safest thing for all of us would be just to rid the world of men. But you wouldn't want that, would you."

She wasn't really asking a question. Face burning, I turned away. Sari had recently learned about my sociology professor and me—it was a thing that was not a thing, not really. And it was over now, besides. But it had been *something*, this non-thing that we both instinctively kept hidden. I was still consumed by it; I thought about it all the time. Him, my professor. Professor Hendrix. Sari did not approve. Now, cheeks still hot, a queasy feeling overtaking my insides, I thought of my roommate. Had I somehow invited this trouble? Had I unleashed it upon her? An unwitting snake with an apple? Only I'd wanted to taste the apple too. I'd wanted to gobble the whole thing.

Sari and I didn't speak of Karlie again. Long after graduation, Sari and I have remained in contact, trading emails now and then. She's an ACLU attorney who works with Title IX complaints, a dedicated person who lives by her principles. I'm a person who has, admittedly, dined out a few times on the story of my roommate's death. Everyone's interested in murder as long as it doesn't touch them. The story makes for rapt listeners, granting me the weirdly exalted status of the true-crime-adjacent, shameful and delicious. I always whisper an apology afterward, feeling the sordidness of my own soul.

They eventually arrested someone for Karlie's death and charged him: a loner who hung out regularly downtown, picking up odd jobs and panhandling—someone most of us recognized on sight—who, it seemed, had developed an obsession with Karlie. He'd previously been picked up only for minor charges: Peeping Tom antics, public indecency. I watched him on the news footage: shuffling along in shackles, mouth agape like a fish flung ashore, bewildered eyes. He had an intellectual disability and lived with his elderly mother. It troubled me, the whole thing. But life, for the living, went on.

And then, all these years later, a letter arrived. From Karlie.

*

The letter was a sort of time traveler—worn with the years, the envelope written over and crossed out, originally addressed to my college apartment. It had made a long and improbable voyage through time after clearly having been tucked away somewhere and forgotten, found, redirected, forwarded. A miracle. I dared not open it.

The letter hit me at a bad time. I was taking long walks by myself at night, thinking, watching people live their lives behind windows, skittering out of the way of oncoming traffic. I'd been having a lot of trouble sleeping.

Karlie had been on my mind even before I got the letter: I'd recently happened on an article online about the guy who'd written *I Kissed Dating Goodbye*. Now he regretted it. He was divorcing his wife and leaving his pastorship. He'd lost his faith and no longer identified as a Christian. It all seemed too sad to warrant any schadenfreude.

I was getting a divorce myself.

My husband and I had spent the year I approached forty debating whether or not we would try to have a third child—a luxury child, my husband quipped, as if the child were an expensive tennis bracelet. This theoretical child, an indulgence, would be wonderful, but wearying, I conceded. We were already too exhausted to have sex, which seemed a necessary prerequisite to obtaining said luxury child. Plonking ourselves down in front of the television, we'd sometimes touch hands. It was the best we could do. We ultimately decided to forgo the metaphorical tennis bracelet in the name of salvaging our marriage. By then, however, my husband seemed to think there was no longer a marriage worth saving. He'd moved on, peremptorily, it turned out. Without my knowledge and against my will.

You're fundamentally unhappy, my husband said. *It oppresses me.*
I'm not depressed.
I didn't say you were. Fundamentally unhappy. It makes me unhappy too. Your unhappiness makes it hard for me to breathe.

He made unhappiness sound like the core feature of my personality. A suffocating force. The way that I looked at the world, pinched and vigilant, bracing for fire ants, falling branches, and tax deadlines rather than celebrations. But my unhappiness allowed me to get things done.

The divorce had turned bitter. There was money involved—my

husband's, originally—and I'd come to the slightly paranoid conclusion he would stop at nothing to keep it. But this wasn't even the part that was getting to me. It was the fact that my husband was now having a third baby without me—with a younger woman he'd met through work, fresh cheeked and fresh egged. It was insulting in such a classic and retrograde way that I felt I couldn't mention it to anyone, that I must feign a carefree attitude about the whole situation. Let some other woman's pelvic floor get busted out like an old screen from its frame. I had better things to do.

I'm sorry, goose. XOXOXO

Karlie had written this on the envelope's exterior, rounded letters along the edge, smudged but legible.

The words rippled through me, giving shape to an inchoate thought that had been dormant inside me for all these years, a virus awakening, tingling through my nerves again.

I decided to find my old professor. It was a damp gray day when both my sons were at their father's. The house was too quiet without them, suffused with a ghostly absence. In the bathroom mirror, the face that stared back at me belonged to a haggard old woman.

My professor and I had not communicated in years. He'd moved during my junior year to take a position at a small liberal arts college in Georgia. But now, he'd returned here, back to the university town where I still lived, the place where he'd begun his career, to retire. I'd heard of this through a loose network of his former students, all admiring, all filled with unrequited intellectual adoration. I both scorned and related to these former students. My professor had seemed old when I'd been his student, but now, of course, he would be a senior citizen inarguably. I worked for a women's health nonprofit, and I wondered if he'd find conversation with current-me engaging. I assumed he was still interested in the things he'd studied over the course of his career: nondenominational Protestantism, cults, the prosperity gospel, televangelism. Younger women.

I could find him. I knew all his old haunts. The youthful me inside myself, still a hopeful girl, alert to every tender shoot, thirsting for beauty, for love, gave a little flutter like a wintering bird catching a ray of light. He is elderly, I reminded myself, and you are very sad. This is nothing, I told myself. You will find him and have a drink, catch up. He is simply an old mentor, an elderly friend. But my skin flushed and prickled at the thought.

*

"Kneel down here," my roommate said.

It was cool outside, the leaves brushed with the first reddish tinge of fall. Karlie had wrapped a long woolen scarf around her neck, and that, combined with her green peacoat, made her look like a girl from a college catalog—bright, perky, ready to learn. Wearing only a thin long-sleeved shirt without a jacket, I shivered beside her. We were in an outdoor amphitheater that belonged to the college, a wooded place surrounded by trees. Her friend Jamie—a born-again kid from Mount Airy, hopelessly blond and handsome, a smiling, musical-loving boy who, it seemed, had translated all his repressed desires into a kind of ebullient evangelism—had come with us. The homoeroticism of the Jesus Jamie described was so painfully obvious, my cheeks reddened whenever he spoke of him.

"There," Jamie said, touching the nape of my neck gently, guiding my head forward. Through the trees we could still hear the sounds from campus, which was not so far away: students shouting, music playing from a boom box in one of the quads.

Karlie and Jamie had brought me directly here from a small on-campus meeting room in which several of us had gathered to listen to Kent, one of the professional leaders of the all-campus evangelical group, sharing his personal faith journey. Kent was older, handsome in the way of an outdoor educator, and his voice had trembled at key moments when he'd spoken.

"Ask him to enter you," Jamie said softly, kneeling beside me. I could feel the afterglow of Kent's testimony still, all that promise. The Holy Ghost was coiled somewhere nearby, ready to unfurl into an all-seeing, all-knowing mist. "Ask Jesus to enter your heart."

Karlie kneeled beside me, her knee touching mine—a meaningful heat transmitted. Or maybe I was just cold. I glanced at her.

"Go ahead," she said. "Ask him."

The sun was already dropping somewhere out behind the trees, the road, the hill, and I could hear the whoosh of traffic. Jamie's eyes were closed. He seemed to radiate peace, beneficence. Karlie too—she tipped her head back, her lips parted slightly, as if she were awaiting some divine dispensation. I wanted that too: I wanted free of my loneliness. Already, I'd gone to frat parties with two other girls from our dorm, pleasantly ordinary college students who wanted all the trappings of a pleasantly ordinary experience: beer pong, formals, all-nighters, pizza. I'd stood in a corner stiffly, until a boy with a pockmarked face had sauntered over and asked if I was in his anthro lecture. When I'd been unable to formulate any answer, he'd left me standing there, alone.

I asked God, forming the words neatly in my mind like a prayer. Jamie gave my hand a squeeze, and I saw Karlie's lips moving, offering some intercession on my behalf.

I waited. Nothing happened.

Finally, as if we'd all agreed to it, we stood up. Jamie and Karlie were beaming at me.

"You did it, Joy," Karlie said, and there was a new lightness I felt in my head, a strange, ebullient, hollowed feeling—but maybe that was the cold, the rush of blood from my head to my feet.

"Joy!" Jamie said, giving my name its full meaning and weight, my name, which had always clung to me like a cruel parody. How had my parents not known better than to give me, their sallow, serious, frowning daughter, a name of elation?

"Thank you," I said, although I didn't know what I was thanking them for.

The next day when I went to my professor's office hours, I felt emboldened. No one had ever taught me to flirt, so my only coyness, my one move, was to play contrarian: I told him what had happened. My recent salvation. He chuckled slightly.

"Another soul saved, another notch on their belts," he said, turning to the shelf of books behind him, moving several volumes to pull out the bottle of bourbon he kept there. From his desk drawer, he withdrew two glasses and poured us each a drink.

I had been meeting him here, after class, regularly for months now, since the day he'd noticed a particular question I'd asked in class about the First Great Awakening. There must have been a clue in my voice, in the way I'd gazed at him, that conveyed friendlessness and hunger. *Preacher's kid,* he'd said, pointing at me with one long, pale finger after the rest of the class had left. *You're lost. I get it. I was a preacher's kid too.* I had nodded, although technically I was unsure if I still counted as a preacher's kid. My father's seizures had grown worse. What for so long he'd managed to frame as a divine gift, the hand of God descending only rarely and electrifyingly, bestowing ethereal visions during his postictal states, had now turned to something vicious and frequent. A curse. It had soured my father's mind, leaving him gray faced and distant, hardly able to get out of bed. *A turning of the spiritual milk,* he

had said. My mother had helped him negotiate a medical leave.
On recent visits, the only times I'd seen him get out of bed was
shuffling to microwave a mug of soup. He hadn't set foot in the
church for over a year. My father, it seemed to me, was now more
lost than I.

My professor told me he'd found himself similarly bewildered
by the vastness of his large university back when he'd first arrived
as a student. Full of questions, just like me. *A familiar story,* he'd
said, nodding knowingly, although I'd actually told him very little.
It felt like a magic trick, the way he'd read me so easily.

"No, it wasn't like that. They're my friends," I said, but the flush
of the cold amphitheater returned to me then, my cheeks growing
hot once more. I wasn't just another heathen converted, a tally
mark on their scorecard.

He shrugged and took a sip from his glass, gesturing for me to
drink also. I did, unable to tell if the burning in my throat was the
threat of tears or the alcohol.

"I'm sure they are."

"Anyway, I felt it," I said, which now, with some distance from
the experience, almost didn't seem like a lie. "It felt different
from before. From back home. In my old church. This felt real."
Already, it seemed, the sip of bourbon was making me bold—or
maybe it was the illicit atmosphere of these meetings, which had
become more and more regular, in my professor's office, sharing
drinks. Something pulled taut between us, invisible, daring one of
us to be the first to pluck it.

"Oh, yeah?"

He raised an eyebrow, his eyes twinkling in amusement. Behind
him, there was a photo: of him and his wife before the Parthenon.
She looked like a nice woman, ordinary—which made me hate her
all the more.

"Yeah," I said, and as we talked about my experience, I could
feel a kind of effortless revision happening: the cold air a kind of
clarity, the rushing sensation in my head when I'd stood up like
being reborn, a God-ghost burrowing into my chest parasitically,
causing a blossoming of my hard little unripe heart.

"Do tell."

"I felt faint. Like something was coming over me. A mystery. It
was weird."

In my mind, I was articulate, sensitive to the vagaries of experience—but with my professor, I still used the crude monosyllables of late adolescence. It was like the blaze of my professor's intelligence rendered me stupid. He drank the rest of his bourbon in a gulp, but I could see through the blur of his glass that he was smiling, trying not to laugh.

"That feeling of mystery," he said, "is probably something we could summon right here. In this dusty little office. It wouldn't take much."

"That's not what Karlie says," I told him. I shared with him what she'd told me of signs she'd received: a message intuited from a bit of green ribbon blowing directly into her path, a butterfly alighting on her nose and filling her with an extraordinary sense of comfort, the time she'd been half asleep and swore she witnessed a seraphic messenger, felt the distinct pressure of heavenly hands on her shoulders while she prayed.

My professor nodded. I could still see amusement in his eyes. He poured himself another bourbon.

"I'd like to meet this Karlie," he said. "She sounds like a real wonder."

I shrugged. Perhaps he was joking, but people did say that about Karlie, who was very convincing, and also beautiful in a soft, womanly way. She had large eyes and a pretty mouth and face, the full arms of an old-fashioned milk maiden. Everyone loved her—Kent, the other leaders of the evangelical group, her peers, the rest of the girls in our dorm. She looked like someone from a Vermeer; I'd seen those paintings in my art history class and had thought of Karlie immediately. The whiteness of her cheeks, that untouchable gaze of hers.

He seemed to intuit my thoughts because he pulled himself closer, scraping the chair across the floor. He let the scoop of his hand fall on my knee, where it rested warmly. His face was across from mine, our breath mingling. This was the closest we'd ever sat.

"I mean as an interview subject," my professor said softly. He was writing a paper on young evangelicals. "If she's willing to participate."

I nodded. Other powers seemed to be working on me then— the bourbon, the cramped space of the office, my professor's hand on my knee.

"I'll show you that feeling of mystery," my professor said, his voice turned very soft, very close to my ear. "We can surely conjure it."

I found my professor at the bar. It was the one nearby campus that he'd frequented back in his teaching days. I'd seen him there many times: flanked by eager graduate students and seniors from his honors seminar, hands awhirl as he spoke, basking in the glow of all that attention. I'd never gone. I'd never been invited, but I'd walked past many times, crunching through the leaves and stealing jealous glances through the window. I was no one, I'd had to re-mind myself—even with those long, bourbon-soaked talks during his office hours, the way my professor had touched the back of my neck just so, a feeling like the Paraclete summoned. I was no one. It was all subtext without text.

Now, my professor sat in the booth alone.

He saw me standing outside and waved. It felt like he'd been waiting for me to appear, like the whole thing had been prear-ranged, predetermined. I pushed open the door and walked up to him, watching his inscrutable smile. There was always part of him, I'd felt, that was gently amused and laughing at me. I found that I wanted to leave already.

"Joy!" he said, like he meant it, my name.

He looked so old, so shrunken and wizened, that I almost couldn't bear it. I still felt the same inside, an earnest college girl, but I wondered if he thought the same seeing me. I was middle-aged; he was an old man.

"What are the odds? Sit, Joy, sit!"

His smile hurt me. He seemed to be recalling an oft-told joke, grateful, like I reminded him of a time he'd loved and forgotten.

"It's good to see you," he said. He was already beckoning to the waitress and ordering me a drink—bourbon, like old times. I didn't have the heart to tell him that it was something I'd only pretended to like, for his sake.

I sat down in the booth across from him and looked directly into his face. Words would not come to me. The unopened letter from my past, from Karlie, was in my bag.

"You could say *It's good to see you too*," my professor said, and his voice was jovial, but I could see the mildest irritation in his gestures, in the way he picked up his glass quickly and drank.

"I read something and thought of you," I said, telling him about the article I'd seen on the *I Kissed Dating Goodbye* guy, the tawdry sadness of it. I mentioned my own divorce, making light of it, easy-breezy, like a fun-time girl. He laughed in his old way again, as if I were unbearably precocious, but then his laughter sputtered to a cough.

I'd never quite liked his laughter, I realized—the smugness it held. My anger toward him was finally coalescing after all the years of uncertainty, and I could feel it burbling up now, like the need to retch.

"Karlie," I said quietly. "Why? Why did it have to be her?"

A look passed over his face quickly, darkening it, but he remained impassive. Carefully, he folded up his napkin into triangles and then took another sip of his drink. There was music playing, an old B-52's song from another era that might as well have been an age of buggies and oil lamps—we were insulated by the music, the clatter of silverware, the voices of other customers. I felt alone within him, in a strange bubble of privacy. *Roam if you want to . . .* Finally, he spoke.

"People are complicated, Joy," he said slowly. With one knobby finger, he traced the circumference of his glass, then held it up to the dying light from the window, as if inspecting it for impurities. "Karlie was very complicated. I think you may never have fully appreciated that."

"She was my friend."

"No doubt of that. I like to think she was mine as well." He sighed very deeply. The B-52's were playing and playing, *without wings, without wheels,* with a Möbius strip–like endlessness, and the dusky bar seemed to be the maw of some sick carnival ride. "It was a tragedy," my professor said softly, in the special, fatherly voice he'd used when I was riled. I'd always hated that voice, which indeed reminded me of my own father—sunken eyed and silent, his uncut hair fanned out against his pillow pitifully, like a failed saint.

"You killed her," I said quietly. "Karlie. My roommate. Or you might as well have. It was your fault. She was so good before she met you. You ruined her."

At this, he laughed, but his eyes had turned hard, bleak.

"Joy," my professor said slowly, dabbing at his lips with the folded napkin. His hands were liver spotted now, with none of the power I recalled. "I know you're under a great deal of stress. With your divorce. I'm going to ignore what you just said. You're beside yourself."

But I could not stop myself. All those old days rushed back to me.

After I'd introduced Karlie to my professor, she'd agreed to participate in his research. They began to meet regularly.

I'm teaching him things, Karlie told me. *I'm sharing the Gospel,* and her eyes shot heavenward, but I could see the way a blush rose up her neck, the extra care she put into her appearance before they met. And I saw the tiny bruise on her neck, a devil's kiss. I'd begun loitering in the hallway outside my professor's office, trying to catch glimpses of them together, trying to comprehend exactly what was going on—although I knew. Of course I knew. I lingered near the departmental building, waiting to see them exit together, watching over time as a casual familiarity grew ever so subtly between them: his arm on her shoulder just so, Karlie wearing his sweater as it got colder.

When I stopped showing up to my professor's office hours after class and he said nothing at all, that was the end of it for me. I finished out the semester but turned taciturn in class, reluctant, careful to do only the bare minimum. Professor Hendrix never sought me out or asked why. It was like whatever we'd once shared had simply been a figment of my own imagination.

"It was your fault," I repeated, although I was hardly sure why I was saying it. Karlie had made her own choices. There was another man in jail, DNA evidence. Open and shut. This man across from me, my former professor, was pitiful now, impotent, a king dethroned. Maybe I was simply cruel.

I put the letter from Karlie onto the table for him to see, like it was proof.

He shook his head and put his hands into the sparse hair at his temples, pressing as if to stop an ache in his head.

"You were jealous," he whispered. "You wanted me to cross that line with you."

"No."

"You hated her."

I thought then of all those days I'd waited outside his office, listening to voices inside—his, Karlie's. She'd laugh softly, he'd murmur something, she'd laugh again, but soon there were other sounds. I'd stood by the door listening, a terrible heat spreading over me.

The truth is that my professor never so much as kissed me, although his every gesture had seemed to promise it: fingers on my shoulders, my back, sending shivers down my neck. His breath behind my ears, at the nape of my neck. The barometric pressure between us thick, ominous. Promises, signals, implications, leaving me like an arrow pulled back on a bow but never released into flight.

"I never hated her," I said.

He shook his head again, like it was all very sad to him. He took another drink. I saw he still was in possession of his most notable attributes: superciliousness, composure.

"Poor lost preacher's kid with her sick-in-the-head daddy."

I stood to leave, my bag knocking over my bourbon and spilling it on Karlie's letter. I gave a little gasp and tried to rescue the letter, but it was already wet. I plucked it from the puddle of liquor.

"I'm praying for you," he said.

I scoffed. There was bourbon dripping from Karlie's letter onto the toes of my boots.

"God, I hate you."

I meant it every possible way.

He didn't answer me. He said nothing when I left.

Outside the bar, I stood on the corner, catching my breath. My teeth chattered. It had grown colder now, but not nearly as cold as I felt, and it was already dark although barely after 5:00 p.m. I pressed a cocktail napkin I'd grabbed against the damp part of the letter.

Karlie and I were close only freshman year. By the time sophomore year ended, I rarely saw her. I'd stopped speaking to Professor Hendrix entirely by then. By junior year, I'd moved to an off-campus apartment with Sari and some of the others I'd met in my women's studies seminar. *Simpatico folk,* we called ourselves. It was a relief not to be seeking some grander plane of being. I felt at ease with my new friends: slump-shouldered former high school nerds made good; vigorous people who invested themselves in things like the college radio station or environmental action campaigns or slam poetry.

With Karlie, I remained pleasantly aloof. We met up only now and then before she died, and we never again spoke of Professor Hendrix. He left for his new job soon after her death.

I tried to shake off the thought of him—a mean old man. Pathetic. I walked away from the bar, ignoring the clusters of laughing students who clotted the sidewalk. Of course Professor Hendrix did not rush out trying to stop me or apologize. I did not turn around to see, but I knew he would be seated peacefully in his booth, finishing his drink in neat sips, untroubled by our encounter.

My husband's lawyer had sent another threatening email to me, trying to get me to sign a bunch of papers, accede to his demands. I hadn't yet. He'd riled the defiant part of me. I wouldn't go down without a fight.

Instead of walking back to where I'd parked, I headed the opposite direction, entering a part of town close to campus where there were million-dollar houses and streets shaded by stately trees. My hands were still shaking, so I stuffed them into my pockets. The boots I wore were a half size too small and pinched my toes. I walked anyway.

I was walking to my husband's house—the new house he shared with the woman who would be his new wife, my replacement. When I got there, I stood at the foot of the drive so I could see into the glowing windows of their kitchen.

There were silhouettes moving: my husband, my sons, the new woman with the baby inside her. I could see them as shapes, like figures in a shadow play. Maybe if I looked long enough, I would really see. I watched them readying dinner and wiped my cheek in the dark.

Karlie's letter was in my pocket, half ruined. It was too dark to read, but I pulled the letter out anyway. I opened the envelope and turned on the light from my phone.

Dear Joy,
I wanted to thank you for introducing me to Prof. H. I also wanted to say I'm sorry—I know in becoming close to him I took something from you. But he's not a good man. And I'm not just saying that to make you feel better or justify anything. I know you've been following me. I've seen you. I saw you duck into the stairwell when we were leaving Howell Hall. And I saw you that day you were standing just

outside his office, pretending to look at a bulletin board. Another time you were sitting at the coffee shop across the way wearing sunglasses, but I pretended not to notice. I didn't want to embarrass you. I don't blame you. I'm not so selfish that it doesn't hurt me to think of you hurt, alone, seeing us together. But you're not a very good spy, Joy, and now that you've started coming to my apartment—watching me at night, from outside my bedroom window—it's too much. Unsettling. You should know I've cut things off with him. The whole thing was a mistake, Joy. So you can stop trailing me after I park my car. I've heard you in the bushes when I leave here at night. Or sometimes when I'm coming home. You don't have to hide anymore, Joy. I get it. I'm not mad. Let's talk, please. Next time I hear you out there, I'm just going to open the door and invite you in. We'll drink tea and eat cookies and it'll be just like the beginning of freshman year all over again. If you'll accept my apology. I'm sorry! I love you, goose.—Karlie

I blinked, and blinked again, then folded the letter back into its envelope. A precious, perishable thing. She'd understood how I felt the whole time. And yet: she was wrong. I'd never been following Karlie. I'd only been following him. My professor. A sick, strange sadness uncurled in my stomach.

A door of the house opened, and out came someone into the dark. I heard the clunk of a trash can being pushed toward the curb. I clicked off the light in my phone quickly and held my breath, motionless.

The wheels of the trash can rumbled closer and closer to me, and then stopped. There, in the dimness, I saw her. She swam into focus, a shadowy woman-shape with the unmistakable swell of pregnancy. Her eyes seemed feline, reflecting ambient light from the other houses.

"You," she said, her voice like a knife. "You again. You're trespassing. I could call the cops."

She moved closer to me, her belly a taunt.

"You've got to stop doing this," she said. "You've got to leave us alone."

I heard the door of the house open again and someone step out.

"Maggie?"

That was the woman's name. It was my husband's voice saying it. I could see his outline, backlit on the porch, as he peered into the darkness.

"You all right?"

I gripped Karlie's letter tight in my fist, but I let the rest of myself slump to the cool concrete. I lay on my back, looking up into the starless sky. Then I let all that feeling course through me. Unlike Karlie, I knew how to do it right. I'd seen my father so many times. I'd watched it happen, an ungovernable force, a wordless thing, like being possessed by something—God, perhaps, or a lesser demon.

"Jesus, John. There's something wrong with her. She's . . . Are you okay?"

"Joy?"

I heard the stricken sound of my husband's voice, his feet pounding down the path—my husband, running to my aid, running because worry is merely one step away from love, and love, one step away from hate.

My arms seized and jerked like I'd been shot through with electricity. I let my head fall back, my mouth foam. My arms stiffened and jerked from their sockets. My tongue had gone rigid in my mouth. I let her scream at it, at my display—she and my husband, hovering over me like two abiding angels—although this time, it truly felt real. Like getting struck by lightning. Or holiness, submitting once and for all.

Trash

FROM *The New Yorker*

I DON'T KNOW why I didn't think of someone like Miss Emily. It never occurred to me to imagine her. I guess you could say I lacked imagination. I married her son after knowing him for only five days. A whirlwind romance.

I was the cashier at the local supermarket. Her son came in on Tuesdays to shop, to get discounts. I thought he was someone who didn't spend lavishly even though he could. I could tell he came from good people. He always wore a nice suit, and he had this beautiful coat, the kind of fabric that made you want to reach out and touch.

Of course, I could never do anything like that. I am not that bold. And, anyway, we weren't allowed to behave that way with customers. I wasn't selling clothes. I scanned bar codes. We were instructed only to take the coupons and the cash, or to press the buttons for the credit-card machines. We don't accept personal checks anymore, we were told to say.

The evening I actually met Miss Emily's son, I was finishing up my shift when I saw him come in. He seemed real glamorous, and I hadn't seen someone like that before so close up, looking right back at me. He certainly was not like the kind of people I'd grown up around. The kind who cuss, grab their crotch, belch. If they didn't like you, you'd know about it and they'd say it to your face. There was no pretending.

I helped him carry some things to his car, and we got to talking. I liked talking to him. He was funny and friendly and polite. That's all I really need to know about anyone. I remember now that it snowed. Large, fluffy, soft flakes that made you think of diamonds. That night, I went home with him, and the rest, as they say, is history. We got married.

I met Miss Emily not long after marrying her son, on a Friday evening. She took the earliest flight she could get to come see her son. She thought I was pregnant because of how sudden it was. I was not.

She was so eager to meet me. She made her son drive her to the supermarket, and they waited in the parking lot for two hours until I finished my shift. I had been on my feet for eight hours, so I wasn't looking too hot or feeling that great about myself. But I didn't think of things like that, impressions—first impressions—what they mean and how people don't change their feelings about you even years after.

I was wearing jeans and a pair of old runners, and a sweatshirt several sizes too large. My hair was tied back in a low ponytail. I wasn't wearing any makeup. Like I said, I didn't think of things like that at the time.

I got into the back seat, where Miss Emily was sitting alone. She took my face in, all its details and pores, assessed what kind of skin care or serum I might need, and kept those thoughts to herself. She smiled politely, and told me she was so glad to meet me—the girl her son had married.

I was family now, she said, and it wasn't up to her to say anything about that. Her son was, after all, his own man.

For as long as she could remember, all she ever wanted was a family, too. Her husband had died a few years ago. Heart attack. Sudden. She had married him right after college. Gone to law school, made partner, owned her own practice. Had three children. Bought property. She could afford to travel and take vacations abroad.

She had bettered herself. She'd worked very hard for what she had, she said. She had been—at one point in her life, so she knows these things—what people called trash. She'd improved herself, she said. Moved on up, pulled herself up by her bootstraps, got to work, and no one could use that word to describe her anymore. She made sure of that, she said.

Over dinner that night, at a restaurant, she told me loving stories of her son when he was a child. How he'd wanted to be a grass cutter at a baseball stadium in a big city when he grew up. His first girlfriend, his crushes and heartbreaks. His prom, and his pets. I loved hearing these stories. She made them so vivid and funny.

The bill came, and she paid. I begged her to tell me one more story. She thought for a moment. And then she told one about a pigeon her son had picked up off the road in front of their house when he was about ten years old. She didn't know that what he had there with him was a pigeon. She thought that he had been injured, that there had been an accident somewhere, but he was smiling at her with all that blood on him, and she was relieved to find out that he just had a dead bird. She said her son was always finding things like that—dead animals, caps and bottles, old books—and bringing them home. She said he always asked her to make something out of them.

When her son drove us back to his apartment, she asked me about my family. I said it was just me. My parents weren't around anymore. They died in a car crash. I should have left it at that, but Miss Emily had spent all evening telling me stories, and she was so open and honest that I wanted to say more. My dad had been drinking and really shouldn't have got behind the wheel. He was speeding. Ran a red light. It was raining. The car, a cheap old thing, was totalled.

I was in my last year of high school when all this happened. My parents didn't have life insurance. The car insurance had expired and no one had bothered to renew it. There were no savings or anything like that. So I had to quit school and get a job to pay rent. I wasn't in a position to spend a few weeks or months sending out résumés, going on interviews. I needed a job right away, and the supermarket gave me one.

I didn't want to live with anyone and was proud to find a place I could have all to myself. It was across the street from a park. It had one window. Hardwood floors, a bathtub, toilet, a stove, and a fridge. I wasn't a person who needed much. I put up bookshelves and set a mattress on the floor. An actress, I was told, had lived there. She gave up the place when she got a big break out in Los Angeles. I thought it was good luck to move into that space. Maybe I would catch a big break myself. I didn't know what, exactly, that might be, but it was something to believe in and hope for, too.

I was telling all this to Miss Emily, and when I paused she asked me if I might quit the job at the supermarket, now that I'd married

her son. I told her I really loved the supermarket. I felt loyal to
the place. I had been there for fifteen years. I'd worked my way
up, too.

It was a grand place. All those shelves of food. You didn't have
to go very far to get anything. The eggs were near the steaks. You
didn't have to spend hours making the perfect cake or rolling thin
sheets of dough to make croissants. You didn't have to own any
land or take out feed or work up the nerve to kill anything that
had a face. Someone somewhere did that work for you, and it was
all there on display. Each and every item was given a bar code of
its very own, everything was kept track of. The feel of the cash-
machine tray as it popped out and hit me on the arm was like an
old friend checking in throughout the day.

But Miss Emily didn't see it that way. She wanted me to go
back to school, get my diploma, go to college, and look for something better. These kinds of things cost money to have, I thought.
I didn't say that to her. I knew she was the type of person who
wouldn't use that as an excuse for anything. She just wanted the
best for me, she said. It was exactly what my own mother would
have wanted for me, if she'd wanted anything for me. I loved Miss
Emily right away then. She was so ambitious for me. And who, really, had dreams for you that you didn't even know you could wish
for all by yourself?

Miss Emily smelled like fresh roses. She was soft and warm. Miss
Emily loved being a mother, and now I was one of hers. That weekend, she took me shopping for clothes. Just us girls, she said. Skirts
and blouses, dresses, trousers, a trench coat. These were things I
never would have dared to buy for myself. They were in fabric you
had to dry-clean. You couldn't throw any of those clothes into a
machine to launder. She was so wonderful to me, really. No one
had ever taken that kind of time with me or cared so much for
me. I was always afraid of troubling the salesgirls at stores like
these. And they usually ignored me, knowing that I wouldn't buy
anything, anyway.

With Miss Emily, the salesgirl was real attentive and friendly.
Miss Emily was so at ease. Talking with the salesgirl, asking her
to bring us things in a size that would be a better fit. Asking the
salesgirl her opinion about what young professional women wore
to the office these days. She told me that, since her son worked in

an office, she didn't want me to feel out of place. I would never buy these things for myself, I said. I don't have that kind of money to spend, I told her. She said she would take care of it. She was so happy to be in a position to help, and all that mattered was that I loved the things I picked out.

After getting back to her son's apartment and putting away my new clothes, Miss Emily began finding other ways to be useful. I honestly thought she would be exhausted after all that shopping. We had been at the clothing store for several hours, undressing and dressing me, putting things back, changing our minds, wanting to see things in other colors before deciding. All that sifting, trying, directing, imagining was a lot of work.

Suddenly, what had been her sweet, warm voice turned hoarse and cold. She became frazzled, asking me to do something—anything, really—to clean the house. Pointing a beautifully polished nail at me. "You," she said. "You do something about this."

I didn't know what had upset her so.

She kept saying, "Can't you *see* this?"

I was honest with her. I didn't know what the big deal was, and, truly, I hadn't noticed all this before.

She brought items up to me as if they were dead animals, holding them with two fingers as she shaped her face into disgust. She brought me takeout boxes and containers, beer bottles, soiled clothes, ashtrays. Then she threw a toilet brush my way and said, "Start with this." I hadn't noticed the stains on the outside of the toilet bowl, or inside just around the rim. I didn't know things could get into those kinds of places, at that angle.

She talked about her son as if *she* had been married to him for twenty-five years and was now emotionally spent. She told me all the things that were wrong with him. How his hair needed to be cut, his toenails and fingernails needed to be trimmed, how he hadn't brushed his teeth for days. She said, "He snores at night! How can you not hear that sleeping next to him?" She then began to describe me with words like stupid and dumb. She kept telling me to think, think, *think*. She said her son had never been like *this* when she had him. She said, "What have you done to him?" She took a spray bottle and sprayed surfaces, and scrubbed and scrubbed. She didn't want to look at my face, she said.

I went outside to the front porch and sat on a step. I wondered where her son was. Why he had been gone for most of the day, and when he would be back. I thought about a mother's love. The incredible generosity it required from you. Her son had taken in a stranger, someone else's child, and, whatever this thing was with the two of them, she felt that she, too, had to love and give everything she had, even if she didn't want to. I knew that, whatever she felt about me, it was true to her, and that there was some truth to it. I wasn't good enough for her, and I never would be. But I wanted her love. I guess it was like a child wishing to see a crowd of gold stars next to her name. Proof that she'd done good that day, and that someone had taken the time to see that. There isn't anything like that for you as an adult, and the feeling of wanting one star—any star—never does disappear entirely.

Just then, I saw a creature crawl toward me. I thought it was a lost cat, but this thing looked large and vicious—it was a raccoon. It reached out at the dark between us, at my little face, and when I flinched it stopped and turned back to where it had come from. I don't know what it thought I was, exactly, what it might have mistaken me for, out there, all alone. I wasn't trash.

KOSISO UGWUEZE

Supernova

FROM *New England Review*

THE ABC TRANSPORT bus headed to Enugu had just reached Lokoja when it slowed and suddenly came to a full stop. Isioma had been asleep at the back of the bus, resting her head against the shuddering window. When the bus stopped, she was jolted out of her slumber.

She checked her watch: 9:30 a.m. She had boarded the bus at 6:30 that morning in Abuja, where she'd been staying with her mother, Josephine, from whom she'd long been estranged. Isioma was staying with Josephine because she had attempted suicide at the NYSC camp in Gombe. She'd swallowed thirty paracetamol pills that turned out to be diluted fakes. Isioma had slept for nearly twenty-four hours until her roommate, Edidiong, insisted she be taken to a hospital.

Now Isioma heard the unmistakable click of gunshots. They were swift, crackling through the air. She sat up, and her first instinct was not to cower but to lean towards the noise. She knew this sound because she had once lived next to the army barracks in Enugu. As a child, she had heard, for months on end, the sound of the soldiers practicing, shooting holes into tin cans and cardboard cutouts. Now the sound came to her like a familiar smell.

Three men climbed on board and the bus shuddered under their weight. The men continued shooting, emptying cartridges into the ceiling as they marched from one end of the commercial bus to the other. Her fellow passengers cowered, but Isioma couldn't tear her eyes from the ceiling where bullet holes now let in rays of morning sunlight.

"Oya, get up," came a man's voice. Isioma saw this man, camou-flaged shirt, a toothpick sticking out of his dark lips. He marched down the aisle, his gun aimed at the ceiling. In the middle of the bus, he stopped and pulled a woman by her braids, yanking her from her seat. When she struggled, he shook her. Then he shoved her out of the bus. Isioma wondered if this was an elaborate robbery or a kidnapping. In Nigeria, it could have been either one.

The bus smelled like a hundred sweating bodies, and it was the first thing that struck Isioma as she lowered her head and inter-twined her fingers behind her neck. A few of the other passengers had begun to beg.

The armed men shouted obscenities.

"Na my time you dey fucking waste," Isioma heard one man shout. Then another gruff voice, "Fuck your Jesus," in response to a woman's pleading.

The men marched up and down the bus. They were laughing like hyenas, and something about the whole scene, the terrified passengers, the bellowing men, was comical to Isioma, so much so that she stifled a snort into her knee. Her head was so low that her jaw met her thigh, her eyes open and staring at her now-dusty shoes. It was impossible to keep anything clean in the Harmattan season, not with the dust that settled everywhere—on tree branches, on car hoods, on her eyelashes. And in the rainy season, the mud and rainwater also soaked through her sneakers, dirtying her socks so that she had to soak them for days in hot water and Omo to get the stains out.

She had her head down for many minutes, counting the small square designs on the bus's floor. Above her head, the men con-tinued to shout. One by one, they picked passengers off the bus. "You, get up." "No, please, I have six children." "Did I ask you? Get up!"

When a hand yanked at her hair and dragged her from the bus, Isioma went willingly. Outside, the sun was blinding. The road had been blocked with tree branches and the branches were ablaze. The heat of the fire struck her like a force. She imagined running into it.

"Move or we move you," one of the armed men said as he struck a young passenger across the face with the barrel of his gun. This gun-wielding man, like his fellow gun-wielding men, was wearing camouflage, boots laced up to his knees. His eyes were bloodshot though he looked young, somebody's baby brother out in the world trying to be a man. He had a hardness that Isioma couldn't take seriously, and though he was wielding an AK-47, Isioma wanted to reach out and touch his face.

He caught her looking at him and his eyes narrowed.

"You," he said, pointing his gun at her. "Oya, march."

"Where?" she said. "Into the bush?"

He looked puzzled.

"Where else?" he said. "March!"

She turned to the forest of tall grass and low trees. The sky over her head was cloudless but gray; the smell of burning fires mixed with Harmattan dust made her nose itch.

"This way?" she said, looking back at the young man.

"If you don't march I'm going to scatter your brains on this red soil," the man said.

"Right," Isioma said, and she began to march.

She entered the forest gingerly, stepping between fallen tree branches. The grass came up to her shoulders. Behind her, she could hear the other passengers, a woman crying, a man begging. The men with the guns continued their verbal assault. "Shut your stinking mouth. Move or I'll shoot."

They continued into the forest for half an hour. Isioma was now sure that she had been kidnapped; robbers wouldn't have gone through the trouble of marching them into the forest. Yet Isioma wondered why the armed men hadn't taken them somewhere more remote. That was how they usually happened; kidnappers dragged their victims out of cars and homes and carried them off to hinterland villages with few passable roads. These kidnappers didn't appear to be amateurs. All of them, with the exception of the youngest, had the hardened look of men who could kill. Yet, here they were, only thirty minutes away from a major road. Isioma was counting the minutes under her breath. She was unfamiliar with the landscape of Lokoja, this transportation hub near the middle of Nigeria. It was a place she had passed through many times but could not quite say she had ever been to. It was like being asked if you'd ever been to London and answering yes, but only to the airport. Not that she had ever been to London.

They came to a stop.

"Oya," one of the men said, hitting Isioma across the legs with his dangling gun. "Sit."

There were seven of them now in the forest, four passengers and three armed men. The passengers were two young men, a middle-aged woman, and Isioma. The two young men had stopped begging but the middle-aged woman was still crying. Tears had pooled in the creases of her face and her nose was running. Isioma found the woman's whimpering irritating.

"Sit!" said a man who appeared to be the leader of the armed group. He was a large man, sweat on his forehead and eyes that darted sideways when he spoke. He was wearing a tight black T-shirt, camouflage trousers, stiff boots.

Isioma sat down as she had been told. The ground was littered with twigs. They brushed against her bare legs and stuck to her skirt. When one of the young passengers, the one wearing an Arsenal football jersey, refused to sit, the large man shook him violently.

"I said sit!" he said. "You no dey hear word?"

The young man sat.

"I'm just a student," he said. "My father doesn't have any money. In fact, I haven't paid my school fees this term."

"Liar," the second kidnapper said. He was slender, feminine, his face covered in pimples. He was wearing slippers and cargo shorts, a dark singlet. "A poor student with iPhone, abi," he said. The other two men laughed.

She had thought about dying every day for six months before she attempted it. Isioma had thought obsessively about how she would do it, whether she would fling herself from some tall height or throw herself into crocodile-infested waters. At last, she had decided on the pills. They seemed easiest, clinical, most certain to work. It wasn't that she was averse to feeling pain, but she had decided at the last minute that it was best to be efficient. Finding a tall building or crocodile-infested waters would have meant journeying out of the city, and Isioma had thought it all too cumbersome for something she wanted to be done with.

She had woken early the morning of her suicide attempt and waited for her roommate, Edidiong, to get up. Edidiong had a beautiful singing voice, one she had honed at church. She had even once dragged Isioma to one of the few Catholic churches in the northeastern city of Gombe, where Isioma had been posted to spend her service year. When Isioma had told her friends in Enugu about her assignment to Gombe, they all cursed the Nigerian government, accusing it of wanting to destroy its best and brightest. And when they found out that she would, in fact, be teaching in a school that Boko Haram had once destroyed, her friends urged her to petition the decision. But Isioma had already become so accustomed to the idea of dying that she didn't care. Instead she went home and Googled pictures of Boko Haram bomb sites.

Now Isioma thought of taking a selfie and sending it to Edidiong. *Forest Babe,* she would have captioned it. Edidiong would have said, *Where are you??* and Isioma would have responded, *I've been kidnapped. I'm in the forest. I hope I die.*

She fished in her pocket for her cell phone. It was the only thing she had on her; her purse was still on the bus.

"What are you doing?" the large man said.

"I was just getting my phone out," Isioma said.

The youngest of the men, the one who had pulled Isioma from the bus, guffawed.

"It's not an iPhone," Isioma said. "Samsung."

The large man gave her a bewildered look.

"Are you mental?" he said. He stepped to her and snatched the phone from her hands. Isioma leaned against the tree stump behind her and closed her eyes. So much for that.

The armed men confiscated all their cell phones. The large man gave them a stern warning.

"You try to run and you die instantly."

Isioma raised her hand.

"Yes?" the man said.

"What should we call you?"

There was a pause in which Isioma couldn't determine whether the man had heard her.

"Call him Chief," the youngest man said. In the dim light of the forest, his eyes glowed. He was cutting an orange with a small knife. "Call him Chief or Daddy."

The sequence of events the morning of her suicide attempt had happened like this. Isioma had complained of a stomachache and told Edidiong to notify the Corps leader when she got to the school. When Edidiong left, Isioma sat up on her bed. She took out her cell phone and thought about writing a suicide note. But there was nothing she really wanted to say. She didn't know to whom to address it either, her mother or her father. If she was going to write a note, she wanted it to be a letter addressed to someone. And when she couldn't decide who would be more impacted by her death, the father who was himself also dead or the mother she hadn't seen in nearly five years, she turned off her cell phone. She fished in her backpack for the pills she had bought at the nearby chemist shop.

After she had swallowed the thirty pills, Isioma stood at the window and listened to the sounds of traffic. Gombe was a dry desert city. Before arriving there five months before, she had never been past Abuja. Northern Nigeria was supposed to be this nebulous no-man's-land. But Isioma found the city and its surrounding environs peaceful, beautiful, full. She liked listening to the early morning calls to prayer, liked that she could have long conversations with the vendors about the weather and the landscape and the best places to get your hair braided or your eyebrows threaded. She was almost sad to be leaving the city behind.

Soon, her stomach began to churn. Isioma tried to lie down on her bed but she couldn't find it. The room was spinning. Her eyes were rolling in her head. She vomited and blacked out.

When she came to in the hospital, twenty-four hours later, her mother was seated at the edge of her bed.

"Forty-five schoolchildren kidnapped in Borno," Josephine said to her daughter.

Isioma tried to sit up, but her vision blurred. She gripped the side of the bed, shut her eyes.

She heard her mother stand up and come to the side of the bed. When she opened her eyes, her mother was peering at her with a worried look. Isioma could smell her mother's perfume, a lavender scent that had always been her mother's signature smell. Isioma remembered that she would follow this smell around her aunt's house in Enugu, and with each passing day the smell would be less potent, and when it was gone completely, Isioma would know that her mother had left her behind once again.

She had known from a very young age that her parents had never wanted to have her. Her mother and father were young lovers, and when Josephine became pregnant her father had fled. Nineteen and studying medicine at the university, Josephine took a leave of absence to have her baby. But as soon as her daughter

was born, Josephine left Isioma with Isioma's aunt and returned
to the university to finish her degree. By the time Josephine graduated at twenty-four, she had decided she couldn't be a full-time
mother to Isioma.

In the hospital ward, Josephine sighed at her daughter.

"I'm not a bad person," she said. "Will you forgive me?"

That first night, they slept on the forest floor, huddled together for
warmth. The middle-aged woman, whose name was Irene, sobbed
through the night. Only one man kept watch, the youngest one,
who told his captives to call him Big Boy.

By morning, Isioma's back was sore. Her mouth tasted like ash.
Big Boy was still eating oranges and there was a mountain of orange
peels around his feet. He was staring directly at Isioma as she sat
up. Isioma met his gaze.

"Big Boy," she called.

"Yes?"

"Where did the others go? Why did they leave a little thing like
you in charge?"

Big Boy laughed. Isioma hadn't expected him to.

"You're a funny one," he said. "But I'm the best shot of all us.
I can take any of you down if you tried to run." He raised his gun
and aimed it at Isioma's head.

"Congratulations," she said. "But you didn't answer my question."

"Where did they go? They went home."

"Like home to their families?" Isioma said.

"Yes," he said. "You think they'll just sit in the bush for days?
Haba, of course not. Chief himself has a newborn baby. Com-
mando's mother might die any day now."

"Is that why they brought us here? So they can go back and forth?"

It made sense to Isioma, seemed efficient, continue to tend to
life's problems while you have people tied up in the bush.

"Wetin concern you?" Big Boy said, standing up. He stretched
and yawned. Irene made a small noise. The two young men, Kingsley and Osita, sat with their heads buried in their palms.

"Big Boy," Isioma said.

"What?"

"How much is the ransom?"

At the mention of a ransom, Kingsley began to wail. His Arsenal
jersey was now covered in dirt.

"Please," he said. "My father drives a bus. We have no money for ransom."

Big Boy laughed a menacing laugh. He wiped tears from his eyes.

"They either find a way to pay or you die."

For the three days Isioma spent in the hospital post-suicide attempt, her mother would read her the news from her cell phone.

"Bomb blast in Maiduguri, oil workers kidnapped in Port Harcourt, fuel scarcity in Lagos." Isioma would listen to Josephine with her back turned.

The day she was discharged, Josephine came bearing new clothes, a pair of jeans and a T-shirt that said "It Gets Better" in faded letters. She watched Isioma put them on.

"Mommy's here," Josephine said as they walked out of the hospital and into the sunlight. "Mommy's here now and she'll take care of you."

The words made Isioma want to shout.

They drove from Gombe to Abuja in nine hours, stopping in Bauchi and Jos where Josephine bought her daughter bananas and roasted peanuts.

When they arrived in Abuja, it was dusk. Josephine pulled into the house in Asokoro. It was the first time Isioma had ever seen her mother's home. For eighteen years, Josephine had visited Isioma at her aunt's in Enugu every six months. Inside the house, Isioma sat in the living room like a guest, looking at the pictures of her mother's other children on the walls, her two half brothers, Ahmed and Musa.

She awoke the next morning to find that Josephine had left breakfast at her bedside. She was in her half brother Ahmed's bedroom. Josephine had married a northerner who had died and left her a small fortune. Her half brothers were studying in California. Isioma had found their public profiles on Facebook a year ago and spent hours scrolling through their pictures, trying to see what it meant to have known Josephine as more than a specter, a vanishing shadow.

On Ahmed's walls were posters of Tupac, Al Pacino in the movie *Scarface*. His closet was full of clothes, and Isioma had thumbed through his shirts and trousers, bringing his caftans and agbadas to her nose until she felt she had mastered his scent.

She rose from the bed and ate the pap and akara Josephine had made, waiting for Josephine to tell her what to do next. Isioma still had seven months left in her service year. She could return to Gombe and continue teaching shell-shocked seven-year-olds about the stars. Or she could abscond like so many people did. Josephine surely knew some high-ranking civil servant who could falsify the paperwork for her, say that she had completed her tenure even when she hadn't.

As she polished off the last akara, Josephine knocked gently on the door and stepped in. She was wearing a bright red kimono Isioma's other half brother, Musa, had bought her in Japan. Josephine's face was radiant, and it was then that Isioma realized just how beautiful her mother was. Her face was perfectly symmetrical, with dark skin, almond eyes, full lips. Seeing her now, barefaced in her kimono, made Isioma think of the mornings when she would sit in her aunt's living room, waiting for her mother to wake. She would sometimes slip into the room where Josephine slept, stand over her, tracing her face with wide eyes. Isioma had become so familiar with her mother's face that when she began to draw at thirteen, she could draw her mother from memory.

Josephine sat at the edge of her bed.

"Sleep well?" she said.

Isioma nodded.

"Just the two of us," her mother said cheerily, as though they spent each weekend like this, breakfast in bed while they gisted. "The two of us girls," Josephine said. "What do you want to do today?"

"I want help," Isioma said. "I want to see a psychiatrist."

Isioma stayed in the forest for four days before the first ransom was paid. Osita, whose uncle lived in Oman, had gathered the five million naira required for his release. He was blindfolded and led out of the bush.

"See," Chief said when Big Boy returned an hour later. "We are men of our word."

That night, Isioma began to count the stars.

"Look," she said to Irene who was staring off into space, her headscarf askew. "We think the light of the stars as instant. But the light we see is actually thirty thousand years old."

"How do you know that?" Chief said, gazing up at the sky.

"I studied it at university."

"Wetin you study?"

"Astrophysics."

"Big brain!" Big Boy said.

"Wetin be astrophysics?" Chief said.

"The study of space."

"You want to go to space?" Big Boy said.

"Yes," Isioma said.

"Like astronaut?" Big Boy said.

"Yes."

Chief laughed.

"From this here Nigeria?" he said.

"Nigeria wants to send an astronaut to space by 2030."

The two men looked at each other. They laughed.

"When we no get electricity we fit put person for space?" Chief said.

Isioma was annoyed by their lack of belief.

When she told her aunt that she wanted to be an astronaut, her aunt had looked at her as though she had said she wanted to be a witch.

"Wait till your mother hears this," her aunt had said. Her aunt, Nnenna, said this often, as though Josephine had just gone to the market for tomatoes and would soon be back. Nnenna was a lecturer at ESUT and made clothes for wealthy Enugu society women on her days off. Isioma's earliest memories were of her aunt at the sewing machine, her feet tapping, tapping, tapping. Her aunt was what people derisively called a barren woman, and Nnenna had raised Isioma and loved her like her own child. Yet the weight of her two jobs meant she was hardly available, and when Nnenna was busiest, during Christmas and New Year's and Easter, she would hand Isioma off to a distant cousin who regarded the girl scientist with suspicion and malice.

Once when she was sixteen, Isioma had sought out her father. She had learned from the distant cousin that he was a surgeon at UNTH. She arrived at the hospital with the birth certificate on which he was listed as her father. Isioma held it carefully in her sweaty hands because it was proof of her existence. But her father refused to see her that day, saying he had no such daughter. Days later, she would find out that he had been killed in a car accident on his way to his hometown in Nsukka.

When the psychiatrist she saw after the fact had asked her why she had done it, why she had swallowed all those pills, Isioma had simply replied that she was bored. It was the only way she could describe the hollowness. It wasn't despair. It was something that had perhaps started as despair but had now calcified into something entirely different.

"Why are you joking about trying to take your own life?" the psychiatrist had asked her. The question made Isioma angry because she had never been more serious in her life.

She had woken one day her penultimate year at the university and found that the thought of going to lectures left her cold. As she stared at the ceiling, Isioma contemplated dropping out of school. This alarmed her because she loved school. She loved her classes, the theoretical ones as well as the practicums, the physics labs conducted with rotting equipment in ill-ventilated rooms. She loved the models she built, the measuring and calculating and weighing. She liked her classmates too; they were motivated and brilliant, capable of working around antiquated textbooks with supplemental research from the internet. During study hall, the lights of their cell phones gleamed in their eyes as they marked up new textbook chapters, updating them with information they found in peer-reviewed journals and online textbooks. Isioma had felt a camaraderie with this ragtag team of budding physicists. But that morning, she didn't want any part in it. She had simply turned over and gone back to sleep.

Big Boy sat at his perch sharpening several knives. With one knife, he sliced open a coconut and ate merrily. When he grew bored, he took aim and shot down several birds. They fell to the ground. Big Boy walked a few feet in the direction of each falling bird, and each time, Isioma considered making a run for it. He would aim his gun and send her down like those birds. But each time, she sat and watched and did nothing.

That night, there were shooting stars. Three of them knifed through the dark sky. Big Boy asked her to explain.

"Shooting stars actually have nothing to do with stars," Isioma said. She sounded like she did in the classroom, and Big Boy sat up. Chief, who was cleaning his gun, stopped and turned his head to the side.

"What are they then?" he said.

"Meteoroids entering Earth's atmosphere and burning up. The trail of light we see is called a meteor. Once that meteoroid hits the Earth then it's called a meteorite."

"How far from here to the moon?" Chief asked, gazing up.

"384,400 kilometers."

"And the Americans went all the way up there? Na wah o."

A week after Isioma arrived in Abuja, Josephine drove her to the psychiatrist. It was a Tuesday morning. They arrived at nine and waited in the crowded waiting room. There were only a handful of psychiatrists for thousands of people, and getting appointments was as difficult as winning the lottery. But Josephine knew this psychiatrist, had worked with him at the national hospital in the Central Business District.

"Here we are," Josephine said.

Then she paused. She looked at Isioma with sad eyes.

"You have no idea how scared I was when Nnenna called me," Josephine said. "Telling me you had been rushed to the hospital unresponsive. I didn't even brush my teeth that morning. Just jumped into my car and started coming to you."

Josephine looked like she would cry.

"Promise me you will try to get better," Josephine said.

Isioma looked at her hands.

"Promise me," Josephine said. "Say it."

Isioma said nothing.

"Say it," Josephine begged.

"I promise," Isioma said.

"Good," Josephine said. Josephine blew her nose into a tissue and wiped tears from her eyes.

In the waiting room, there was a man mumbling under his breath, a woman who could have been his daughter looking around embarrassed. The man's eyes darted around the room. His eyes settled on Isioma and there was fire in them, his dark pupils rimmed by a rage that Isioma understood.

She would see the psychiatrist every Tuesday. After the first day, she drove herself in her mother's sedan. The psychiatrist, Dr. Tim as he liked to be called, asked her every Tuesday morning why she had done it, unsatisfied with her answers.

"I can't help you if you aren't honest with me," he said.

"I don't know what you want me to say," Isioma said on their second meeting. "I came here because I thought you could give me something, some type of drug to make me feel better."

"I want you to tell me the truth," Dr. Tim said, ignoring her. He was a thin man with bushy eyebrows and a haughty stare. Isioma wondered how much he knew her mother, what he thought of Josephine. Had he known that Josephine had a child in Enugu? More importantly, how could he help Isioma? Isioma wanted to know if Dr. Tim knew a hollowness so vast that it swept up everything in its path. She wondered if he ever woke in the night with dull voices whispering mayhem into his ears.

Dr. Tim asked her on their third meeting whether it was her grudge against her mother that made her attempt to take her own life.

"Were you so angry that you wanted to punish her?"

Isioma knew now that Josephine had told Dr. Tim all about her. In the office, Isioma stared at the potted plant behind Dr. Tim's head. Then she looked him squarely in the eye.

"I'm not angry," Isioma said. "I was never angry."

"Anger can take many forms," Dr. Tim said to her. "Sometimes what we feel as sadness is actually anger in disguise."

"Will you give me something to help me sleep?" Isioma said.

"I could give you a sleep aid," Dr. Tim said. "But unfortunately, the antidepressants you requested, the ones you've clearly researched on the internet, are in low supply across the country. You'll have to do other things."

"Like what?"

"Like talk to your mother, try to see things from her perspective."

A week in the forest and there were only two of them left, Kingsley and Isioma. Irene's family had managed to negotiate the ransom down to three million naira. She had been escorted out of the forest the afternoon before.

Chief had taken out Kingsley's sim card and was now using his iPhone as his own. Isioma's Samsung now belonged to Big Boy.

"You say your parents are doctors," Chief said. "But they don't want to pay ransom. They no like you?"

"My father is dead," Isioma said. "My mother is a psychiatrist."

"Ah ah," Big Boy said. "Your mother no like you? Big brain like you?"

Isioma didn't know how to explain that it wasn't that, at least that wasn't how she saw it. She saw her mother simply as a person who had made a definitive choice eighteen years ago to compartmentalize her life between her past and her future. On the subject of whether she was a good or bad person, Isioma also didn't think it was a fair question or the right question. Her father had left her too, and perhaps this was even more significant.

But in Gombe, Isioma had thought briefly of driving to Abuja, finding her mother's home, and killing herself by blowing herself up right in her mother's front yard. She imagined that she would go like a supernova, hot and pressurized. A pressurized dot. And maybe that way, all her energy would have finally burned bright.

She didn't return to Dr. Tim for three weeks. When she finally did, it was less because of him and more that she liked the routine, liked that it gave her something to do. Edidiong had called her and asked her once again why she had done it.

"I found you there," Edidiong said in distress. "Sleeping so peacefully. But then you slept and slept and slept, and when I checked your pulse, I couldn't find one. Why did you think death was the only way?"

Isioma was tired of this question.

"I was so fucking bored, you know," she said. Edidiong hissed.

Isioma realized her mother had been spying on her when Isioma returned home from the market where she had gone to buy euca- lyptus soap. Dr. Tim had told her to indulge in sensory pleasures, to try and see if she could regain a lust for life. She had bought ice cream and soap and a scented candle with the money her mother had given her that morning.

In the kitchen, Josephine was cooking egusi soup. Isioma gave her a noncommittal wave as she headed up to Ahmed's bedroom. She took a shower with the eucalyptus soap, which filled the bath- room with its powerful smell and made her think for a brief mo- ment that perhaps she could try to live.

Her mother had set the lunch table and was waiting for her

when Isioma returned downstairs. Josephine looked up from her cell phone. She gave Isioma a smile that didn't reach her eyes.

"Why didn't you tell me you weren't sleeping?" Josephine said in a distant voice. Isioma stopped. She knew Dr. Tim was feeding her mother information and vice versa, but the nonchalance with which her mother had revealed this breach of confidentiality made the blood rush to Isioma's head, like she was hanging upside down.

"Did Dr. Tim tell you that?" Isioma said.

"I've been trying," Josephine said. "And yet you still see me as the enemy."

"He's been telling you everything I've been saying," Isioma said. Josephine sighed. She closed her eyes.

"He says you are one of the most difficult patients he's ever had," Josephine said.

Isioma didn't know what came over her. Perhaps it was her mother reaching for her, as though to pull her into an embrace. Perhaps it was her mother bursting into tears when Isioma slapped her hand away. But Isioma picked up a vase of hibiscus flowers and flung it across the room. She didn't wait to watch it shatter against the wall. She went upstairs to Ahmed's bedroom and tore his shirts from their hangers. She smashed the mirror. In the morning, she boarded the ABC Transport bus headed to Enugu, to Nnenna.

Two weeks in the forest and Isioma was now the only remaining abductee.

"You must be a problem child," Big Boy said. He was tired of being in the bush, tired of shitting in holes he dug with a shovel.

When Chief returned the next morning, he sat on the stool Big Boy had vacated and cleared his throat.

"Why don't you go home, Big Brain?" he said.

Isioma was leaning against the tree stump.

"Surely there's someone out there missing you." Chief looked at Isioma with a pity that annoyed her. She chased an army of ants away from her bare thighs, the stench on her unwashed body filling her nose.

"I think I'll stay a little longer," Isioma said. Then she closed her eyes and fell asleep.

This Isn't the Actual Sea

FROM *The Idaho Review*

AS I APPROACHED my friend's house, I could see by the number of cars on the street that many people had been invited, far more than I expected. I considered turning around. Instead, I let myself in to a clamor of voices and the barking of my friend's poodle. The long living room windows swam with gusts of color as guests circled in their bright sweaters.

"Come here," she said. "You look older! And I thought you were timeless." She hugged me and I hugged her back, and when I pulled away my ring snagged in her hair.

"I'm sorry," I said.

"It was silly that we went so long without seeing each other," she said, dipping her head as I disentangled the ring, like a child letting its mother work out a knot. She smiled over my shoulder at someone. "You humiliated me."

I pulled two long, crinkled strands of her hair from the ring, a flat, square, algae-green-and-black-speckled stone, set in gold. It wasn't my wedding ring. My husband and I didn't wear wedding rings. Mine gave me a rash, his he'd misplaced sink-side in a restaurant in LA, gone by the time we went back. The thought of wearing someone else's wedding ring seemed unlucky to me, darkly incantatory. (Probably it had been sold.) We'd decided not to replace it, and now, as I released my friend's hair from between my pinched fingers and watched it drift to the ground, I wondered if this made us weak or strong, reckless in our indifference to the totems of our pairing. My friend moved to the center of the room and thanked everyone for coming, and I took a seat on the couch sandwiched between two others. The poodle was sprawled on the floor in the middle of everyone, and people would reach out their arms and legs occasionally and give his side a swipe. Guests leaned against walls, crowded out of the kitchen. It was a happy, eager group, willing to give themselves over to art, to be transformed by an encounter with what they would remember later as intellectual beauty. One always remembers one's first time with intellectual beauty.

"It's been twenty years since I did this," my friend said. "I was twenty-nine when my first film was released. I never expected it to be received the way it was. I never thought it would become something of a cult favorite. It took on a life of its own as I married, raised twins, saw them off to college. Recently, at a party, I overheard someone talking about it. He thought it was by Peter Bogdanovich."

A redheaded man raised a tremulous hand. "That was me. Sorry. I thought it was his juvenilia."

"I told myself what I'd had was enough," my friend continued. "Why would I deserve anything more? No one expected a second film from me, and for a long time it seemed as if there wouldn't be one. I'm not going to say I was writing even when I wasn't writing, because I don't know what that means. It sounds good, like the mind is a ledger and nothing is lost, but the truth is more like I *wasn't* writing even when I was. I'd start something and it would turn into a to-do list . . ." Her voice trailed off and she gestured toward a white bedsheet unfurled in front of the fireplace. "And then there was this. I give you *The Park*."

The lights dimmed, and the movie began playing. It doesn't matter, just now, what it was about. When it was over, everyone applauded and thronged my friend to congratulate her. I watched them say how much they cared about the characters, how she made them care, how they didn't expect to care so much but they did. The darkness outside was now complete, and I was reminded of a sensation from early childhood, of waking from a nap and feeling that the heart, the dense bud of the day, had disappeared and I was left with misplaced time, an hour I didn't recognize, silty and mournful and gray.

My friend took my elbow and drew me into the kitchen. "Did you like it?" she said. "I thought it would be different this time, but it's not. If anything, it's worse, because I'm older. I should know better."

I told her I did. I said these quartz countertops were the pathetic kingdom of doubt, and she must leave it, she must leave it forever. "If behind every great man is a woman, behind every great woman is a panting blob of doubt and insecurity, a fanged blob nipping at her heels," I said.

"I just think it sort of sucked," my friend said.

"It did not suck," a man who'd approached without us noticing said. Our heads rolled in his direction.

"I don't mean *sucked* sucked," she said.

"Oh, it's false modesty, is it? A relic like a shard of pottery or something?" To make sure she got the friendly spirit of his delivery, he reached out and touched her arm.

She laughed. "Here lies the museum of false modesty. Do you have a ticket?"

I slunk away.

I couldn't fall asleep that night. "Let's have sex," I said to my husband, but he didn't like the way I broached the subject, and we quarreled. I rose from bed and scuffed into Birkenstocks and walked outside to the park across the street from our house. Leaves massed above me like filigreed clouds. Trash cans waited to be emptied, filled. Their inhuman patience leveled my racing heart. I, too, had given things to the world—let's say poems, but they could be stories or novels or simply my opinions—that I felt, immediately, I wanted to take back, and hated with a sickening intimacy. Why did I feel that way? Here is the shuddering dark inside of my brain, these things seemed to say. Here is my religion. Bear in mind I am not religious.

My friend and I had avoided seeing each other in order to avoid falsehood, because to not speak of what had happened between us, what had caused our break, would be a lie. To not speak of what we had gleaned of one another, for while I had seen vulnerability in her so had I seen an adherence to hierarchy, to an idea of who should do her bidding and how that bidding should be done, while, for her part, she had seen something stubborn, disloyal, in me. To speak of this would expose us to scrutiny and take every last bit of her strength, the strength she was using to make her movie. It was only when she'd finished, when she had proof of some sort, that she decided she could see me again. The proof wasn't the movie; it was the survival of her secret self. After all, her friends weren't making movies, the woman who taught her yoga class wasn't making a movie, the twins weren't making movies, her ex-husband wasn't making a movie, the neighbors who stopped her for small talk weren't making movies, and so she—the *she* they knew, the *she* in the material world—wasn't making a movie, either. It was some hidden, grotesque part of her, some immaterial urge that roiled inside her like steam in a bottle that was making a movie. She must've known that there were other women who were making movies (and had seen some of them, the few that eked through), she just didn't know these women personally. She texted me the next day, a Saturday.

> That guy
> The ticket guy?
> I slept with him
> What!
> A rando as the twins say
> Listen to you with the youth's lingo.
> Yes cheap perfect words

I shut my phone in a drawer and ate a yogurt and tried to work. When I checked it again after what felt like at least forty-five minutes, twelve had passed. I was rewarded with an invitation for coffee.

How different a house looked after a party, its facade flattened, washed of responsibility. In the kitchen, the poodle sniffed my crotch until I pushed his head away. The coffee maker burbled; my friend poured. She placed two steaming mugs on the breakfast table, a sugar bowl, cream. Her hair was pulled back with a tortoiseshell clip. Her ears were very pink, and I was reminded of the peppermint pig my husband brought forth each Christmas after dinner. He placed the pig in a velvet bag, and invited our son to smash it with a little silver hammer. It was a tradition from his childhood—eating a piece of the pig was supposed to mean you'd be prosperous in the year ahead, but I rebelled against the idea of treating prosperity like something to be heralded, hoped for, coaxed forth with rituals, placed at the zenith of human ambition. Give me insight, I always thought as I let the peppermint dissolve in my mouth, which was in its own way rapacious, an invisible acquisition, sometimes undependable.

"You left early last night," my friend said.

I made a what-of-it face.

"I know, okay. I'd never met him before, a friend brought him. Afterward I cried from some kind of ancient exhaustion and we ate leftovers."

"Which leftovers?"

"Those almond horns."

"And then you felt better?" I said.

"About me. I won't see him again. I'm over it, the drama. Give me a good meal, good weather, a comfortable bed."

"You already have those things."

"The weather's only mine when it's bad," she said.

"I know what you mean."

"We're so *blind*," my friend said exultantly.

I felt very close to her then.

My friend couldn't stand the idea of her movie being ignored or reviewed. Both scenarios were terrible to her. Being ignored would confirm her invisibility, while being reviewed would dissect her presence. It was more than the individual circumstance of her releasing a movie, I imagined she thought. It was historical, societal, gendered. The pathway one took when considering one's success was wide and well groomed, and branched off in several places; the pathway one took when considering one's failure was narrow and icy, and circled fatefully back to oneself. Her movie played at a few art theaters in New York (but not at any of the Laemmles here), and when she found out it was to be reviewed in the Sunday *New York Times,* she asked me to come over and read the review first. I did so with a mean need for it to be panned. If her movie was panned, I would find some fuel for myself, a source of heat, a jagged, terrible pleasure. It wasn't panned. It was well reviewed, and I felt, too, genuine happiness for my friend, and shame at my animal thought.

I was sitting on her front stoop. She took the newspaper from me and read it herself and then rattled it decisively closed.

"It's too generous," she said.

"It's not. It's very perceptive."

"You don't mean it. I can see it in your eyes."

"My eyes lie!"

"I think what I'm most afraid of is never having another original thought again."

Her street was lined with ginkgo trees that had turned yellow and were shedding their fan-shaped leaves. It was early December and fall had finally arrived. Even so, the cooler weather could erupt at any time into heat like the brush fires that broke out near highway exit ramps, long tongues of smoke in the distance. Now, though, the air was clear. Leaves plastered the sidewalk. I had once been afraid of the same thing, but I went so long without an original thought I forgot what it was like; in my maze of the familiar I forgot how grand the strange could be.

I saw her in the grocery store. We were at opposite ends of the freezer where bags of fish were kept. I saw her ask an aproned clerk a question. I saw her not like how slow he was to respond, for she brandished her phone in his face, causing him to step backward into someone else's cart. They both turned to this third person, an elderly woman who'd approached with fragile steps, and apologized profusely. I saw her face move from anger to concern; I saw how swiftly and shamelessly she camouflaged herself inside separate moments and the forces that made them. I saw her see me and come forward explaining before she even quite reached me that she'd had to scold the boy for scrolling at work. I asked if he might not have been searching for music, as my son so often claimed he was doing when I caught him gazing dumbly at his phone, and she said no, he was watching someone skateboard off a roof. "A roof!" my friend said, as if had it been steps it might've been different. As if all human effort must go through her, her body a sieve with the heavy organs caught in the bowl of her and the rest running out.

She was invited to screen her movie at the women's college in our town, and she asked me to accompany her. The campus was a lush collection of bougainvillea- and fountain-filled courtyards that seemed designed less for the delights of the mind than the senses, the plashing of water, the wax-paper weight of the sun. In a velvet auditorium, a professor of gender and sexuality studies introduced my friend. The lights dimmed and the movie began. Ten or fifteen minutes in, I became aware that students were leaving, swiftly up the aisles, the shushing of their leggings. Afterward, the professor opened the floor to questions. The questions asked by those students who remained were deeply skeptical of the movie's depiction of the lives of middle-aged women as lives of frustration and anger and shame. You could tell they didn't think their futures would bear any resemblance to that. Their futures were like stacks of soft-folded sweaters in a pretty store with a salesgirl whose hair was cut in a style they would soon see everywhere. Some girls were nearly soothsayers that way. The movie, no, the movie didn't feel that apt. It felt a little irrelevant to be honest.

My friend nodded vigorously as they spoke. She said she understood. She used to feel that way herself. But everything changes when you get married, she said. I thought of her ex, a slight man with slick lips who had disappeared early each morning onto a train that took him into LA to work at a podcast production company. The most shocking thing about him was that he was missing a nipple. My friend had felt he didn't take her seriously and had only tolerated her creative ambitions. I had a recurring fantasy about him, or not a fantasy exactly but a sequence of thoughts I summoned when I couldn't fall asleep: I was dying and asked to see him, and he walked into the dim room where I lay quietly, and he held my hand and confessed his regret, and I realized I didn't have any regret and that was the great, the only gift of dying.

After the Q&A, we had dinner with the professor of sexuality and gender studies and her wife at an Italian restaurant. The professor apologized for the students. She said it was ironic, their objection to the vision of women the movie presented, for had my friend's movie depicted women as reduced figures in entirely functionary sexual roles they would've been fine with that. My friend came to the students' defense. To the professor it must've seemed like generosity, but I knew the choice my friend was being asked to make was to align herself either with the bitterness of age or the shiny glaze of youth, that icing-sweet shellac that cracked in skittish lines at a fork tap. After dinner we walked home, politely drunk. She'd chosen the side with all the joys and disappointments still to come.

I understood what my friend's movie was about the first time I saw it, but I was too distracted by the other people in the room for it to sink in. (I tended to succumb in other people's presence to an awareness of their presence, a closed loop.) It was only after my second viewing that I realized how little she'd changed about the incident that had caused us to stop seeing each other. It had happened shortly after her husband moved out, in those early weeks of her aloneness. She had asked me to dog sit for a few days while she went to soothe herself at a hot springs. Of course, I agreed. It was a midweek trip, so the poodle couldn't stay with her soon-to-be-ex. The poodle was used to having someone around—it wouldn't work for him to be left alone all day. My friend dropped him and his bed and leash and kibble at my house on a Tuesday morning, and I told her to have a wonderful time. She was traveling to the hot springs with another of her friends, a woman I knew only slightly and who was so beautiful I felt like an old, cracked log in her presence.

Later that day, I decided to take the poodle to the dog park. It would be fun, I thought, to see him loping about, and to pretend that he was mine. I loaded him into the car and we drove there, and there he bit a small dog, badly, on the neck. The small dog let out a cry like a peacock's, and gushed blood. My friend was very upset when I called her and told her what had happened. She drove straight home, came into my house, and dropped to her knees to inspect every inch of the poodle, who had sustained no injury and was lying in his bed panting with residual angst. My friend said she hadn't told me to take the poodle to the dog park, and I said I assumed it was somewhere he had been before, and my friend said it was, and it had been fine, but she'd sensed the park's potential for chaos, for violence. But it was your dog's potential for violence you sensed, I said. My friend began to cry. She said I was selfish, a selfish person willing to blame others for their own suffering. Then she piled the poodle's leash and kibble into the dog bed, and left, the poodle trotting after her with a hung head. He knew we were talking about him.

I had disavowed my relationship to the poodle right after he sank his teeth into the small dog's neck. The small dog's owner and I had been chatting so pleasantly before the attack. Oh my god! He's not mine! I had cried, though the small dog's owner was too busy kicking the poodle off her dog to respond.

Seeing my friend's movie a second time, I noted how brusquely the friend who was dog sitting treated the dog after the attack, how completely she shunned the animal, and I realized that my friend identified with her dog very closely. I thought back to the attack again, trying to picture exactly what had happened, and I remembered that the small dog had sniffed the poodle under his muzzle right before the poodle bit him. Raised his little head and sniffed the soft, vulnerable throat so pink beneath the poodle's lambswool coat. The attack appeared unprovoked, but it wasn't. It wasn't justified, but it was not unprovoked.

As I swam laps, I considered how to talk to my friend about her movie. I knew she'd deny an explicit connection. If pressed, she might say a movie is a dramatic experience, and the filmmaker won't be around to explain it, so of course I was free to interpret it any way I liked. Putting it that way would undermine my authority quite nicely while seeming to argue for the autonomy of art and the independence of the viewer, for an authentic relationship between two entities which were both, in their own ways, staged. My friend might quote Gertrude Stein, who said she wrote for herself and strangers. *Everybody is a real one to me, everybody is like someone else too to me,* Stein had said. I began to backstroke, droplets from my fingertips falling into my mouth. The ceiling panels were open to pale parcels of sky.

I emailed my friend's ex-husband to ask if he'd seen her movie. He had not been at her house, and I didn't know if that was because he hadn't been invited, or had declined to come. (My husband had declined to come.) I wrote, *I felt it didn't imagine enough,* filled with a sudden desire to commiserate with someone who must, himself, wish my friend had done more work creating rather than replicating, building something new. I sent the email before I could stop myself. He replied politely, with no insight.

My friend was raking leaves in her driveway, her car parked in the street and the poodle sniffing about the yard. It had rained the night before, and the mountains were covered with snow. Palm trees in the foreground, white mountains in the background, the sky a heartrending blue. I sat on her stoop and said the name of her ex.

"What about him?" she said.

"Do you see him regularly?"

"We're very friendly." She turned her head and called to the

poodle, then turned back to me. "We don't have to explain ourselves to each other anymore. We can be more generous."

I had heard this before, or some version of it, and indeed it
made sense that those who had suffered divorce's pain would also
want to broadcast its freedoms. Like swimming in an icy lake and
feeling very alive, very awake, in intimate contact with the elements.
A genuine feeling, an admirable one, though I wouldn't for any
reason, not for clarity or moral forthrightness or inner rectitude,
choose an icy lake over my eighty-two-degree pool. She called the
poodle again more sharply, and he came and sat at her feet and
despite this act of obedience, or because of it, she picked up his
leash from where it lay coiled next to me and leashed him.

"Why do you ask?" she said.

"I've been thinking about him for some reason. And you. You
seemed so happy together."

She snorted. "You can't know what it's like to be another person,
not really. This is what we depend on."

She loved Ingmar Bergman, especially *Wild Strawberries*. I objected
to his depiction of women. She said that to dramatize an ideal,
one always exaggerated. I said ideals were for cowards. She said
my thinking was too grim. I said hers was too accommodating,
stretching to fit the flatness she had been given and asked to believe was profundity. She said I needed to smile more. I said that
was what men always said about women. She said that was because
unsmiling women scared men, but she wasn't a man and I didn't
scare her. Why then? I said. You just look better when you do,
she said. Bergman and Fellini and Cassavetes and Coppola and
Anderson and Fincher, all that male weather, sun storm, deluge,
drought, downpour.

And then came a few weeks during which we did not see each other,
for no reason. Just a stretch of being idle. But I was aware as the
weeks went by that although there had been no incident this time,
every day we did not see each other brought us closer to not seeing
each other again. How telling myself I'd be fine before—when we
really *weren't* seeing each other—meant in fact I would be fine,
though something would be lost. How you can lose something and
still be fine. How the lost thing is more present when it's lost.

*

Sometimes my thinking about her was clear, thrillingly absolute. Sometimes my thinking was laden with regret. One might say it was really about myself though it felt so precisely about her.

I was driving into the foothills, listening to an interview with Bruce Springsteen on the radio. He was saying when he first met his wife they had so much in common. "It was like, before you were you, you were me," he said. I stopped at a red light. A car with a loud muffler pulled up next to mine and rumbled in place and when the light changed took off in a series of ignominious putts. The road rose and narrowed. We go to music not to learn something but to be reminded of something, Springsteen said, and I turned onto the street where I'd arranged to meet my friend, parked, and got out. She was leaning against her car, staring at the mountains. She had brought water and I hadn't, and I imagined asking her for water, whether I could or whether it would seem too forward, drinking out of the same spout. Of course, I could unscrew the lid and sip from the bottle, or she could unscrew the lid for me before handing it over, a sure indication she would not like to share the same spout, though it was also possible it would mean she thought I was about to do so myself and trying to save face by beating me to it, or even that she was simply being helpful. I determined to trudge through my thirst. We donned hats and set out on our hike and she began to talk about her movie, about how she was trying to scare up more interest in it. Attention wasn't something she wanted, but needed. She supposed it was the people who wanted it that got it. She was grateful her movie had been reviewed in the *Times,* but it hadn't been reviewed anywhere else. No one had approached her for an interview, no film festivals had contacted her. She was getting no publicity and her window of relevance was shrinking every day.

"My little performance at Shelton College might be it," she said.

I mentioned that I knew an editor who may be interested. "Send me a link."

"Thanks. I'll give you a DVD, too."

We were climbing on loose, pebbly dirt past gray-blue agaves and manzanita trees whose dried-blood bark seemed to run in rivulets down the trunks.

"You know, I've been thinking a lot about what I said to you in the kitchen that night. I was wrong," she said. "I'm better than many. I'm downright good. If others can be, why not me?"

I told her I agreed. I said her next movie would be her best, meaning it as a compliment, meaning it would be more elusive, more mysterious, that it would range farther afield and might surprise her, but it sounded as if I were saying that what she'd made wasn't enough. To make up for it I decided to tell her about what I was working on now. She had given me this story, and I realized she could take it back by uttering two or three condemnatory words, or smiling with a little question mark at the corners of her mouth, or allowing a glaze of disinterest to come into her eyes. We walked higher and higher until we had a view of the valley, cars swimming through the milky smog, flitting close behind one another like fish in an aquarium about whom one inevitably thinks, *Do they know this isn't the actual sea?* Then we walked back to our cars, and I followed her to her house and idled out front while she ran inside. She re-emerged and handed a DVD to me through the car window, and I could hear the poodle barking and smell something coming off her, a stab of deodorant, a sort of unnatural hope and exertion, and I felt then the terror and promise of friendship, the daily encounter with what the other dares to be.

It Is What It Is

FROM *Electric Literature*

KHORSHID, WHOSE NAME in English translates to *Sun,* arrived from Canada on a dreary February morning. I had been warned that she wouldn't answer to *Sun* because her family only ever spoke to her in Farsi, telling her softly, Khorshid *bia* and Khorshid *nakon* and Khorshid *bia bebin chi vasat kharidam,* her favorite of the three commands because it meant a treat had been purchased for her, a sliver of fish or a thread from which lush multi-colored feathers had been strung for her pleasure. Her fate, which had been mostly favorable, had taken a horrifying turn. She had lost her family, a set of parents and their twin children, on the eve of January 8, 2020, in an explosion at dusk over the Tehran sky. The family was returning to Canada after a brief visit to their homeland to attend a wedding. The pilots had barely drawn the plane's wheels into the wheel well when it was shot down by two surface-to-air missiles twenty-three seconds apart. As the plane dribbled down the night sky, it appeared to the confused gaze of bystanders to be the descending sun ablaze.

For days, I sat at the kitchen table in my apartment in Chicago scrutinizing the videos of the explosion. I traced the missiles' upward trajectories as they carved their way toward the passenger plane and then watched the plane light up from the impact and tumble down the bruised sky. I scrolled through social media searching for posts about the explosion. That's how I found Khorshid. I saw her photo on Twitter. The caption, written by her pet sitter, read: "Cat needs to be rehomed. Owners died. Victims of flight 752 that was shot down in Tehran." I stared at Khorshid's high cheekbones and exaggeratedly long whiskers, her green eyes through which she looked out at the world in shock and concluded that her owners' deaths had been a kind of disappearance. No bodies had been recovered. They had turned to ash midair and taken their place next to all of the unburied dead. Next to my father who had never been found.

I wrote instantly to Khorshid's pet sitter: "I will take her. I will love her with all of my soul."

I was aware that my language was over the top. I didn't care. The situation was uncertain, dire. I needed something to be definitive, even if that something was the tone of my voice. I didn't bother to tell my roommate, Fereshteh. I could hear her furiously typing away at her dissertation on Mahmoud Darwish in the next room. She always typed with aggression, offensively pounding the keyboard. I once asked her why she typed that way.

"When I write I'm taking revenge on the world," she said curtly and I never brought the subject up again.

I stared out the window at the passersby in their long windproof coats, their heads wrapped in wool, walking crookedly, making little jumps to avoid the puddles of black ice that always clog the arteries of Chicago in winter. Then I leaned into my reply, my plea which was also a pledge, and DM'ed the pet sitter again: "I will pay for her to be put on a plane this instant; she is my Khorshid, I can feel it in my bones." If Fereshteh were to protest, I would tell her that adopting Khorshid was my version of taking revenge on the world. That, I decided, would settle it.

Then I put my coat on and walked to the lakefront. I stood there in the harsh wind and watched the water crash and rebound against the breakwater. I watched the foam and froth lift into the air, shattering into a million brilliant droplets before they dropped again into the black depths that reminded me of the Caspian—just as moody, just as much of a trickster, pulling swimmers into its entrails and yanking them around until they go limp. A sea disguised as a lake, hemmed in by land and in a rage because of it.

I paced around restlessly for hours, hunched up with homesickness and sobbing in my grief. Then I went home and called the pet sitter who had written me back with his name, Roger, and phone number. "Here with my ear to the phone," wrote Roger. Then, "Other interest, call quickly."

Roger's voice was deep, guttural. He told me that on the morning of the accident, at the family's cul-de-sac home on a quiet tree-lined street in Toronto, Khorshid had sat expectantly at the picture window. The gray domed sky beyond it had dumped snow onto the city all through the long dark winter. Roger was convinced that Khorshid sensed that her family was due to return *any minute now* because her eyes, fixed on the wide concrete path on either side of which shoveled snow had been piled high, betrayed an expression of longing.

At least that's what he'd thought initially, he said, pausing gravely, before describing to me in greater detail the view from the window where Khorshid had conducted what had appeared at first to be a ritual act of devotion to her humans. He repeated several times, his tone progressively more confessional, that that's what he'd thought was happening: that the cat was yearning for the familiar scents of her beloveds, that she was anticipating the hour of their approach. But then, as news of the explosion surfaced on all of his life's screens—the multiple televisions affixed to the walls of the family's home, the Twitter feed on his iPhone, and then again on the YouTube channel he'd opened his laptop to—he'd begun to feel that he too was engulfed in flames.

He paused again, and in the deafening silence of his retreat I thought of my father. My father, the poet Ali Shafabaksh, who had disappeared along with a busload of other poets. They belonged to a literary group called the Truth Bearers. That's all I know. It happened before I was born, when I was just a fetus. The poets' remains were never found. They were likely dumped together in an unmarked grave in a remote province of Iran.

"Anyway," Roger started up again, somewhat irritably. Uncertain about what to do to find relief from the intense heat, from the invisible flames that he felt were devouring him, he'd run outside into the cold where he'd suddenly snapped back to attention. That's when he saw that the cat's eyes bore an expression of horror and disgust not unlike his own. An even stranger feeling had come over him then, Roger said; an inability to recognize the world, and for a moment, which had seemed to him to last an eternity, he felt unable to tell himself apart from the cat. He had seen in her distressed face his own. Khorshid's pupils, he told me, were dilated, static. Her brow was locked in anger. Her mouth was turned down in grave lament, and as he looked at her, he had the strange sensation that his own mouth was sliding off his face.

To this the sitter added that in the days that followed he had not known how to speak of the disaster to poor Khorshid, who had begun to lick her sides raw in response to her family's sudden collective death on the other side of the Atlantic. He'd failed, he said, at soothing her. "She must have sensed the end approaching," he muttered breathlessly into the phone. His voice kept shifting registers, exposing his distress.

"It's entirely possible," I said, sensing an opening, then I closed my eyes and saw the concrete path Khorshid had studied through the windows. I don't remember what the sitter said next. In my mind's eye, the sidewalk, cracked from the cold and exposed to the elements, suddenly morphed. It became elongated, as though it were made of rubber, and took the shape of the lit runway at Imam Khomeini Airport from which the family's passenger plane had taken off—the same runway from which I'd fled decades earlier, once my mother had given up on waiting for my father to reappear—and my whole body shuddered.

"Are you still there?" the sitter said.

I confirmed that I was. I told him not to worry, that I would adopt Khorshid and give her the best Iranian life ever. I said this so emphatically that he was taken aback. I felt myself getting nervous, growing taut with the energy of madness that stretched me from limb to limb every time I thought of my disappeared father. What does one do with the unburied dead? I filled the silence when I should have kept quiet. I said, "Don't worry, I promise the samovar will be going at all hours, releasing cardamom vapors, and that she will always have her share of white fish served on decorated ceramic plates." I spoke as though I were relaying a message of comfort directly to her dead beloveds. I was convinced that any pleasure I provided her with would be conveyed to her deceased humans.

I didn't explain any of this to the sitter. Sure, he was tender-hearted. But still, I considered, this pet sitter, sensitive as he may be, was not *my people*. There was no one planting grenades at his feet or watching his thermal shadow on a screen or tracking his every move convinced that he was a purveyor of violence. His life, I'd thought, remembering again the black ribbon of the runway which had taken on a liquid aspect as the plane on which I'd fled Tehran took off into a sky stripped of stars, was not conditional. I refrained from providing explanatory notes. Neither did I care nor think about how this transmission of pleasure from Khorshid to her family, who had been eviscerated midair, would take place. I just needed to believe that it would.

It took a few weeks to settle the adoption. In the interim, Fereshteh and I barely spoke a word. She'd taken the news about Khorshid in stride, perhaps because her attention was elsewhere. She was exhausted from her looming dissertation deadline and a severe adviser she was convinced had a mood disorder, a young aspiring poet on his first tenure gig who changed his hairstyle every semester and who had an uneven email habit that drove Fereshteh mad.

Occasionally, she would come into the kitchen, where I did most of my reading, to make herself some lunch and call home. She would leave her computer open on the counter behind her. The Skype screen displayed her mother, her *maman,* seated on a sofa beneath wide windows through which I could gleam the triumphant ring of mountains that crown Tehran, making it difficult for the pollution to escape. Each time I saw the Tehran sky on the screen, it appeared to be heavy with artillery, full of ashes and the soot of the dead. Her mother and I would wave at one another politely and shake our heads, as if to say *I have run out of words.* Fereshteh's brother, Iraj, a famous wrestler, had been at Evin prison since the Green Movement protests of 2009. No one had heard from him in years. Her uncle, Ahmad, a defender of the Islamic Revolution, had disappeared in the Iran-Iraq war in the early '80s. A second uncle, alive and locatable, lived in Beirut. There were framed photos of the two missing men—Fereshteh's brother and first uncle—hanging on the wall behind the sofa where her maman sat. Occasionally, I'd steal a glimpse of their faces. They looked alike: round tanned faces, plump cheeks, a full head of black curls except that Iraj had a clean-shaven dimpled face and bright blue eyes and Ahmad had a wiry speckled beard and piercing black eyes sunken beneath a unibrow. Looking at their faces helped me to imagine my father's. I'd never seen a picture of him. All ties to him had been destroyed to preserve my life.

In the days leading up to Khorshid's arrival, Fereshteh and I barely spoke. She was always in a gloomy mood. If we did speak, it was to exchange verses from the latest Darwish book we were reading together and which we kept on the living room bar cart next to the bottles of Arak we had accumulated over the years. That week we were reading *Memory of Forgetfulness*. Every time we crossed paths in the living room, one of us would pick the book up and recite, "Are you well? I mean, are you alive?" The other, having memorized slivers from the book, would answer, "Don't die completely," or, maybe, "Don't die at all."

That was the extent of our exchange until Khorshid arrived, bald, her skin raw from all of that anxious licking. The day of her arrival I stood on my toes and squinted beneath the bright overhead lights that lined the low ceiling of the Chicago airport. I strained to look over the beanied heads of passengers and those who'd come to greet them, eager, expectant. My heart was racing. I was trying desperately to spot her crate, sweating despite the fact that the airport air was damp with a biting winter chill. I kept imagining her fearfully pressing her face against the bars of the crate. That face of hers which I'd first seen on my Twitter feed and that had stolen my heart, seized it instantly and with such brute force that later, once she'd settled into our apartment, I would come to forget that I'd ever lived without her weaving between my legs, licking my tired eyes, yawning in my face at dawn.

I kept thinking I'd spotted her amid the parting airport crowd and would squeeze Fereshteh's hand and whisper "Khorshid!" with a sigh I suspected she found grating but which she nonetheless echoed in solidarity. After all, things had been taken away from our lives more often than they'd arrived. It was hard not to feel giddy.

When I finally saw her, I grew ecstatic. I thought my heart was going to explode. Fereshteh was smiling too, a broad smile that momentarily shattered her icy dissertation mood. On the way home, I said Khorshid's name over and over again. We drove along the belt that hugged the curves of the lake, so blue that day, bright and full of an unexpected light. Khorshid occasionally emitted a reluctant reply which we took as an indication that she knew she was safe again, that somehow, by the grace of god, if Khorshid, unlike us, was one to believe in god, she'd made it through the worst of it.

Halfway home, Fereshteh's mood shifted again. She turned serious, austere. I was convinced that the anticipation of sitting again at her desk was making her shut down. Wide shafts of light came through the car window and made her fingers, white from gripping the steering wheel, look translucent. In that oxidized light, she looked to me like a ghost. She turned to me and said, "Today, while I was finishing my second chapter on Darwish's oeuvre, I had an awful feeling that the world is a book and that we are all characters trapped in separate chapters, on different levels of reality that don't necessarily intersect, and that the whole thing, this book that is our lives, will be torn to bits soon and that we will all be floundering in a sea of sorrows." I was alarmed. She was so seldom dramatic. Prosaic in conversation even less often. She was a woman of few words.

I said nothing. I stopped speaking to Khorshid. I looked at the lake. It was beautiful, glittering, immense. I wondered if Fereshteh was quoting Darwish, but I couldn't recall having read those exact words. I had read almost all of Darwish. I had already finished my dissertation, a study of "revolutionary madman writers" who either lived solitary monkish lives in exile or who, like my father, had disappeared, but who, unlike my father, had left letters and sheaths of poetry behind. I looked over at Fereshteh. Her eyes were shining with remorse, as if she'd betrayed a secret she'd been entrusted with and had been unable to bite her tongue.

I tried to make sense of her words.

"Do you mean to say we need a new script?" I asked. "That this life as we've come to know it is about to expire?"

"Worse," she said, fixing her gaze on the road, "like our lives are going to gradually disappear from us, rather than the other way around, and this vanishing of our lives will feel to us stranger than death, than dying, than the disappearance of our brothers, uncles, fathers, that we will be alive, able to see and hear the world, but we will lack all understanding of how to operate within it."

"Just us?"

"No. Everyone."

I didn't say a word. I thought of what Roger had said, of that odd sensation he'd described to me; how the boundaries of his body had become diffuse and merged with Khorshid's and pictured his mouth sliding off his face. I thought to myself, great ruptures have happened before. Empires have collapsed. Civilizations have gone extinct. I wished I could read my father's poems. That some piece of paper, some scrap existed in the gossamer of the universe with his words. I wished my mother had memorized his poems and recited them to me, transcribed and published them under a pseudonym. But she hadn't and besides, she'd passed away a decade ago.

I looked again at the lake. It appeared swollen to me, as though the water levels had been rising by nearly imperceptible degrees. Up above, the sun was lit. A thousand flames shot out of it. It looked like a wheel caught on fire; it was branding its burning tentacles onto the immense lake.

"I'm telling you," Fereshteh said, turning to look through the passenger side window at that sun, "something sinister is afoot. I can feel it."

I opened the crate and put my hand on Khorshid's arched back and felt her slim body twist to find a new shape. I felt her muscles relax. Her engine, that little roar, ancient, subterranean, came on. The sound of her purr kept my heart beating steady even though I could see shadowy figures rising from the glassy blue horizon, plumes of gray smoke being sucked into that rabid sun.

By late April, Khorshid's fur had mostly grown back. She appeared to be in the spring of her life. In the afternoons, I would often find her pinned to the hardwood floor by a slant of auburn sunlight coming through the east-facing windows. If I approached her she would roll on her back and her soft doughy stomach would spread on either side of her; she'd elongate her legs, expose her claws, and let her head bob from side to side in greeting. She was most active at dawn and dusk, during the twilight hours, those electric libidinal hours of uncertainty that impart awe on us feckless humans. I began to suspect that her activities during those charged hours of possibility—her crooked runs at top speed across the length of the apartment, her acrobatic jumps and backflips, the way she crouched in the shadow of an armchair with her nose pointed straight at the floor—were simply a mechanism for communing with her dearly departed, evidence that she was in league with the dead. It was not a leap to think so. Roger, who I hadn't spoken to since the first time, believed that she had intuited the disaster, that her body had registered the loss before it became a known fact of her life, or to be more precise, that she had perceived the disaster at the exact moment of the explosion. When I shared my thesis with Fereshteh, she merely shook her head in disbelief.

"She's an average cat," she said. "Stop projecting on her."

"But you saw the pandemic coming the day we drove her home from the airport," I insisted. She said nothing. "Don't you think it's possible that Khorshid was intimating news of the cosmic violence we are engulfed in?" I cried in a supplicant tone.

"Coincidence," she emitted tersely, "and besides, the only prophet here is Darwish."

The next time she spoke to her maman on Skype, I brought it up again. Maman was slicing a watermelon in their kitchen. The neon-green soot of the Tehran sky was visible through the rectangular window over their sink. For a brief second, before her maman turned her head to look into the camera, I thought I saw Iraj and Ahmad's faces swimming in that green sky, their curls and Ahmad's beard bright orange flames of fire. Maman pointed the knife she was holding at us and said: "Life is short. There's a pandemic raging. It's summertime. You two should go out and buy yourselves some watermelon. I had to queue for over an hour to get this." She was always trying to be instructive for Fereshteh's sake, unaware that seeing her mother whip herself up into false decisiveness when her realm of control was ever diminishing only made Fereshteh feel more weighed down, as if lead had been poured into her veins.

"Seriously," I objected, "think of all the reasons why cats were revered in ancient Mesopotamia!"

"Hearsay!" Fereshteh whispered under her breath. Maman simply replied that there's nothing special about our Khorshid, or nothing especially special she said, and brought the knife back down into the rind of the watermelon.

"See?" Fereshteh said glaring at me with the white of her eyes. "Don't confuse myth with life!"

I said nothing. We ended the call shortly after that and Maman vanished from the screen with the same electric swoosh of her disappeared family member's faces as they dragged their tales of fire along.

Days passed, monotonous, tense, foreclosed. All through June the atmospheric humidity in Chicago was unbearably high. Everyone walked around slick with sweat, moist masks obscuring their features, shoulders slumped as they ambled through air loaded with humidity and death. It was like the days of curfew in Tehran, the long nights of silent terror, of searchlights and distant sirens when the march of war was interminable, taking everyone hostage. If only my father had lived to see those days. What would he have written? On the streets of Chicago, strangers neither greeted nor acknowledged one another. They marched past one another like zombies, as if they belonged to separate planets and had happened to coincide on earth by way of a terrible accident they had no recollection of, but which they foolishly believed would be reversed, restoring them to the lives they'd known so intimately before the pandemic. Our neighborhood was largely a ghost town except for a few bars and restaurants that had cautiously reopened; they had placed their tables and chairs six feet apart on the sidewalks between giant planters of green elephant leaves, hydrangeas, dense blazing stars. Such remarkable flowers.

By midsummer, our lives had shrunk to the size of a coffin. Fereshteh and I became increasingly plagued by feelings of homesickness. We barely ever left the house. We felt we were in Tehran again. I would be going about my business—washing dishes, refilling the water in the samovar, reading at the kitchen table—when I'd suddenly hear the awful thud I'd heard when the wheels of the plane detached from the tarmac at Imam Khomeini Airport. I'd hear the plane whistle into the thick of night and feel a yawning void in my guts, an abyss that sucked my heart into its bottomless depths. Then I'd turn around to realize it was the samovar signaling a boil. Every once in a while, Fereshteh would lift her head from the sofa where she'd be laying recumbent, reading, and ask, "Do you remember the sound of the creeks in Darvand?"

Yes, I'd say, and I'd hear the water gurgling over the ancient rocks and smell the tender green leaves of the trees. Her mood had softened. She hadn't seen her adviser in months and his absence from her daily life combined with Khorshid's presence had changed her in subtle ways only a close observer could identify.

"Did you play hopscotch on the roof?" she'd ask, and I'd see the numbers I'd drawn in chalk appear beneath my feet. I'd smell the bitter scent of hot asphalt. I'd see the courtyards of the neighboring houses with their pruned roses and shallow pools. I'd hear the salt seller as he worked his way down our network of crooked streets, pushing his wheelbarrow of salt around, yelling *namaki,* even as the war raged on.

After that, Fereshteh and I began to call each other across the apartment that way. *Namakiii,* we'd say emphatically. But no sooner we'd uttered the word, we'd retreat in anger at the seductive call of nostalgia, its vampiric hunger for snatching souls in the night, leaving bodies to burn from the sting of emptiness. In those bitter moments, I'd find Khorshid at my feet, waiting to receive me as if we were one spirit knocking on the gates of death. *Pishi,* I'd say, *pishi* . . . and we'd trail to my room and lay like suicidal lovers in bed.

In the morning, I'd find her next to me purring, squinting her eyes ever so slowly, her front paws stretched out before her like a phoenix. She'd pretend she hadn't been hunting down messages from the dead all through dawn. I'd lay there, and admire her shiny patches of fur which were orange and full of tiny white stripes that looked like commas, semicolons, em dashes. I would say to her, "You are as beautiful as language," and she would purr louder. "Just as mysterious," I'd say and she'd rub her mouth on the crease of my thumb and index finger. She was striking in her simplicity during those lazy morning hours.

Once I got up, she'd move along with me: first to the kitchen where I'd drink my morning coffee—always Turkish, with a generous spoonful of sugar—and then to the dining room where I would sit on the turquoise blue velvet armchair I'd purchased at Goodwill and light a cigarette. I read the news while she languished the morning away sniffing at the window screens, her pupils as narrow as a sentence. Our day would progress calmly, statically, until dusk would arrive and her routine of cartwheels and message retrieval would begin again.

By July, Fereshteh and I decided we needed to bring the noise of Tehran back into our lives. That we should live as though we had never fled Tehran. This impulse, too, I attributed to Khorshid's presence, as if she were demanding such a life from us, a life that refused to recognize its difference from that other life we would have lived had we never left, a cheap copy, a butchered mimicking job. She was drawing the past back into the apex of our lives, resuscitating memories we had given up for dead.

When the midsummer festival of Tirgan came around at the start of July, we celebrated. We put small bowls of water all over the house and encouraged Khorshid to slap the water with her paws; Fereshteh and I would say to her, look *Khorshid jan,* like this, and we'd dip our hands in the bowls and flick the water onto one another. Fereshteh played the Daf in the evenings, and as she dragged her slender fingers against the taut sheepskin drawn over the frame, it emitted a deep guttural sound that attracted Khorshid's attention. The cat would sit at our feet the whole time, and

I would read a few lines by Rumi or Khayyam to the rhythm of the Daf, and we'd close our eyes and sway side to side in ecstasy. In those moments, I felt my father was standing next to me. My father whose face I could not picture. My father who had been reduced to energy.

One morning while I was lying in a bath I'd drawn to cool off from the terrible heat, I heard a leak. Khorshid, who was perched on the edge of the tub grooming her tail and paws, stopped instantly and stood in a frozen rictus, attempting to perceive the origin of the noise. It sounded like water was running over the tub, across the floor, coming down the walls in a thin but steady sheet. I wondered if I had gone so deep into homesickness that reality had begun to part altogether in order to clear access to the great beyond. For a moment, I had the odd sensation that the floor was opening up beneath me, that the tub was going to go through it and eject me on the other side. I felt as though I were being birthed again. As though I were floating around in my mother's uterus and a sudden unannounced pressure were being exerted on me, a force larger than life emerging to suck me through the narrow channels of her groin. For a moment, I thought I heard my father cooing, reciting cliché verses of doves and cherry trees, telling my mother that her face was more beautiful than the full moon to encourage her along. An inside joke, those lines. A wink, as though he was saying to her, the system wants only these tired words, so here they are . . . *your hair is like a river, your mouth sweet as nectar, your breasts soft hills I yearn to climb.* Then, again, I heard the water spreading across the floor. I closed my eyes and saw my father for the first time, a thin man, a defeated man with a gaunt face whose pride has been broken, whose spirit has been crushed, standing blindfolded in a soiled linen button-down and brown slacks with his hands tied behind his back at the edge of a ravine. I heard the woosh of a bullet as it spliced the air and broke his skin, as it ripped through his flesh and buried itself in his heart which closed around it like a bloodied fist. I saw him stumble backward over the precipice and as his body tore through the air I heard him say *down with the shah* and the water spread shhh shhh shhhhh until he disappeared from view. It was all very odd. I'd never had a memory of my father before and it seemed impossible to be having one now. I opened my eyes to Khorshid letting out a loud and urgent meow and pointing a stiff paw at the fogged pane of the bathroom window beyond which I could see the white palette of the sky smeared with blood.

Fereshteh appeared at the door with the spent aspect of those returning from a long and brutal war. She was carrying her laptop, the screen open to a news channel. "Another plane!" she said. Khorshid kept rubbing her ears with her paws, first one, then the other. There was something disturbing about the intensity with which she kept flattening her ears. Shrill voices came through the speakers. I felt my vertigo kick into high gear. I climbed out of the tub, hastily wrapped a towel around me, and stood next to Fereshteh, whose eyes were fixed to the screen, her face aglow with its pale blue light.

"Look," she said, and shoved the laptop into my arms. At first, I didn't know what I was looking at. I could see a cloudless sky recorded by an unstable camera. The patch of sky kept bouncing up and down. The screams grew progressively louder. An F15 fighter jet appeared. So did the wide white wings of the passenger plane. I saw the beaked mouth and elongated sting, the sharp, sturdy wings of the fighter jet as it approached the passenger plane with an intent to kill, or to say, *Boo! You can't see me but I have my eyes on you and I'm ready to draw your blood.* Then, as quickly as it had appeared, it departed into the white horizon. The camera flipped to capture the passengers. A man looked numbly into the camera; a river of blood cleaved his face in two. His head was bleeding. He tried, unsuccessfully, to reach for one of the oxygen masks that were dangling from the overhead compartment, but he failed. His hand moved imprecisely through the air. His lips turned blue as the blood dribbled down his chin onto his shirt. The camera panned around to capture weeping children; their mouths looked like shriveled rolls of old bread. In the narrow, carpeted aisles, next to the restroom doors at the rear of the plane, two bodies lay motionless, their eyes closed. It was Fereshteh and I. I was convinced of it. It was as if we had multiplied: one version of us stood in our bathroom in Chicago, warm from the steam coming off the tub, and another version of us was lying supine on the dirty carpeted floor of that plane, flying over the Al-Tanf garrison in Syria, leaving Tehran for Beirut on Mahan Air. I stood there staring at the screen, trying to figure out what had come over me. Was time bending in recognition that we had been split in two? Were the individual lives of who we'd been in Tehran and who we'd become in the land of the free separated by a wall that acted like a looking glass through which we could view one another without touching? I looked over at Fereshteh. We sat on the floor, Khorshid at our feet, our only witness, and sobbed for so long we felt our ancestors shiver in the heavens above us and in the ground below us, deep inside this dark brown earth.

Weeks passed. It seemed to us, or perhaps we wished, that time would soon cease to exist, that the world which was a book would soon turn to dust, that the days would end their relentless march, that the seasons would stop their eternal change of clothes.

One morning, unable to take the monotony of our days any longer, I decided to leave the house, to go to the lakefront, take a swim even if I had to risk proximity to others. Khorshid climbed into her backpack. As the door shut slowly behind us, I heard again the squeal of that plane as it lifted into the starless Tehran sky and turned westward. I felt like a fugitive, an eternal refugee adrift on the streets of the world. I felt I was running out of time. Time for what, I did not know. I felt as though something momentous was on the precipice of revealing itself.

I walked through the tunnel that runs under Lake Shore Drive and across the lawn to the concrete steps overlooking the water. I noticed there was something sublime in the air, a euphoric energy. People had come to the lakefront in droves despite the restrictions of the pandemic. There were colorful towels spread on the lawns. There were beautiful earringed boys in bright pink and orange speedos tanning together, their limbs oiled and slippery as fish. Chicago's buildings, handsome and glassy and blue, stood erect as soldiers surveilling the waters from a distance. The lake was green and even. An unblemished surface. Each time someone dove into the water with their legs drawn into their chest, plopping through the surface like a bomb, the lake sealed over them and instantly reestablished its calm indifference. I heard the beautiful boys cheering the divers. Then my cell phone rang. I picked up. It was Fereshteh. I could hear her screaming on the other end.

"Beirut exploded," she said. "It exploded!"

"What do you mean?" I asked, in disbelief, feeling instinctively for the heat of Khorshid's body against my back.

"That's where my second uncle lives, remember?" she said, breathing in gulps, "the one who didn't disappear in the war."

I pictured a third photograph going up behind her maman's sofa, a third martyr, all of them gone to inconclusive causes, disappeared or dead—a framed face all that's left of them.

"When?" I kept asking. "When?" I repeated the question as though I had gone stupid.

She couldn't answer.

She breathed heavily into the phone. I sat down and held the cell to my ear. I looked at the lake. I detected an odd movement on the horizon, the water cresting as if it were being rolled back the way I'd sometimes seen her maman roll her Persian carpet on the screen through which we observed her life. I got up with the phone still to my ear and walked closer to the edge of the water. The liquid horizon appeared to be trembling, as if somewhere at the edges the water was registering that distant perturbance in Beirut. I felt the void in my guts open its jaws. I walked even closer, more slowly, as if I were walking toward the water for the first and the last time. I heard Khorshid move around in the bag. I turned the backpack toward me and looked down at her through the clear bubble of her carrier. She looked more orange than ever. Brighter. Warmer. Shinier. I whispered Darwish's words into Fereshteh's ear. I said, "There's no end, no beginning, no first, no last, no presence, no absence." In the background I could hear Trump's voice streaming through a boy's iPhones, his rotten lips moving on their screens which glowed as he said, *it is what it is, it is what it is, it is what it is.* The beautiful boys had gotten up and begun to dance. They were joining their voices into a chorus, singing: *It is what it is, it is what it is, it is what it is.* They began to choreograph a dance. They kept putting their masks on and tearing them off, flexing their bronzed arms, moving their lips with the same disturbing suckling motion. They sang with mock astonishment, *It is what it is.* I looked away from them. We were trapped in different levels of reality. I kept staring at the horizon where the water had begun to move ever so slightly at the edges.

And then it happened. A deafening roar boomed through the air and blasted the lake open. I saw the water shoot out into the sky, shatter into a million shiny droplets, then sink back into the belly of that lake so eager for a hunt. The silver gleaming needle-shaped buildings in the distance reflected the rising waters. Khorshid began to emit a terrific orange light, and her shafts shot out of the holes carved into the bubble of her carrier.

I heard Fereshteh's voice come through the phone. She was finally speaking, reading Darwish back to me, whispering, "Intense bombardment of Beirut! Intense bombardment of Beirut!" She was chuckling nervously in my ear. Her mind was sliding through her hands. I could hear her losing her grip. The cratered surface of the lake made the void in my guts open its jaws even wider. A merciless light came on. A sickly crimson mushroom cloud billowed out from the lake and rose further and further into the sky, a fist of fire rising to land a punch on eternity's ancient face. *Beirut is on fire. It is what it is. Beirut is on fire. It is what it is.* I heard the choir chanting those words as I staggered home. I called out, "Father! Mother!" I felt my confusion turn to an icy panic. I asked myself, *Whose death shall I mourn?* Khorshid and I looked at each other through the bubble of her carrier. I felt so much love. Love spread through my body the way the water had spilled over the tub, shhh shhh shhh, and in that quiet susurrus I heard the song of my ancestors. *Whose death shall we mourn?* I asked, and they answered, *We are all here together.*

Moon

FROM *The Paris Review*

THE PACK OF boys had released their first album in Seoul two years ago, and now they were selling out corporate arenas and Olympic stadiums all over the world. I was familiar with the story of their explosive ascent, how the premiere of their latest music video had triggered a power outage across an entire Pacific island. I knew they were performers of supernatural charisma whose concerts could leave a fan permanently destabilized, unable to return to the spiritual attenuation of her daily life. I also knew about the boys' exceptional profundity in matters of the heart, how they offered that same fan her only chance of survival in a world they'd exposed for the risible fraud that it was.

At least this was what I'd derived from hours of listening to Vavra. As her roommate, I was subject to her constant efforts at proselytization. But the more she wanted me to love the boys, the more they repulsed me. The healthy communalism of feeling they inspired, almost certainly a strategy to expand the fandom, desecrated my basic notion of love. I could love only that which made me secretive, combative, severe—a moral disappointment to myself and an obstruction to others. So when Vavra knocked on my door to announce that her friend had fallen ill, freeing up a ticket to the boys' first-ever concert in Berlin, I declined.

"But this concert will change your life," she said. "I just know it."

"I don't want my life to change," I said. "I want my life to stay in one place and be one thing as intensely as possible."

Vavra widened her eyes in affected compassion. In the year since she'd let me, an online stranger, move into her apartment in Wedding, her tireless overtures of care and my circumventions of them had come to form a texture of cohabitation that could almost be called a friendship. What I feared most wasn't death or global cataclysm but the everyday capitulations that chipped away at the monument of seriousness that was a soul; my spiritual sphincter stayed clenched to keep out the cheap and stupid. Still, Vavra was inadvertently training me in the art of self-delimitation, and for that I couldn't help but feel a bit grateful. I returned my gaze to the open book on the desk before me.

"You look like a scholar," Vavra said. "But you aren't one."

"Thank you," I said, gratified.

"What I mean is, you don't do anything with what you read. What about teaching? You could be shaping young minds."

"How? I can't even shape my own."

"If the boys were to think that way, they wouldn't be where they are now," Vavra said. "They're unafraid to leave a mark on other lives, possessing as they do an unshakable faith in their own genius."

She shut her eyes and disappeared into worship. When she opened them again, she smiled with condescension, as though she'd just been to a place beyond my understanding. But her return to normalcy, to a world of stultified passion, struck me as a failure of commitment. I realized then that if I'd yet to follow her to this other place, it was only because I knew I might never come back. It wasn't revulsion I felt but fear that I would befoul myself beyond recognition. Irked by my cowardice and seized, too, by perverse curiosity, I wondered for the first time what it would be like to love the boys.

Two hours later I found myself following Vavra into a crowded arena. Our seats, located toward the rear, offered a meager view of the stage, forcing my attention onto a screen that served as the backdrop. This screen, as large as a Berlin apartment building lying on its side, reproduced the happenings onstage with astonishing clarity, so that when the five boys drifted in as if by accident, heads bowed and hands clasped over their stomachs, I couldn't fathom how their real bodies, as small as grains of rice from where I stood, would survive an evening at the feet of their gigantic images. Thousands of women erupted into shrieks. I remembered Vavra telling me that incidents of shattered eardrums at the boys' concerts were rising, prompting the entertainment company that managed them to recommend earplugs. But I saw none being worn by the fans around me. They were finally breathing the same air as the boys; now was not the time to be less of a body.

The boys stood in a line, their heads still bowed. They appeared freshly reprimanded. Their outfits began with black derby shoes and black trousers, blooming into tops that spoke to their individual personalities. Each boy was named after a celestial body; it went without saying that none of them was named Earth. I didn't know which boy was called what. Vavra was shouting for all five again and again, taking care, on principle, not to say one name more than another.

But I was no egalitarian. I'd already decided that the boy on the far left bothered me most. He wore a pink silk button-down with oversize cuffs that obscured his hands save his fingertips, which gripped the hem of the shirt with desperation, as if he might fly out of it. His hair was a shade of blond that matched his complexion exactly; skin seemed to be growing out of his head. He looked up, revealing an unremarkable face, somehow flat, eyes narrow like the space between two slats of a window blind. But his plainness seemed a calculated strategy to foreground the intensity of his gaze, which discorded with the stony coolness of his pallor. The pose he held should have been impossible: his trunk was perfectly vertical, but his neck jutted ahead at an angle so wide that his head, held erect, seemed to belong to another torso entirely. It was the neck that disturbed me. Long and smooth, it implied the snug containment of a fundamental muscle that ran down the body all the way to the groin, where, I imagined, it boldly flipped out as the penis.

The stage lights turned red and shuddered into a new constellation, casting long shadows down the boys' faces. Music began—atonal synths encased in a rib cage of driving percussion—and the boys erupted into dance. They never used backup dancers, according to Vavra, because they considered it a cheap trick to pad themselves out with a horde of comparatively homely boys. So there they were, five lonely specks on a vast black stage. They faced one another in a circle and passed between them an invisible ball of energy. Upon the heady climax of the chorus, they turned around and flung out their arms, palms upturned, as if giving their prismatic harvest over to the surrounding emptiness.

The boys sang: "What does it mean to die on this planet? Aloneness, despair, confusion. A human being is a particle of dust in a galaxy. And what does it mean to live on this planet? Creation, desire, collision. A human being is a galaxy in a particle of dust."

I remembered Vavra saying that most nights the pack of boys, after the rigorous training of their bodies, washed up and then gathered in their living room to study the classics of literature and philosophy. Like a civilization, the boys entered new eras, one for each album. In preparation for their current era, they'd pored over a Korean translation of Sophocles, troubled by Oedipus's decision to blind himself. Yes, he'd been woefully ignorant of the truth—why not, then, gouge out two new holes on his face, for two more eyes, for double the sight? The album was a statement of protest against Oedipus's capitulation to darkness; it celebrated too much seeing, too much light.

My eyes kept returning to the boy with the disturbing neck. The others conveyed depth of feeling by exaggerating their movements or facial expressions; I could understand the terms of their engagement with the world. But the boy with the disturbing neck followed an inscrutable logic. I could never predict his next move, but once it came along I experienced it as an absolute necessity. He seemed to control even the speed at which he fell from the air, his feet landing with aching tenderness, as if he didn't want to wake up the stage. His movements: fluid, tragic, ancient. Every flick of a joint happened at the last possible moment. He never geared up. He was always already there.

Each boy stood at the head of a triangular formation in turn and sang a bar, prompting the screams in the arena to peak five times. When the boy with the neck surged forward to take the helm, my eyes filled with tears. Confronted by the tetanic twitching of his individuality under the smooth skin of teamwork, I saw all the more clearly what was different about him, and I knew I loved him because I liked him better than the others.

His voice was a pink ribbon whipping in the wind: "I used to stand still in one place to observe the world with care. Now I'm running as fast as possible, seeing as fast as possible, yet even this isn't enough, for all I can see at any moment is the street ahead of me before it disappears over the horizon. Will you please flatten out the earth so that I can see ahead of me forever?"

I'd never been able to keep Vavra's exhaustive profile of each boy tethered to a name or a face. But the body onstage extracted details from the depths of my memory, and they spun like thread around the spool of a particular name: Moon. I remembered that Moon, at twenty, was the youngest in the group. He'd been the child prodigy of a ballet company in Seoul, performing every lead role until the age of fourteen, when he was recruited by the entertainment company. Four years later, he'd almost failed to earn a place among the pack of boys because the company president, known as the Music Professor, had been skeptical of Moon's ability to subordinate the idiosyncrasy of his dance to the needs of the group. Details that had been vivid without meaning, applicable to any one of the boys, were now indispensable to the evocation of Moon. It made perfect sense, what Vavra had once told me, how he ate heavy foods right before bed because he liked waking up to find his body slim and taut, proof of the metabolic intensity of his dream life.

I was being sent to the other side; I was having what Vavra had once described as my First Time. But unlike losing my virginity, which I'd anticipated with such buzzing awareness that I'd been more certain I would have sex than die someday, I'd never known to expect Moon. My First Time, experienced at the age of twenty-nine, made me wonder about all the other first times out there to be had. The world suddenly proliferated with secret avenues of devotion.

Several songs later, the boys returned to standing in a line. As Sun, the oldest member at twenty-four, spoke in Korean, translations in English and German trickled across the screen. The boys were halfway through their world tour, he said, which had begun two months ago in Seoul, after which they'd traveled east to meet their fans in the Americas. Their journey had now taken them to Europe, he said, and they'd decided to surprise their families by flying them out to a continent that they, the boys included, had never visited before.

Each boy faced the camera that fed into the screen to deliver a statement of gratitude to his family. Only Moon, last to speak, walked to the edge of the stage, shielded his eyes from the lights, and peered directly into the crowd.

"Mom, Dad, Older Sister," he said. "I can't see you. I love you. Therefore, where are you?"

His use of *therefore* stunned me.

The sound of string instruments, melancholic and slow, filled the arena. Moon approached center stage and stood there, alone.

He was wearing a black blindfold. Everyone in the crowd raised their phones, situating thousands of Moons before me.

He sang that there had been a time when he couldn't bear to cross a room in the presence of others. He didn't want anyone to know the shape of his body, so he wore shirts that hung down to his knees. The fact that he had a face distressed him. If only it could remain hidden like the secret of his groin. But then he met me. Finally, he could bear to be seen. I looked at him so much, more than anyone ever had, that it left him no room to look at himself. That had been the problem, the looking at himself.

"Cock the gun of your eyes," he sang. "I will make myself easy to shoot."

In unison, everyone raised a hand and stretched their thumbs and index fingers apart into pistols aimed at Moon. I couldn't follow along, as my arms were crossed in order to thwart any flare-ups of agency that might disturb my state of perfect passivity, which I needed to maintain so that Moon could act upon me as much as possible.

In the instrumental, a pistol was cocked and fired. Thousands of wrists spasmed. Moon, struck in the chest, stumbled backward. I thought he would fall over, but instead he began pivoting on one foot, submitting to the long stream of the crowd's bullets. His chin went first and his arms followed, then his torso, which, dense with organs, forced his other leg into swinging accompaniment. I finally understood that his shirt was the pink of a newborn's tongue. He was tasting the air with his body. It would always be the first day of his life.

He came to a stop and tore off the blindfold. My eyes moved between the screen, where I could see the contours of a bead of sweat dangling from the tip of his nose, and the stage, where his entire body was a tiny blur. I didn't know which I wanted more of, the precise reproduction or the imprecise actuality. He began to walk down a runway that extended from the main stage all the way to the center of the arena floor. On the screen, I saw the bead of sweat wobble, then fall off and disappear from view, likely splattering the floor. Moon tucked in his chin and gazed up at a sharp angle, as if seducing the person he was fighting. And this person was me. He was walking right in my direction.

I began pushing through the crowd. Angry strangers tried to block my way. I couldn't blame them, I was being a very bad fan.

But I felt no solidarity. I excised them from my perception of space. All went quiet in my mind. Moon and I were alone in the arena, headed for each other. I would jump onto the stage and force him to look into my eyes. For a single moment in time, I would be all that he saw.

Moon grew from tiny to small, from small to less small. I begged him to become as large as I was to myself, but the closer he came to reaching the size of a normal person, the more I sensed he'd never get there. We stopped moving at the same time: he reached the end of the runway, while I couldn't penetrate the crowd any further. He threw back his head in dreamy surrender, exposing a limestone column of neck almost as long as his face. The cartilage supporting his larynx protruded like a spine. Blue veins ran up the neck and branched off across his mandible. Life swarmed just under his skin. The neck's language was of suppression, unlike that of his face, where the jungle inside his body oozed free through his eyes, nose, and mouth. Vavra's mistake had been to draw rational strokes of narrative, compelling me to understand everything about Moon at once. But all I'd needed was to begin with the singularity of his neck.

A steel cord descended from the ceiling. Moon lowered his head, throwing his neck into shadow, and attached the cord to a buckle on his waist. Every light in the arena was pointed at him. He stood still and endured it. He was a gift forever in the moment of being handed over. But he couldn't be had. Hunger pierced me. I wanted something, and I wanted all of it, but I didn't dare want Moon, because if it were that simple, it was also that impossible.

"I will be you when I grow up," he sang. "You will be me when you are born again."

When the cord lifted him away into the dark firmament of the arena, I didn't say goodbye. I knew I would see him again, that I was doomed to see him always. He had his arms hanging at his sides and his eyes shut, as if surrendering to the controls of a divine force. His hands were curled into loose balls. It made me sick to imagine just how moist his palms must be.

I worked from home as an English copywriter for an Australian expat's business in canned artichoke hearts. My job required me to credibly infuse the vegetable with the ability to feel romantic love for its consumer. I'd always felt a kind of aristocratic apathy about the task, but in the days following the concert, I avoided my boss's calls altogether, nauseated by the prospect of speaking seriously about such unserious work.

Instead, I spent hours copying a long note that Moon had written by hand for his fans on the occasion of his twentieth birthday. I coveted his handwriting: narrow and angular, flowing across the page with energy and spasming in its higher reaches. I had no Korean handwriting of my own, having grown up speaking the language but almost never writing in it. I cried out in Korean whenever I accidentally touched scalding water, but the slower, thicker pain of conducting the relationship I had with myself— this required English. "I like aging before your eyes," Moon had written. "It makes me feel like a story you'll never get sick of." By the fifth time I copied the note, I could compose the text from memory. His hand, even his ideas, had begun to feel like my own.

My phone bleated from my bed for the only reason it was now allowed to bleat: Moon was about to begin a livestream. I entered to find him lying across the crisp white sheets of a hotel bed in Dubai, holding the phone over his face. I lay on my stomach and gazed down at him, phone flat on the mattress. His eyes were heavy with exhaustion. I hoped he would do nothing interesting; his normalcy steeped the two of us in a new intimacy.

"Hello, Liver," he murmured.

The pack of boys called their fans "livers" because we weren't just "expensive handbags" they carried around. We kept them alive, like critical organs. I suspected they used the English word *liver* because it sounded like *lover*. They could be coy like that. But I would much rather be Moon's liver than lover.

"I just returned from the buffet downstairs," he said. "There were a hundred different kinds of food to choose from, yet I managed to fill my plate with only the wrong choices. Have you at least eaten well today?"

"Please," I typed in English. "Save your insipid affection for the others. Meals shatter my focus. I can't believe I have to eat three times a day. Where's the ritual that matters?"

His eyes skittered wildly as he tried to read the comments flooding the chat window. Almost as soon as a comment appeared, it flew out of view, overtaken by another, usually in a different language. One fan, a vegan, had looked up the hotel's menu and was now cataloging every animal represented therein so as to love Moon

282   ESTHER YI

"without illusions." But what I sensed was the fan's desire to be masticated by Moon, just as those animals had been, and to bring him comparable pleasure.

I could hear the bedsheet rustle upon the slightest movement of his body, but he couldn't hear the collective din that his fans, numbering in the thousands, were making on bedsheets all over the world. I tried to pretend that no one else was there, that Moon and I were floating alone in virtual space. This exercise fatigued me, especially when I found myself wondering whether I should keep my lips open or shut. The fact of the matter was that he couldn't see me. Even the possibility of looking dumb in front of him was a privilege beyond my reach.

Moon began to laugh deep in his throat. He plushly shut a single eye. He was the only person I knew who could wink sincerely.

He said, "You're up all night worrying about whether I'm getting enough to eat."

He wasn't wrong.

"When my belly is gone, you miss it. But when my belly returns, you miss how my ribs protrude. So what is it you really want?"

He was completely justified in asking.

I tapped at my phone with vigor: "I hope you do skip the occasional meal. When you're on the thinner side, your soul becomes more visible, almost hypodermic. You become a pure streak of energy, like the blue flame of a blowtorch. But the entertainment company better not put you on a diet. That would be disgustingly presumptuous. You know best how to flagellate yourself. No company can be as perverse as yo—"

I'd reached the maximum character count. I pressed Enter and watched my block of text disappear into a stream of far pithier messages.

"So much English," Moon said. "Let me run some of this through a translator." He fiddled with his phone and squinted. "Based on what I'm seeing, you're either poets or idiots. And here, it's not even a translation. It's just the Korean pronunciation of the English words. The English words must have no correspondents in Korean. My god. What's this inconceivable thing you want to say to me?"

He released a soft groan. Sensing he would log off soon, I begged him to lower the phone so that I would know what it was like to have his face close to mine. He froze, seeming to lock eyes with me. A luxurious docility permeated his expression, and his lips cracked open into a smile that hinted at the black velvet rooms inside him. And then the whole video blurred.

His left eye filled the frame. It was wide open, tense; I gathered he was no longer smiling. I had the strange feeling that I wasn't witnessing the transmission of a reality as it unfolded thousands of miles away in Dubai but awakening to that which had always been in my bed. This eye had always been lurking among the tired folds of my sheets, rigid with attention to my small life, even to the dark wall of my back at night. I drew closer to the screen. Beyond its quadrilateral parameters lay the rest of Moon's face, his neck, his whole body. We regarded each other without moving or speaking. I knew better than to think that he'd read, much less chosen to obey, my request. But this was of no importance. I didn't need the help of wild fortune to be alone with him.

I wrapped my arms around his neck and held him tight, turning us away from the world and toward each other. The radiator was pumping heat into my room, and the lights were low. The image resolution was so poor that I couldn't tell where the brown of his iris ended and the black of his pupil began. I was transfixed by this circle of inchoate darkness. But the more I searched it for a flicker of anima, the more it flattened out into pure color, and abruptly the eye dislocated itself from Moon, becoming hideous, hieroglyphic.

"I'm sorry," Moon said. "But my arm is very tired."

His eye shut, and the screen darkened. The sheets underneath me suddenly went cold.

"All of me is tired," he said. "In my stomach there is camel meat, but in my head there is nothing."

Then he logged off. His voice had cracked while saying "There is nothing." I made an hour-long loop of that phrase alone so that I could study this moment of unbelievable cuteness. "There is nothing," he blared on repeat, making my speaker shake. Vavra pounded angrily at my door. I clenched my fists and bit down on my tongue. Given all that I felt, I needed to do more. I looked around the room, then picked up a book from my desk. "There is nothing," Moon said. "There is nothing." I flung the book to the floor. My heart softened at the sight of its forbearance, how it lay butted up against the wall in quiet recovery. I got on my knees and turned to the first page, promising to read with care. But panic burned in my chest as the words streamed past me. All I wanted was a single sentence that radiated truth, yet I found myself turning page after page, faster and faster, accruing small cuts all over my hands, as if I were grappling with the mouth of a rabid dog.

Contributors' Notes

Other Distinguished Stories of 2022

American and Canadian Magazines Publishing Short Stories

Contributors' Notes

CHERLINE BAZILE is a Haitian American writer from Florida. She graduated from Harvard University and received her MFA in fiction from the Helen Zell Writers' Program at the University of Michigan. Her work has been supported by the Paul & Daisy Soros Fellowship, the Mass Cultural Council, the Andrew W. Mellon Foundation, the Vermont Studio Center, and others. She is working on a novel and lives in Los Angeles.

• The voice came first, a character who was so wounded, so caught up in telling her side of the story, that she couldn't be there for her friend. This was more obvious in the first version of "Tender." It was nonlinear, and the protagonist withheld the moment she witnessed her best friend's dad yell at her. Eden knew her friend was experiencing a familial fracture but chose to make her best friend's recent transformation about herself.

I love tenderness as the guiding mood of this story. To be tender-headed is to feel like you've gone bald from a comb slashing through your coarse hair. Death by a thousand forceful tugs. So intimate, to be nestled in someone's thighs as they make something from your pain. Many have done my hair, friends and strangers. It requires trust. So much could go wrong.

I played with the possibilities of intimacies gone awry. What if you didn't trust the person doing your hair? What if it was your best friend? What if you and your best friend wanted the same things, or thought you did? What if you were so fixated on a perceived competition that you couldn't show up for them? What if you were the awful one, you were the one who dealt the first wound, and they still loved you?

The first image of "Tender" was two friends on ice, reaching for each other, unsure how to bridge the chasm that had solidified between them, unsure if it was temporary, imaginary, worth dismantling, worth fortifying. I wanted the story to scrape at the corrosiveness of comparison, while also showing how comforting loneliness can be, how sometimes we choose it.

MAYA BINYAM is the author of the novel *Hangman*. Her work has appeared in *The Paris Review, The New Yorker,* the *New York Times Magazine, New York, Bookforum, Columbia Journalism Review,* the *New York Times Book Review,* and elsewhere. She is a contributing editor at *The Paris Review* and has previously worked as an editor at *Triple Canopy* and *The New Inquiry* and as a lecturer in the New School's Creative Publishing and Critical Journalism Program. She lives in Los Angeles.

• My father is very mysterious. When I was a child, he told me stories about when he was a child, almost all of which he made up. The stories weren't lies. They helped contextualize the stories that were true, which I could hardly believe. He had been orphaned? And then imprisoned? His old life looked nothing like my young life, but I sensed that my father still had something to do with me, and that the connection between us would be forged through language. I tried to make my writing tell me the stories I knew he wouldn't. That writing always failed, but I became interested in that failure, which seemed fundamental to representation, more broadly: I would never be able to manufacture the thing itself. In trying to imitate my father, I produced someone else, a character familiar and also surprising, the figure you might project when you know you're on the wrong side of a two-way mirror. That character became the narrator of many discarded stories and, eventually, "Do You Belong to Anybody?"

TOM BISSELL was born in Escanaba, Michigan, in 1974. He is the author of ten books, including two story collections: *God Lives in St. Petersburg* (2005, winner of the Rome Prize) and *Creative Types* (2021). "His Finest Moment" marks his third appearance in *Best American Short Stories*. As a screenwriter, he co-created the Apple+ show *The Mosquito Coast,* based on Paul Theroux's novel, and contributed three episodes to the second season of the critically acclaimed *Star Wars: Andor* for Disney+, which will air in 2024. Currently he is working on a book about the history, theory, and practice of literary adaptation for film. He lives in Los Angeles with his family.

• "His Finest Moment" grew out of the dismay I felt when an old writer acquaintance—"Friend" is too strong a word, but this is someone whose career I played a role in advancing—was accused of violent, predatory behavior by a number of women. First came my initial shock: How could this man have done what he was accused of doing? This was followed by a more disquieting realization: It was, in fact, incredibly easy to believe he'd done what he was accused of doing. His self-professed libertinism, his wild stories of affairs and chance encounters—he'd been telling people who he really was all along. We just chose not to hear it.

I found myself fixated on how a man like my erstwhile acquaintance would begin to explain to his teenage daughter what he was being accused of and why. How would that conversation go? What could he *possibly* have said? Soon I was wandering the haunted house of an imagined mind.

"His Finest Moment" was the first thing I tried to write after the death of my father, who, unlike the deluded wretch of this story, was a profoundly decent man. I'm a better person than I might have been thanks to my father. I dedicate this story to his memory, and I thank Oscar Villalon and Laura Cogan for continuing to give my fiction a home at *Zyzzyva*.

TARYN BOWE'S recent work has appeared in *Epoch, The Sewanee Review, Indiana Review, Bellevue Literary Review,* and *Joyland.* She lives with her husband and daughter in Maine, where she serves as the associate director of the Maine Writers & Publishers Alliance.

• "Camp Emeline" was the first story I wrote after my mother died. I remember feeling like I had lost not only her but everyone I cared about because of how deeply her death had changed me. I would go for walks in the woods and search for colorful birds, signs of her lingering, but I never found any, just woodpeckers.

During this same window of time, I volunteered to teach creative writing at an overnight camp for youth who'd survived suicide loss. While I spent only a couple of days at the camp, the experience shook loose so many memories of my one summer serving as an overnight camp counselor in New Hampshire. Even more significantly, seeing these young campers bond and support one another, while lugging around such heavy burdens of grief, reminded me that the human connections I find most magical are the ones that occur in hard, dark moments when people on the verge of sinking still somehow manage to lift each other up.

DA-LIN was made in Taiwan to be an electrical engineer, but after an almost-PhD in decision science, she made a very practical decision to become a writer. She has won the PEN America Emerging Voices Fellowship and the James Kirkwood Literary Award at UCLA Extension. Her stories have appeared in *Colorado Review* and *New England Review.* She is working on a short story collection and a multigenerational mystery that spans one hundred years of Taiwanese history.

• "Treasure Island Alley" is a real place, a fascinating and terrifying recess in my childhood geography. The story is autobiographical, except for the parts that are not, the death scene obviously. It is as yet my wishful thinking to die at 105 while dreaming of Monkey King, who, along with Doraemon, was my hero when I needed to escape as a kid. My ex-husband is not a venture capitalist, although he did suffer, not least from reading draft after draft of this story.

Everyone has a life situation, and mine is that death and birth appeared so entangled in one moment that I struggle with mortality, connection, and being anchored in some sort of meaning of life. Some Buddhism teachers say that you can use any situation to wake up or cling to old ways and stay asleep. I find that challenging but inspiring.

This story is one of the earliest I started when I began taking writing classes. It was the first that meant something, or rather, everything, to me. My impulse was to weave real moments of pain and real moments of transcendence into something whole, something more beautiful and meaningful than I can make in real life. At first, I tried to write a braided essay, a form that I love in hands such as those of Eula Biss, who juxtaposes lynching with the invention of telephone poles in "Time and Distance Overcome." But my rendition satisfied neither readers who wanted memoir nor those who wanted quantum physics.

A year after drafting the essay, I chanced upon Mark Haddon's short story "The Gun." The story showed me how to jump between one day and a lifetime, and I thought Haddon's ending—a question and an answer of not knowing—was more perfect than anything I could have dreamed of. All at once I had my story.

As if it was that easy. Even though most of the final draft appeared in some form in the first draft, it took almost eight years to jettison real events that did not serve the fiction, invent elements that made the fiction truer, and smooth out the time jumps that remained clunky for a long time.

My story could not have existed without Mark Haddon's story. I am grateful for Haddon's blessing for my last sentence to mimic his. After Xuan-Xuan tries to dazzle in the act of vanishing, as a magician did when he said, "Watch me disappear," on his deathbed, as recounted in the documentary *Consider the Conversation*, and after Xuan-Xuan dissolves into everlasting elements (the closest a materialist gets to reincarnating), as Bill Bryson framed the breakdown of a body in the opening of *A Brief History of Nearly Everything*, Xuan-Xuan is left with the unknowable, where Buddhists and many other philosophers have also arrived.

I exist. I vanish. And in between, I am not at all sure of anything. That is perhaps magical enough.

BENJAMIN EHRLICH is the author of *The Brain in Search of Itself* (2022). His work has appeared in *Scientific American, Aeon, Paris Review Daily, LitHub, The Gettysburg Review, New England Review,* and *Nautilus.* His first book, *The Dreams of Santiago Ramón y Cajal*, was published in 2016.

• I was born and raised Jewish. I went to Hebrew school, where, as in the story, one of my teachers was a veteran of the 1948 war, and also where, for the first time, at around ten years old, I saw images of the Holocaust. The year of my bar mitzvah was the year I stopped believing in God. My favorite counselor at Jewish summer camp, whose father had committed suicide, was an atheist. I could not deny the air of solemnity and gravitas in the temple sanctuary, with the Holy Book inside the ark, but in time other books became holier to me. I never learned how to recite all the prayers, and so my prayer became silence.

The character Bernstein is based on an usher at my childhood synagogue. We used to see him everywhere. It became a running joke. To me, there was something supernatural about him. My family saw him as friendly and generous, but I portrayed him as mysterious, even sinister. I am not sure why.

After nearly two decades of academic education, as an intellectual, and a student of literature, I find myself less determined to know and more open to not knowing. I wrote "The Master Mourner" before I could have articulated that, but the ending of the story, it is clear to me now, is an invitation to either know or not know, perhaps both at the same time. The narrator navigates this; the reader navigates this.

I do not know why I wrote this story. I do not know why I write at all—thank God.

SARA FREEMAN is a Canadian-British writer based in the United States. Her debut novel, *Tides,* won the Bridge Book Award and was named one of the "100 Must-Read Books of 2022" by *Time* magazine.

• In the summer of 2013, after graduating with an MFA in fiction, I began to work on a novel, my first. I knew little about what writing a novel entailed, but I had a character (her name was Leah; she was seventeen), a setting (Montreal in the late 1970s), and a sense of the kind of story I wanted to tell (intergenerational, intimate).

And so I wrote, and in writing, I discovered the texture of Leah's life and consciousness, the vexing and exciting nature of her psychology with its equal parts desire and self-effacement. When I didn't know what to write anymore, I wrote "The End" and hoped for the best. But not surprisingly, upon rereading the manuscript, I found that what I'd written barely hung together. I hadn't identified the necessary shape to contain my character's complexity, the necessary tension to sustain her story. After a few years of trying to rewrite the manuscript, I decided to put it aside completely, to accept defeat.

In the year that followed I didn't write; I found it nearly impossible to read. I wondered if I had it in me to be a writer at all. I was devastated.

But slowly, as happens, unimaginably, in the wake of great creative disappointment, I began again. When I finally sat down to write, I was dismayed to find that what came to my mind was not some fresh idea, but Leah again, old friend, insisting on her second chance. This is how "The Company of Others" came to be. Having spent many years in Leah's company already, the writing of this short story, set more than a decade later than the novel, came relatively easily; the particular slant of Leah's mind, the exact shape of her past, were embedded in each new sentence, in each new scene that I wrote.

I had to write an entire novel and abandon it in order to arrive at this short story, but in doing so I finally found the correct container, the necessary narrative pressure to bring this insistent character to life.

LAUREN GROFF is a three-time National Book Award finalist for *Fates and Furies, Florida,* and *Matrix.* Winner of the Story Prize and the Joyce Carol Oates Prize, she was named one of the Best of Young American Novelists by *Granta* and has been published in thirty-five languages. Her seventh book, *The Vaster Wilds,* will be published in 2023. This is her seventh story to appear in *Best American Short Stories.*

• "Annunciation" is a story I've been trying unsuccessfully to tell for twenty years. There had been, in life, a fairy-tale pool house in California, two separate journeys to the West to become a different person, a pair of hot Brazilians having tantric sex on the youth hostel floor, a soul-crushing job in a Department of Human Services office, etcetera. My agent, Bill Clegg, on receiving earlier drafts would gently bat the story back to me, saying that though there were pretty pieces, the story as a whole didn't quite sing yet. He was always right. Some stories linger in the mind until the writer has lived enough to do them justice. The story languished during the darkness and anxiety of the COVID pandemic and reanimated when the danger lifted enough in May 2021 for a long-delayed stay at Civitella Ranieri in Umbria. This was a time of tremendous outward bursting toward life, roses and sunlight and incredible food and Piero della Francesca and beauty redounding. In that golden light, the story allowed me to finish it.

I'm grateful to the Civitella Ranieri Foundation's staff and my fellow fellows, every one of whom had some hand in making the story emerge. Thanks to *The New Yorker* for publishing it; thank you to Min Jin Lee and Heidi Pitlor for choosing it for this anthology.

NATHAN HARRIS holds an MFA from the Michener Center at the University of Texas. His debut novel, *The Sweetness of Water* (2021), won both the Ernest J. Gaines Award for Literary Excellence and the Willie Morris Award. It was also long-listed for the Booker Prize, the Center for Fiction First Novel Prize, the Carnegie Medal for Excellence in Fiction, and the Dylan Thomas Prize. He was honored as one of "5 Under 35" by the National Book Foundation.

• Urban legends have always intrigued me. I found The Grootslang particularly fascinating. I also saw in some dark corner of my imagination the eponymous mine itself, which carried with it a specific type of horror, an emotional horror—one rife with elements of exploitation, a deep sense of ongoing trauma for every single individual who had stepped foot in that place. I wanted to put those images, and those emotions, onto the page. All of which, naturally, seemed to flow through Nicholas, who is in charge and carries the responsibility of the multitude of poor souls who answer to him. He is also, symbolically, held accountable to all those individuals who passed away toiling in that mine so he himself might prosper. I myself felt burdened by a narrative that suddenly felt substantive. A story had to be told. So I sat down and put pen to paper.

JARED JACKSON is a writer, editor, educator, and arts administrator. Born in Hartford, Connecticut, he received an MFA in fiction from Columbia University, where he was awarded a Chair's Fellowship and a Creative Writing Teaching Fellowship. His writing has been published in the *New York Times Book Review, Yale Review, Guernica, The Kenyon Review, n+1,* and elsewhere. He has been awarded residencies and fellowships from Mac-Dowell, Yaddo, the Center for Fiction, Baldwin for the Arts, Tin House, and Plympton's Writing Downtown Residency.

   • In many ways this story was the beginning of everything. I was in the second year of my MFA at Columbia University. It was fall and I was in a workshop with Victor LaValle. When the story came to me, I realized I didn't just have this one piece, but a vision for an entire project, a story collection, *Locals,* that, among other things, centers the lives of Black and brown adolescents in Hartford, Connecticut. With "Bebo," as with most of my stories, I knew a couple things that would happen before starting it. The rest was discovery and craft.

This isn't to say the story simply fell into place—quite the opposite. This story took multiple drafts. I'm fortunate to have had many generous eyes on it, from master practitioners and my astute agent, Meredith Kaffel Simonoff, to my peers among both writers and readers. Following Victor's workshop, I brought the story to the Tin House Winter Workshop, where I worked with Nafissa Thompson-Spires. From there it returned with me to Columbia and took a tour in my spring workshop with Paul Beatty. Addressing matters of craft along the way, I still struggled with answering a question I felt, if figured out, would unlock the rest of the story: Why is Collin the one telling it?

I put it away. I worked on other stories that will be in this collection. I published a couple. A few years later, I revisited what would become "Bebo" (it once had other titles) with newfound energy and perspective. I came to realize that a big part of the story, as the deputy editor at the time, Elliott Holt, wrote in a mini-essay on why *The Kenyon Review,* where the story was originally published, chose it, was about "the emotional work of friendship and loyalty," and with that came Collin's failures. I needed

Collin to be honest, to sit in his discomfort and still be vulnerable in spite of it. That's hard to do in real life, and it's the same in fiction. Most of us, including myself, fail to have the courage to consistently show up in this way, for ourselves and others. I hope I, we, can be better; I know we can. But going back to that first workshop, one thing Victor taught our class was to be merciless, and therefore honest, with our fictional characters. And personally, I've always felt, if I can't be honest on the page, where it's just me and blank space, where can I be? Once Collin was able to confront the truth of his decisions, the beginning and ending of the story, which had eluded me for some time, became clear.

I'm thankful for this story. For the doors it opened. The patience it taught me. The questions it asked. The revision it demanded. And I'm beyond grateful for the readers who believed in it along the way, and for it to have found a home first in *The Kenyon Review* and now, humbly, here.

SANA KRASIKOV was born in Ukraine and grew up in Georgia and the United States. She is the author of the collection *One More Year*, a finalist for the PEN/Hemingway Award and winner of the Sami Rohr Prize for Jewish Literature. Her novel *The Patriots* won France's Prix du Premier for best international novel. Her next book, *The Shelf Life of Evelyn Shine*, will be published in 2024. Her short fiction has appeared in *The New Yorker, A Public Space*, the *Atlantic,* and the O. Henry Prize anthology. She has also written extensively for radio, in particular for the international narrative podcast *Rough Translation,* which she cofounded with her husband.

• Although I began to write "The Muddle" not long after the Russian invasion of Ukraine in 2022, I think this story came to me in pieces years before that. One side of my family is from Crimea, and when the peninsula was illegally annexed by Russia in 2014, rifts began to form within the familiar network of friends and relatives. Some people were appalled by the unchecked Russian aggression, while others drank toasts to "Krym Nash" (Crimea is ours). These simmering resentments spilled over into a boil when the invasion of the Ukrainian mainland began. I wanted to write about the war from the angle I was witnessing it: as a kind of civil war among fathers and sons, wives and husbands, something that tested long-standing bonds of friendships. Shura, a Jewish immigrant from Ukraine, and Alyona, a Ukrainian woman married to a Russian man, arrived almost as mirror images. At various points in their lives, each has felt a sense of both connection to and estrangement from her own country. Exploring these women's relationship to their physical land, whether a dacha tended for survival in Ukraine or a front yard groomed for appearance in New York, felt like a good starting point to exploring these larger questions of connection, estrangement, identity, and independence.

DANICA LI is a union lawyer based in the San Francisco Bay Area. She won the Eisner Prize in Prose as an undergraduate at UC Berkeley, where she also received her law degree. Her writing has been published in *The Missouri Review, The Iowa Review, Citron Review,* and *California Law Review,* and nominated for the Pushcart Prize and the PEN/Robert J. Dau Short Story Prize for Emerging Writers. She is at work on her first novel. Find her at www.danicaxli.com.

• As a lawyer, I often think about work that involves reporting stories of great grief and cataclysm to the public, such as that performed by journalists and lawyers. I think about how the weight of the stories accumulates on psyches and bodies. With this story, I wanted to explore the life of a character who carries a weight like this one, her reserves of motivation and vulnerabilities. At the same time, I live in the SF Bay Area, an epicenter of alternate realities and virtual technologies. I regularly meet engineers and artists who work on the cutting edge of these technologies, whose work enables the world to live more and more of our lives online. The dialogue between the main character and her brother is my questioning of the tensions that exist between living in the real world and inhabiting virtual ones, the ethics of escaping reality, and how these technologies are changing how our needs for connection are met, or not.

LING MA is a writer hailing from Fujian province, Utah, and Kansas. She is author of the novel *Severance* and the story collection *Bliss Montage,* which together have been translated into nine languages. Her fiction has been honored with a Windham-Campbell Literature Prize, a Whiting Award, the Kirkus Prize, the Story Prize, the National Book Critics Circle Award for Fiction, and others. She lives in Chicago with her family.

• I can't remember when I first noticed that the story in Lydia Davis's story "Happiest Moment" echoes an anecdote from Mark Saltzman's memoir *Iron & Silk,* a book I had read a few times as a kid. Every once in a while, I would think about this coincidence, this strange overlap. It was a pebble in my shoe that I carried around for years.

One day in spring 2020, I was jogging around a runner's track near my apartment, and I started forming this fragmented narrative that begins with *Iron & Silk,* then loops around to the Lydia Davis story. This trail of thoughts seemed diaphanous and almost flimsy. It was almost as if I were trying to compose an essay, though I already knew it was a story.

As I ran, I noticed that city workers were putting up wire fencing around the track—maybe a measure taken to discourage people from congregating during the early pandemic—and I realized this would be the last time for months that I would be able to access this area. I jogged poorly for a bit longer, trying to thresh out a couple more ideas before the track closed to the public. (I think if inspiration comes to you unexpectedly, it's not a bad idea to remain in the same place for a while, doing what you're doing, until the visitation is over.)

When I got home, I laid out a partial outline of fragmented sections that followed a loose narrative. Some sections seemed to represent sides of a long-running argument I'd been having with myself, about the ways that the second generation creates cultural capital of their immigrant parents' experiences, and questions about how non-English-speaking characters are supposed to be conveyed, particularly in first person.

I worked on a draft on and off over the course of a year. I didn't know what the last sections would be. If I got lost, I would look at the partial outline. It was leading me to complete a thought. Once I realized what form the final section would take, I also realized it was important that this section feel immersive, that it should read as a story in its own right.

The process for "Peking Duck" was straightforward compared to other projects. I take this as a sign that I'd been thinking about these ideas long before I tried working them into a story. Among my stories, it is not one I love most, but it has seemed the most inevitable, if that makes sense. It felt necessary to complete it.

MANUEL MUÑOZ's most recent collection, *The Consequences,* was short-listed for the 2023 Aspen Words Literary Prize. A 2023 Simpson/Joyce Carol Oates Literary Prize finalist, he is the author of the novel *What You See in the Dark* and two collections, *Zigzagger* and *The Faith Healer of Olive Avenue;* the latter was short-listed for the Frank O'Connor International Short Story Award. He has been recognized with three O. Henry Awards and a Whiting Award. This is his second appearance in *Best American Short Stories.* He lives and works in Tucson, Arizona.

• When I first started submitting fiction in the late nineties, I had difficulty placing explicitly queer stories. One prominent journal went as far as to write back, "We don't publish gay fiction," though the central figure was a father mourning a dead son who had remained largely off the page. About the same time, in queer literary circles, I was encountering resistance to stories of the closet and its ramifications. Their ubiquity—at least to a white audience—was the problem. Yet for communities like mine, which were only starting to get on the page in sufficient numbers, the critique felt like a divisive narrowing. It was the start of letting go of many assumptions I used to have about receptive audiences and community.

This story came from a failed date I had many years ago with a man who had only recently left his family. Around the holidays, he was moved to return to them, concerned about their very young child. When I told some friends about this, their snap judgments surprised me. "Great way to fuck up your family," I remember one saying. The lack of empathy stung me.

It seemed clear-cut to my friends that the light of the opened closet was the real story—the only story worth listening to. The sooner he entered that light, all the better.

But I refused to judge this man or his decisions. This was where he was. I had learned a long time ago that the act of listening was far more important than the act of telling. That's what guided me here. I still had the corrosive effects of those old arguments lurking in my head, the refusal of someone else's pain when one's own might have already been assuaged. *We've heard this before,* the old voices kept saying to me. I finally got bolder in answering: *So why does it keep happening?*

JOANNA PEARSON'S first novel, *Bright and Tender Dark,* which grew out of the story "Grand Mal," is forthcoming in 2024. She is the author of two short story collections, *Now You Know It All* (2021), chosen by Edward P. Jones for the 2021 Drue Heinz Literature Prize, and *Every Human Love* (2019). Her fiction has recently appeared in *The Best American Mystery and Suspense 2021, Colorado Review, Electric Literature*'s "Recommended Reading," *The Sewanee Review,* and *The Missouri Review,* among other publications. She lives with her family near Chapel Hill, North Carolina, where she works as a psychiatrist.

• I'm pretty sure it was my dear friend Alice who told me in college that if one was ever attacked, the thing to do was to go limp and pretend to throw a violent fit. I have no idea if this advice has any basis in fact, but it still rattles around my head whenever I find myself walking through the dark, outside, alone. Probably it's just one of those mental talismans that so many of us, especially women, carry through our lives in hopes that they will keep us safe. The illusion of control holds such appeal. We long for it, especially when the world seems always to be bending toward entropy. This longing, I think, also has something to do with questions of belief, our search for order in disorder. Over the years my interest in these problems grew into "Grand Mal," the story that appears in this anthology, and later served as the kernel for a novel, *Bright and Tender Dark.*

SOUVANKHAM THAMMAVONGSA is the author of four poetry books and the short story collection *How to Pronounce Knife,* a finalist for the National Book Critics Circle Award and winner of the Scotiabank Giller Prize. Her stories have won an O. Henry Award and appeared in *The New Yorker,* the *New York Times, Harper's Magazine, The Paris Review,* the *Atlantic,* and *NOON.*

• I didn't know my family and I were what people would call trash. It isn't that we have no ambition for ourselves or that we didn't pull ourselves up by our bootstraps or that we do not work hard. It's really that we came here with nothing. And just want to live. I think that is our greatest triumph. I think there's tremendous intellectual rigor in someone like the cashier in the story who will always find something to love about what is there and what they have.

What I loved about writing "Trash" is what happens at the turn and with the word "too." For a long time we are told what is said and told to the narrator. We don't see or hear Miss Emily's voice in dialogue tags until the turn in the story. And once we hear it, the tone of the story changes, and even more so if we reread it. What seems polite, nice, kind, helpful is actually quite awful. The word "too" is not all that grand or profound in itself, but a writer can make it so. If we follow how this word is used in the story, we see how ambitious it is, but also how so very doomed. Another thing I love is the confidence the story has in its brevity and clarity.

KOSISO UGWUEZE was born in Enugu, Nigeria, and raised in Southern California. Her short fiction has recently appeared in *Joyland, Gulf Coast, Subtropics,* and *New England Review,* among others. Kosiso is the winner of the 2023 *New England Review* Award for Emerging Writers, and in 2020 she received a Barbara Deming Memorial Fund grant for feminist fiction. Other awards include residencies and fellowships from Kimbilio for Black Fiction, Ox-Bow School of Art, the Vermont Studio Center, and the Napa Valley Writers' Conference. She recently earned an MFA from the Writing Seminars program at Johns Hopkins University, where she was the managing editor of *The Hopkins Review* as well as a recipient of the Dr. Benjamin T. Sankey Prize in Fiction. She is currently the senior editor at *The Hopkins Review* and an adjunct lecturer in creative writing at Johns Hopkins University.

• "Supernova" began as a prompt in one of my graduate writing courses. The prompt was to write about a character in physical danger. I've never really used writing prompts before, and this is my shameless plug for them. But I started with this story about a girl on a bus and men with guns and then it took off on its own. When I began writing the story, I wanted to capture the incongruence between how we sometimes react to trauma and how we are *supposed* to react. And the thing that stayed consistent through multiple revisions was that incongruence. Isioma's inability to react "properly," even as her own life hangs in the balance, is at the center of the story's forward movement. The story came together quite quickly; I wrote most of the first draft in one sitting. And I think that's the great thing about writing prompts (another plug!): you already have something to guide you.

A huge thank you to Lori Ostlund for believing in the story, to Katharine Noel for the prompt, and to the team at *New England Review* for publishing it!

CORINNA VALLIANATOS is the author of the novel *The Beforeland* and the story collection *My Escapee,* winner of the Grace Paley Prize in Short Fiction and a *New York Times Book Review* Editors' Choice. Her third book, the story collection *Origin Stories,* is forthcoming.

• This story came quickly after I decided, for lack of a better plan, to allow myself to write about women trying to make art. The secrecy of their ambition, and what happens when that secrecy is punctured, as it inevitably is, by marriage, friendship, conversation, failure, even success. And that meant the story had to curve close to my own life and experiences. My sensibility had always saturated my writing—what I thought was funny, what I thought was tragic, the little moments of slippage and misalignment I noticed and stored away—but I'd felt it was somehow more serious to invent scenarios and characters who bore little relation to me, especially in the stories I wrote when I was younger. Now, though, I decided to invent only in order to clarify, to more purposefully articulate something true.

Thanks to Jessica Anthony for the title suggestion. "This Isn't the Actual Sea" was always a phrase in the story, but I hadn't thought to fish it out.

AZAREEN VAN DER VLIET OLOOMI is the author of the novels *Savage Tongues* and *Call Me Zebra,* which won the PEN/Faulkner Award for Fiction. She received a 2015 Whiting Award and was a National Book Foundation "5 Under 35" honoree for her debut novel, *Fra Keeler.* Her work has been supported by the Radcliffe Institute for Advanced Studies at Harvard, a Fulbright Fellowship, the Aspen Institute, and a MacDowell Fellowship, and her work has appeared in the *New York Times, The Sewanee Review, Yale Review, Granta, The Believer,* and *BOMB,* among other publications. She is a professor in the University of Notre Dame's MFA Program in Creative Writing and a fellow at the Kroc Institute for International Peace Studies. In 2020, she founded "Literatures of Annihilation, Exile, and Resistance," a conversation series focused on the intersection of the arts and human rights.

• I wrote the story in response to a line from *The Odyssey:* "It is his homeland he missed / As he paced along the whispering surf-line / Utterly forlorn." The narrator of "It Is What It Is" echoes Homer's sentiment when she walks along the shores of Lake Michigan in Chicago. The line in the story goes: "I paced around restlessly for hours, hunched up with homesickness and sobbing in my grief." At its core, "It Is What It Is" is a story about the gravitational pull of homesickness and the paradox of communication technologies as a means of connectivity and of witnessing violence. The characters in the story resist the oppressive conditions of their exile by exercising intuitive modes of communication with their literary and genetic ancestors, with their mysteriously telepathic cat, and with nature.

ESTHER YI was born in Los Angeles in 1989 and lives in Leipzig, Germany.

• This piece eventually became the first chapter of my novel *Y/N* (2023). The narrator, a woman living in Berlin, attends the concert of an internationally successful Korean boy band and sets her eyes upon Moon, the youngest member, performing onstage. She is permanently changed; obsession proceeds. Her journey to come can be seen as the following question imaginatively prolonged: Was her fatal encounter with Moon a blessing or a curse?

Other Distinguished Stories of 2022

Aguda, 'Pemi, "The Hollow" (*Zoetrope: All-Story,* vol. 25, no. 4)

Alcott, Kathleen, "Temporary Housing" (*Harper's Magazine,* May)

Almond, Steve, "I'm Not the Only One" (*South Carolina Review,* vol. 54, no. 2)

Anderson, Derek, "Napalm" (*Arts & Letters,* no. 44, Spring)

Andrew, Rick, "Couples Therapy" (*Ninth Letter,* vol. 19, no. 2)

Arp, Chris, "The Holes in Our Souls" (*Chicago Quarterly Review,* vol. 36, Fall)

Aurora, Bipin, "The Terrorist" (*The Journal: A Literary Magazine,* vol. 46, no. 1)

Auster, Paul, "Worms" (*Harper's Magazine,* April)

Barrett, Colin, "Rain" (*Granta,* no. 161, Autumn)

Baumann, Joe, "There Won't Be Questions" (*Fantasy and Science Fiction,* January/February)

Bazzle, Bradley, "Where the West Begins" (*New England Review,* vol. 43, no. 3)

Bell, Matt, "Empathy Hour" (*Slate,* March 26)

Bevacqua, Dan, "Riccardo" (*The Paris Review,* no. 240, Summer)

Blackburn, Venita, "Not a Donut" (*The 2022 Short Story Advent Calendar*)

Boyle, T. Coraghessan, "Princess" (*The New Yorker,* November 7)

Campbell, Corey, "Everybody's Good" (*The Gettysburg Review,* vol. 34, no. 1)

Castleberry, Brian, "Night of the Dark Ritual" (*Michigan Quarterly Review,* vol. 61, no. 2)

Chakrabarti, Jai, "A Mother's Wish" (*One Story,* no. 294, October 20)

Chakrabarti, Jai, "Lilāvati's Fire" (*Conjunctions,* no. 79, *Onword*)

Chung, Gina, "Attachment Processes" (*The Idaho Review,* no. 20, June)

Citchens, Addie, "A Good Samaritan" (*The Paris Review,* no. 242, Winter)

Clarke, Taylor, "Live Free" (*Shenandoah,* vol. 71, no. 2)

Cline, Emma, "Pleasant Glen" (*The Paris Review,* no. 240, Summer)

Conklin, Lydia, "Sunny Talks" (*One Story,* no. 285, January 27)

Crain, Caleb, "Easter" (*The New Yorker,* September 26)

Crotty, Marian, "What Kind of Person" (*The Iowa Review,* vol. 51, no. 2)

Crouse, David, "The Arm of the Lord" (*The Kenyon Review,* vol. 44, no. 4)

American and Canadian Magazines Publishing Short Stories

Able Muse
Adroit Journal
African American Review
After Dinner Conversation
Agni
Air/Light
Alaska Quarterly Review
American Literary Review
American Scholar
American Short Fiction
Another Chicago Magazine
Appalachian Review
Arts & Letters
Astra
Baltimore Review
Barrelhouse
Barren Magazine
Barzakh
Bayou Magazine
The Believer
Bellevue Literary Review
Bennington Review
Blackbird
Black Warrior Review
Bomb
Booth Journal
Boulevard
Bridge Eight
Bright Flash Literary Review
The Brooklyn Rail
The Brooklyn Review
Capsule Stories
Carbon Copy
The Carolina Quarterly
Carve
Catamaran
Catapult
Change Seven
Cherry Tree
Chicago Quarterly Review
Cholla Needles
Cimarron Review
The Cincinnati Review
Clarkesworld
Cleaver
Cloves Literary
Cold Signal
Colorado Review
The Common
Conjunctions
Copper Nickel
Cowboy Jamboree Magazine
Craft
Crazyhorse

Cream City Review
Cutbank
Cutleaf Journal
Danse Macabre
The Dark Magazine
Dark Matter
December
Denver Quarterly
The Dodge
The Dread Machine
The Drift
Driftwood
Ecotone
Electric Literature
Epiphany
Epoch
Event
Exposition Review
Fantasy Magazine
Fast Flesh Literary Journal
Fence
The Fiddlehead
Fireside
Five South
Flash Fiction Magazine
FlashFlood Journal
Flash Frog
Foglifter
The Forge Literary Magazine
Freeman's
Frigg: A Magazine of Fiction and Poetry
The Georgia Review
The Gettysburg Review
Gordon Square Review
Granta
The Gravity of the Thing
The Greensboro Review
Gulf Coast
Guernica
Harper's Magazine
Harpur Palate
Harvard Review
Hawaii Pacific Review
Hayden's Ferry Review
Hobart
The Hopkins Review
The Hudson Review

Hunger Mountain Review
Hypertext
The Idaho Review
Image
Indiana Review
The Intima
Invisible City
The Iowa Review
Iron House
I-70 Review
Jabberwock Review
JMWW
The Journal: A Literary Magazine
Joyland
Juked
The Kenyon Review
Khabar
Kweli Journal
Lady Churchill's Rosebud Wristlet
Lake Effect
LatineLit
Laurel Review
Leo Weekly
L'Esprit Literary Review
LIGEIA
Lightspeed
Literary Matters
LitMag
Litmosphere: Journal of Charlotte Lit
LitroUSA
Little Patuxent Review
Longleaf Review
Los Angeles Book Review Quarterly
The Louisville Review
Lowestoft Chronicle
Magazine of Fantasy and Science Fiction
The Maine Review
The Malahat Review
The Massachusetts Review
Masters Review
Maudlin House
McSweeney's
Menagerie
Michigan Quarterly Review
MicroLit Almanac
Milk Candy Review

The Missouri Review
The Muleskinner Journal
The Museum of Americana
Narrative
Nelle
New England Review
New Ohio Review
New Pop Lit
The New Yorker
Nightmare
Nimrod
Ninth Letter
Noon
n+1
The Normal School
North American Review
North Dakota Quarterly
Northwest Review
No Tokens Journal
Obsidian: Literature & Arts in the
  African Diaspora
Off Topic Publishing
Okay Donkey
One Story
Orange Blossom Review
Orca Literary
Orion
Oyez Review
Oyster River Pages
Pangyrus
Paper Brigade
The Paris Review
Passengers Journal
Pembroke Magazine
Persimmon Tree
Pigeon Pages
Pithead Chapel
Ploughshares
Pontoon
Porter House Review
Potomac Review
Prairie Schooner
The Public Domain Review
Quarter After Eight
The Quarter(ly): Myths, Fables, and
  Folklore
Quarterly West

Raritan
Reckon Review
Reed Magazine
Room
Ruby
Ruminate
The Rumpus
Salamander
Salmagundi
Salt Hill
Santa Monica Review
Saturday Evening Post
Sequestrum
The Sewanee Review
Shenandoah
Short Story Advent Calendar
Slate
Slice
SmokeLong Quarterly
Socrates on the Beach
Solstice
South Carolina Review
The Southampton Review
Southeast Review
South85 Journal
Southern Humanities Review
Southern Indiana Review
The Southern Review
Southwest Review
Split Lip Magazine
Statement of Record
Story
StoryQuarterly
Stranger's Guide
Substance
Sundog Lit
Swamp Ape Review
Tahoma Literary Review
Third Coast
Threepenny Review
Tough
Trampset
Transition
TriQuarterly
Twin Pies Literary Journal
Variant Literature
Virginia Quarterly Review

Vol. 1 Brooklyn
Water-Stone Review
West Branch
West Trade Review
Wigleaf
Willow Springs
Witness
Women on Writing
World Literature Today
Wrath-Bearing Tree

The Write Launch
Wyngraf
X-R-A-Y Lit
Yale Review
Yellow Medicine Review
Your Impossible Voice
Zoetrope: All Story
Zone 3
Zyzzyva

EXPLORE THE REST OF THE SERIES!

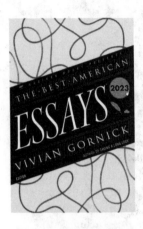

On sale 10/17/23
$18.99

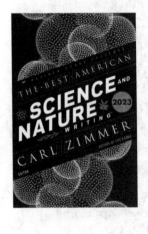

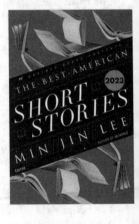